The
PROSPECT
of
THIS CITY

Being a novel of the Great Fire

EAMONN MARTIN GRIFFIN

✜

Lord, have mercy on London

DEDICATION

For my parents.

CONTENTS

ACKNOWLEDGMENTS

First, huge thanks to George Green and Lee Horsley for their enthusiasm, insight, support, latitude, ideas, questions and prompts. This couldn't have happened without you.

Thanks also to beta testers Joanne Pearce, Maxim Griffin, Chris Dows, Paul Roberts, John Ashbrook, Lisa Fox, "Kev G" and Jo Foster who each read at least some of the novel in its various forms and were kind enough to give feedback. Thanks as well to Harry Sidebottom for some words of encouragement along the way.

PROLOGUE: THURSDAY 23RD AUGUST 1666

Midnight made a mirror of the window-glass. Grand Pensionary Johan de Witt's reflected face was as immobile as a portrait. He must have heard Rufus Challis be admitted into his offices, but had made no reaction. Instead he stared, his back to Challis, unblinking into the outside dark.

Challis stood in the centre of the room, left hand over right. De Witt's desk was a scrabble of documents, papers tumbling over each other. Official correspondence, hastily-printed street pamphlets and hand-bills. Challis did not need to read them to know their contents. There could be only one reason why he had been invited, so secretly, to attend on the Dutch chief minister.

A smaller, secondary desk to one side. Somewhere a secretary might have sat and taken notes. Mathematical charts, writing equipment, a courier pouch.

After perhaps five minutes, de Witt spoke. His English was good. 'Sometimes I talk to myself aloud when I am alone,' he said. 'To organise my thoughts, nothing more.'

This was it.

'The news is all across the Republic of the Seven Netherlands. All Dutchmen have learned of the recent atrocities the English have wrought. We might be at war with their King Charles, but our battles are at sea. Navy against navy, fighting like good Christians and honourable gentlemen despite our differences.

'But no.' De Witt stopped.

The old pain flared in Challis's right hand. A harbinger, a premonition. He breathed through his mouth to ease the ache.

De Witt rubbed his eyes. A deep draught from a glass of almost purple wine. 'A fire-ship attack on our port of Schelling. Frigates burned in their berths, honest merchant-men losing their livelihoods. Worse, though, the sacking of the township. Women cut down in their homes. Innocents slaughtered. This,' he drank again, draining the glass, 'must not go unanswered.'

'So I stand in solitude.' De Witt's voice quietened. 'And I pray.'

Challis bowed his head and closed his eyes.

'I pray that I am forgiven these violent imaginings.

'I pray that we Dutch are given the year to rebuild our lost vessels and recruit fresh men. That we will right the wrongs done this week by Charles of England. That renewed, we will take this fight back to England in the Spring.'

Challis's right hand pulsed. It felt full to bursting. This was no infected war-wound, though, but a holy thing. An engorgement with the spirit of the Lord.

'But,' de Witt continued, 'this destruction, this murder cannot remain unaddressed. I pray that the sparks of the same fire that burned Schelling are blown across the water to England. That God brings down His fire upon the English and that we Dutch are avenged. That we are spared the necessity of retaliation in the new martial season.'

Challis opened his eyes. He went to the pouch on the secretary's desk and checked inside. Papers, money. More than he needed for the enterprise. He took the pouch, cupping it in his throbbing, precious hand.

'I pray that this is done soon, so that God's will is seen,' de Witt said. 'Amen.'

Leaving, Challis turned at the door.

De Witt remained at the window, his back still to the room.

Throughout, he had made no acknowledgement that Challis had ever been there.

THURSDAY 30TH AUGUST 1666

Tom Farriner pulled the oak die from his pocket. He turned it in his hands while his brother got more drink. The die was three inches long and a little more than half an inch thick, squared off on its four long sides. Three sides were scored: one mark, two marks, three crosses. The fourth side was blank. This was called a Long Lawrence, and it only had one use.

Taff, the landlord, was not to be seen. The custom was to help yourself to the keg and leave the money in the beaker left on the stool where Taff usually crouched. If there were strangers in, then one of the regulars would either take over or supervise. Often as not, Tom found himself helping out.

Daniel came back with the refilled flagons. He sat down awkwardly, his height making it tricky for him to get his legs under the table. He took a sip. He put the clay pot back down again, staring into the foamy remnants of the head as though the ale would give him answers.

Daniel had been like this for the last few long hot days. Distant, uncommunicative. That was why Tom had asked him to come next door to the White Hart. But his tongue wasn't being loosened by the drink and he wasn't taking the opportunity himself to tell Tom what was eating him up.

Ah, bollocks to him, Tom thought. If he doesn't want to, then he doesn't want to. Sooner or later the fever would break. It had to. And if it got unbearable, then Tom would ask him outright.

Maybe a game would take his mind off matters. Tom stood the Long Lawrence on its end, then flicked it over. He stood it up once more, and again toppled it, this time with the bottom of his mug as he lifted it to drink.

'Can't afford to gamble,' Daniel muttered.

Oh, so he could speak. 'We'll just play then. We can square up after. If I win I'll give it back to you.'

Daniel shrugged. 'If you like.'

The game - Put and Take - was simple. You agreed the stake - a penny was usual - per player. You paid into the pot and you each rolled the die in turn. Roll a blank and you did nothing. The side with one mark on it meant you put a penny in. The side with two marks meant you took a penny out. Roll the side with the crosses and you won what was in the pot.

The first few rounds were inconsequential. But it passed the time, and Daniel's shoulders were relaxing. He was out of his worry and into the game. Good, Tom thought.

This round, the pot grew. There must have been a couple of shillings in pennies in the pile. 'Another?' Tom asked, indicating Daniel's near-empty tankard.

'Go on.' Daniel paused, then rummaged in his purse. 'And get some change from Taff.' He held a florin - another two shillings - for Tom to take.

'Thought you didn't have money to gamble,' Tom grinned.

A smile back. That was something. 'Sorry,' Daniel said.

Tom got more drink and Daniel's change from Taff's stool. One hand cupping the money, the other hand grasping the two tankard handles, he crossed the floor slow to not to spill anything.

Damn, but Daniel wasn't alone any more. Tom had hoped that he was ready to start talking. But he'd never say a thing with someone else there, and especially not someone such as Lizzie Corbet.

Lizzie worked out of the White Hart most nights and drank there most days. She was the ringleader of the handful of girls that landlord

Taff let operate. She was big and loud and sad at the same time. Word was that something had broken inside her with the coming of the plague. That she'd lost her man and a child and with them her soul, and that since then she tried to fill the hole in her heart with swiving and wine.

'Tom,' Lizzie said. 'Daniel. Thought I'd sit in with you boys a while.'

Lizzie was a good enough sort, but a nuisance. Doubtless the money had attracted her across. She kept herself to the usual table she shared with her cronies, unless there were fresh men in to try her luck with. Lizzie liked a drink. She was flush with it now, pink-cheeked and shiny with sweat just under the skin. She'd hang about until either she won herself some ale-money or until one of them took pity on her and bought her a jug. Lizzie had some respect, though. She'd known them since Tom was young, ever since they'd come to London. She never tried to swive either of them. Daniel would say no, of course, being too holy for that.

As for Tom, he was sure that she still saw him as a child, not a man of almost eighteen years.

Besides, there were always plenty of others for Lizzie, both regulars and passing trade, who'd see her right for her doss and drink in exchange for a tumble.

Lizzie threw a penny in.

'You can't come in half way through,' Daniel said. 'How fair is that?'

She retracted the coin with a single finger, dragging it slow across the table-top. 'You can't blame a girl for trying.'

'Come in with us on the next round,' Tom said. 'That's no problem I'm sure.' He glanced at Daniel, who said nothing.

The tension was back in his brother's shoulders. There'd be no discussion with him now.

Tom swigged his fresh pint. 'See? No issue.' He rolled the die and came up blank.

Daniel threw the crosses on his next turn. Lizzie shrieked in glee and clapped her hands. Daniel scowled. He counted up the coin, arranging it in piles of a dozen apiece in front of him.

They played some more, five or six rounds. Lizzie joined in with each, joshing and making asides throughout. Tom kept the conversation circling, trying to fill the gaps Daniel might have taken up had he not gone back into his gloom.

After the sixth round, Lizzie's banter ceased. A penny between thumb and forefinger. 'Last one,' she said. 'Last one.' Silence from her, before she spoke. 'Thanks for the game, lads.' She slid the coin back into her skirts and got up.

'One more and we're off,' Tom said. 'Refill for your pot?'

Lizzie smiled; awkward, like sunshine and rain together. 'That's a kindness,' she said. 'But no thank you.' Then the drizzle cleared. Her smile was almost convincing.

A racket from behind them. Taff coming through from the back room and whatever he'd been doing in there. He nodded over to Tom and then sat on his stool to count the money in the cup. It didn't take long.

'We having that last one?' Tom asked. Daniel shook his head. He downed his drink and Tom did likewise. No point staying here, he thought.

'I've a drink in,' Tom said to Taff. 'Lizzie can have it if she wants.'

Taff looked from Tom to Lizzie and back to Tom again. He didn't believe a word of it. He nodded anyway. Tom knew he'd be paying for that drink in the morning.

Lizzie was back in her corner with the girls she ran with. Their banter had a shrill edge to it.

Daniel was already at the door, holding it open. Then others came in. A couple of regulars Tom knew by sight, then two men who were strangers to him. One was tall and thin enough to look it and his opposite; short, stout and ruddy-faced.

The little round man was leering, rubbing his hands together. He squeezed past Tom on the way through. Behind him, and before the door swung shut, he heard Lizzie, strident and friendly, approaching the incomers.

Doubtless she was making the best of what she had so she could get herself through the night.

Tom felt bad. Bad for Lizzie, who'd spent all but her last copper. Worse, who'd gambled it into his and Daniel's pockets. Bad for Daniel, who could not share whatever was preoccupying him. Bad for himself for not dealing with matters more directly.

The sky was turning from blue to violet. Darkness was only an hour or so away. The short, hot summer nights meant that sleep was a luxury. The morning would be here soon enough, Tom thought. He prayed it would bring the strength to take his elder brother on.

#

Challis was tempted to let the woman live. After all, she was simply pursuing her trade.

Nevertheless, Challis thought himself vigilant, not just to the subtleties of the Evil One, but also to those of Christ Jesus, who spoke to him in many ways and who tested Challis just as He had been trialled by Satan.

Challis cast the temptation off, seeing the sparing of the woman's life for the false charity it would have been.

She would have to die.

Challis had crossed London Bridge from the Southwark side and was walking north. His immediate concerns were for basic lodgings, somewhere off the main road. A place central to the city where there'd be little regard paid to a travelling stranger, and quiet so he'd not be disturbed at his supper by carousing bucks or the self-important crowing of some boldface trader. So he'd diverted off the wide road, Fish Street Hill, which pointed up away from the bridge. He turned right then took a side-street left. There'd surely be such an establishment as he had in mind hereabouts.

Little more than a lane, this new street was narrow and steeped northwards in mimicry of its greater sibling. There was none of the late evening bustle he'd encountered crossing the Thames to get here. A mix of shop-signs and there, cutting into the dropping darkness, a hanging tavern-board painted with an image of what he took to be a white deer.

Challis re-shouldered his bag and made for the sign. That was when the first disturbance came.

Sudden movement to the side from a narrow cut-through between the tavern and its neighbour building.

Challis halted, his left hand coming up to his right wrist, and to the blade concealed in the sleeve.

A man came out of the gap, tucking himself in. He turned, facing up the lane, and put one hand out to the wall for support. His balance reasserted, he went up the hill. He glanced at the tavern door in passing as though contemplating a nightcap to warm him home, but he moved on without stopping. He made no indication that he'd determined Challis's presence there.

Challis waited for the inevitable slattern. She came at him in a heavyset rush, all hands and yellow grin snapping at him.

Challis let the knife-handle go.

'And will you swive me, sir?' There was drink on her breath and meat-grease on her straining clothes. Her hands were already around him, one to his balls and one seeking a way within his coat.

Challis grabbed her wrist, pulling her fingers back off his cods. He pushed her backwards, hard enough to make her stumble against the wall by the alley.

'And are you clean?' he asked.

'Shiny as silver,' she said, all sly, tugging back against his grip, seeking to slide them back where she'd come from.

Challis let her pull him in.

The alley reeked of piss. There was dusty earth underfoot, little bits of wood. Dry animal bone. Then a sharper noise, a discarded bottle being kicked against brick. That made Challis tense up again. The woman must have mistook his cautious stiffness for lusty urgency, because she twisted to loosen herself from his fingers, then reached again for his breeched member.

No. Challis slammed her grasping arm up against the wall. He listened for confirmation that their scuffling or the bottle-sound had roused no attention.

The street was quiet. The tavern gave off no noise from inside.

He brought her pinned arm down to her mouth, pushing in to gag her with her own forearm. Her gasp was cut short but there was playfulness and business in her eyes. She must have thought herself to be trading with a feisty one.

She squirmed now, and it was clear to Challis that her shuddering was a parody of pleasure for his lustful benefit.

'Shh,' he said.

She was a sign. A microcosm of the capital, sent by the Lord. A drunkard and a fornicator, a glutton and a night-time opportunist. Like London, like England, like its navy. Like its King.

Challis would show her the way.

He accepted the gift the Lord had given him.

Until that point he'd made sure to disguise the lack of thumb on his right hand. The instant of its revelation to a newcomer was always a point of curiosity to him and much depended on the reaction given it.

Challis brought his right hand tight over her mouth, at once clasping her jaw and encasing her lips. The ridged scarring from the severing of his thumb was pressed under her nose.

Then she showed fear.

She snorted; twin smears at her nostrils. She could not breathe. She gagged, struggling, but she was outmatched. Her eyes bulged, tears at all corners. He held her firm.

Her cheeks inflated like a pig's bladder. She bucked and writhed but her panic was nothing compared to the surety of his grasp.

She stopped. Eyes wide open and dark mottling about her face. Challis gave it a count of ten to be sure that she was dead. Then he let her head fall to one side.

The body slumped over. The mouth yawned open, leaking fluid onto the dry ground.

Challis stepped back and kicked the body's legs until they were deep in shadow. He took a handkerchief from one of his many pockets and wiped his hands clean as best he could. He'd wash anon. His right hand would hurt in time, as it always did.

And then there was the sound of a single footfall, a scuff of leather or wood somewhere. The noise made Challis halt. He checked up and down the narrow street. There was nothing in either direction. Good. Nevertheless, he waited. A repeat or a continuation of the noise did not come.

Maybe it had been nothing.

Challis shouldered his bag again, and made certain that the alley bore no outward evidence of the despatching. She should be proud to be the first, he told himself, and then he went to see about his lodgings.

#

Daniel usually slept sound. But these last few nights there had been a worry-rat gnawing at his innards, a beast that would not let him slumber. And God knew it was difficult enough to get any bed-rest in this swelter even without Daniel's restlessness.

Christ, Tom thought. Now he's getting out of his bed. Tom held still, pretending to be asleep. He could tell by the footsteps that Daniel was going to the small side window. Then silence.

At least his shuffling had ceased. Tom thought that he'd get some sleep. Let him stand there. But then his brother started muttering to himself. Trying to sort whatever was vexing him, doubtless.

But no. Daniel said the same words again, louder. Tom was being addressed.

'At it again.'

'What?'

'In the alley.'

'What are you going on about?' Tom sat up. There was no point in lying there.

Tom kept a beaker of small beer to hand for thirst in the night. He drank from the cup, but the watery ale was as warm as the heavy air in the room.

'Your whore friend from the White Hart.'

'She's not a-' Tom stopped. There'd been no explaining some things to Daniel since he'd turned so wholeheartedly to Christ. All he recognised was what Lizzie did, not why. Her sin, not her need.

Daniel now sat on his own bed opposite.

Tom's sight was adjusting to the dark. His brother reached out for the drink, and Tom passed it over.

Go on. Ask him.

'What's wrong with you?' Tom asked.

Daniel drank, and then set the beaker down so gentle on the floor that it made no sound. He hunched forwards like he was squatting on a privy.

Tom went to the window, hoping for a face-full of breeze. The air had been still for weeks. There had been no rain since the early summer. Even at night it was as hot as the bakery two floors below them. A dry determined heat with no relenting.

There was no relief from the night.

Tom could not help looking down to see what had riled his brother.

Two figures in the pewter grey below. A chinking noise that must have been coin being exchanged, then one of them - the man - making to move off.

Almost directly above, Tom not could make out his face. No way to tell if Tom knew him or not. A shame; there'd be no gossip to swap with Alice in the morning.

He knew the woman though. It was Lizzie.

She would have been a fine sight to see once, all tumbling dark curls and overfull breasts and a smile as wide as a shovel-blade. But Tom only saw her in her cups or in the working towards, cowing the other girls in her gang so she'd get first pick of any trade.

It was a surprise to see her in the street, even so. Lizzie was a crafty one, Taff had grumbled to Tom more than once, often as not gulling her swiver into paying for a room for the night so she'd not have to go back to her empty home alone.

Lizzie left the alley. Tom was about to try once more to get Daniel to talk so that there'd be some peace. It was too hot to sleep anyway. But Lizzie was back in a snatch with another man in tow and Tom could not help but watch.

Perhaps the two had egged each other on to get themselves a woman. Maybe there was money involved, some ale-driven bet or other.

Lizzie's customer shoved her against the wall. That was odd. Tom had seen enough to know that it was the girls who took charge. They were practiced, skilful. Efficient. Get the mark to spend himself and his money in the shortest time possible, the better to be earning again or sat back at their trestle with another drink set up. That was their tactic.

This fresh one looked like a hunchback because of the bag on his back. He must have been a traveller staying at the tavern, wary of leaving his possessions unattended while he took his pleasure.

Again Tom wondered why she'd brought him outside. Perhaps the price for her to room with him for the night was more than he was willing to pay.

Tom turned to one side so that he could see more clearly. He pressed himself hard against the plaster. The rough warmth from the wall made him prickle.

A single hollow clatter; in moving, he'd tipped the beaker over. Tom trapped the cup under his heel and held still, not wanting it to roll and cause more noise. He didn't want Lizzie to know there'd been an audience. Moreover, he did not want to rouse his father in the room below. Baker Farriner guarded his sleep, like so many other elements of his life, with a jealous anger.

Tom took his foot off the cup. It stayed in its place.

Daniel was still hunched at the edge of his cot. He made no movement.

Leave him to it, Tom reckoned. Daniel had always been a creature of bell-clapper moods, forever swinging back and forth, resounding with some new rapture, else with an echoing melancholy. Lately though, that clapper swung one way only.

By now Lizzie's mark had spent himself. He backed up, sorting his long coat, adjusting his bag-strap. He stepped away, making for the Lane proper.

The man waited a moment in the entrance to the alley as though listening, then made off up the hill.

Tom turned back to Lizzie, but she had gone.

No. There she was, toppled over to one side.

Something shone down there, a brighter gray against a hundred dull metal shadows. A liquid shine. Puke at best, blood at worst, oozing out from Lizzie's mouth and into the dust around her face. She was not coughing, nor crying in pain. She was not twitching or spasming in her voiding.

Tom was already pulling on his clothes but he knew it was useless. There'd be nothing he could do.

And besides, he had seen death before.

#

Taff spat onto the tavern floor. The White Hart was quiet for a Thursday. It was too hot again for a fire to be lit, and so the room was darker than usual for this time of year, light being cast only by a few lanterned candles and the glow from tobacco-pipes. Drinkers had scattered themselves among the trestles. Chatter was patchy. No-one was spending, no-one was gambling, no-one was obviously drunk.

The last two girls left, lumpen Martha and her shadow Salt-Lick Jane, were sullen desperate creatures tonight. They crouched over their drink, Martha counting and re-counting their coppers. Jane sat opposite her, sucking on her salt-stone, nodding at the reckoning, agreeing with the tallies.

Hadn't Lizzie Corbet been with them? Yes, she had. There were two more pint-pots on the table. Lizzie must have snared someone and taken him out for service. At least someone was turning over silver tonight, Taff rued.

Trade had been off for days now. You'd have thought that the dry heat would have sent Londoners scurrying to alehouses to breach their thirst. But no. Not at The White Hart at any measure.

Only one room let too; there was no making up for slow drink sales with lodging monies. His rooming guests were a curious pair, as ill-matched in size and shape as could be designed. Taff looked them over. The little one was tubby and moonfaced, balding with a boil on his crown that he scratched every few minutes. And his travelling companion, as thin as woman's piss and just as pale. A foot or so taller than his friend and as silent as his fat opposite was chatty. Even now, Tubby was jabbering, smiling, making his points with little gestures and pulled faces, only stopping for another gulp. Pissface sat, not appearing to listen, the only colour about him the wine-stain on his lips.

They were showmen of some kind, a remnant of one of the illegal fairs that had cropped up. With the Bartholomew Fair cancelled because of plague fears for a second year there were plenty who craved the entertainments only show folk could provide. Enough of them were willing to risk the edict to provide the same.

The second year's ban was bad for business and unpopular too; plague had all but deserted London, if the mortality bills were right. Next year, thought Taff. Next year. A Fair to remember. If only he could keep the place running until then.

This two must have been doing well, Taff thought. They got through meat and drink for twice their number.

Taff, sat on his stool by the ale-casks, wondered if he could get away with closing up early, getting upstairs with his Daisy, and seeing if she was feeling wifely. Their bed had been as quiet as the drinking-house this last week. Taff reckoned that he was past due his rights.

The latch on the door shifted. That didn't help, having the door shut, Taff thought, and got up. He'd need to tie it open again. Maybe that would bring in a couple more punters.

Taff was now halfway across the room. Whoever was outside was still fumbling with the latch.

One of the drinkers, face crumpled with ale and annoyance,

turned round towards Taff.

'Got something to say?' Taff grunted. Taff knew him as a semi-regular, one of the market traders, but he couldn't recall his name or what he sold. Just another shouting face in the hot, dry crowd.

The drinker gurned, his stinking black midden of a mouth hanging crookedly open.

'Go home, Walter.' That was his name, was it not? Walter? Bollocks if it wasn't. Taff was tired. Maybe the name would come to him in the morning.

The latch rattled again. And then the sharp snap of metal freeing itself as the mechanism was forced up and open.

He'd have to attend to the lock before shutting up. Grease at best, a hammer and bolster to the thing at worst, if the latch bar was catching in the keep again.

Taff had half a mind to get on with the job now. Christ Jesus knew it was getting late enough and, there not being much trade, he'd be grateful of the distraction before the last of these pissheads slinked back to their doss holes.

The door swung open and darkness stood there. Taff squinted, expecting light rather than shade, a street-lantern in a traveller's hand or a light-boy seeing his client to the door. Not this. Not black on black.

Taff took a step back, then another. He almost lost his footing, catching his heel on something behind him. A thought that Walter, if that was his bloody name, had kicked a stool behind him in jest.

The door closed firm behind the dark figure standing on the highest of the steps which led down from the street. Taff found himself focused, not on the man, but back up to the mechanism.

The latch had clicked shut as though nothing was wrong.

Taff felt himself redden: his neck, the backs of his hands, his cheeks.

And in his own place too, the place he'd raised from nothing, turning the shell of a disused storehouse to a tavern with his own hands, making everything from the tables to that damned fallen stool.

The place he'd stuck with through the last twelve-month of pestilence and drought, when trade had either run from the pox or died from it.

All that and Taff had never felt like this: nervous and embarrassed in front of his regulars.

Though Taff didn't look, he knew what the others were doing. Nothing. Hooded eyes staring back into their drinks; no-one seeing anything.

The incomer stepped down to the bare floor. And then he took off his hat, glanced around, and asked for a bottle and a glass and a moment of the landlord's time.

#

Tom made down the stairs as quiet as he could. He paused on the first floor landing, listening for evidence of others being awake. For sounds he did not want to hear. On one side, the corridor that led to the back bedchamber that had once been Daniel's. On the other, the passageway leading to his father's room.

Tom knew that houses have heartbeats. Rhythms and personalities, smells and quirks all of their own. The Farriner household had changed so much this past year or so. The silence from Daniel's old room did not surprise him.

That there was nothing resounding from his father's chamber, not snoring, nor worse, was some relief.

Tom found the stair-rail in the gloom and made his way down to the ground floor. His boots were not to hand, but his clogs were.

He left himself out by the back way, went up the passage on the far side of their bakery to the tavern, and came out into Pudding Lane, knowing a body waited to greet him.

#

Taff put down the bottle and let the stranger pour himself a drink. The newcomer let the liquid - dark like muscovado sugar from the Indies and the best the house could provide, not the weak light jaggery-brown filth Taff usually sold - coat the insides of the glass.

The stranger swirled the drink until he seemed satisfied. He took the glass in his left hand, held it there, tasted, met Taff's eyes again, and then swallowed the measure.

He kept his right hand in his pocket throughout.

Taff felt the hairs on the backs of his hands prickle. He kept his eyes on his own glass. He did not touch his drink.

'That,' the stranger said, 'is very good indeed.' He poured himself another, more this time, almost filling the vessel to the lip.

Taff now took his glass and drained it in one swift movement. Brandy-wine was not to his taste, never had been, and it burned all the way down. He opened his mouth to avoid gasping or coughing. Then he nodded, both to acknowledge the compliment, and to further disguise his discomfort.

'To business,' the stranger said.

'Yes?' Sizing up was part of the game of running a tavern and Taff prided himself on his abilities to read a person. The world of letters might have beyond him except where bills, invoices, and lists of inventory were concerned, but the face of a man was plain for Taff to interpret. Bad drunks, gambling cheats, swindlers, brawlers and wheedlers; Taff had not just eyes for them but a nose as well. Where needed, he backed this with landlord authority, and beyond that he had his fists.

Taff's hands were neither clenched knuckle-white in fighting anticipation or in show of superiority, but placid and pink, nails down, either side of his glass.

Taff had no feel for this man. That was enough to provoke unease.

'I need lodgings for a few days,' the stranger said. 'Perhaps five. A clean room to myself and good plain food. If this is any indication,' he said, indicating the bottle, 'I'll not be let down.'

Taff took his glass, now refilled, in hand. He prayed that his fingers would not betray him, that the surface of the brandy would not rock with his discomfort. 'I'd hope not,' he said.

'Too often in these troubled and profligate times,' the stranger continued, 'men take advantage, profiting through greed and the misfortune of others, using their position to better their own ends instead of proper reliance on honest work rewarded by Providence.'

The appearance of deferral to the opinions of others was a necessary weapon in the landlord's arsenal. Taff mouthed an amen.

Together they drank and then, glasses drained once more, Taff noted an opportunity to make a point and to secure some trust. He took the bottle by the neck and poured two more.

'In uncertain days,' Taff said, 'more than ever before, your words are true. Men should look to the Lord and to the King and to themselves.' Taff raised his glass. 'King Charles the second.'

The stranger did not hesitate. 'King Charles,' he said, almost to himself, and finished his brandy in one slick draught.

Taff relaxed a little. There'd been no pause or reluctance whatsoever in toasting the restored monarch.

The stranger slid a pouch onto the table: a pouch he then pressed into Taff's palm. It felt thick with coin. The stranger's left hand rested on top of Taff's, a gesture which almost felt comforting. 'Your discretion is valued,' he said.

'Indeed, sir,' Taff said. Quite where the note of deference had come from, Taff couldn't say. It might have been the lateness of the hour. It might have been the drink. Whichever it was, the conversation had concluded with Taff allowing the stranger a key for the few days he required a room, to have cold meats and coffee available at his request, not to disturb him unbidden, and not to draw attention to his presence.

On the latter point Taff found that he had three reasons, each as compelling as the last, not to gainsay his guest. For one, the purse, upon checking later, contained enough coin to buy a fortnight's accommodation. And for the second, the stranger had an air about him of studied vagueness, such that Taff could not recall with precision any specifics other than his favouring his left hand. And the third reason was plainly that the man had not offered a name, and that Taff had neglected to enquire.

#

The whole street was dark, no candle at any window, yet Tom found himself scarcely daring to breathe lest he cause some disturbance which would wake someone or summon a curious night-watchman. Not that the latter was likely. For the pittance the night-walkers got for their patrols people expected little more than the hours called out and that not always. Tom was surer, thinking the matter through, that the watch would be sleeping off drink in some corner or down by the waterside, idling in banter with dock workers or gambling with fresh arrivals from the afternoon tide. They'd be doing anything other than their allotted duties.

Tom stood still in the blackness. But for occasional wisps of smoke from the last of the day's fires, the night sky was clear enough for stars. The smoke drifted slow, there being little air to stir it. There were noises, yes, but from the Thames to the South. Distant labour, shouts and laughter, boxes being humped and winches swinging loads from dockside to deck or back.

Their own home, Farriner's bakery, was shuttered up. Tom's father's room was the one facing out into the Lane from the first floor.

Higher, the small room in the attic space that Tom shared with his brother. The side window was un-shuttered but had been closed. Daniel must have latched it after he'd left.

Now Tom stared deeper into the cut between the bakery and the inn. There was nothing to show that a body lay inside.

Then Tom's attention was caught. Something moving; a slyness at the top end of the street. A dog. It stopped, raising its head as though to inspect Tom, to determine if he was a threat or not.

They'd killed many dogs in the previous two years, he and Daniel. Too many. It was well thought that dogs might be responsible for spreading the plague. So there'd been a price on their hackles, two pence a hide, dogs and cats alike. They had trapped them in pairs; his brother with poisoned meat and a pitchfork, Tom with the barrow to porter the carcasses to payment.

With each dead cur, Daniel had a muttered a prayer for their mother. That had been when Tom first appreciated the change in his brother. As though killing the dogs would murder the sickness that had taken their mother. As though making the bloodshed holy would scrub clean the taint from his soul.

The money was good, and almost made up for the drop in passing bakery trade in the plague year, but killing always has its price.

Dogs took their revenge in Tom's darker dreams.

Tom locked his eyes on the dog. It was as black all over except for a splash of white fur around its cheeks which served to accentuate its mouth, splitting its doubtless hungry grin fully from ear to pricked-up ear.

The dog's teeth did not shine, appearing instead dull and grey. Perhaps they were not fully bared; perhaps they were still greasy from some earlier feeding which had not served well enough to quell its ravening.

Perhaps it was a shade, a devil-dog intent on avenging its cousins. London was ever full of ghosts.

Tom made to move but his feet were unwilling. More than that, these clogs would clatter. The racket might alarm the dog. Worse, it might encourage it.

Then came another set of sounds, from the North this time, from up the hill and beyond the dog. Men in drink, rough songs rising in the still air. Old battle rhymes.

The dog turned as though to hear better, and Tom used the moment. He darted to the shadow-safety of the jetty overhanging the Farriner' shop window.

He strained to listen for movement, the clicking of claws on stones.

There was nothing, Jesus be praised, Christ be praised.

He dared to look; the dog had turned back around. Tom conjured thick veins under the fur, sinews and muscle and the bulge where the jawbones articulated.

Tom stepped out of his clogs. They would clatter otherwise if he had to run.

Jaws that would grasp and pierce, then crush and break, tear and bite and swallow.

The cobbles were mercifully cool under Tom's feet.

But the dog was just a dog, and distracted into the bargain. Its body followed its nose, uphill and away, toward the sounds of revelry, away from Tom.

Tom's prayer-words still at the front of his thinking, pressing into the backs of his eyes like the head-ache that comes with tooth-ache, he watched the cur slink off. It moved low and careful, more like the foxes Tom knew from his Norfolk childhood than the upright strut of a well-fed city hound.

Tom missed Norfolk. He missed the rest of his family, the home they shared. He missed the open spaces and the wide sky. He missed the clean water in the streams and the wells, the cold salt of the sea. He missed the mill turning. He missed the inexorable power of the machine, its grinding stones smearing wheat into flour.

There were times he thought he'd run away, run back and be as free as in the days when he'd hide in his mother's skirts from his tickling father. Free to jump in clear puddles, to scare sheep in their pens, to throw sticks at his friends, to pretend to be fighting the Wars again.

Taking turns to play Cromwell and the first Charles with Daniel, each having their head cut off in turn and the other laugh as it was lofted for the crowd.

But he was no child any more, and his mother was dead.

Mother was dead and he had a man's work and a man's responsibilities. Not all the responsibilities that he wanted, but he would have them soon enough, if Christ willed it so.

London had its attractions. Never mind the hard work and the smoke in the air, the tight squeeze of the buildings and the myriad grappling stenches of the city, the river and, worst of all, the people. And never mind his father.

Never mind Thomas Farriner the elder, baker, a man who thought Tom little more than a wheedling child despite his seventeen years, fit only for fetching and carrying, for keeping quiet and grafting six till six, an apprentice first, a son second.

Not like Daniel, who was indulged by their father in the faith he'd claimed since their mother's death. Tom was a second son in all meanings.

Despite all of this London had its charms. Or rather, one person who embodied its mysteries and wonder, its splendour and its grace, its pleasures and its chance festivals, even when there was death all around. That person's hair was straw-white and she was shaped like a wine-bottle, slender and long-necked.

That was Alice.

Tom followed the building around to the alley which separated the bakery from the White Hart. Now he could smell vinegar-sharp vomit, piss, and dust.

The tang brought him back to this moment. To the reason he was here.

Tom got closer, still barefoot, so that he could see.

#

Challis could not yet sleep. The brandy still burned a little in his mouth. It had been some weeks since he had taken so much liquor in one evening. Then again, he reflected, he was in England, where drunkenness was commonplace, and more than that, he was in London, where the state seemed nigh compulsory.

The room was more than adequate; in the eaves of the building, with a roof that sloped somewhat, compelling him to stoop at times on account of his height. A window at the side that, if he bent his neck a little so he did not stare at the similarly-constructed building opposite, gave a pleasing enough view of rooftops and still, at this late hour, smoke lifting directly from scattered chimneys. The night was both warm and still. He could not fathom why they would persist in burning fires so close to midnight.

With that, he smiled. And that smile brought his mind around to the reason for his travel.

He laid his bag onto the bed. The satchel was fashioned after the carrying pouch a military courier might have, though it was somewhat larger. It had been made to order. He unbuckled the bag and spread it open. He shifted a layer of clothing onto a three-legged stool.

The removal of the clothes exposed a swatch of soft leather that acted as a partition. He lifted this up and over, and his eyes shone, not from the candlelight, but at the gleaming of what he revealed.

The wallet containing his blades. The box holding his pistols and weapon-works. His letters of introduction and of creditworthiness. The purses with together some two hundred new-minted guineas between them. A leather-bound and brass-clasped Bible.

He picked up the book. He opened the clasp by its sliding catch, and let the book fall open.

A name, all that he shared with his father, was inscribed on the flyleaf. Rufus Challis. He turned the book to the page marked with the slim woven cord incorporated into the book. The bookmark revealed the point that pages had been cut away to form a hiding place.

Challis tingled again with the glee-memory of the day he'd taken a knife to his father's Bible.

He didn't need the words in the book. He held them true in his head and in his heart.

Challis tipped the dead book forwards to retrieve the items inside. They fell into his hand. He closed the book, and then went back to the window.

Some drunk had lost their shoes. They lay in the roadway. Challis glanced up into the night.

Smoke aside, the sky was still clear, as apparently it had been for the entire summer. The landlord had chuntered that there'd been little rain since late Spring. This lack pleased Challis.

What also pleased him were the twin items now in his hand. He replaced one in the Bible and considered the other.

A stoppered vial of good Dutch glass. It contained a thick red fluid. He swirled the liquid around, though there was little space inside the almost full vessel. So he upended it, allowing the glass to catch candlelight on one side and starlight on the other.

A single bubble wobbled up through the red liquid before resting on the inverted bottom of the glass.

Challis righted it, and unstopped the vial, which opened with a firm and reassuring pop. He raised it, and brought it to his lips. 'Blood of Christ,' he said. He sipped, taking in the metallic scent from the bottle and the rich taste, acid and fruit combined.

Then he sat the bottle back in the Bible with its twin and closed the book. He removed one of his pistols from the carrying box and sat on the rush matting on the floor under the window and closed his eyes. He cradled the pistol in his thumbless right hand, and let it rest against his face. Only then he allowed himself to swallow.

The woman, alive.

An embodiment of London. A gift from God. A specific before the generality.

The woman's face in death.

There'd been a noise as he'd stood over her.

Now there were shoes in the street.

Someone had seen. Someone had gone to find out more. They'd crept up, not wanting to make a disturbing noise.

The lack of a hue and cry.

That was interesting. Perhaps someone fancied themselves an investigator.

Challis half-cocked the pistol to enjoy the sound it made.

The morning would come soon enough. Challis willed the new day towards him. Who would find a body in the night and not bang on every door?

The liquid was burning his throat, but it was a white heat, a purifying flame which stripped away all the pain and every sin. A flame which made him clean.

Already his phantom thumb was hurting less.

#

Tom took care placing his bare feet in the alley. He squatted by the corpse.

The air about Lizzie's body was rich with coiling sweat and drink vapours. Her eyes were wide and shot with blood, her face darker than it ought to have been.

No obvious wounds.

There was nothing lumpy in the vomit he could see that might have caused her to choke. Even so, Tom put his hands into the bile. The spew had not yet cooled. He ran his hands through the gruel, but there was nothing, no half-eaten food or similar, that might have made her retch herself to death. Reaching out further, he could feel nothing that she might have spat out or dropped.

Lizzie had been a toper and a whore. But these were not her choices, nor had it been her choice to die out here. All this had been forced upon her.

Tom was sure that she'd been murdered, that the man with the bag was the one to answer for it. If he was rooming in the Hart, then he'd be there in the morning. If not, then that'd be the place to begin asking questions.

Tom wiped his hands on his shirt. What best to do for Lizzie? She was a dead 'un and that was it.

Alice would take the news badly; they had been friends along with the rest of her crew that had worked out of the Hart. And Taff would be sad, in his own way, to see her gone. His wife, less so.

There was no point in raising a cry now. That would only put Tom in the middle of questions and accusations, and perhaps attract unwanted attention. From his father, for one. From the man with the bag and the long black coat, for another.

Better that Lizzie was found in the morning. And by someone other than him.

There was a chance here. A chance to show that Tom Farriner was more than a drudge. That he was a man in his own right. Not an all-but ignored second son, not a child any more.

He would have Lizzie's death repaid.

Tom backed out of the alley and collected his clogs.

He washed his hands inside the bakery and wiped them dry. He snuck back up to bed. Daniel was sleeping, which was something. Tom reopened the window. He did not look down.

For the longest time he lay on his bed. He stared up at the ceiling until he was sure that it was dawn and that he had remained alert through the night.

And then he woke, and knew that his dreams had been of nothing but unproductive wakefulness.

FRIDAY 31ˢᵗ AUGUST 1666

'Tom?' The shout was ragged. His father could well have been calling for hours. 'Tom!'

Tom fought to get dressed in clean clothes. There was no point in yelling back down to the kitchen. Quick as he could, he pulled a fresh work-shirt over his head and made for the door.

Tom was as careful as ever on the top staircase. It was steep and ill-made, as though an afterthought by whoever had decided to make use of the attic space. Planks creaked in complaint against his hurrying down.

Tom made it to the first floor, and then he ran along the corridor, past what he now knew to refer to as Alice's room, not Daniel's, and went along to the back stairwell that led down to the kitchen areas. His hurrying raised both dust and more shouts from below.

'By God, what are you doing up there?'

Then a softer voice, almost as though it was his mother. 'He's but a lad.'

'A lad's not what I need, it's a man. There's two men's work and more here to be done here, and nought but me, a woman and a child.'

A child? He was almost eighteen years old. Yes, he might be small for his years, unlike Daniel, who was six feet tall and more, half a head taller than their father, but Tom was strong. Not the strength which his father valued, the strength which made lifting sacks of flour no task at all, but the other kind.

The strength to see past his father's huffing annoyance, past his bluster. The strength to work so that one day his qualities would become obvious and he'd be properly valued for them.

The strength to keep his head down.

And what of Daniel? Free, it seemed, to pursue his calling, as his brother now put it. Standing with a chap-book sermon in one hand and a cup for coppers in the other, charming alms through his words and the power of his eyes, as clear and blue as the vitriol crystals displayed in apothecaries' windows. As clear and as blue as Norfolk water.

Daniel was still asleep even now. Curled on his pallet, hand on his cock and doubtless torn between lustful dreams and guilt for the same. Rising only when the Good Lord stirred him for another day of wheedling and praising, shaking with the fervour of the righteous, the better to rattle his begging-bowl in the faces of those captured by either his words or his charm.

Two brothers, two sets of household rules.

In the meantime, though, there would be sea-coal to fetch, wood to chop for kindling, trays to scrape clean of crusted baked-on matter. There was water to carry and jugs of ale to hike in. There were messages to courier: to customers and suppliers and to the Naval Offices alike. There was the shop frontage to keep clean. There were pies and bread to bake for and to hawk in the streets. There was flour to sift and salt to measure, cooked loaves to stack, and baked biscuit to cut from sheets into portions and then to pack into barrels.

And then there was Alice.

Two years ago – and how the years seemed to be gliding by faster, like clouds across the sea before a summer storm – Tom had travelled back to Norfolk with his mother, summoned by a message that her father was close to death. The news proved true. His grandfather had already been buried by the time they got there, his grandmother lasting just long enough to die with her new-returned daughter trying to feed her milk-dipped bread.

Tom was there when she died. She was so thin: her skin like muslin, pale and creased. It draped over her bones as though they were somehow shameful.

Grandfather had wasted away slow, over weeks they said, a tumour in his belly eating the fight in him from the inside.

Grandmother had been taken quicker. If Tom's mother knew it was the plague, she had not said. She just bade Tom keep some distance. He had watched from the doorway, as she tried to bring comfort with blankets and honeyed warm water.

Then Tom's mother withered and died too; the pestilence took hold of her as well. She gave her life willingly, uncaring, to the contagion.

There was discussion as to whether Tom would stay, but his father demanded by letter that he be sent back to the city.

His return in the spring found Alice already in place.

The plague had followed Tom towards London, and then passed him on the road somewhere.

Thomas Farriner's explanation was brief, as befitted his bluff manner. He had taken Alice in, showing right Christian charity by offering a roof in exchange for her labours. Daniel, whose reaction to his mother's death had been to begin his leaning towards Christ, asserted the same.

At first she had worked in the days, he said, returning to her family in St. Giles in the Fields at dusk. But as the plague took over the city after the comet, she lost her own family, all taken in one week so she'd told him, and so had come to live under Farriner's wardship.

This did not happen at once. Alice had, for a time, been part of the loose gang of whoring girls who did business out of the White Hart. Tom had heard gossip afterwards that she'd had Farriner in her aim for some time. Tom tried to not to concern himself with the insinuations.

What did it matter anyway?

Besides, with once-willing hands driven off by death or its shadow all across the city, good workers were hard to find.

At first Alice had earned her keep through the very chores that Tom now performed. Now though, she was like baker Farriner's third hand, proving an able student, quick to learn. She'd learned mixes and baking times, the ways to craft different loaves from the same base ingredients. She'd learned to tell quality ingredients from bad, pure flour from that adulterated with sawdust or milled chaff or riddled with rat turds or clumped with cat-piss; how to re-work stale bread by dampening it and baking some of the moisture back off quick so that it might be sold the next day. She'd learned how to make pies and pasties, ship's biscuit, baked sweetmeats and savoury tarts. And she'd proved able in other ways too, having an eye for decoration and the presentation of bakery goods which was beyond Farriner's simple tradecraft.

And then there was Alice herself.

Tom stood at the foot of the stairs. He had to watch her. Her hair, all creamy-light, was caught up and held in place with a wooden comb. She was sweeping up some small spillage. Her body, which swayed as she moved, flexed with each flick of the broom. And then her eyes, which caught his as she turned from the door back into the shop proper, as sharp and as green as nettles in summertime.

She smiled, a slighter thing than was usual for her; like the brief impression nails leave on a palm when fingers are clenched and released. Tom did just this, his hand curled tight in on itself as though he was bracing against some expected pain.

This was not physical hurt. The loss of his mother, this woman being placed here instead. The way he felt nothing about it at times, unlike his brother, who was consumed.

Christ, but all of it now ached in him. A gripe that did not ease as he followed Alice's slim smile over to where she'd shifted her gaze. Towards his father.

Thomas Farriner, supplier of ship's biscuit to His Majesty's Navy, stood hands on his apron-belt, blocking the doorway which led through to the bake-room.

'Good morning, father,' Tom said. There was no point in making apology for being late to rise. Late was late and that was bad enough. Excuses on top of tardiness would not help.

Farriner stepped out of the doorway. 'There's food on the table.'

Tom squeezed past his father, who clipped him on the back of the head as he passed. The blow was not hard enough for Farriner have meant it to hurt. Tom knew that from experience.

Tom resolved to eat fast and get on with his tasks.

How best to escape from them and see what news had spread? If any, that was. Information usually ran faster than rats off a gangplank.

Had the body been found? What about the man Tom had seen?

If Lizzie hadn't lost her money at dice would she have gone out into the alley? Had the drink he'd pledged her been the one that had led her to trade without due caution?

Was this his fault?

If it was, then what could Tom do to make amends?

There was bread and a bowl of mutton scraps. Tom ate, surprised at his hunger, washing the food down with mouthfuls of small beer straight from the jug. The mutton was still moist, fatty and rich; the bread was fresh, not yesterday's stales, sometimes served for economy or rebuke.

Tom licked his fingers, listening, trying to hear. Father and Alice were talking, but their voices were low.

He could not bear it any longer. He had to know. Keep your voice even, Tom told himself. 'What are you two fishwives chuntering about?' He busied himself again with the food.

Alice spoke to him first. 'Lizzie Corbet's dead, Tom.'

Tom caught the emotion in her voice. Her smile was weak today because of her dead friend. Maybe even because it could have been her instead, had she not found a refuge here.

'Johnny Hasleby found her,' Farriner cut in. 'Coming back from portering nights on the wharves. Stopped for a piss, he said. She'd passed out in the alley, they reckon, and puked her guts up. Choked on 'em in drink, the constable reckoned.'

'The alley?'

Farriner indicated the wall. 'Other side of there. Right under our bedchambers. Dead as mutton.'

Tom winced. The meat congealed in his throat.

'She was a good girl,' Alice said, her words hardly carrying.

Farriner snorted. 'Maybe so, but a drunk and a tosspot as well.'

'That's no way to speak of the dead.' She had turned away and was facing towards the front door.

'It's the living we need to be concerning ourselves with.' Farriner clapped his hands, a dry hard slap. The conversation was done.

It couldn't be as simple as that, surely? Tom had seen the man. Lizzie'd not been alone when she died.

But how to find out more? Tom kneaded his mind for an excuse, anything, to get away from his duties and find out.

There was one job which Tom knew that would keep him, if not quite out of sight or mind, but most likely beyond reach of his father's firm hand. And it would give him time to make enquiries next door. Perhaps Taff had seen something, the men she'd left the tavern with perhaps.

Tom left the last of the mutton, took a gulp from the jug, and turned to the cellar door.

'I'll sort out the trays,' he said.

Farriner raised a glance. 'Not like you to volunteer for that.'

Tom shrugged. 'It'll take my mind off Lizzie.'

His father was going to snap back with something, but he held fast, not speaking.

'I'll just fetch some more small beer first,' Tom said. Farriner waved a hand over his shoulder. Tom took that as assent. Besides, he rued, he owed Taff for a pint.

#

Challis awoke later than he had anticipated. Light was full through the window. Usually his sleep in new lodgings was more cautious, stirring him at every unfamiliar creak and scurry.

A continuous low rumble of daytime labour resounded from outside: carts over cobbles and the urging on of animals. He shut his eyes and the clamour continued anyway.

He would have to be more careful with the dosage.

Jesu, but his thumb ached. A miracle, as it was not there. He flexed the hand careful and slow. Each year it got worse.

They had tortured him well, all those years ago. First, by withdrawal of food and sleep. Every time he became drowsy, his collected piss was flung in his face.

Then they started with their ingenuity. Tied to a chair, a rag stuffed into his mouth. Water poured over the cloth to get him to the point of drowning, then the rag being snatched away.

They asked him questions and he quoted back scripture. They beat him about the kidneys and he recited psalms.

A table was brought in. Heavy thumbscrews had been bolted into the work surface. They left him to look at the equipment for an hour before they used it.

True torture is anticipation. The worry of what might happen is always worse than the eventuality. The tactic is twofold. First, trust in your reasons. Second, become the eventuality yourself.

They had left him again, his hands trapped by the thumbs. Challis took the option open to him. He twisted and applied pressure, breaking his right thumb. He sheared his skin against the screws, sawing through the flesh until the table was slick with his blood and the thumbscrew workings were oiled enough from the wound for the hand to slither free.

The hard part came later. Taking a hatchet, heated to scalding in a campfire, to his own hand. Cleaving the ruined digit like he was portioning a capon. Cauterising the wound with the same blade.

Now, and he breathed through the grinding under the skin as he flexed, testing his hand's willingness to embrace the day.

The thumb was his mark and his burden. And it was also a sign and a proof; a sign that He had graced Challis with His favour and had underwritten his expeditions, a proof of His passion in reminding Challis of Christ's agonies on the cross.

He was being paid for this job by the Dutch, but he worked for a higher authority.

Challis would have to take better care of himself. The thought of another nip from the vial had already sailed across his mind, but he let that idea drift off to port.

One dose a day was the discipline.

He passed water into the pot, shoed himself, verified that he had left his satchel packed and buckled, and satisfied that he had, stowed it back under the bed.

Challis went downstairs in search of something to eat.

The tavern was busier than the previous night. Some were taking their breakfast beef and bread, others beer alone. One, a thickset rough with a freckled bald pate and a stripe of tufty hair around the ears, was deep in conversation with a newsbook and a bottle of wine. Challis observed this from the stairs. Ah, he was not in conversation, but was reading aloud in a somewhat halting voice, as though public speaking was a talent he was not altogether familiar with. Other patrons were enjoying the reported account given from the journal, judging by their expressions and occasional comments in rejoinder.

The two whores there last night were sat at their same trestle. The fat one's face was streaked with tears. Her hair was being stroked by her partner, who alternated between taking sips from a jug and suckling on what looked like a chunk of limestone. A red-headed serving girl stood over them, half-engaged in keeping an eye out for customers wanting service, but keen also to stick with her sisters. None of them were speaking.

Challis could feel different kinds of grief emanating from them, such as he'd been party to in the past in the aftermath of battle. The emptiness at the loss of a loved one, the selfish punch in reckoning how you might be affected yourself, the awkwardness at not knowing what to say.

'Some ale or food?' The Welshman who had taken his money so readily stood running his hands through a cloth tucked into his waistband.

Challis nodded in response, finding a seat as far away from the whores and the reader as was practicable. 'Whatever you have to eat, and perhaps a glass of wine.' Today was going to be arduous, with much to do. There was little point in beginning on an empty stomach and with unbalanced humours.

'There'll be a roasted beef ready for noon, sir. Cheeses, cold meats and bread in the meantime.' The offering was cut with derision from across the room.

'Sir? Hark at Taff.' One man, already drunk, bowed as low to him as being seated would permit, before collapsing into unmanly giggles with his cronies.

'Watch your mouth, John Hasleby, else I call you to account,' growled the Welshman.

The whores stirred at the drunk's interruption, the fat one half-rising before slumping back to her seat to be comforted by the other.

'Ignore him,' the Welshman - Taff, it seemed – said. 'He's been drinking for free for hours.'

Challis said nothing. To ensure that Taff kept talking.

'We had a death in the night,' Taff said, dropping his voice. 'One of the girls that drinks here. She must have fallen in a stupor and drowned in her own puke. John there finds her at first light. He's stopping for a piss, on his way home, so he nips into the alley. And there she is.

'Course,' Taff continued, 'he knocks me up cause she – Lizzie – well, she's a known face, so I'm the one that has to sort it all out while he takes a bottle to settle his nerves. I'm surprised you were not disturbed, because there was a hollering and a banging for a while.'

Challis shrugged.

'Anyways,' Taff went on, 'there we have it. Not a bad lass in her own way, if you catch my meaning.'

'Once you got to know her?'

'Aye.'

So there it was. All cleared up, the body carted off to a pauper-grave unless there was family to claim it, and nothing more to be said except to raise a cup in the woman's name when it crops up in bar-talk. And eventually that would fade too.

But someone had been there, not long after the woman had forfeited her life. That person could well have seen him. They might suspect him. But maybe they'd just taken their chance and robbed the corpse. Maybe worse. Challis had witnessed many perversions conducted in the name of pleasure.

There was nothing to suggest murder had been determined. The place was draped in a respectful quiet. They'd lost one of their own.

The man with the newspaper must have sensed an opportunity for an audience. He began to read aloud from the print, but was cut off almost immediately by a flung drinking vessel from the body's finder. That set the women to wailing and cursing his name, as though he, by bringing the fact of the death to light, was somehow responsible for their miseries.

Taff wasn't slow in restoring order. He grabbed the drunk by the neck and twisted, pulling so that the man had no option but to stand and be led. Taff took him to the door, muttered something harsh, and slung him out into the street.

Challis was impressed. Taff could handle himself.

The women calmed each other. The redheaded one that had been standing throughout gave up any pretence at working and sat with her friends.

The drinkers went back to their food and pint pots, and the reader resumed his telling of events from his *London Gazette*.

The paper was full of speculation concerning the Dutch and the French, as was only to be expected. At the mention of Johan de Witt, Grand Pensionary and therefore day-to-day ruler of the Dutch States, Challis half-closed his eyes and clasped his hands under his chin, affecting a moment of contemplation before the rigours of the day, rather than betray concentration on the topic of comment.

He imagined London Bridge. Silence. Then, a series of explosions. Stone flying, brick walls rupturing. Glass shattering. Screams. Buildings blowing outwards, debris collapsing forwards into the street, backwards into the water below. The smoke clearing to reveal sundered arches, blackened bodies in the churning Thames.

A bridge no more.

Soon.

Challis opened his eyes.

The man with the *Gazette* not only held court, but knew it; he bristled with pride in the attention his oratory brought.

"'De Witt-'"

'De shit,' someone shouted across the room, to laughter. The place started to feel like a tavern again.

"'De Witt,'" he continued, affecting annoyance at the interruption with a shake of his head, though Challis detected a smirk in his voice at the sophistication of the wordplay, "'continues to lick his wounds like the burned dog he is, with his vessels either sunk or in dry-dock under repair following his recent besting at the guns of Charles' glorious navy, and his sailors similarly confined, either to the hospitals of the Dutch sisters or in winding sheets at the bottom of the ocean.'"

At this there was some cheering, though Challis noticed that one or two shook their heads at the mention of Charles Stuart.

He looked up, distracted. Bread, with cheese and cold boiled ham, had been slid onto the table. A glass of wine and a tankard stood beside it. Taff stood beside the trestle, presumably hanging on for some sign of approval.

'Good news is it not?'

'If news it be,' Challis replied, turning his attention to the meat. He prodded it left-handed with his knife, then cut and lifted a sliver to his mouth in one fast movement.

'The Dutch will sue for peace, I'll wager,' the landlord continued. 'They'll not suffer another beating such as they took on St James' Day. Five thousand Dutch souls lost, they say, in one day's sea battle.

Their vessels either sunk or blown almost to a point beyond repair.'

There was another tatty cheer from across the tavern. Challis, who had stood on the Rotterdam docks not three weeks previous and who had watched the returning Dutch fleet rope themselves up, chose his next words with care, allowing himself the soft pleasure of good meat well-cooked between his lips while he thought. 'I heard tell that less than a thousand were killed in battle. That the Dutch lost but two vessels, and that De Witt cares little for the outcome of one encounter when he knows that Dutch numbers will prevail, as they did in the Three Days' Battle, come the Spring.'

The landlord sat unbidden, opposite. Challis let his eyes hold the Welshman's for long enough for him to register two things; that no invitation had been offered, and that he was prepared to overlook this indiscretion for the sake of an interesting conversation. He cut himself another mouthful of the meat. It was still just pink in the centre of each slice, and though cold, the taste of blood was within it, as though it had been seasoned by death. It was quite delicious.

'I've not heard such things reported,' the landlord said, his hand tracing the tankard's handle. 'Not in the newspaper reports, nor in conversation.' Challis noted he had strong fingers and clean, short nails. There was no injury or disease about them.

Challis wetted his lips with wine. 'Times of war bring all manner of rumour. The foolish speculate, and those befuddled by strong drink or excessive coffee and with an audience to charm or amaze will often resort to fancy. You'll know this as much as the next man.' He waved the tip of his blade towards the man with the *Gazette*, the journal now spread on the table in front of him, one page held down by his pint pot.

The landlord nodded agreement.

'That being said,' Challis continued, 'I have occasion to talk to diverse fellows, despite and to some extent because of these present difficulties. And sometimes, because of their intolerance for strong drink and business combined, or because of an odd compulsion to prove themselves trustworthy by betraying confidences, I hear rumours.'

Taff nodded again. 'I know such men.'

'Indeed you must, operating such an establishment as this.' Challis took a slice of the meat and laid it on top of the hunk of bread. 'The point is this,' he said, then bit down. He continued with his mouth full. 'The journals may print one of three possibilities: a true record of events, the version that Charles's spymaster Arlington feeds them, and that version of events which will find favour with their readers and so have their subscription and popularity increased.

'Thus, I find it prudent to accept all opinions, and weigh them in the light of experience and understanding of the source of that opinion, rather than allowing myself to be over-swayed by an individual utterance.' He finished his bread and meat, and allowed the Welshman a space to think. 'This is very good, by the way.'

'The ham hock?'

'The manchet too.'

'Bakery next door. The meats I like to prepare myself.'

Challis waved his knife to indicate again his satisfaction, and then set the blade down.

Taff watched the knife, then spoke. 'You believe that Charles' recent success is overplayed in the public record?'

'I have reason, in part drawn by such confidences as I have indicated to you, that this may be just the case. All the Netherlands, the Dutch Republic, call it what you will, knows that England can be bested in sea battle, and they know likewise that the dark events of the past year have left London both weakened and eager for respite.'

'But the death lists show that the plague has been gone from London since last Spring.'

'Yet parts of the city are not recovered. Many who fled the contagion have not returned, through finding themselves new lives in other towns, or through having met their ends, having merely taken the disease with them.'

Challis went on. 'The Bills of Mortality do not tell the whole tale. Is there a man here who has not lost some family, or a neighbour or a workmate? Is there anyone of your acquaintance who has not suffered, either in heart or purse, through loss of business, customers, or through lack of willing bodies to labour for them?'

'You speak true enough. I-,' Taff hesitated, catching his breath. Some private grief there. Challis allowed him a respite from the conversation.

The cheese was good, soft, crumbly stuff. It was white as chalk and with the same light bitterness to taste. It stuck slightly to Challis's fingers as he broke off pieces and put them to his mouth.

'True enough,' the landlord repeated at last.

'And this is the fear that I have heard expressed in the coffeehouses and the ordinaries, by the docksides and in the merchant-houses, by guildsmen and labourers alike. That the Dutch know of this weakness of ours, that London, if not all England, is a brave but weakly child who needs more than a winter to recover from her recent injuries. And that the winter brings its own torments, and that not all the enfeebled will survive the frost and the long dark nights.' Challis rubbed his fingers clean on the napkin that had been provided.

The landlord sat sullen for almost a minute. Then, without speaking, he picked up the platter, stood, and took the remnants of the meal away. The public reading had apparently ceased some time ago. The fat woman was still crying. The men had gone back to their drinks and had retreated into their own silent worlds.

#

Tom made busy with the biscuit trays, the job he knew his father despised more than any other. It was a task often delegated to others, but baker Farriner would never deliberately let slip his distaste for an errand. Tom had made volunteering for the trays a personal ritual, a way of reaffirming approval in his father's eyes.

Daniel never bothered with such tactics. Tom was not sure if this was stupid or wise. Either way, there never seemed to be any comeback on Daniel. He was left to his own whims.

Farriner supplied ship's biscuit for the Navy. Of course there were loaves and pies for sale and often the use of the Farriner oven by others, at a price, for baking off their own goods or roasting their meats. But the backbone of the business was feeding sailors.

Since Alice had become part of the Farriner operation, the baking of goods for sale had become more important. That which had once turned a few shillings a week as a side-line now made more substantial gains. This was welcomed by Farriner; income had sustained itself through the plague in no small extent through Alice's enterprise. He let her have her way, at first as an indulgence, and then as a money-spinner. Besides, Farriner's heart was not in shop-work, but in the military.

Farriner, Tom knew, felt he was as much a part of Charles's glorious Royal Navy as the most lauded sea captain. It was his biscuit that ships ran upon, and with each man rationed two pounds of hard tack a day with their beer, there was ample opportunity to serve His Majesty.

Tom had overheard from Farriner's discussions with the Navy Office agent Harrow, a delicate and precise man who called once a fortnight with fresh requisitions and advance indication of His Majesty's needs, that the Navy contract yielded modest profit at best. Tom suspected more than once that Farriner had cut his price per barrel of biscuit in order to secure more orders. Navy work was dull, didn't pay, and its manufacture did not tax the baker's art. More than that, the Navy was less than prompt in the settling of accounts. It felt, both in the manner of the King's agent and in the lateness of receipt of payments, that the act of serving at His Majesty's command was deemed reward enough.

But Tom had heard his father speak with pride about his work a hundred times. For Farriner, the return of the King to England was first a fervent hope, then a glorious reality, and one he spoke of often.

These were the snatches of childhood that Tom treasured most. Sitting by his father at the kitchen table, shaping salt-dough into cake-shapes, decorating the circles with triple-pointed crowns made from rolled-out strands and dough-balls. Being told that one day he would bake for the Monarch, and that young Tom would be the finest baker in the land.

Sometimes Farriner would tell old stories of Hereward the Wake or of Robin Hood. Tom would feature in these stories, and always his skills would save the day and the King.

He was told of Much the Miller's Son, except this was now Tom the Baker's Son, who had taken his loaves to Nottingham Castle and who bribed the guards holding the imprisoned Master Hood and Little John with some of the bread, and who had been allowed in turn to take a last meal to the condemned men. And that they had taken their loaves with them on the back of the cart to the gallows, and had been allowed to break bread at the last dawn before the nooses, for the evil Sheriff liked to be seen to be gracious in victory. And that Tom had baked the bread with weapons concealed inside, and that Robin and John had fought and escaped and mocked the Sheriff in doing so, and that they all feasted that night in Sherwood on stolen venison with Tom acclaimed as Master of the Revels.

His father had mimed the ways in which Robin and Little John, Will Scarlet, the maid Marion and all had bowed before him, because that night Tom Farriner was King of the Forest, and because of him Robin had lived another day to further disrupt the evil plans of Prince John and the Sheriff, and so protect England until the true King's return from battle in Outremer, the holy land beyond the sea.

Tom remembered the way his father had spoken of Charles' return. Tom had been there back in '60, still small enough to be sat on his father's shoulders at the parades. Farriner described the procession as though it was as fresh and as yet as distant as last night's dream. A dream of fountains filled with wine, of strong meat roasting for all, of songs and music and laughter and hugs and kisses.

And all the while, his father's strong arms were there to lift him up. In those arms were comfort and reassurance, safety and strength and the promise of a fine future. That was Thomas Farriner, and that was why Tom had been proud to share his name.

And yet he worked him like a pony.

There were trays to scrub for the next batch of hard tack. The baking of biscuit was straightforward enough; a simple dough of flour, salt and water, rolled and baked twice. The dough was mixed and rolled out onto the trays, then the sheets of dough pricked, to divide the dough, once baked, into individual biscuits. The trays had to be well-greased or the dough would stick, and even with the thickest application, some would still break or, worse, remain baked-on.

Pig-grease was the stuff to use. For one thing, some pork flavour worked its way into the biscuit. For another, the biscuits smelled good when fresh, even if they tasted of little over time. And often as not, its use prevented having too much spoiled goods and wasted effort.

The first baking cooked the biscuit; the second was necessary to dry it so that it would keep for months in storage in Navy warehouses and then on board ship. Even so, spoilage by rats, weevils, leaks on board or theft by sailors was invariably put down to poor baking or barrelling by the supplier, and would be charged back in due course.

Tom had tried, of course, to eat the stuff. Sailors had all manner of names for it; hard-tack, yes, tooth-breaker, and worse besides. You had to smash it to get a piece small enough to fit in your mouth. Some would suck on a lump of it as they worked. Others would dunk or soak it in beer to soften it, and either eat it wet or else spoon themselves the resulting gruel. Others would add it to broth to thicken it. Some refused to eat it altogether, and traded with it, bet with it, or used it simply as bait for the rats which infested all ships, Navy or not, and would catch and eat the vermin instead.

That, for Farriner, was their business.

For Tom, his business was twofold, and to hand. First, to clean and prepare as many of the baking sheets as he could.

This left him with the second matter.

Lizzie. The man he'd seen. The impossibility that her death had been a natural one or an inevitability of her drinking life.

Tom grabbed the beer jug. The trays could wait.

#

At first Alice had been like an elder sister to Tom, sometimes sheltering him from his father's ire, like the time he'd not ensured that the oven was out and the hearth-fires all extinguished. His father's face had been fury; shouting about the dangers of unattended flame. That fire was a dangerous tool if left unguarded, and that fire and flour together was as much a risk of explosion and flame as any tinderbox, magazine or armoury. Alice had taken baker Farriner, who would surely have striped Tom's back in anger otherwise, and had calmed and soothed him.

Alice had washed Tom's clothes. She had cleaned him thoroughly once, when he had become lousy. He recalled how that felt, half-shivering in nakedness, half boiling with unformed lusts. She cooked their meals; mutton stews laced with ale, oyster soup, baked eel, partridge pie. She had kept him clued in with the gossip from Pudding Lane and Fish Street; who was sick and might have succumbed to the plague, whose husband was carrying on with whose wife, whose children had more in common with the drayman or the tinkers – anyone but the man who was raising them as his own.

She had let him brush her hair through with the comb she used to bind it up with. Alice's hair framed her face like the pale stone around a church window. Like St Magnus's church on Sunday mornings, the early light washing through the East window like coloured dreams.

Men bought pasties from her for the sake of a moment's conversation.

Lately, Tom had found himself studying Alice more. He'd watched, sitting on the stairs, when Alice was passing trays to his father to be baked off. From behind the shutters when she was in the street, yarning with passers-by.

Once, when Alice thought she was alone, through the open door of her room – Daniel's old chamber - she was sat on the edge of her bed, skirts hitched above the knees. She had swung her legs like a little girl, not letting them touch the ground. Tom could have watched that for hours. The ways the sinews in her ankles flexed as she shifted her feet. The way her toes arched.

All of her.

Tom had heard Alice speak of love many times; chatter with the girls from the White Hart, in fragments of songs sung herself, in fending off advances, both clumsy and confident, that came her way from callers and customers.

From what she'd said and sung and talked to others about, Tom knew. From the way he found himself behaving in her presence, awkward and foolish, he knew. From the way he felt, queasy and desperate, full and empty at the same time, he knew. From the stabs of anger and the bubbles of frustration he found popping in his head when she spoke to other men, even his own father, he knew.

It was easy to love Alice Corbould. Too easy.

She was there now, all trace of her previous distress at the news of her friend gone. She was laughing with some woman in the street, taking money for a loaf, paying Tom no heed as he slid out into the already hot sun.

It was as if Lizzie had never existed.

#

Challis left the Welshman and returned to his room. There, he retrieved certain items from his bag. His documents, some coin, a knife in a leather sheath which he'd had made some time ago in Antwerp. He tied the sheath to the inside of his forearm, handle end out. Then he adjusted his sleeve and checked that the device was unobtrusive yet ready to hand. He checked this twice, with his greatcoat off and on. The blade was discreet and drew fast each time. Challis then took his coat off again and laid it out on the bed.

The coat was heavy and had cost more than he could then afford to be made to his specification. He'd had pockets made to precise measurements, and had returned to the leatherworker three times for fittings. Some pockets were secret, and designed to be undetectable. Into some of these he slipped his documentation and some money. Other pockets were intended to deceive in other ways, such as the twin pouches he'd had inserted into the inside under the armpits. He took out his pistols, ensured they were primed, and slid them into these pouches. Satisfied that they hung with comfort yet did not disturb the flow of the garment, and were thus unobtrusive, he rubbed his fingers through his cropped dark hair, and hatted himself. He'd never been one for wigs, though they had their uses in matters of disguise and in such occasions where the resemblance of a gentleman was useful.

Satisfied with his appearance, he replaced his bag under the bed.

Temptation came to him then; to take a vial from the Bible and carry it on his person. To have it to hand.

The urge was as strong as it had ever been, but Challis knew it for what it was. A test, not dissimilar to the woman he'd been challenged to not kill that night.

The vial was another test he would not fail.

The notion faded.

Challis had work to do.

The landlord was at the premises' front door, blocking the way out. He was passing the day with some youth sent out for a jug of beer. He was swinging the vessel by its handle. By itself the fidgeting meant nothing, but on top of that the young man was shifting his balance. Left to right and back again on the balls of his feet. His free hand came up and swept damp hair back; there was sweat on his face also.

Challis had no doubt that this lad's guts were roiling too. He stank of nervous apprehension.

And then their eyes locked over the Welshman's shoulder. Challis did not need to press his gaze; the effect was almost instant. Fear has a universal face. There was no mistaking it here.

The lad did what he could, but the damage was done. He'd revealed himself in the genuineness of the reaction to having Challis there.

The Welshman picked up on it too, shifting attention from the lad to Challis. He stepped out into the road, unblocking the doorway. 'Didn't hear you coming there,' he said.

Challis kept the youth firm in his sight as he stepped outside. 'Don't worry yourself,' he said. 'I'm in no pressing rush.' He flicked his hat brim towards the youth, and smiled. 'Morning to you.'

'Morning.' To his credit the reply was not stammered.

Challis then turned to Taff. 'I suppose there's just the one topic of conversation today?'

'And you'd be right at that. Just telling Tom here all about it.'

Tom. That was his name. 'Dreadful business. So sad to hear of another, even a lost soul such as the unfortunate seems to have been, meeting their maker before their time.' Challis paused. 'Isn't that right, Tom?'

'It is.' He had recovered some of his composure. His voice was firm, the eye-contact was direct and he'd got his fidgeting under control. Challis approved. Caution and control were wise bedfellows.

'Busy day ahead, sire?' Taff seemed to want to move the conversation on, to get back to his work perhaps, or just to shift matters away from dead women in the street.

'Some business appointments. And, please, no need for formalities. Rufus will do just fine.'

'Very well, Rufus. If you have some time for pleasure between your meets, you'll find enough going on to divert you.'

'Oh?'

'Well, though Bartholomew Fair's not been official these last two years, there's still a city full of counting pigs, three-titted women and suchlike out there, all trying to lever themselves some of your money. You'll not be stuck for distraction. I've got a couple of the fair-folk lodging here, so I've heard all about it. There's a square off Chequeryard, by the Plumbers' Hall. Travellers meet there if you've a mind for stagecraft and sideshows. There's carousing late into the night, so I wouldn't expect an early start from them though. Late morning onwards there'll be something to amuse you, I'd say. Just watch your purse.'

'I'll bear that in mind.' Challis tipped his hat once more to Tom.

'Good day,' the lad said.

'Yes,' Challis said, now facing up the hill. 'I expect it will be.'

This Tom knew something. He gave himself up in that first flicker. He was a sack of worry, sick to his tripes because – why? – because he'd come within reach of someone he believed to be a murderer.

Yet there'd been nothing to make Challis believe that the woman's death was being thought of as anything other than a tragic inevitability, and one soon to be forgotten. But this Tom felt different, and was saying nothing about it. Again the same question; why?

Because he feared if he came forward he'd be ridiculed or disbelieved? Because an accusation might make him a suspect in turn? Neither of these possibilities sat right. It had to be something else.

He suspects but is not sure.

He is scared but he's trying to find out more.

Oh, thought Challis, and barked laughter at the realisation. A woman with a basket of fish scowled at him as though he were mocking her. Challis waved her off.

He fancies himself an intelligencer. He wishes to investigate me.

There might well be sport here, extra butter on the meat of his visit.

Let the lad do his worst, Challis thought, as he rounded the corner into the wider street at the top of the hill.

And if he were to become any kind of annoyance, then Challis was certain that God would show him what to do.

#

Tom followed Taff back inside the White Hart. Christ, but he was tight with fear, his skin clammy under his shirt.

Taff got him his jug filled and came back with a couple of mugs as

49

well. 'Sit down,' he said.

Tom drank first. The liquid rushed straight to his belly. Almost at once he began to feel better. He drank again, emptying the mug. He refilled it from the jug. 'Thank you.'

Taff waved it away. 'I don't know if she had it coming to her,' he said. 'But if you don't care for yourself, why should the Almighty?'

'It wasn't a natural death. I'm sure of it.'

'And I'm sure you're right. But we won't all make it to three score and ten, no matter what the Bible says, and we won't all die warm in our beds with family all around us. City life, Tom. She made her choices.'

'No-' Tom cut himself off. Taff had the matter boxed off in his thinking. A shame to lose a regular and all that, especially one who'd like as not kicked some of her whoring monies back to him. Lizzie's body had been taken away and any mystery had gone with it. 'No,' he repeated. 'I'm sure you're right.'

Tom poured another from the jug. Taff didn't say anything more.

Tom spoke, hoping that the action would make his next question pass as casual gossip-searching. 'So what's the story with the black-coat?'

Taff shrugged. 'Turned up late last night, staying for a few days. Bit private, mind, one of those who reckons his business is a bit special.'

'When last night?'

'What's your interest?'

'I just thought-'

'That he'd been around at the time Lizzie met her end?'

There was no point denying it. Tom nodded.

'No, I'm sure of it. Quiet night last night, just the usual dregs in after you and your brother left. Was thinking about shutting up shop sooner rather than later.' Taff drank from his cup. 'Lizzie'd already gone out by the time he turned up. He arrived afterwards.' Taff finished his ale, drawing the back of his hand across his mouth. 'Like I said, he – Rufus, wasn't it? - got here later. So he couldn't have seen her here. Like as not, Tom, she was already dead by the time he opened my door.'

Tom fumbled coins onto the table. Enough for the jug of ale, for it to be refilled to account for the extra he'd just drunk, and to cover Lizzie's last drink.

Taff's hand hovered over the money. A pause, as though he was going to push a copper or two back. Then he picked the coins up, all of them, and got back to his work.

#

Preparing the baking sheets was good for one thing; you could get lost in the routine of the work. Your mind was free to consider other matters.

Rufus had to be the man Tom had seen. The huge coat he was wearing was what he had on in the night. He'd have had a bag with him too.

And there was a manner to him, all confidence and surety. Tom knew a hundred merchants and a thousand traders, and there was none of the brittle charm of the hawker about him, nor the world-weary acceptance of having to take a price-beating in order to secure a sale.

Merchants tended towards showy in their dress-sense, but this man, in leather and black, was altogether more sombre. There was a fine quality to the stitching in the leatherwork though, a lightness in the way the doubtless cumbersome garment hung about him that spoke of both pride in appearance and a certainty in how he wished to present himself.

Those eyes as well, like a hunting bird. Except this hawk was not restrained by any jesses or creances about his legs that Tom could determine.

So what was his business in London? And what reason could he have to kill Lizzie?

No, that was wrong thinking. He had come to the Lane to find a quiet place to stay; close to the centre of the city, but a little out of reach. So he had reason or inclination to privacy.

That meant that Lizzie's death had to be an accident, some unintended matter. If he'd come here for the express purpose of killing a woman, then surely he would have walked off and lodged himself anywhere but next door to the body.

If he'd happened on Lizzie already dead, then why had he not raised the matter immediately?

Because that's not what happened, of course.

That raised another question. Supposing this Rufus had found himself, in whatever circumstance, committing a murder. Why had he stayed around?

The answers thudded into Tom like fists into dough. Because life held no consequence for Rufus. Because he'd killed before. Because he was used to death.

Because he could kill and leave no outward trace.

Because he was at ease being death's cause.

So why kill Lizzie?

There it was. Because he could.

Tom drew a breath, the air rushing into him as intoxicating as brandy vapours. He put down the tray he'd been cleaning. He took a few more breaths, big gulps this time; they served to bring him round.

Rufus killed because that was his response. That was how he approached the world around him.

But what to do about it? Tom had nothing but suspicions, notions. Who would hear this yarn with credence? Not his father, nor Taff. Not Daniel nor Alice.

There wasn't anybody. Maybe, just maybe, Martha and Jane from the tavern, but they'd cling to the idea that their crony's death had been anything but accidental because that would make sense to them, not because they believed it were true. They'd take succour for themselves that her death had been a cruel blow by the Fates. But they would not be believed in turn; they'd be seen only as shrill harpies, desperate slatterns who'd slander a working man to apply salve to their abraded consciences.

Tom could think of no-one.

He would have to unpick this matter, and this Rufus, alone.

Tom stood back from his work. His flowing mind had released him from thinking on his duties; a hefty stack of cleaned-off baking trays stood in confirmation.

Then Tom remembered what Taff had said about the gathering by the Plumbers' Hall, and an idea came that might bring some measure of justice for poor Lizzie's soul.

What he had in mind would need a measure of luck.

Tom went to get some.

He slid his knife into his hand and went to see Mother.

#

Tom was afraid of the cellar. It was an addle-headed thing to confess to, but there it was. It was not so much the darkness nor the cold, nor the musty smell of dried-up mouse-droppings, nor the saltier tang of the cured hams that were sometimes stored there. Not even the closeness of the room, with its low roof and squat dimensions, or the way the air was textured with cobweb so that each gritty nose-full made him want to choke and sneeze. The accumulation of these factors however; this was what weighed upon him.

That and Mother. Mother, who sat on the stool at the bottom of the stairs, forever waiting.

Tom took a lit taper in hand and held it out into the open doorway. The light was thin, adding little at first to the sunlight now at his back. Tom peered down the stairs. The light did not penetrate through to their bottom. Careful and slow, he began down the stairs, flame in one hand, and his work-knife in the other.

Mother sat in her pot at the bottom of the steps. When Tom had asked why the sour yeast preparation they used to make their bread rise was named that, Farriner's eyes bronzed. 'Mother provides all,' he said. 'She feeds the dough and allows it to grow, to rise. She gives it air and food as my mother, as your mother and grandmother in their times, gave life to you and I.'

Mother had to be kept cool because that prolonged her life. This was why she lived in the cellar. That and the smell, which some customers found too earthy, too ripe for their sensibilities.

Mother had to be fed every few days with a little flour and water. And with this food and drink she grew. And with each batch of bread, a little piece of Mother went into the mix, and the loaves would rise.

It made no sense to Tom how such a thing could work. Father said that it was another proof of God the Father's design and of His faith in turn in good King Charles, under whose reign all prospered. Alice said simply that Mother worked, and that we should never question that which worked well and without complaint.

Tom found himself wary though. He approached Mother with his blade out and the taper held high. She bloomed out of the pot rather like a cauliflower might out of the earth, like a cloud fallen from the sky.

There was barely an inch of the feeble light-stick remaining as he cut into Her.

His father had told Tom that Mother was precious, that she was as close to a holy thing that a baker could possess. She was like saints' bones to papists, like a cross-staff or a backstave to a ship's captain. He'd told Tom that pieces of Mother were worn around the neck in pouches by bakers attending to armies, partly to restore should the whole encampment's supply be lost to cannon fire, partly for their own protection.

Tom cut a slice. He did it without touching Mother directly, instead steadying the pot with his left hand and using the knife with his right. He curved the blade around, taking the top of Mother's head off in one attempt. Mother was soft to cut through; less heavy than dough. It was like bread, light and airy, just not baked. Tom could not understand it.

Cupping his left hand, still holding the remnants of the taper between his fingers, Tom speared the slice and made his way backwards up the stairs. At the top of the stairs, the taper gave out, but Tom was back in the daylight.

He slid the piece of Mother onto a section of clean cloth. Then he checked around. No-one was in sight. He cut a small square of the material, perhaps three by three inches, and dabbed a sliver of Mother into the middle. Then he closed this swatch around the sample. He made sure that Mother was wrapped tight, then Tom nicked holes in the ends of the cloth, and slipped a thin leather cord through the holes.

Tom tied the necklace he'd made around his neck, and tucked it under his shirt. It felt itchy next to his skin. Somehow he felt safer. Braver. Like someone about to charge across a battlefield with uncertain outcome, but protected with a charm.

He was ready to gabble some excuse but the shop was busy and it was easy to get to the street unquestioned. Maybe the charm was working already.

#

Daniel was outside, standing by the alleyway where Lizzie had died. He was staring into the gap between the buildings.

Tom was tempted to skirt past him. Leave him to his God-struck idleness. But Daniel was muttering under his breath. Fast words, a gabbling tumble, to no-one.

He was saying his prayers. Prayers for Lizzie.

That was more than Tom had done.

Tom put his hand on his brother's arm.

These were no prayers that Tom knew from church, though, but a running together of scraps of scripture. Throughout, Daniel gazed into the shadows. Then he stopped, turning his head slightly to acknowledge Tom's being there.

'Brother?' Tom asked.

'She died alone, Tom. The first of many.'

What do you mean?'

'Whoso killeth any person, the murderer shall be put to death by the mouth of witnesses: but one witness shall not testify against any person to cause him to die.'

'What? What does that mean?'

'It means what the Lord intends, nothing more.' Then a blink, and Daniel faced Tom. 'No-one should die alone.'

'No. Are you-?'

'I am fine, brother. I needed to say something. Some words for your friend. Not all prayers are for churches.' Daniel rubbed his eyes. There was redness there that might have been just from the rubbing. 'You away?'

'An errand.'

'Of course.' Daniel's expression was distant. 'Take your time. I'll cover for you.'

None of this was like Daniel. Not these days. Tom felt pulled in two directions. Half of him wanted to stay with his brother, to get him to talk about whatever it was that was turning his insides. Part of Tom wanted to be far away from him, from his strangeness.

'I won't be long,' Tom said.

Then he ran to the Plumbers' Hall.

#

Crossing London was perilous enough if you stuck to the main thoroughfares. Carts, horses, sedan chairs, the thrust of crowds, and the ever-present threat of stumbling into a dozen different kinds of obstruction.

The snickets and smoots that cut across the streets offered faster ways through the city, but the potential cost was even greater, be it through lurking thieves, rapists who'd like as not wrestle a young man to the ground as a woman; distempered dogs, hidden half-rusted nails in wood, even middens.

That danger was high in Tom's mind, and part of his plan. Anything could occur off the main roadways, and poor Lizzie was the proof of it. Tom's plan was simple enough; sneak through to the Plumbers' Hall and point Lizzie's murderer out to some rogues. He'd have him marked as a rich target and let them take his revenge out unwittingly.

He walked fast, first down the hill and then left across Fish Street, and then kept going in as straight a westward line as he could, making

56

his face a mask of business that would not be dissuaded.

#

Dust swirled under carriages and cartwheels. That morning's discarded shits were cracking and dulling in the sun. Fat flies danced, dazzled by the choices open to them. Challis thrust his hands into two of his more ordinary pockets and headed on.

Some of the streets still bore evidence of contagion. Houses and shop premises were boarded up. Some had once-red crosses daubed up on them. Properties once secured with nailed planks had since had these measures corrupted. Challis wondered if it had been by looters breaking in, or by the walled-up diseased breaking out. Had the houses been entered and the corpses removed to the plague-pits, or were there still rotted English barricaded in their homes?

Dust was everywhere, drifted into corners like ancient snow. Dwellings were thick with the stuff to the ground floor windows. The only moisture evident was puddled piss, either hoisted out from chamber pots above, or deposited by animals or people on the ground. The English were beasts, thinking nothing of crapping in any corner, grunting and spitting as they voided their precious beef. One street had fresh weeds growing through the cobbles. The plants may have been pale through bleaching and thirst, but had nevertheless made their way through to the surface, had not been beaten down by feet, hooves or wheels.

The people, too. Though some were all bustle and swagger, or slouch and smoke as their nature, humour or immediate task dictated, others appeared lost or beaten, lurching through the streets. Any circumstance might have led to this; loss of family or business through the plague or its consequences. Loss again through the on-going wars with the Dutch; a husband or a son. Perhaps just the weight of suffering all around, coupled with the selfishness of the city, the desperation of the poor, the retreat into drink or other abandonments, the loss of faith in Christ Jesus, and all under the rule of the restored idolater Charles.

Charles, whose reign had been marked by rampant whoring and

feasting, by the squandering of monies levered from Parliament, by excess and indulgence, by mockery.

Mockery of the office of King.

Mockery of the right rule of Parliament.

Mockery of the Redeemer.

Instead, Charles had behaved how many of subjects had feared he might; like a fat child with access to a pantry. A fat child, moreover, with the weaknesses in character of a sot and a sybarite, a head inflamed by toadyish trucklers who debased themselves to his whim, crawling through ordure for a kiss of his boot heel, giggling at his farts, nodding in profound affectation at his vapid observations, hanging on his every word as though Lord Protector Cromwell had never existed.

A fool and his court that, at the first whiff of the plague-pits, had absconded the city and their obligations and had set themselves up in Oxford, returning only when they deemed it safe. Little wonder the street-people had the ash faces of the penitent, and the blank eyes of the blinded prisoner.

Challis was now in a square; an open courtyard sided by taverns and stalls.

His knowledge of London's geography was not precise, but he knew where he was. He'd meandered the streets to where he'd been directed by the landlord. It was the noise that had brought him here, he reckoned. Illicit or not, there was no disguising the raucous din of a fair.

He'd not seen a guild hall in the area, but then again, how grand an establishment would plumbers have?

Finding himself with a mild thirst, Challis took a seat. Straightaway, a boy brought him ale.

'Are you here for the show, sir?'

'The show?'

'Yes, sir, the next performance. About to begin.' The lad motioned across the courtyard where a wagon had been secured with chocks under the wheels. The cart was mounted by a gaudy tent, all reds and greens, a cloth sketch of a castle. 'I'd move closer sir, or stay back and stand on the table to watch. The crowds, sir, you see.' The boy was off, refilling vessels from a seemingly bottomless jug and taking money fast.

Perhaps two hundred had assembled around the cart. An assortment such as only the largest cities could bring together. He'd heard a word for such crowds: gape-seed. There were fops; ruffles and lace, brash colours and ornate embroidery and each of them bewigged in unseasonable manner. Most were accompanied by females, a few of obvious bearing and expensive dress, happy to slum it with the masses, others were the opportunistic kind, drawn to men with money for drink and busty companionship. There were idlers and gawkers, sober-attired merchants, jowly old bastards and their "nieces", barrow-boys and sneak-thieves, traders, hawkers, dullards and dolts. All drawn by the tent and its promise, or else by opportunities presented by the crowd itself. There'd be more than one purse cut here today.

A barker patrolled the tent's frontage. He was little and round and quite drunk, a fat full moon of a face split into a grin either rouged or wine-stained from a broad-lipped cup.

He was cheeky with the children, lascivious to the ladies, mock-solemn to the gentlemen. He waggled a little finger through a split in his breeches, glanced down and pretended to bawl at his lack.

Then he scratched at a boil on his head and Challis remembered him.

He was lodging at the White Hart. Somewhere here there would be his tall and ascetic companion, perhaps behind the curtain on the wagon.

Once the barker had the crowd's focus, he bid them be silent, all the better to raise a huzzah for the Lord of Misrule himself.

He counted the crowd down in a shouting mock-whisper back from five to one.

Then a cheer from the crowd, and a partition opened in the tent. Challis saw the show for what it was, and found himself surprised.

A puppet-show of the Italian kind. What surprised him though was not the performance itself, which seemed little more than could be staged in any town by any itinerant showman, but by the crowd's reactions to it. There was silence at first, then such laughter at the antics of the glove-puppets on the cart.

The main character was Puchinello, all crookback and reedy wobbling voice as might be expected, though the others were new to him.

As Challis gave more attention to the show, he understood. There was little story; merely a succession of escalating scenes, each ending in Puchinello beating his counterpart around the head. But such a series of opponents. First his wife and his child then a puppet dog made themselves known, and Puchinello, or "Mister Punch" as he was here called, bested them all. Then, another puppet, with bald head and screwed-up face, came onto the stage, and was announced as Sobersides Cromwell; and he too was butted repeatedly in the face by Punch.

The crowd roared its approval at the punishment. Then Death appeared, cowled in black, and boasting about the contagion and the souls that had been harvested with His infernal scythe that year, and boasting moreover that his shadow had ensured the Fair was cancelled - there were jeers at that - and Punch faced him down and beat him up. Again the crowd cheered, clapping as though they were children and this was some great Christmas treat.

And then a final puppet. This one was dressed in purples and reds, with lace and ribbon around him, and was adorned with a black wig that almost reached the character's waist. It wore no breeches, the better to display the pendulous puppet cock swinging there.

'Do you know my name?' the bewigged puppet thundered. Punch gawped on, first to his addresser, then to the audience, and then back, as if in puzzlement at his royal tone.

'Yes,' cried several in the crowd. 'Yes!' Others whispered and giggled to each other.

'Oh no, you don't,' the puppet said, teasing.

With glee, the crowd chorused back, 'Oh yes, we do!'

Then Punch came to the front of the stage. And in his swazzled voice he called 'And I know him too!' And with that Punch beat around the head of the other puppet until his black wig fell off. The crowd cheered as one, and this now bald puppet slumped to the stage. If the crowd had been raucous up until this point, what came next sent them into peals of laughter, abandon and amazement. Punch dipped out of sight, to reappear a moment later. Some gasped. The crippled puppet now wore a crown.

The crowd cried out their bravos and shouted for King Punch to take his bows, which he did over and over again.

The puppeteer, gaunt and serious, came out from around the tent. He bowed to the audience, and accepted a tankard passed up to him. He toasted the crowd, drank it down in one, and held out the cup for monies. Though many simply applauded then went on their way, chattering about the audacity of the show, enough left offerings to make this seem a profitable, if borderline treasonous, enterprise.

It was not the playlet but the reaction of the crowd which intrigued Challis. Such merriment at the violence, infantile rapture at the mayhem, even that done to the last figure almost gave Challis pause.

Perhaps they would welcome the storm he was bringing.

The barker counted the money in the tankard then made a show of throwing a couple of standing somersaults. This brought a handful more coins, the feat being all the more amusing because of his wide round body.

The puppeteer had vanished somewhere. No, he was back behind the curtain, because Punch was watching the capers.

Punch cast about the fading audience. When he came in direct sight of Challis, he paused. A puppet hand came up and waved.

Then Punch disappeared behind the red cloth.

The crowd had by now dispersed, some leaving the courtyard in search of other diversions, others remaining to attend to their thirsts. Challis fancied calling the serving child over and taking another beer from him, but the boy was not to be seen.

No matter. If London was full of anything besides corruption, it was full of chances to get drink, be it in one of the hundreds of taverns, inns, ordinaries and alehouses which made up one in ten premises hereabouts, or yet one of the coffeehouses where any of the imported libations, coffee, chocolate or tea could be obtained, and with it the cachet these fashionable new beverages purported to offer. Even water was freely available, there being standpipes at the end of most of the wider streets. Perhaps there was work for plumbers after all.

It would, though, be a warmer day than this, Challis reflected, before he'd take a mouthful direct from one of those. Too often he'd seen the cramps, sweats and fevers resultant from drinking bad city water. There was no accounting for what manner of vile humours might be collected through the pipeworks, through the piss, the shit, the guts and the rotting slime that made itself into the Thames and Fleet rivers, and thus into the mouths of the thoughtless.

Challis took off across the square, cutting into a narrow alley he fancied would lead him quickly to Dowgate and thence to Thames Street, where he had the first of his arrangements to make.

The alley was a dank strip, barely a yard and a half wide. The clear sky was almost obscured completely, through overhanging timbers or by clothes strung on lines between houses so close that one might pass items across from upper-floor windows across the alley's divide.

Challis was ten paces down the alley when he heard the whistle. A shrill; the sound a child might make with grubby fingers in his mouth. He turned to see the ale-boy who'd served him. Then the child ran off.

So that was it.

Challis checked his coat to see where he'd been marked. There it was; a line of dry white - chalk most likely - daubed on his flank. Challis was impressed; he'd neither suspected the boy nor felt any touch.

He'd been marked out as a swell. An easy target, but for whom?

There were two of them. One at each end of the alley. At this end, a hulking brute of a man. Over six feet high and almost as broad, Challis reckoned. He was there to block off an escape route, his fists and bulk his primary weapons. This left the other end of the alley.

The second man was running at him, fast and silent, arm outstretched. He had a blade. Not a sword; it was too short and too wide. Something more easily concealed and which could be carried with good reason. A fish-filleting knife perhaps, or a butchery tool. Fifteen inches long, and two inches broad at its widest. The blow would come low, hard and fast. Under the ribcage and up, treating Challis like one of the carcasses it was usually wielded upon. Death would be swift if the blade struck true. If it did not though, his demise would be slow and agonising, bleeding out in this alley or else on a barber-surgeon's table later, if he could be brought to one in time.

The runner dropped his arm, bringing the knife down with it. The sprint would give him momentum; he intended the stroke to be a killing one.

Challis discounted his firearms. Too noisy in these environs, and questions would be asked. A hue and cry was not in his interest, despite the obvious utility of a swift resolution.

Challis made his choice and stood his ground.

The knife was rising, the runner perhaps four yards out when Challis stepped forwards. He kicked out to the side, knocking the knife-arm out of true as it rose. The blade struck the wall to the left of Challis's shoulder. Its wielder came after the knife, which had been strapped into his hand for purchase. Knocked off course by the kick, he too hit the wall.

Challis followed the kick with a punch, deep into the man's gut. He grunted a foul expulsion of air as he took the hit. The knife-arm dropped, all its pent up energy spent. Then Challis withdrew his own knife from the hidden sheath. In one move he put it to the rogue's chin, delivering a bladed uppercut. Up and through the mouth, shutting that festering gap, and up into the brain; there was the briefest resistance as the steel forced its way through.

The would-be butcher's eyes bulged for a second, and then the pressure behind them subsided. Challis held the man up until he was sure that he was dead.

Dark liquid began to leak from the pinned mouth. Challis withdrew the knife, and turned to the near end of the alley. The body slumped sideways along the wall, and then flopped to the ground. He was as silent in his death as he had been in the few moments Challis had seen him alive.

This brought a roar from the ox, lurching into the alley. His fists were out, great hams that scarcely fit into the confined space. Challis was minded at first not to kill him, but the thug was not to be reasoned with. He charged at Challis, bellowing wordless anger for the loss of his conspirator. He threw a punch, an awkward attempt as the narrowness of the passage constricted his swing. Challis slashed out at the man's forearm, catching it before the blow could be landed. The blade cut across just above the wrist joint. The man shrieked as though he'd not experienced pain of the like before. Anger was replaced with confusion. Distracted by the wound, he didn't see the next blow being delivered.

Challis jabbed twice, both punchy cuts to the throat. The second must have severed the windpipe. The hulk scrabbled at his throat, wetness bubbling through his fingers. He dropped to his knees near his compatriot, one arm out and bleeding, the other gloved in deep red from his neck.

Challis checked up the alley. There seemed to be no attention being paid, so he waited until the fellow tumbled over next to his friend, hand still under his jaw.

Challis waited for the pain in his right hand to pass. He blinked away flecks of dancing light. Angels in celebration, rejoicing at this minor victory. He breathed in three, four times. The angels parted. He did not examine his hand.

Challis wiped his blade and then sheathed it. He made two cursory checks. First he rifled the bladesman's pockets. This search revealed no money but a couple of useful-looking items: a hank of tough twine; a tinderbox. These were pocketed. And second, Challis checked his own clothing, which seemed clean of gore.

Satisfied, with that he left, continuing onwards towards Dowgate and from there, the environs of the river.

#

Tom held back from entering the square by the Plumbers' Hall until he heard cheering; some new diversion had commenced. This was what Tom was waiting for.

If Rufus had indeed come here, then he'd be in the crowd, facing whatever show was being put on. Tom could be sure of not being seen if he lurked back here.

A serving boy came out from a doorway, a heavy-looking jug being carried two-handed: by the handle and also supported underneath. Tom nodded him over.

'You thirst?' His hair was close-shorn, doubtless to stave off lice. His mouth was a jumble; children's teeth, empty gaps and still-furrowed adult teeth half-showing. Clean streaks across his face where he'd drawn a sleeve over his mouth to wipe off ale-swigs.

Tom shook his head. 'I'm on lookout for someone.'

'What's that to me?'

'He's rich. A pocket full of gold.'

'Oh?' The lad affected disconcern.

'Long black coat,' Tom said. 'Hands in pockets, most likely.'

A pause before reply. 'Why hands in pockets?' So he was here.

'As I said, full of gold. That's why.'

'So?'

'Don't tell me a smart one like you doesn't take the odd shilling for marking out a prospect.'

'I'd be lucky to get a sixpence and boot up the arse.'

'Better than nothing at all.'

'Aye.' The boy nodded to one side of the gathering. 'That the one?'

And there he was, smiling, seemingly equally at what he

determined of the audience as with the puppet-show that they were gathered around. 'That's the man.'

The boy put the jug down and made two moves. First he shifted across the square and skirted past Rufus. Then, looping around and back towards Tom, he opened his hand and flashed something, a white rock, in his palm. Tom didn't see who the gesture was intended for.

The boy came back to his jug. 'You want a slice of his gelt?'

Tom shook his head.

'Just as well. You'd not get it. So why the interest if you don't want a share of what he's got?'

'It's personal.'

'He'll get hurt.'

Tom shrugged. Rufus would get beaten so hard he'd be shitting blood if there was any justice.

Cheering from the crowd, some whistles and much applause. A fat juggler was pulling tricks and wheedling money from the gathering. Tom stepped back into the shade of an awning.

'No stomach for it?'

Tom felt a gauze of coolness from the shadow, but blushing shame soon cut through it. Perhaps the darkness hid his face from the boy. Maybe it would obscure him from Rufus, should he turn in this direction.

There he was, still as a dead tree as others dispersed around him, caught by the little puppet peering out from the upraised stage. Then his attention shifted and he moved off.

Someone small and fast – not the boy, who had taken again to hustling beer – ran past Tom, ducking into a narrow cut-through. Rufus was headed in the same general direction, but towards a parallel alley. The boy was talking quick but not paying much attention to a new customer.

Now Tom could see what the lad was looking at. First, the runner, then second an enforcer, a shire horse of a man coming up also. Threats and muscle, Tom supposed. Ox and plough.

He hoped they cut him from arse to mouth, splitting him open for flies and hungry dogs to snaffle. Tom thought about staying, but counselled himself against hanging around.

He walked back towards the bakery, taking the streets this time. Lizzie had been killed and this man was responsible. Now he would pay a price for his violence.

He'd been freed of a blockage inside. The griping in his belly was gone. There was a balance in justice being meted in a side-street. This felt right.

Tom prayed that Lizzie would find her rest in whatever lay beyond. As he made that prayer he held onto the talisman he'd made earlier. The softness of the pouch and the heavy yeast smell were comforting.

By the time he was three streets away, the matter was out of Tom's mind.

#

A little bell sounded when Challis opened the door; fairy laughter. Already he did not like this place.

A man sat at a bare desk facing the door. A second desk to one side, apparently placed to extract maximum benefit were a fire lit in the adjacent grate, was its opposite, cluttered with papers, writing implements, a wine bottle and a glass.

The walls were shelved out from floor to joists. Each shelf was loaded with ledgers and bundles of parchment. A doorway curtained off with a heavy cloth.

The man at the desk stood as Challis entered. A further insipid ringing over his shoulder as the door clicked shut.

'Yes?' The man affected an imperious tone. He leaned forwards, spreading his hands out like slim pink spiders on the waxed wood.

Challis took out a letter of introduction. 'James Jephcott.'

'You are expected?' This was said in a manner indicating that such a state of affairs would be most unlikely.

'We have a standing arrangement.'

The clerk looked Challis up and down. 'Very well-?' The words trailed.

Challis did not supply the vacant space with his name.

'Very well,' the clerk repeated, in as decisive a fashion as could be mustered. 'If you would wait.' He retreated through the doorway in a flurry of topcoat and breeches.

The curtain billowed again almost immediately, filling like a mainsail catching its first draught of open sea air, then collapsing as though a spar had snapped under the fresh tension. A fat flustered man came through, pulling his wig into place. He had gone perhaps a week without a shave and judging by the yellow-stained linen tucked in at his neck, he'd been disturbed at his luncheon.

His words were obscured, first by chewing and swallowing, then by industrious swabbing around the mouth. 'Jephcott, sir, James Jephcott.' He did not hold his hand out in greeting, but instead snatched the letter from Challis.

The clerk peered over Jephcott's shoulder for a view of the papers. Jephcott waved him off with a flick of the cloth, then used the same napkin to usher Challis through beyond the curtain.

#

Jephcott led Challis along a corridor not to another office, but into a kitchen. There was food and drink on the table, and a plate bearing the remnants of a meal. Cold beef and pickled onions. A pot of mustard. A small fire burned unseasonably, more smoke than flame.

'Sit, sir, sit,' Jephcott said. 'If you'd excuse the informality of the surroundings, I'd be obliged.' Jephcott smeared mustard onto an offcut of the meat and then took a bite. As he chewed, he wiped his knife on his napkin and, after brief inspection of the sealed note he'd taken from Challis, drew the blade through the wax.

Jephcott's eyes flicked over the letter. He then got up and laid the paper on the fire. Jephcott stood until the paper curled, then blackened, and then was consumed. He took a poker propped up by the fireplace and riddled the ashes until there was nothing to indicate an incineration.

Jephcott sat heavily down.

Only then he returned Challis's gaze. 'Well, sir,' he said. 'You come with the most-' he paused, 'compelling of references.' He stroked his stubble. 'Some days I wish that full beards were more fashionable. As it is, I find that I have neither the patience to sit in a barber's chair nor the skill these days to attend to my whiskers with any great dexterity.'

Jephcott consulted a watch he wore as a pendant. The single hand indicated that the hour was between noon and one. 'Of course,' he said. 'I really should have offered you something in the way of hospitality.'

'Think nothing of it.'

'Indeed not, no. Saying that, these are inhospitable times that we live in, And I'm not the man to make that the more so. Though neither am I the man to abide the vanity and falsity of manners at the expense of humility and plain speaking.

'Nevertheless,' Jephcott continued, with a sigh, 'I have made my bargain and am satisfied that is a right one to have made. The monies have been deposited as per our understanding, and so I am in your debt till the work be done.'

Jephcott stood, and Challis did likewise. 'Come, sir,' Jephcott said. 'We have matters requiring our attendance.'

#

Jephcott led Challis back towards the front office. Jephcott's wig was lousy; Challis could see the ticks crawling. At its crown there were signs of patching and re-stitching. As though aware of this observation, Jephcott removed the hairpiece and ran his fingers through his silver-white hair, itself as patchy as the wig.

Jephcott scratched with vigour. His fingernails had been left to grow; they were long and uneven, albeit for the most part clean enough. Jephcott knocked the wig against the door-frame when re-entering the office. Dust and Lord knew what else dropped from the wig in small white puffs. The knock had the effect of rousing the clerk.

This man brought his head up from his crossed hands fast. He might have been sleeping, or praying.

Jephcott stuffed the wig into a cubbyhole and clapped. 'Mister Raftery, if you would,' he said. 'Quick to it man.'

Raftery reached into a drawer for paper, ink and quill, and made ready to take down instructions. Working for Jephcott evidently often involved long periods of indolence and then random, sudden activity.

'Much more like it, man.' Jephcott seemed renewed. Purpose had slapped vitality into him. 'Take this down.' Jephcott then spoke fast, and Raftery wrote quickly to keep pace.

Raftery read back to Jephcott, who pronounced himself satisfied.

Raftery took the now-dry note and folded and sealed it with wax-stick and a stamp.

Watching them helped Challis keep his mind from the twisting agonies emanating from his ghost-thumb, as taut as a fully-pregnant belly. The two who'd attacked him earlier had deserved their fate. They should not have taken him on.

No, they should not have. Challis knew that he made a fearsome impression on some. Two low thieves would surely have been inclined to choose easier prey.

The square had been full of potential. So why mark him out?

No, why was the wrong question.

Who.

Who would do such a thing?

'Much obliged, Raftery.'

'Sir.' The words snatched Challis back into the room.

Jephcott examined the note, snuck his wig from the cubbyhole he'd stashed it in earlier, and offered Challis the door. He then returned the paper into Raftery's still-outstretched hand.

'I might be the rest of the afternoon,' Jephcott said. 'Be a good fellow and lock up at five if I'm not back.' He waved, wig still in hand, and closed the door behind him.

A muffled tinkling.

Outside, Challis walked ahead a few paces. Then, once clear of

Jephcott's windows, he turned to the man a step or two behind.

Jephcott was smiling. 'Raftery is good enough in his own way,' he said, catching up with Challis and then overtaking him. His gait livened; he was not wholly the corrupt figure he'd first presented. 'His writing is excellent, and his secretarial proficiencies without measure. In the active dissemination of professional, dispassionate, and discreet service in the business of agency and factoring, there's no equal.

'However, in my trade, the-,' Jephcott paused, wig still in hand, 'the bringing together or yet maintaining a barrier between importer and wholesaler, landlord and tenant and suchlike, professionalism alone is insufficient. Discretion is the watchword.'

Challis allowed the man to jaw on. He had an inkling where this would lead.

'So. Raftery,' Jephcott said. 'Industrious and one to whom much might be reliably trusted.' Jephcott stopped in the street, an act of physical punctuation. 'But not everything.'

'Oh?'

'As I said, sir, he has as intimate a knowledge as I of my daily particularities.'

'He is indiscreet?'

A yellow grin split Jephcott's salty beard. 'The very word. Indiscreet.' Jephcott resumed walking. 'Clerks and secretaries, through message-carrying and so on, are liable to meet in taverns, and they talk, sir. They talk.'

'I see.'

'I have suspected him in the past of trading information. Not gossip. Gossip is in many ways the fat that greases the wheels that grind the meal for this city. But information? That is a different matter. So, with Raftery, I take what precautions as may be prudent. I may let slip a falsehood, for example, or be vague about my whereabouts from time to time. As for today, sir...,' Jephcott let the sentence peter out, for Challis to ask the question.

Challis felt inclined to not disappoint. 'Yes?'

'I have sent Raftery on a fool's errand. He is despatched to one Joseph Morton, a wholesaler of rope for the rigging of ships, who deals from a coffee-house Westminster way on, for he likes his business done with a bowl of chocolate. Morton has one distinction. He is, sir, the most verbose and yet the most careful trader in this city. He can put me, whom I am sure must appear to be overly fond of the sound of my own voice to one as taciturn as yourself, sir, to shame.'

Challis said nothing.

'Just so. If words were soldiers, he is a general perpetually engaged in siege tactics against his conversational opponent. He will keep Raftery in abeyance for some hours.'

Satisfied that his point was made, Jephcott held out the hand which still grasped his wig. He opened his hand out. Nestling inside, like a fresh-laid egg, was a key.

Jephcott extracted the key, slipped the hairpiece back on, and pointed forward. To the grey stone bulk of St Magnus' Church, and beyond it, to the bridge.

#

When Tom got back, a Navy Office agent was waiting in the bakery.

There were two who called upon the Farriners. One, elderly, round-faced and ebullient, always licked his lips at the food, and, often as not, at Alice too. He was inquisitive, always asking chirpy questions about flour prices and how - precisely - ships' biscuit barrels were sealed to make them water- and air-tight for storage.

The other was here today. He was perhaps half the age of his colleague, and not just the junior, but the less interested in the Farriners' work. He asked nothing about process, betrayed little in terms of curiosity about what they did or in the pretty girl who helped. For this at least, Tom was glad, though the man's disinterest was as unsettling as his partner's lasciviousness.

His name was Harrow. He nodded once to Tom at his arrival, an awkward stiff-necked movement, which made him appear like a stringed marionette.

Noise from above, footsteps approaching. Farriner came down; he'd changed into something more formal, something less like a working man's garb. 'Alice?' he called.

'Yes?'

'I'm away to talk with His Majesty's man,' Farriner said. 'More orders from our brave boys to quell the Dutch, I trust.'

Harrow nodded. 'Indeed so. Our stores will need filling as will our sailors' bellies if we're to best the enemy.'

Farriner then glanced at Tom. 'Back are you?' he grunted. 'Work as Alice says now and I'll be back by nightfall.'

Farriner and Harrow went out, the agent with something of a bow, again wooden-stiff, towards Alice. They turned to go downhill towards Thames Street, where there were many taverns.

Tom caressed the little bundle on the cord around his neck and went back to work.

Laughter started almost immediately.

Alice was talking through the open door to Molly, one of the serving girls who worked in the White Hart. Molly, all curly-headed, was beaming as though in pride, nudging and jostling, almost play-fighting with Alice. Whatever it was, she seemed pleased about it. Probably some fresh man-friend or other. Tom didn't listen to the words, just to the tone of the chatter.

Molly's voice rose and fell like a ship on the sea. Great peaks of excitement and crashes of laughter. Alice chipped in with a word every now and again, as though piloting the craft.

Again, that sense of Lizzie being gone. Not just dead, but gone.

Tom left them to it, and found himself a job to do which meant that he needed to go upstairs.

There were washed and dried clothes in the kitchen. Tom scooped up his clean shirts and breeches and carried them up to his room. Once there, he left them on his bed and opened the small chest which served him for storage.

Daniel's bed was the one by the front window. From there he could lie on his mattress and gaze down on the workers about their trades in the Lane without rising. The bed was empty, blanket tousled on the floorboards, doubtless kicked off when he'd eventually awakened. And then Daniel had slunk out somewhere. Out of sight, out of mind, as far as baker Farriner was concerned.

He might have covered for Tom earlier; he might have not. He was not in the bakery now.

There had been a time when Daniel was an ever-present. Both an apprentice to his father and a mentor to Tom. But he was his mother's child. Her death had hit him hardest, but he was not one to volunteer the hurt. Better at giving advice than taking it. That was Daniel.

The break with Farriner had come with Alice's moving in. Daniel had changed, become first more withdrawn, then as the religion in him developed, more outward-looking and disengaged from the bakery. Alice repelled him. More than that, their father's developing relationship had. Never spoken about, never acknowledged save the one request that the lads now shared the top room. A sharing that was now unnecessary.

The shift was a transaction. Farriner dealt in business terms, or at least thought he did. Tom reckoned that was how he saw the arrangement with Alice: an accommodation on both sides. A contract, but not one bound in marriage terms.

And the man who he reckoned to have killed Lizzie? Broken in a dead-end, of there was any justice. Best not to think more of it. An end to the matter, cut off in the same way as Lizzie's memory had seemingly been.

One of the shirts was not Tom's. It was too broad across the chest, too long in the arm and too well-worn. It was one of his father's. The shirt, once white but now the creamy-grey colour of milled wheat, would have taken two of Tom.

He picked up the shirt, deciding to leave it in his father's bedchamber on the way back down to the shop. Tom's hands were shaking. Blood, murder, death. He waited for them to cease.

#

'Why this was not repaired, I'll never know,' Jephcott said, treading with care across wooden boards scabbed and black with ancient fire-damage.

Challis followed, matching his steps. The factor was making too much of a fuss. The wood felt solid enough, though Challis acknowledged that it did not always look the part.

Wood was all around them, a patchwork of repairs of variable quality over the singed or otherwise decayed levels below. More planking stood to each side, either supporting ruptured buildings or protecting travellers from a drop of some twenty feet to the waters flowing fast under the bridge.

Viewed from St Magnus' church at the north entrance to the bridge, it had seemed that great repair works were underway; such was the amount of temporary materials. But up close the cheap truth was clear. The bridge had been lashed back together in haste after a fire of, what, thirty years earlier, and had been ill-maintained since.

And the noise! The rushing of the Thames through the culverts below would have been enough on its own. But the racket was magnified by the enclosed wooden structural work, by the churning of the water around the pumping wheels that some ingenious fool had seen fit to erect; the din was tremendous.

The wheels were not turning. Either they only operated in one direction with the tide, or else they had been disengaged from their gearing for yet more repairs. Either way, water was not being pumped into the city.

It had been an arid summer. There would be empty wells everywhere.

Challis had cause once to slither into a ditch and play dead in one of his less noble excursions, and found himself tumbled together with battlefield corpses. He'd pulled bodies over and around him, hoping to be mistook for a dead 'un by the searchers. But the fellow he'd dragged over his face was still alive. He had been sliced from his left shoulder to his right hip, a great scooping slash that had cut him to the rib-bones. That was the sound of the bridge; the echoing, swallowing, omnipresent rush he'd heard that time, ear to the breast of a doomed soldier.

The first third of the bridge was denuded of proper buildings, being instead a semi-permanent promise of reconstruction; and then houses began. It was hard to credit that such fabrications should stand in any part of a city supposedly as great as London, let alone on the sole bridge over the Thames this side of Kingston ten miles upriver.

This was typical of their thinking; such arrogance and foolhardiness, stupidity and weakness. One river, one crossing. That callowness would be their undoing.

And Challis was the man to unpick that knot.

It was apparent through ground-level markings that many buildings had been demolished in the wake of the conflagration had previously corrupted the bridge. The still-standing houses were undeniably precarious things. Lofty and insecure, like peacocks, they were cantilevered over the sides as though leaning out for a better view of the water. Some reached three and four storeys into the air, others arched fully over the roadway down the centre of the bridge leaving scarcely a carriage-width of clearance.

Every few dozen houses there was a break which acted as a passing-place, such as one might find on a narrow track on some forsaken Scottish hillside. In such spaces congregated idlers and fruit-sellers, oyster-merchants. Sutlers and strumpets, buskers and pissing drunks. Some buildings were homes of prestige if the fancy clothing hanging out drying above was any indication. Others were shops of regard; perfumes and silks, tea and sweetmeats all on offer. Wine merchants and good tailors were abundant. The buildings were slick with sea-salt and coal-smoke, with dark pitch for waterproofing and with ill-aimed piss-puddles and shit-dollops from the upper windows.

That combination of idleness, stupidity and sheer malice again. That some emptied their chamber pots into the street rather than the river gave Challis pause, if only for the amount of time it took for Jephcott to employ his key and to tug at his elbow.

'In here,' he said, indicating a now-open door.

This building was an abandoned shop. There was a ground floor for making sales, and two more floors above for stores and accommodation. There were faint traces of paint on the door, livid smears of red both against and with the grain. A faded cross and some words. There were further signs of these premises' recent past in the door-jambs; lines of deep holes where nails had been driven to close up the building from the outside.

This place had been nailed shut.

Jephcott tugged again. Challis turned to him. The man was already across the threshold, a cloth to his mouth and nose. His voice was urgent. 'Quick!' He had no desire to tarry.

Challis stepped in and closed the door behind him. Jephcott shuddered at the noise. Challis sniffed the air, detected nothing as foul as the streets outside, and strode past the quivering Jephcott, who he left in the grimy shop window.

There were two rooms on the ground floor. The shop front was fitted out ceiling to floor with shelving, drawers and a long serving counter with display cabinets behind. There was no obvious scent which might have indicated a previous use. No spices, for example. Not tobacco or ambergris either. A second downstairs room behind the first gave views from two small windows over the river. This room was perhaps twelve feet square, and empty save the stairs up, which he took.

Jephcott came bustling up behind. There were sounds as though he was struggling with catches on the window frames. Challis left him to it and continued upstairs.

The first floor, too, was bare. Two more rooms off a narrow hallway, and then stairs continuing again. Both rooms seemed larger than below; maybe they over-hanged the ground floor on the river side.

Downstairs, Jephcott was shouting something, but Challis ignored his bawling.

The second floor was divided into three rooms. First there were two small rooms to the back of the property, again with windows over the Thames. Then there was a larger room to the front that must have served at some point as the main bedchamber. There were scuff-marks on the floorboards indicating that a bed of some size had been here once. A window, oddly small, gave some view down into the passage between the houses below.

On leaving, Challis stooped. The lintels were low on this floor, there being less clearance up here than the floors beneath. As he raised his head from its dip under the opening, something shiny attracted him.

It was a nail head. It had been burnished bright by being driven hard into place.

Challis checked around the door and then returned into the bedchamber, allowing it to close behind him. There were scratch marks on the wood on the inside of the chamber. Scrapes and gouges on the wattle around the doorway and at a split floorboard proved what Challis had suspected. Someone had died in here, and not well.

Perhaps those who'd remained outside the door but within the house had thought themselves safe as a consequence of this walling-in, and that as they were now both close to and far enough away from their loved one they had done the best they could.

Challis again assessed the dimensions of the rooms and checked the width of the stairwell. He did his calculations.

For all his bluster the factor had his uses. The house would serve well.

Jephcott was not downstairs. He had retreated outside, and was pacing back and forth as though in desperate need of a privy. Almost before Challis was out into the street, Jephcott was re-locking the shop. He still had his handkerchief dabbing around his nose, as though cautious of being seen guarding his self from the possibly noxious, though undoubtedly scentless, premises.

'It does me no good to be seen here,' Jephcott said, moving off towards the London side of the river. 'The bridge attracts many and there's no credit to be found emerging from a place such as that with one such as you.'

Challis did not have to say anything before Jephcott began retracting his words. 'I meant no disrespect, it's just that-,' he waved his hand from his mouth towards his companion, 'well, from a distance, in your black, your hat and coat and all, you might seem to be dressed as a doctor of the,' he paused, 'late unpleasantness. If rumour of returned pestilence - and my association with it - were to spread, then I would be ruined.' There was perspiration on Jephcott's brow. Yes, the day was warm, and yes, the appointment was perhaps onerous for Jephcott, more accustomed to dealing with merchants and moneymen than with sterner folk, but even so. His part was little more than he would expect to perform in his usual commercial activities.

On the face of it, Jephcott had little to be concerned about.

Challis smiled. 'Perhaps I have dressed with little regard for the season,' he replied. Then, moving on, he asked Jephcott about the deliveries he should have arranged.

'On the morrow, by noon.'

'And all as requested?'

'Oh yes, that is, I have heard nothing to indicate otherwise.'

'And you will be here to supervise the consignments?'

Silence.

There it was. The reason for his vexed behaviour. Jephcott's next words were stammering, stuttering their way from his throat. 'I had thought that my involvement would be concluded with my handing over of the key and my good faith assurances that all requests had been dealt with.'

Challis put his hand over Jephcott's shoulder as they re-approached the unfinished repairs. The din in the area, with the throbbing sound of the water below, the shouting of passers-by, the barking of dogs, the horse hooves and cartwheels on the uneven and unstable roadway surface, made it difficult to be heard. So Challis leaned in and spoke with quiet insistence.

His words did not carry far.

Jephcott swayed, as though the repair work under his feet was failing him. He did not look well; pale in the face, almost as grey as his untended chins. And there was water in his eyes. It might have been dry muck thrown up by the traffic that caused him to blink wetness, but Challis did not think so.

By way of reassurance, once the bridge was crossed and they were close by St Magnus', Challis dropped something into Jephcott's coat pocket. The weight in the something must have given Jephcott pause. His hand went straight to the fresh bulge.

The cool of the coin in his doubtless sweaty hand must have given him new resolve. 'Of course,' Jephcott said. 'It's only proper that the factor is there to ensure his customer's order is fulfilled to his requirements.'

'Indeed so,' Challis agreed. The long slow hill they called Fish Street rose up ahead of them. The street was packed, side to side, fore and aft. Shops and dwellings two, three and four storeys tall crowded each other out. Chimneys everywhere, some quiet, a few spilling listless smoke up into the still air. Grander buildings, guild halls most likely, here and there. And churches. Everywhere there were churches. Steeples and towers dominated, either holding up the sky from the city below, or pressing down upon the tiny people, crushing them with the weight of their stones. And largest of all, the thickset bulk of St Paul's, its own tower huge and dark against the pale blue sky.

Challis knew the place well. These days it was part church, part booksellers' haunt, part building site, part quarry. Some of its stones had been robbed for other building projects, one vanity exchanged for another. Now the place was as much a market as a site for worship, its precincts and yards given over to stallholders and printers, bookbinders and pamphleteers. Paper was replacing stone.

Challis indicated a side-street. 'Perhaps some refreshment? The places here are little more than cattle-troughs, I'm afraid, swill-holes for porters and drovers.'

Jephcott seemed surprised, not unpleasantly, by the invitation.

'You have somewhere in mind?'

Challis had. And he had something in mind too, something beginning to grab at him. That overly-nosy assistant of Jephcott's. 'Indeed. Just a handful of yards this way.'

Jephcott led Challis to the right down a side-street, and then gestured left into an even narrower lane. They passed the bakehouse, bread in the window-hatch and a sheaf of corn as a sign above. And then there was the inn and above it another sign, that of a deer or a hart.

Challis declared this to be a more than serviceable establishment with the additional benefit of some of London's more comely serving girls.

Jephcott was leering at one of them, a fresh-faced curly-haired poppet, gossiping in the street with another of her kind. Ah. There it was. Those new-minted guineas were already working their way out of his purse, their gleam lighting the path in his imagination to depravity's door.

Challis resolved to let the man have his moment; besides which, the notion concerning the man's secretary had formed fully, and this diversion might prove useful in making that idea bear some rich red fruit.

Challis held the door open for the weak old goat, and followed in behind.

#

Tom lifted the latch to his father's bedchamber. He laid the shirt on a still-rumpled bed. Farriner kept his garments in two places. Some longer items, his coat and suchlike, were hanging on pegs hammered into the cross-beams supporting the ceiling. Shirts, hose and the rest were folded and kept in the chest at the foot of his bed.

The chest was locked. An iron padlock.

Tom worked his knife in the fat keyhole until the click came. It was an old lock, and had always been a simple device to out-wit.

A pouch of coin, a wad of documents. Clothes; and under them, the folded banner.

Tom understood the true reason he kept the chest locked. That piece of material alone was worth the gesture of security.

Tom had never seen the banner unfurled, but he had heard about it from his father, tales told when the sweet wine he favoured had loosened his tongue.

When the drink was minding him, Farriner had liked to tell the young Tom stories. But these were not bedtime tales of Arthur, Robin Hood or of the valiant Drake vanquishing Philip of Spain's Armada.

These were stories of war. His father's war. The war that had almost torn the country apart forever.

Farriner had told Tom, cow-eyed at the telling, of Naseby-Fight in '45. How he'd been part of the supply train supporting Langdale's cavalry for King Charles. Apprenticed to a baker and little older than young Tom was then, he'd been in the Royalist camp, had often seen the King and his generals, and once had occasion to wait at his table.

'Tom,' he'd said, his face flush with pride and wine, 'I served the King, and he patted my head as I stood by him the day before battle.' His face would then darken, pink to red, like clouds above the setting sun.

Whenever he told this story, he never embellished it. The words were always the same, as though he was making easier for his son to remember. 'And we lost the day. Langdale was repelled by Cromwell's troops, and with that, our advantage could not be held. I was there when the King's standard fell. I saw it drop, the bearer hit by some coward musketman from the damned Roundhead lines.

'I couldn't help myself, son. I ran into the field, though all around me were scattering, it being plain that though not even noon, the field was lost. The standard was in the mud, and Ironsides' men cheering at our rout. But I took it son. I wrested it from the earth and I ran. And Cromwell's men paused, and the Royal army took heart and roared me back to our lines.'

His face would shine, fever-bright. Yet his eyes would be clear: no rheum or tears. 'I was taken again into His Majesty's presence. He was hurried, as there was rumour, which proved right, of traitors in the camp who would betray their King's movements for favour or coin, but he took time for me.

'For me, lad. A bakehouse rat. He stroked me soft on the head, and called me "son". "A true son of England," he said, those were his very words. "A true son of England." And with those words he brought out the banner I'd fetched from the field, and he kissed it. He kissed it and he handed it to me. "Hold this," he said, "in trust". And then he turned to his advisors and asked, I think as much to himself as to them, what might have happened that day with a hundred such lads as me, brave and loyal subjects all.

'There was sadness in his eyes. He knew there were few pages left unwritten in the book of his life. That Cromwell's grasping hand would find him, and he'd pay for it twice over, with his throne and his head.

'And that was that. His Majesty was taken away by his counsel, grim-faced and still soiled with battle. And they left me in the King's private quarters, all England in my hands.'

The banner. Folded and torn, a patchwork piece of bright-threaded cloth, tucked in tight at the bottom of the chest. Tom dared not touch it.

Instead, Tom closed the lid. He snapped the padlock shut. It gave a shearing, twisting click. Perhaps something had broken inside it. Bollocks.

Tom laid the shirt on the lid. He could always claim to have not touched anything. Then he went downstairs.

#

Jephcott was three drinks to the good and calling for more. The wine had eased him, and that blush had returned to his cheeks. He guzzled, passing the back of his hand over his mouth to wipe away excess. He did not employ the cloth used earlier as a mask.

Challis sipped his watered wine. When he'd called for the first jugs to be brought, he'd ensured that two different drinks came to their table. He'd no wish to be foxed by grapes. He'd also slipped something extra into the curly-headed serving girl's hand, now she'd come back in from her jawing outside. She'd laughed at his whispered instruction, and Jephcott had picked up on that, joining in with what he'd assumed to be bawdy commentary.

The girl had kept a look out for their table since, and was across whip-smart when Jephcott raised a hand for service.

A pretty enough portion, all curls and skirts, she brought fresh wine, leaning right over so Jephcott got a fine face-full of her bawbies.

'And so,' Challis said when the doxy had left, Jephcott's hand trailing out from under her behind as she skitted away, 'what of your future?'

Jephcott snuffled his fingers, distracted. 'Oh,' he said at last, rubbing his digits together under his nose, 'retirement, I should think. A few years of rest by the fire before the coffin claims me. Somewhere quiet, a day or so away from the distractions of London.' He dipped his fingers into his wine, and sucked the wetness off them. A droplet rolled down the back of his hand and christened his cuff. 'And speaking of retirement-,' Jephcott looked around; she was already on her way back to him.

Jephcott threw a glassful into his mouth, and poured himself another. 'If you don't mind …?'

The girl brushed past behind Jephcott, her hand draping across his shoulders. She moved to the foot of a staircase half-shrouded by tobacco smoke and stacked boxes.

Challis raised his eyebrows.

Jephcott, taking this as either approval or resignation, stood. 'Until the morrow.'

'Until the morrow.'

And with speed, if not grace, Jephcott went to the stairs and then up, the swish of curls and skirts two steps ahead of him all the time.

\#

'Alice?'

She didn't turn around. She leaned on the door-jamb, arms folded, taking in the street. Her hands had crept round her sides like she was comforting herself. Street-dust and kitchen flour floated around her. The lane was quiet; too hot now to be standing around nattering. Too hot to be gathering warm loaves. A day for shade and cool drink.

It didn't matter what Daniel said about her; about all women. About how it wasn't their fault, by which he meant hers.

That was the reason, Tom was sure, why Daniel could not bear to be near her.

Daniel had preached before in public, and in private to Tom, about how a woman couldn't help but be temptation. It was in their nature, their essence. 'Pigs snuffle in shit,' he said. 'That's their nature. A dog will eat anything if it's hungry enough. That's a dog's nature. And a woman will try to snare a man. That's her nature, that is. With her cunny, with her wits, by trading on a good man's desire to raise sons and to provide for family. With a sharp tongue if possible and soft bedroom words if necessary.'

'Be on your guard,' Daniel had said. 'Not just for your life, but for your soul. A woman caused Adam to be cast out from the Garden. When Eve ate of the fruit of the tree,' he said, 'her eyes were opened and she knew good and evil. Was it not her selfish willingness to listen to the serpent which led to Man's banishment?'

He never spoke this way before their mother's death.

Alice pushed her hand through her hair. Sometimes she wore a headscarf, but not today. There were flashes of white from where she'd run her fingers, leaving smears like the glow from a halo.

Then darkness in the doorway, and banter outside. Laughter; farewells and promises to meet soon.

Farriner stepped over his threshold. He was early; he never came back so soon. These meetings were his excuse to carouse, to tell war-stories. To wench, as he supposed his father must do now mother was gone, Tom had long assumed.

Farriner's face was bright, too. But not with radiance, like Alice, and not with drink as was usual on these meeting-dates.

He rushed through into the bakehouse, hands clasped together, smiling. He did not bark his usual enquiry about the afternoon's takings, nor check the money-drawer without asking, as was his alternate custom.

Farriner took Alice's hands in his.

He was talking to her. Tom could see him doing it, but could not make clear the words. It was as though they were under water. His father's hands were over hers, cupping them like she was a bowl of hot porridge. His words came to her fast and intense, but they made no sense.

'Tom?' Then again. 'Tom?'

'Sir?'

'Well?'

Alice cut in. 'Check the stores, please Tom. Flour, sacks of. Barrels, number of. Salt, pounds of. And quick to it. His Majesty waits on us.'

'Struck deaf, were you, lad? Did you hear nothing? Fresh orders, and twice the usual consignment. And in the normal delivery time too. War, Tom, that's what this means. Charles intends to take the fight to the Dutchman, to sink his remaining ships in their berths. They'll think themselves safe in their dockside stews till the Spring, but we'll show 'em, eh?'

His hands were still tight around Alice's. Tom could not move his neck. He could not force his gaze to break.

'Harrow at the Navy Office waits on our word. He'll be back within the hour with a credit note for supplies. We're to start at once; double-time on the ovens all next week and we'll need your brother to assist. Where is he?'

Farriner then broke Alice's grip. She did not snatch her hands back. There was no embarrassment at being rudely seized by her employer.

'What else?' Farriner asked. 'What else do we have in the ledger, Alice? We must accommodate this work, but are there orders we might have to delay?'

Alice's brightness had not diminished. If anything she was more alive, more alert, more beautiful than before. If before she was blossoming, now she was full-bloomed.

Alice weaved around Farriner. 'It's in the top drawer with the writing materials as always, Baker Thomas.' There was laughter in her words, and something else also.

Tom felt sick.

She stood at the little desk and opened the drawer. Farriner stood behind her, looming over her shoulder as she drew the book out, untied the leather cord which bound it shut, and opened the volume.

They must have assumed that Tom was attending to his errand.

Farriner murmured something close to Alice. Words that caught. She giggled. The noise a naughty child might make if caught licking honey off their fingers by an amused parent.

Farriner kissed her neck. She giggled again, leaning slightly to allow him more room. He shuffled closer as she murmured protest. But she lifted herself on her tip-toes anyway.

His hands were on her. On her waist, on her hips. Then one hand around her midriff, pulling her closer still, as his other hand pushed free the hair that gathered around her neck, exposing her skin.

Tom backed away, out of the room and toward the stores. Out of sight, he knocked something over, shouted whatever words came to him by way of apology; he knew not to whom. He blinked through the counting he'd been sent to do, and shouted out the tallies.

Tom did not cry.

No.

Then a realisation. A fist to the belly. This was the reason for Daniel's torment. This was why he preached against womankind. Why he avoided the bakery.

Little wonder he could not sleep. Alice being fucked by Farriner every night, their panting secret lustings in the room below

Daniel hated the woman who had taken his mother's place in his father's bed. And he hated himself for the doing so.

Tom had to find Daniel. Fast. Before he did something stupid.

#

Challis winced at the sun as he left the tavern. As clear a sign as one could wish that the Almighty despaired of excessive drink in daylight hours was the squint when one went from squalid tavern darkness to the reviving slap of His bright hand. Challis would note this in his pocketbook.

The streets were not as busy as one might have expected the capital to be. There was hurry but no bustle, masses but not quite crowds. Nothing of the verve of Amsterdam, the flash of Paris, the swagger of Hamburg. Here, there was one overriding sense, that of corruption.

Yes, there was the hot stink of human piss and animal droppings in every runnel, the warm grimy sweat from every porter, the damp scent of flowers and fruit masking foul breath and the wet heat of pox from street-girls and boys alike.

But there was something else as well. Signs that gave reason and form to the air's rotting taste.

One shop in four was shuttered. Doors bore other faint traces of being marked in paint as plague-houses, similar to the premises Jephcott had procured. There were dogs everywhere. Some must have been house animals, pets or guard creatures, but even so. Curs ran all about, ribby and itching creatures, nipping under carriages and between houses, shaking and shitting in any shade they could find.

Some of the narrower streets displayed other signs. Weeds and grasses grew in odd corners, breaking through cobbles away from the track-marks worn by carts and barrows. There was urgency in the hawkers' hollering. Not the full-bodied barking of lively competition, but a shriller tone, piercing and insistent. Pleadings, not exhortations, little better than begging cries. Less shouts for sales than pleas for alms.

It was in the scrawniness of children playing in gutters, clinging to their mothers. In the bruised eyes of women, their drab colouring, the sweat-stains and the ill fit of their garments.

It was in half-empty shop windows, in the dust coating them

inside and out. It was in the heat that clung to your neck as though you had a lecherous drunk whispering clammy indignity from behind.

The sky was a stained horsehair blanket barely held off the city by the thin spires of empty churches where, if anyone prayed, they prayed for themselves, and only for the selfish forgiveness of sin.

These observations reaffirmed to Challis as he made his way back to Jephcott's offices that this city's time had come and gone. All it required was for someone to strike a spark. In His name.

It was going to be a pleasure to blow up London Bridge.

#

Challis waited for Raftery at the street-corner.

Raftery would return to the offices after his time-wasting errand, continue at his work until five, and then lock up and leave as instructed. That was who he was; punctual to the point of unpleasantness, as though adherence to the clock was a virtue. He reasoned further that Raftery was accustomed to his employer's habits, and that Jephcott would often return late from luncheon appointments, sometimes not at all. Thus Raftery would feel free, as long as he was on the premises and had chores on hand to disguise any questionable behaviour, to be able to pry, to solicit written confidences for later exploitation. The only question Challis had concerned where Raftery might go after five o'clock.

His protestations notwithstanding, it was plain that Jephcott's trade was in information as much as in the management of property or business affairs, and Challis was confident that confidences were not kept as thoroughly as they might be.

But Jephcott was predictable and mundane in his desires; table, coin, glass, bed.

Raftery, less so. It was possible he traded secrets for money, and that Challis's business would be opened to scrutiny. Worse, Raftery might be one of Secretary of State Arlington's little toadies, proffering snippets of intelligence for either coin or kudos. Either way, he warranted attention.

#

Raftery emerged from Jephcott's as bells all around claimed the hour. He still had the key in the lock as Challis shifted; he didn't allow the man a chance to turn.

Challis was on him fast, clapping a shoulder as though surprising an old friend. His other hand held the blade from his sleeve. The Scotsman he'd taken it from had called it a "dirk". He liked that. A short sharp word suiting the implement and its function. He'd babbled in dying, the Scotsman, bad Latin in a stupid accent, for his Pope and The Virgin to save him.

The dirk went under Raftery's chin and up, pushing against his jawbone.

'Back inside.'

Raftery did as instructed. Once in, Challis swiped the key and locked the door. He guided Raftery through into the kitchen area he'd been in earlier, blade still to his throat.

Challis shoved Raftery onto the chair where Jephcott had sat to eat. The table was as he'd left it, scattered with food scraps and drinking vessels. There was another knife on the table; better suited to cutting cheese than flesh, but Challis swept it onto the floor anyway.

Then he focused on Raftery.

Jephcott had indicated the man's fastidious nature before, and this was borne out by what Rufus Challis had in front of him. Raftery was thin and still, with long clean fingers and nails which had never seen wet-work. His clothing was dark and plain, and he wore no wig, electing to have his hair tied back at the nape. The single aspect of his appearance implying vanity was the slim black ribbon used to tie the hair off, leaving a small tail, dandling like that of a prize pony at a horse-fair.

The ribbon had a coin threaded onto it; a shilling piece into which a series of holes had been stamped.

Challis had seen this device before.

Raftery's skin was brown, a touch of the Italian to his complexion. There was something of the Roman to his shape of his face too; his colouring aside, his lopped head might have passed for the bust of some minor emperor.

The thought of Raftery cut off at the neck did not entirely displease Challis. He pressed the blade to Raftery's throat again.

'You're Arlington's man, are you not? One of Bennet's grass-snakes whispering back intelligence to the Crown? But not for profit. You've got a whiff of the justified about you. A man who believes in his work, not the payment.'

Raftery said nothing. That was confirmation enough.

Challis traced a knife-point line across Raftery's throat. There was pleasure in the way the skin tone changed under pressure, paling and then regaining its lividity under the cutting point's examination.

The man was fixed on Challis. He did not waver. He was putting on a creditable show, but it was a show nevertheless. The artery in Raftery's neck was pulsing, faster than any man's ought. Challis shifted the knife-point across to that spot, applying the same pressure as before. Again, the neck-skin blanched momentarily; olive to cream, ale to foam.

'I remember the first time I saw a man kill a pig,' Challis said, adopting a conversational tone. 'It was quite the thing.' Challis shifted a stool over with his foot, and sat down beside Raftery. 'The trick, of course, is catching the beast. Pigs are clever, you know, clever amongst animals at any rate. My father told us children the same jest at supper-times about why sage, the herb, went swell with pork. Sage, you see. Clever.' This was true. His father was a maunderer, forever masking his inadequacies with jokes and funny faces.

'But once you've trussed your swine,' he continued, 'and it's best to get assistance for that, the rest is easy.

'He was not a butcher by trade, but the best in town with a cleaver and by no means the squeamish type. He liked the attention, and seemed born with the skills. We boys gaggled around at the killing times like vermin at a split sack of barley.

'The pig was trussed, front feet and back feet together, and hoisted up by the back legs a yard and a half. He'd had a jib and pulley made for the purpose. And under the beast, though often there was a large barrel, on this occasion he used an iron cauldron. Quite witchy, we thought, us boys.

'Sometimes the pig, because I went back many times after that, as you might imagine, was quiet. He'd stun them first with a poleaxe or the flat of a shovel. But sometimes it came around and screamed. And did that first pig scream.'

Raftery blinked a little too long. His vein felt full under the knife-tip.

'It knew, being clever. It knew that its life of muddy snuffling was over, that it would gorge on kitchen waste and sprouting grain no more. It knew then that it had been fattened for this reason, for today. And it screamed.

'He, the butchering fellow – an ugly mister he was, with a face swollen and marked as though he'd been burned as a child - showed us boys the tools of his trade, and then he showed them to the pig.

'You must have heard childhood tales of torturers of old, how they'd show their prisoner the instruments before they'd set to them to extract their confession? That's what he did. Of course he was playing up to us children, and we loved it. He stood, blade in hand, stripped to the waist except for an apron so ridden with gore it looked as solid as armour.

'Except it wasn't a plain knife like this,' Challis said, indicating with a sly twist of the tip into Raftery's skin. 'No. He preferred one blade, one instrument to do all of his work. The kill, the slitting of the belly and the removal of the tripes, even the sectioning of the beast into sides, then joints and hams and whatnot. He used a cleaver sharpened on two edges, top and bottom.

'So after his little pantomime, and with the pig's yelps shrill in our ears, he'd let the animal spin a little on its rope. Left and right, backwards and forwards. And then his hand would flash, and the cut would be made.

'That first time, I don't believe I saw the blade part the beast's flesh. A sensation of movement, like sunlight off a looking-glass, and then a thin red line across that sow's gullet.

'Its keening ceased immediately. The silence was a pure thing. I'm sure I wasn't breathing, and I'm sure my fellows gathered with me weren't either. And then the blood ran.

'Do you know,' Challis asked, his voice as sweet as honeyed milk, 'how much blood a pig holds?'

Raftery did not respond.

'More than a wine gallon. At least eight pints. Over half a stone of black puddings' worth. First squirting and pumping, then running, then dripping into the container underneath.

'It's not as though the first cut makes the kill. It's the blood leaving the body, not the shock of the knife. That's what does the deed. That pig lived for a good five minutes. It thrashed at first, the rope stretching as it wriggled, but that only hastened its end. And as the flow slowed, so did the pig. Only when the dripping slowed to a spotting did that pig's existence extinguish.'

Challis stood and dove his right hand into a pocket. He took out a shank of twine, one of the articles he'd lifted from the alleyway opportunist earlier. He laid the cord on the table, Raftery watching all the way.

Challis wanted him to see the hand. He wanted him to wonder.

'I need you to write something for me. Then I'm tempted,' Challis said, 'to ask you to bind your feet together, and then I'm minded to half-hitch your hands behind your back.'

God love him, but Raftery tried some banter. 'Is that quite necessary?'

'I'm afraid,' Challis said, 'that it just might be.'

#

Tom stayed in the stores until he heard fresh conversation; his father and Harrow. Their voices carried the jovial bluster of good deals fresh made. Father sounded as happy as he'd ever been.

Tom kept his head down as he came out. He did not want them – her, if she was there – to see him. He did not want them to revel in his stupidity, in his childish ignorance.

93

He wanted to talk to Daniel. Where was he?

Tom wanted the rushing in his ears to cease. He wanted his heart to choke him. The walls were pressing in. He had to get out.

He had to find his brother.

#

Challis admired the letter that he'd had Raftery scribe. It was near enough perfect. He let it dry, then folded it in three and laid it on the table. 'And if you'd address it.'

'To whom?'

'Henry Bennet, Lord Arlington, care of the Post Office, should suffice.'

Raftery picked up the quill with his unbroken hand. He dabbed the nib into the ink. Challis held the paper still for him as he wrote. His writing was still strong and clear; you'd never have surmised that he'd written it against his will, one fresh-shattered wrist tied behind him.

The breaking of the hand was inevitable. The one hundred and forty-fourth psalm put it well: rid me, and deliver me from the hand of strange children, whose mouth speaketh vanity, and their right hand a right hand of falsehood.

The scriptures were plain enough. Challis's mark was his hand, and the mark for him to interpret in turn was the hand of others.

When Moses slew the ram, one of the three points on the body used to anoint with the ram's blood was the right thumb; his hand was no ordinary injury but a mark of anointment.

These signs were undeniable.

The perfection he'd seen in Raftery's hand matched with the vanity of his hair-ribbon.

This was a strange child before him, and deliverance was due.

Raftery put the quill down when he was done. Challis dried the address-work first with sand and then with a wave in the air. 'That's very good,' he said. 'Not long now.'

Raftery didn't bite at that remark. And good for him.

Challis checked about. It would be here somewhere. Ah, there it was, an iron ring recessed into the floorboards near a back door that presumably led to a privy. The boards around the ring ran counter to the flow of the others, the hatchway they represented being perhaps a yard square.

He pulled the ring, uncertain which way the opening was hinged. It shifted easily enough, revealing rough-hewn wooden steps down. A waft of must, cool and damp, came up.

There were no wax droplets on the slats leading down into the dark. No smell of stored cheese or hung hams. No grooves, runners or nicks to indicate that much had been dragged, dropped or rolled up or down.

The cellar would be empty. And Jephcott would not think of searching down there. He'd probably never been down there since the day he inspected the property for purchase.

Shuffling behind him. Challis dropped the hatch lid, letting it fall open. Raftery was curious at last, jiggling against his bonds to see what was going on.

Challis came up behind him, two fingers up the man's nose. He yanked back, pulling Raftery's head hard against the top spar of the chair's backrest. Raftery's eyes rolled up to meet his.

'Good hand on the table, if you'd be so kind.' He was not sure if he would acquiesce. Then again, it didn't matter much either way.

Raftery grunted, straining. So he wouldn't let things go without a struggle. A fighter to the last was Raftery.

So be it.

Challis brought his free arm under Raftery's neck. He didn't want to use a blade. The mess might cause problems, if only in the clearing up. He locked his arm around Raftery's neck, holding him as still as he could. Raftery thrashed under him, free hand flailing, scrabbling around his nose.

Challis braced himself. He leaned in, locking Raftery's neck still, then let go of the nose and reached around the man's head.

Raftery must have realised, because his hand came over Challis's, trying to pull it down. But he didn't have the purchase, what with one ruined hand and two ankles tied well and good to the chair.

Challis twisted once, then twice. Raftery held for the first pull, but not the second. His head whipped around, tendons and veins shearing inside his neck. His head flopped uselessly forwards. Already bruising showed right around the neck. But the skin wasn't broken.

Good.

Challis gave himself a few seconds to recover; he was breathing hard. Then he put Raftery's loose hand on the table. He came around the corpse and took out the knife he'd had in his grip earlier. He inverted the blade and brought the pommel down onto Raftery's still-elegant fingers. He did this until he was sure the bones were broken. It took six strokes.

When it was done, Challis recited the twenty-third and twenty-fourth verses of the eighth book of Leviticus.

Satisfied at last, he dropped the crushed limb into the corpse's lap. Standing behind the body, he tilted the chair onto the two rear legs and walked it left foot, right foot, until it was beside the cellar opening.

Challis slit the bonds at the ankles and the bound left hand, and then he tipped the body into the hole like it was a barrowful of shit being dumped in a midden.

Raftery's head cracked against the edge of the hole. The body twisted as it fell in, hitting the stairs and collapsing forwards, lumpen into the darkness.

Challis stood over the cellar opening. He couldn't see the body from the kitchen. Good enough.

He closed the cellar, replaced the chair, tidied up around the kitchen table, pocketed the letter and left.

If he was lucky, he'd find a boy to run the letter around to the Post Office right away.

#

Daniel didn't say anything for the longest time. He sat on the edge of his bed, hands round his alms-tin. There was good money in the metal; three or four shillings in pennies and ha'pennies.

Eventually he set the cup aside. 'This is my mistake, brother. My error.'

'How so?'

'For too long I have been exercised at father since Alice moved into the household.'

At last. He was finally breaking.

'I was vexed, I admit. Over the relationship beginning at all. And so soon after...so soon. And the nature of it.'

'The nature?'

That is was dishonest. Unblessed. That there'd been no wedding.'

'Not even a conversation with us.'

Not even that. And because of that, I did you a disservice, brother. I made assumptions.'

'You thought I did not know?'

'I assumed you were blind to it. That you were still a child.'

Tom's words took time to form. 'Of course I knew. Everyone knows. There's neither secret nor shame.'

'Then why didn't anyone say?'

'And why should they? The sun rises each day, yes? So do we wander out and act astonished each morning? Of course not.'

Daniel took a penny from the cup. He sat in his palm. 'We don't because it's natural. We're used to it. And it happens every day and we see it for ourselves. So we don't feel the need to talk about it.'

Daniel turned the penny. The single digit on one side, Charles' bust on the other, laurel-wreathed and imperial.

Tom tried to reach out. 'The fault is not with you, brother.'

'Then with who? With Alice, for following her nature, as you've said before? How can someone be blamed for what comes naturally to them?'

Daniel let the coin fall from one hand to the other. Over and over, palm to palm. Sometimes the coin slid, sometimes it tumbled. 'I should have warned you. I should have said something; not let my assumptions take hold of my tongue.'

Daniel grasped him, cupping Tom's hands in his own. Between

them, the coin; a warm circle against Tom's knuckles.

'Look at me.'

Tom met his brother's eyes. There was sadness there. Daniel let go of Tom's hands. The coin dropped to the floor between them. It hit the floor spinning.

The penny's edges blurred with speed, then regained permanence. Once solid again, it stuttered and fell, juddering till it lay still, head side up on the floor.

When Tom looked back up again, it was Daniel's head that was bowed.

A black thought welled inside Tom, a thought about his brother's concern for him and whether it masked something else, something of Daniel's own.

Tom bid the idea leave.

'Brother,' Daniel said, his voice quiet and his head still down. 'Come with me tomorrow. I'll work alongside you in the morning, hard enough to earn you some grace at noon. I've got things to say. Things that can only be said in public. It's important that you're there to hear.'

'You're preaching?'

'At noon, as I say. I've an offer of kinds, and I'd like you to be there to hear it.'

'And until then?'

'Are we not our father's sons?' Daniel spoke with a bleak smile. 'We'll bake, brother. We'll bake.'

SATURDAY 1ST SEPTEMBER 1666

Challis was visited with the same urge as the previous day; to take one of the vials with him into the city.

He considered this twice, first when sat on the edge of the bed then second when at breakfast.

He paid scant attention to the other tables in the tavern; enough to recognise and nod a good morrow to the mismatched pair of travelling puppet-show performers, and then to the two whores. Any pall the previous day due to the death of one of their own had lifted. Life was trundling on as if uninterrupted.

His hand was in his pocket. His pocket was found to hold one of the glass containers. The full one.

The test was surely not in the decision to carry or not to carry a vial. That was a simple aye or nay. No, the test was to endure ongoing temptation. As He had been trialled in the desert, this was a torment being set before Challis.

The little fat jester grinned, a dribble of ale like a still-wet scar on his chins. His companion was impassive, but there was movement at table-height. He was toying with his puppet, letting it mime eating a crust from his platter, then dunking his curled beak into his cup. The puppet shook like a thirsty horse at a trough.

Punch waggled himself dry then swivelled round to meet Challis's gaze. A puppet hand slid into a pocket in its costume. The fat one farted and guffawed. His partner remained impassive. Then Punch slid under the table.

The landlord cut between them, making small talk, asking if there was anything else to be got. Challis must have shaken a no.

To be able to carry the tincture and its promise of ease with him and not yield to it? That was the purpose here.

Challis would not fail. He'd best this demon. He caressed the bottle and made his way out.

He turned right to go down the hill. He snuck a glance at the passageway where he'd dispatched the woman. Just another gap between buildings. An unremarkable place. There was nothing there. No shade, only shadow. Challis only believed in one ghost.

He thought he heard a gasp when passing the bakery's open door. Another step though, and the notion was already retreating, being pushed out by the wall he was constructing in his imagination between the weakness of his mortal body and the soft womanly voice of temptation, of the djinn held stoppered in his pocket.

#

The sun was bright and still low, catching Challis between buildings as he walked towards the bridge. It was early enough for there still to be the last of the night's cool around, yet it was busy already; there were queues ahead, horses, wagons, and carriages, porters with barrows and labourers with sacks over shoulders crowding towards the access to the bridge. Some were taking breakfast; hunks of bread, hard-boiled eggs. Discarded shells crackled underfoot. There must have been a seller nearby. Tavern barkers were crowing the advantages of their establishment's wares over those of the competition.

Even from this distance, perhaps fifty paces from the bridge, Challis's nose was filled with the river's stink. It hung in the air like the midges. Maybe they helped fan the stench of muddy corruption from the water. Maybe their swatted bodies helped cause it.

'You want a pipe, you do,' cackled some crone. She was swathed in a once-black headscarf and a faded yellow coat that looked stolen from a battlefield. The only thing clean about her was the creaminess of the clay pipe clamped in her over-biting jaw. Grey smoke clung to her as though embarrassed for the wretchedness of her appearance. 'A pipe, that's what you want.'

She patted her side. A brittle rattling. She must have had a pocketful of clays for sale. 'Smoke will keep 'em away, makes your air smell sweet, sir. Drives off noxious vapours and thickens the blood it does.' As she spoke, smoke drooled from her. 'Will you take a pipe from me?'

Challis shook his head, walking on. There was a break in the melee queuing for bridge access, and he made for it.

'Thick blood's what you want sir. Makes your pizzle as fat as an ox's!' Laughter and coughing behind him.

The old woman might have had some wisdom in her puckered skull though. As he pushed further into the crowd, Challis was struck again by the ingenuity and complexity of the odours around him. Smoked fish and meats, animal and human piss, faeces, ale puke, then something clean and astringent like vinegar. Coal smoke, tar, hot bread, clothes that had been sodden with sweat then dried and worn over many times. A passing lungful of flowery sweetness. Grease and coffee and fresh-cut wood. Tobacco might serve to mask this.

The noises too. Arguments and bluster, swearing and pleading. An inevitable child's ignored crying. Animals; cages of hens, geese, pigeons: all clucking and cawing. The drays themselves, horses, cows and donkeys were all employed. Grunting and pushing and shoving and clattering, metal and wood on cobbles either slick with crap or dry enough to beat dust from.

His hand was on the vial throughout it all.

The bridge served to calm the clamour, its one-in, one-out system regulating the nuisance. There was room, just, for foot traffic alongside the carts. Challis was borne through, stepping into the space being carved by a flat-sided wagon loaded high with stacked and roped-down barrels.

The wagon lurched as it encountered loose or missing boards.

Sunlight flashed across and from below, through the slatted fencing protecting the half-rebuilt sides of the bridge span, off the water being churned by collision with the unmoving pump-house wheels. A wider gap in the side walling, and Challis saw the sun leaving the reverse of a shadow, a great yellow streak down the river from the horizon. From the sea.

The long light was caught in the skeleton workings of moored and sail-less shipping as if – then the moment was broken, the observation incomplete as foot traffic on the other side of the bridge shuffled past towards the city, excising the view. Then Challis was walking again at a livelier pace, because he'd determined the wagon and its contents in the new light.

Challis released the vial.

He knew what was being carried on the cart. And he knew where to.

#

Usually Daniel was a crumpled snoring pile. He always wanted to be warmer, forever swathing himself in more covers, sometimes stealing Tom's if he'd kicked them off because of the trapped summer heat.

A flat fuss of blankets. Daniel was gone.

Tom was a dolt to have been taken in by his brother's promise of work; words which jingled like the promise of wagered coin, now snatched away just as quick.

Sounds from below; the house was awake. That meant his father, and that meant industry.

Tom pissed and emptied the leather jug they used as a chamber pot out of the window. The window did not open far. The jug was a necessity for its spout alone.

No shouts from under the window at least. The sky, what little Tom could see between the jetty and the roof opposite, was a pale clear blue. No clouds. It would be hot again, and dry.

Tom got dressed and went downstairs. Loud enough to be heard coming down, slow enough to tell himself he did not relish it. He turned, eventually, at the bottom of the staircase into the bakery.

The door to the street was open. At once, a spasm of darkness and a flurry of long leather coat.

How could Challis still be strolling around? The deed done, he'd put the matter out of his head. Injustice, then justice. A balance restored. Challis should be dying or dead in a tunnel.

And then Daniel's troubles over Alice had crowded his mind. There'd been no space to think more on Lizzie's killer.

'Morning, slugabed,' Daniel said. There was flour on his boots and sweat across his forehead. The fire door to the oven was open and he was standing with the peel in his hand. He leaned the flat long shovel against the wall while he ran the back of his forearm across his head. Hair stuck to his forehead in its wake.

Tom stepped back towards the stairs.

Daniel laughed for once. 'Don't act so surprised.'

Tom cursed himself twice, once for doubting his brother, and once for not thinking yesterday through. This Challis, if he was the ruthless killer Tom supposed him to be, would not be bested by a couple of road clinkers.

What if he suspected that he'd been marked by a spotter? No, he'd think of the ale-boy. And if he questioned the child? Then the lad would spill, the truth or his blood, maybe both. Challis had already shown he'd kill without qualm.

Tom coughed, and with it brought up a mouthful of gut soup.

Daniel shook his head, but with apparent good humour. If he chided any more as Tom barged past to take a slug of small beer to wash the tang of bile from his throat, then Tom didn't hear it.

His head was full of possibilities and none of them good.

#

The cause of at least some of the jamming of carts, sedan chairs, horses and pedestrians on the bridge soon became evident. Jephcott. He leaned rather than stood against another flat-bedded wagon which, though it had been pulled over so that it butted up against the rented building, left little clearance for carriages. Jephcott was flushed, the fishy pink skin showing his off-white beard and broken veins around his nose in clear relief. Around him, two porters worked silent and quick, accustomed to hauling goods at pace. The wagon, which must have held two dozen barrels when fully-laden, had most been cleared off by the time Challis was within hailing distance.

Jephcott had papers in his hand, receipts or invoices, and was ticking off against his lists with a stubby bit of charcoal, the kind a pleasure garden artist might use in sketching cartoons for the amusement of ladies. The writing implement seemed too dainty for his hands. It left dark marks, more shit-streaks than bruising, on whatever Jephcott touched.

He was sweating like a papist on the rack.

Challis did not speak as he approached, preferring to observe the work. The first wagon now empty, the porters nodded to Jephcott, then unhitched the horse from whatever hook or nail it had been tethered to, and walked the beast and cart on. There was not room here to turn, though Challis assumed that there were passing-places where there'd be enough clearance to walk the horse about, pivoting the cart on itself.

The second cart drew up, and Jephcott shivered. Perhaps his hackles rose. Maybe he smelled brimstone. By whatever means, he determined that Challis was near.

Challis nodded. But Jephcott did not at first fully countenance him. He was as though struck with cataracts. Then he blinked them away.

Challis had appeared before Jephcott the way a demon might. Jephcott's jaw slackened. He took a half-step away, almost losing his footing. Then he recovered, reaching back to the wagon for support. Perhaps for security.

Challis waited. That's what you do when you have that effect. You wait. You allow the effect to double, and then subside. And you watch.

'Ah, yes. There you are, sir, and prompt. Early in fact.' Jephcott cast backwards and forwards, both sides of the thoroughfare and to both ends of the bridge. 'Unlike some that I could mention.' He was about to say something else, but he checked himself a second time and took a different tack. 'But no matter. No matter.'

A workman grunted, having clambered onto the cart and struggled to loosen a knot apparently designed to come unstuck with a single pull. Instead, the rope tightened, constricting the twine bolus. Jephcott took the distraction to gather his wits. 'As you see, we're well on with the specified deliveries. We'll be done within the hour-'

'Fucking thing,' the workman muttered, before halting himself. 'Begging your leave.' He brushed fingertips to where a hat brim would have been, and then drew a knife.

It was old and worn. The blade had been reground many times; it was too slim for the handle. There were spots of rust on the shaft and on the rivets holding the wood in place. The handle, too, was worn. It fit the worker's hand perfectly, as though cast from a mould, the wood having been abraded through time and sweat. This knife had seen much duty.

His co-worker came across, all sunken eyes and thin precise grabby hands. He climbed aboard, taking position to hold the uppermost barrel. He braced himself and nodded, and the first man sliced the rope under the knot.

The stroke was good; the sharpness of the blade more than a match for the corded hemp. The rope snapped under tension, whipping around and snaking under and between the cartwheels. The horse juddered against the shift in its load. Squirrel-man took the difference well, the top barrel scarcely bucking. He gave it a count out loud of three; yan, tan, tethera, and then hoisted the barrel to his shoulder on the fourth count, methera.

'As I say, within the hour we'll be done.'

'And the goods have been roomed according to my instructions?'

'Just so, sir, just so.' Again, Jephcott glanced up and down the street.

'First load to the bedchambers, this second to the first floor rooms and the third, to remain on the bridge level rooms, should be here in,' and here he folded his chin into his whiskers in consulting the watch hanging around his neck, 'in but a few minutes.'

Challis pulled him by the upper arm, firm enough to make clear his intent – direction, not caution – tugging him out of the way of the porters. Around them others grumbled at the unloading; wasn't this night-work, best done when the bridge was quiet? Weren't there by-laws? But it was the everyday chuntering of petty discomforts, nothing more, and no-one official-looking came bustling up to interfere.

'Ah, yes, thank you for that. One should not inconvenience the labouring man, particularly when there's urgency to the task.' Jephcott's breath was sharpness gone stale; wine that morning over wine last night.

Challis kept hold of Jephcott's arm, leading him into the house. He took him through to the rear windows. Behind them, the porters continued; heavy footfalls up and softer steps on their return from the first floor.

'I, that is, can I ...?' Jephcott struggled for his words. Boats on the water, little skiffs ferrying one or two passengers. The river swell made the rowboats seem dangerous, rising and falling as they were buffeted, occupants clinging to their headgear or sides of the vessels.

The water was streaked, clear blue towards the middle of the river alternating with, and then giving fully over to clay browns at each bankside. There were ink-spots of children on the mudflats, playing or scavenging. One boat crossed left to right loaded with lobster pots. There were shouts and squeals, screams and distant high-pitched giggles. Bits of wood bobbed here and there. A fat bird sat on the water, then spread its wings. They opened wide, wider than Challis had reckoned they might.

'Hmm?'

'Offer further services, is what I was intending to say. Is there anything further?'

'Ah, yes. That is, no.'

'Then our contract is concluded?' Jephcott's tone rose, half questioning, half submissive, as he finished.

'On delivery of the third consignment.'

'Which shall be here momentarily, I am assured.' Again, that wheedling note.

'Then with its carriage through to these rooms we will be at accord, and you released from your obligations.'

'And the documentation mentioned at our earlier meeting?'

Challis let go of Jephcott's arm. A wherry cut across his field of view, empty save for the rowers. The rear of the two men in the craft was either chewing something gristly, or was arguing with his companion out loud. He bubbled and flexed, caught in an imperfection in the glass, and was then restored.

'You'll have your coin.'

A shuffling sound; Jephcott might have attempted some obsequious gesture.

Challis used his flattest tone. 'And I'll be assured of your discretion.'

'Most assuredly, sir. Most assuredly.'

Darkness behind them. Challis turned to find the doorway blocked. The workmen had finished and were waiting on their gratuity. Jephcott had gone to them, arms open, and was ushering them outside. His words were the awkward kind they who fancy themselves gentlemen use when dealing with the labouring sort. Words which would return little but resentment masked with professional blankness.

Then the cart pulled away, and Jephcott was left in the porch, once more agitatedly scouting the bridge traffic.

'Confound him,' Jephcott said.

'Confound who?'

Jephcott turned, startled. 'I'd thought you still at the casement, engaged in your observations.'

Challis indicated he was disobliged to repeat himself.

'My man Raftery. I'd anticipated his attendance in this matter. Indeed, I'd left a note to that effect at my offices. Saturdays being his half-day, he's there the earlier in the morning and I confess it unusual that he'd not already arrived when I left. That being said, I was a-rush being late to my bed as, as you might,' he paused, 'appreciate last evening, and I woke with a heavy head.'

'You left written instructions for Raftery to come here?'

'And damn the man, but he's seen fit not to comply. Thinks too much on his own feet. Capital he may be in other respects, but he has an independent streak in him that seems to be widening.' Jephcott tugged out a napkin with which he swabbed himself down. 'And damn this heat too, though I daresay it'll sweat out some of my fatigue.'

Challis read the watch that dangled upside down on Jephcott's front. There was enough time to deal with this. Just.

'And the note? You were clear in your instructions?'

'Like spring water in diamond goblets.' Jephcott sounded sad.

So be it.

#

The oven had not stopped all morning. Tom had lost count of the trips he'd made to get more faggots for the fire. Trays of once-baked biscuit were stacking up; having Daniel in the bakehouse made it cramped and difficult to work in – Tom had been caught with the scalding edge of a tray once already, leaving a pink smear across his forearm - but they were turning out goods fast.

Farriner kept his distance. He knew not to interfere, and had merely nodded in assent after seeing their first hour's production. Yes, take from noon to do with as you will, if a day's work and more be done by then.

And Tom knew he'd have other reasons to wish that. With them out of the way, he'd have the run of the place. The baker and Alice together.

Something flicked out at Tom. A rag, the one Daniel used to handle the Devil's Claw with when he was raking out ashes, the one he wrapped around his hand when shifting hot trays. Tom ducked, but not in time, the rag catching him smart on the ear.

'Don't slacken off, brother. Keep at it. Not far off now.'

He was right. Daniel always was. Keep working; keep your mind full of flour, salt, and heat.

Daniel flicked again, but Tom was ready, snatching the rag. He tugged back, trying to wrench the cloth from him.

'Ha!' Daniel pulled back, stepped to one side. Tom stumbled forward, sprawling onto the floor.

His brother stood over him.

Alice wasn't in sight; probably gossiping with Molly from the tavern. Praise God for that absence at least. Farriner was in the street, pushing a broom and maintaining distance.

Keeping an eye on her arse.

'Pull me up then,' Tom said.

Daniel held the Claw out, handle end first.

Tom got up and crossed to the oven. It was an over and under design; the hot box above where the baking was done, the grate below where the fire burned. Tom lobbed a couple more split logs in. They settled with crackling, the impacts crushing wood already burning. Tom would have taken a passing satisfaction in that on another day.

He gave the new fuel time to catch. It didn't take long, smoke folding around the wood like water around rocks. When it took to flame, Tom thrust the Claw in. He held it close to the fire like he was making toast.

'What are you doing?'

Tom didn't reply. Instead, Tom ground the Claw into the meat of the fire, stubbing and stabbing at the same time. It felt stupid and necessary. Tom riddled the burning logs again.

Tom did not know how to feel. He was thankful that his brother, for once, held his tongue.

'Come on,' he said, at last. His eyes were prickling with heat. That was what it was. Of that he had no doubt.

So much life and death around him. His mother, long gone. Lizzie, dead barely a day. His father and Alice, lost in themselves in keeping forward momentum, not daring to look back at what had been. Not thinking of what consequences there might be for others. Challis, responsible but not yet held accountable.

The red of the fire; lust and sin, blood and iron, wine and meat.

There had to be something more than this. There had to be some sense in it all above the immediate.

'Come on,' Tom said. He put the Claw down, his hand now clammy from transferred heat. 'We've much to do if we're to be away by noon.'

#

Challis bought some fruit from a hawker who'd chosen the cramped northern part of the bridge as her patch. The apples were small, doubtless because of the dry season, but they seemed ripe enough. He tossed one to Jephcott who caught it with both hands. The catch was a firm one, his hands snapping around the fruit with confidence. There was a touch of old age to his fingers, a curl to the knuckles, but there was no fault with his grip.

Jephcott nodded thanks and took his first bite. He went at the apple with an efficient snappy bite. He sucked as he took the second bite, drawing in any juice that might fall. Challis remembered doing that as a child, gorging himself on sweetness, fast in his determination to extract maximum pleasure not only from the eating but also from his father's despairing, impotent glances.

Challis brought out his blade from his sleeve. He did it deliberately; it might be interesting to determine Jephcott's reaction to the metal.

Challis could peel an apple in one movement. He'd learned such pastimes during wartime. Battle was waiting, after all. Waiting for orders, waiting for intelligence. Waiting for camp to be struck or to be set, for food to be ready. For daylight. For death.

You could pass time in prayer, in weapons checks, in coaching those who would listen. You could spend it in whoring, in gambling, in drink. For some, army life had been just that, a moveable feast, a travelling caravan of pleasures.

But that was a mark of true soldiering, how you took the tedium.

Long days on the road and cold nights on watch. The stratagems undertaken to quell the boredom mattered little as long as they accorded with a man's conscience and they did not impede his effectiveness when killing focus was critical.

In waiting, Challis had learned his Bible entire.

He let the blade curl around the apple, stroking it before he made the first incision. A slice. He snicked the segment of apple off the flat of the knife into his mouth, taking it in without biting. Only when it was quite inside did he chew. It was good and fresh despite its appearance, being full of honeyed water.

He let Jephcott see the scar reflect along the blade of the knife.

Jephcott was finishing his apple, taking the green-white flesh to the core. He would pause, chew and swallow, then continue. Then he bit off the bottom half of the core and ate that too. He ended up with just the stalk, which he used to dig with between his teeth.

Jephcott was not a gambler at hazard or other games of chance where the correct play of a hand might depend as much upon the reading of one's opponent as on the cards and the odds. He was a child's chapbook, so easily read.

So he claimed he'd left a message for Raftery. But had he? Was he expecting the man to arrive, or did he not know where he was but wanted Challis to believe the opposite?

Either way, it was clear Jephcott did not trust the situation, Challis thought. But then again there was nothing much in the situation to engender such a trust. Money buys, it does not earn, when all is said.

Business conducted in written instructions that had been couriered in secret. The same confidences pressed through monies advanced and promised and by threats oblique but tangible. Names not exchanged. Jephcott's part in this was significant, though but one element of a broader design, his part to secure the leased premises and to arrange for the transportation of these barrels from warehouse to the bridge. The barrels had been in storage three days, having landed from the continent not long before Challis's arrival. Neither the merchantman that'd brought them abroad nor the storage agent nor this factor knew of their provenance or their true contents. The barrels delivered and stacked thus far evidenced no tampering or swappage; they were distinctive enough to avoid mistake or forgery, and their sealing and caulking was comprehensive and well-engineered enough to dissuade both the idly curious and the opportunist thief.

Either way, Jephcott had no reason to believe Raftery was not alive, whether he truly expected the man to present himself or not.

And either way, Jephcott indicated that he was expected and would be missed.

The simplest solution would be to do nothing. Let Jephcott alone to his money and his petty indulgences, to his gluttony and his defilement of what little of His image was preserved in the man's dissolute frame.

Look at him, gouging between teeth, affecting boredom and impatience, the coddled warmth of fear rising off him like steam from a fresh horse turd.

He wants nothing but to be away, Challis reckoned. But now he cannot leave. If he's waiting for Raftery, then he has to wait. He must realise that I'll not grant him leave to check for the man. There would be no point. Wait here with me he must, at least until the third cartload is off the transport.

Challis sliced himself more apple.

There was merit in both positions. Life was life, and Jephcott had played his part as he'd promised. There'd been no fault in his services. Did he deserve to suffer on that account? But damned he was, sure to burn on account of his avarice, his wanton and lustful fornications and yes, his treachery towards his King and his country in failing to ask questions for the love of money. And if damned he was, then he'd burn the longer the more he lived his life the way he did, his protestations of longing for a bucolic retirement aside. He'd find his peace not in pressing flowers and in country walks but in farmers' daughters and in continued ill-treatment of his frame until either surfeit or the pox claimed him.

It might be a kindness to kill him.

It might save him part of eternity writhing in torment.

Challis finished his apple and licked the knife clean.

#

Daniel was muttering to himself. Tom couldn't catch what he was saying; the word-sounds travelled, but not clear enough for him to determine any meaning.

Daniel was away somewhere, eyes half-closed. He continued his labours as he spoke, working like some mechanical marvel, as unthinking yet productive as a windmill's worm-drive.

What was it like, to have the Holy Spirit moving within you? That was surely what was happening. Daniel was being directed, not through his body's working and his mind's will, but with something else, something higher. He was – Tom fumbled with the word - inhabited.

Tom had seen faith a hundred times, but he had never understood it. All around him, in churches, in overheard conversation, in the bawlings of those supposedly possessed with the divine will, in the certainty of his father's tales.

How many Sundays had he stood in St Margaret's church and felt nothing but the cool of the walls and the slow ache of time passing? Then a time when he'd felt only the fearful immensity of the church around him. Not just the building but the whole of it. Heaven and hell and Jesus and Satan, righteousness and redemption and charity and hard iron nails in soft white flesh. Rules to live by and consequences for good or ill; the promise of bliss and the heavy hand of forever if His will was not done.

He'd heard the words. The pleadings and entreaties, the threats and the promises, the seductions and the inducements. The thick language of the Testaments uttered from the pulpit, alive with age and possible meanings, had swirled around him. And he had been scared into some form of belief. Frightened to do otherwise because he had been brought up to always do what he was told.

But did he feel it? No.

It was a strange admission, but it was true.

It was not the same with Daniel. Daniel believed. Faith was surety and certainness with him. And his belief communicated. It rose from within, like the fed and cared-for Mother, like bread itself. It reached like a kindly relative, not a grovelling beggar. It neither wheedled nor snatched, but encouraged and nurtured; acknowledgement and forgiveness in one.

Daniel's heart was open. Tom was sure of that. Who would deny the truth of His goodness if it came to him? Perhaps there would be something in Daniel's preaching later which would offer some guidance.

Perhaps that would fill the hole inside his ribs. A space which had only room for one thing. One person.

Once, that had been his mother, once it must have been Alice, once, maybe Lizzie. And now that she, that all of them, was and were gone, Tom was sore from the wrenching out, and the remaining hollowness.

#

Challis left the house to allow the carters to move with more freedom. The third consignment had arrived and was already filling the street-level rooms, the workers able to unload all the faster without stairwells to contend with.

Jephcott was also in the street, pacing like a child desperate for the privy. He was chivvying the workmen on with little comments and busy gestures, ushering them like he was some farmer's wife and they geese. In fairness, they paid him little more attention than the previous deliverymen had; bearing him with silent efficiency or with the detached amusement that so often comes with labour without responsibility.

And then they were done. Jephcott palmed them some drinking money and off the wagon pulled. Challis used the diversion of the handover to slip back in the property.

The blade was secure inside his sleeve.

'And so we are done,' Jephcott said. There were barrels all around him, some stacked three high against the walls. There was space in the centre of the room, and the windows were not obstructed, but it was as though the house had been furnished entire with storage containers.

The room stank of coffee. The smell came off the barrels in waves. Out in the street there was too much in the way of competition for your nose's attention. Inside it was different.

The coffee warranted an acknowledgement. The Dutch were nothing if not efficient and forward in their thinking. The aroma would provide a ready explanation for the barrels' contents without further examination should the bills of lading not suffice, and the use of barrels in themselves would have been a disincentive for the opportunist thief. If someone wanted to steal a handful of coffee beans for their own pot then it was far easier to snick a sack than to bash open a cask. The same went for wholesale theft. Sacks were ubiquitous, easier to carry, and could be hidden inside other, larger hessian sacks, painted, sewn or scorched with appropriate disguise if necessary.

'The job has been well done.' Jephcott's words hung in the scented air.

'Ah.'

'So, I'll bid you good day and wish you fortune in your endeavours,' Jephcott carried on. 'We are left with the vulgar yet necessary business of remuneration. You have a letter of credit for me, I understand.'

So he did. Challis had an idea.

He reached for an inside coat pocket, brushing against the handle of one of his firearms. He took the papers out, tapping them against his other hand as he spoke.

'And here we are. Your notes as agreed. More than adequate to set a minor gentleman up in a rural retreat.' The papers were ribboned, the seal, which Jephcott had broken on first examination previously, almost matching up.

The papers were genuine and the accompanying instructions, as with so many given to Challis, somewhat open-ended.

Challis held the papers out with his left hand. He offered his right as though in friendship.

They were back from the front door which, while open, gave little direct view of where they stood. From the outside there would be little to see but darkness.

Jephcott came forward. There was relief in his face and something else. Greed, perhaps. His hands came out, one to take Challis's in fellowship, the other to accept the papers.

Challis took the offered hand. He kept hold of the ribbon around the papers. They shook once and Jephcott pulled back, expecting the papers to come with him. There were several leaves bundled together, and with the pull on the ribbon, they came apart. Some fell to the floor.

Jephcott was quick, too quick for his own good. He was already bending down and reaching to pick them up before he realised that Challis had his right hand held firm.

Challis slid his left hand into his right sleeve. As Jephcott glanced up, open-mouthed in puzzlement, Challis pulled the blade free from the guard strapped to his forearm.

Jephcott's left hand came up in defence, but the man was off-balance. Challis tugged once with his clasped right hand, bringing Jephcott's head up a touch.

His mouth was still open.

Challis filled it with metal. The strike was not clean, catching and cleaving a tooth as it went in. Challis' aim was in and up, driving for the roof of the mouth, but instead it struck soft tissue at the back of the man's throat before jarring against the point where backbone meets skull.

Challis withdrew enough to jab a second time. This was a stronger blow, at once pulling Jephcott almost upright and pushing him back.

Challis advanced, stabbing again and again into the brain from the mouth. Jephcott's maw was filling with blood, red flecked with white, at first trickling and then squirting over his tongue. Each blow slamming the knife's small hilt into the man's lips.

More cracking; teeth again, then something more resonant. His jaw.

Jephcott, now as close to the wall as could be, back arching over a barrel, spasmed. Convulsions wrestled his body as the knife scrambled his brains. Challis' hand was covered in blood. Something else also. The man must have vomited. There was pulp – apple, doubtless - giving clumpy texture to the gore.

Challis let the blade slide out slow. Jephcott's body toppled over off the barrel and pitched forwards onto the floor.

Challis kicked the door shut.

He listened, breathing hard, by the closed door. Nothing but street-noises, ordinary clatter.

Blood spread around Jephcott. Some soaked into his wig, which had come askew. Eventually, the pooling stopped, ruby juice finding space between floorboards.

Challis examined his hand. There were little fresh scars like mouse bites on the leading edge of his forefinger where the thin hilt had not protected him from the broken teeth. He flexed; the cuts did not open. Good enough.

Challis wiped his fingers clean, then the blade. He frisked the corpse. Some money, snuff tobacco, a grubby sneeze-filled rag, keys. Nothing else.

He perched himself on one of the casks and studied the body. Face down and doubtless mashed by the blows, still and soon to be cooling.

Whatever soul this vessel had once contained had gone. This was meat, nothing more.

Challis said a prayer anyway. For himself. Then he got onto his haunches, taking care not to let his coat trail in the mess, and lifted Jephcott's head enough to slide the linked metal chain over. Then Challis sat back on the barrel and examined his prize.

This face was not broken. The thing still ticked. It seemed well made enough. The single hand pointed between eleven and twelve on the face, more to the former than the latter.

The man had been as good as his word, and the work done on time.

There was more yet to do. The docks and the meeting this afternoon and then there'd be work into the night for certain.

First, though, Challis decided to check on Jephcott's premises, and ensure the man had left nothing incriminating by way of correspondence.

The puddle of gore around Jephcott glistened, as shiny as melting butter. It would take a while to dry. He decided to leave the body where it was. He had no wish to get blood on his clothing.

Besides, the others could shift it later when they arrived.

#

Daniel grabbed a crate from the alley between the bakery and the White Hart. The wood was sodden; Daniel's fingers were immediately stained with green slime from the box. There'd been no rain in the night. There'd been no rain for weeks.

'Pissing drunks,' Daniel smiled, wiping his hand on his arse.

She died there. That was her essence poured out onto the wood, or else evidence of desecration of the nearest site Lizzie would ever have to a grave. Tom felt a new grasping in his ribcage.

Shouts from the tavern; raucous free laughter. Someone stumbled out of the alehouse, a round-faced little man, grinning, moving at speed and already with fingers to his groin. He jostled Tom as he passed, shouting some good-natured apology over his shoulder. Then he slid round the corner into the alley.

Stop doing this, Tom thought. Perhaps Daniel will provide some kind of answer.

Daniel was striding ahead up the hill. Tom hastened, in part to get away from the tavern, in part to catch up. There was purpose in Daniel's gait; the swinging of the box indicated his determination. Liquid flicked off the wood at the top of its arc.

Daniel turned left at the crest of the hill. A carter cut through between the two of them, hauling a barrow stacked with grain sacks.

Tom lost sight of his brother for a heartbeat. Others cut between them in the wake, as though he'd created a ford through a river of people.

Daniel was ten, then fifteen yards ahead, his head bobbing in and out of sight from moment to moment.

Blood thudded in Tom's ears. Daniel hadn't said where he was going. What if they got separated? What if he couldn't find his brother? What if he missed this promised revelation? Daniel had been clear; he wanted Tom to hear the sermon.

He had to hear the words as they were spoken.

The stream broke, Tom hustling a child over in his stumbling forward. The mother swore twice, first in anger as though she'd thought the bairn had wrenched itself free from her grip, then second in worry, higher in pitch, as she realised that was not the case.

Tom surged on, Daniel still fifteen yards ahead. There were new shouts behind him; the child's shrieking, the mother's cursing, laughter from others.

Ten yards ahead. Tom ducked under a porter with a basket of eels on his shoulder. Fish stink was swept along with him, then other smells. The sweat of the crowds. Coffee and beer. Roasting meats and frying fat. The wet musk of raddled whores. Flowers and salt and shite and pepper, poxy sores and bacon.

Five yards. Daniel was distracted; someone must have yelled a greeting. He waved the crate in answer, pointing onwards with it. He kept it aloft and it seemed to Tom that the box had become a standard and that he and others were following it.

As if in response to that, Daniel spun the box around in his hands, holding it now by its base, open side to the heavens. The street crowded in around Daniel, the rooftops here four feet at most from their neighbour across the roadway. Between them, a pale blue streak of clear sky, the sun high in the air, and ahead of them the tower of St Paul's.

#

Jephcott had been as good as his word. There were curt written instructions left on the front office desk in his premises, held in place by a bottle. Wine had trickled down the neck and onto the note. It had left a dark crescent, a blood moon on the paper.

Challis took the note and shoved it into a pocket. The watch was there. So was the vial. So was something else; the tinderbox he'd taken from the would-be street assassin.

Mementoes. He took mementoes.

Trophies.

The letter aside, he'd taken nothing from Raftery. Nothing to keep. Not unless you considered the perfection of his form. Challis recalled the cracking of the man's fingers under the heel of his knife when he'd broken them.

That was worthy of reflection. Perhaps it allowed the dead to live on in some way. Maybe the taking of trinkets and powerful memories was His design; a method to remind His humble servant Rufus Challis of the fleeting nature of human existence. Small tokens signifying that they had given their lives for something, for an element of His greater imagining, His stratagem of which Challis was humble to be a part.

Challis held his hands out in front. The left was common enough. The right though; it was beautiful. Beautiful and terrible, burning with an inner flame relit with every movement, every gesture, every kill. A sampler of His passion, an omnipresent reminder of the twin truths of the crucifixion and of the promise of damnation. That pain has no memory. So learn to endure it now and take its message well in this life, or face the alternative in the next.

The tokens would have to go, of course. One's pockets were not bottomless, even in a coat as well-constructed and as expensive as this. But not before they had been given due consideration. Not before prayers had been offered, even though actions in His name required no forgiveness. Not before he'd had a chance to make a note of their significance. For such tokens would not present themselves if there was nothing to be gathered by their acquisition. They held meaning.

The watch, for example. It was surely too trite to infer from it that time was of the essence. No. Time was always precious; need was always great.

Time. It was time he held. Ticking made the watch reverberate. It was as though he held some fragile creature, its heart thrumming, afraid to move.

Time. That was the sign. It was time. A sign that he was right. That his acts would be remembered, even if he were not.

Challis scouted around the office space and again in the kitchen back room, but apart from evidence of another hurried meal or perhaps of one perpetual snacking, the place had been as he'd left it. The upper floors held nothing of interest; clothing, some reading matter – mostly cheap little chapbooks in French with flamboyant though accurate and detailed illustrations of women displaying their privy parts – and boxed sets of client accounts.

Satisfied there was nothing of importance, Challis locked up with the keys found on Jephcott's body. The search had not taken long.

He had time to find something to eat before moving towards the riverside areas where his afternoon business would be conducted, and time also to take one last look around the city before it would be changed forever.

He made his way to his lodgings. There was an unresolved matter there.

Challis went, not into the White Hart, but into the bake-house next door. A big man, once muscled but now turning to yellow fat through city living and heavy meals, was trowelling ashes out from a fire-grate. A young woman was serving, leaning out through the window-hatch that was hinged to make a stall jut out from the night-time shutters. She was haggling pleasantly enough with the little fat barker from the puppet-show. He was intent on buying as much as he could for as little as he could manage, leering that the week's trade was all but done, and she'd be away to her husband the earlier if she sold up soonest.

'How much for a pasty?' Challis cut in.

'Two pence.'

'And I'll give you a shilling for the lot,' the barker said. There were half a dozen pasties there. They looked good, brown and full, almost burned where filling had seeped out of the crimped pastry.

Challis offered a shilling. 'For one.'

The barker clapped, delighted. 'For one, says he! And I'll still give you my shilling for the others. Two shillings for a shilling's worth of pasties! You'll be abed before the hour's out, you'll see, your husband there'll give you another shilling's worth of meat for your supper as well, or I'm a Dutchman.' His tongue flicked his lips, shoulders already hunched as he shrugged towards where the baker had turned, hackles raised. 'Just a bit of fun, master baker!'

'A shilling for the one,' Challis said.

She handed him the savoury and slid the coin into her apron pocket. 'Enjoy,' she said.

'Oh he will, won't you?' The fat little man's face was split wider than ever, glee all about him. 'Meat and flour, oh yes, or The Bottler's not my name!'

The baker was glowering in the background.

'Just the two of you this afternoon? No help in this hot kitchen?'

The baker cut in, now over her shoulder. 'Aye. Some of us must work, not having shillings to squander on cozening up to working women, or on trying to gull an honest man out of what little profit there is in providing food.'

'And,' continued Challis, not breaking eye contact with the young woman, who was more than pretty enough and had a dangerous confidence about her, a quality that someone older and warier – like the baker, for example – would find both a source of intoxication and a never-ceasing disquiet whenever she approached by another man, 'where might I find some entertainment while I eat this?'

'Try St Paul's,' the baker said. 'It's where everyone else is today.'

'Thank you,' Challis said, again to her, and with his pleasantest smile, if only because it would make the baker stew the more.

So that was where the lad was.

#

Pasty in hand, Challis walked in the direction of the cathedral. Churches meant people, and in a city of this size, people would mean opportunity for refreshment and diversion.

And besides, he still needed to hire someone to act as a guide. The throng would provide that also. Someone young. Someone keen. Someone who needed the money and had the sense to respect confidences.

Someone who knew when secret was safest.

Challis needed to have a conversation with the baker's son. And the outcome of that talk would be either the offer of a little work, or it would not.

#

Tom broke into the open space around the cathedral. People funnelled in between the houses and shops now behind him and into the street he'd just left. Against them, others pushed Tom further up the hill, an incoming tide working its way up runnels in the silt.

Stalls were everywhere, fencing the stone bulk caught within. Sellers shouted, hustled, barked. Beyond them, as Tom squeezed between a trestle table loaded with cheeses and a girl, arms loaded with sprigs of heather for luck and gaudy nosegays for warding off stink, a second rank of stalls. This was where the booksellers could be found.

For years St Paul's had been home to as many traders in books as men of faith. They rented space in the nave or in the crypts for storing their more precious stock. Some stalls butted up to the stone walls, studious-looking fellows leaning back to take in the cool afforded by the limestone. Tables, stalls, flat barrows were all employed as trading surfaces. Some had covers, tented roofs offering both shade and protection from bird droppings. Some had rigged awnings to the scaffolding which clad parts of the cathedral, the seemingly never-ending repairs still being undertaken. Others had nothing so elaborate; just books stacked high or propped spine side up. Manuscripts were bundled together; one stallholder, gaunt and bald, used a tight scroll as a pointer, jabbing at browsers to warn them off his precious papers.

Daniel walked on, skirting the books, dodging round the buyers, the loiterers, the beggars and scroungers. Tom was almost back to where he'd begun, within two steps of his brother. The crate was still held ahead and aloft.

Catching up, Tom saw that Daniel was not present. He had gone to that other place, the place he claimed his inspiration. By whatever contrivance it was wrought, that was where he was, attending to the transaction.

Daniel shifted again, and his face was lost to Tom. He was gazing ahead, to the new-looking steps and columns at the west end of the cathedral, and to one side, the cross where a crowd was already gathered.

#

Challis bought another apple. That last one had been good, leaving him with a taste for more, redoubled after the salty savour of the pasty. This time, though, he would not use his knife.

He wanted to bite flesh. Killing had always given him an appetite.

There was noise; some entertainment. Good.

He ignored the fruiterer's cajoling, waving off his pleadings to take some more, a handful say, home to the wife.

No puppetry today though. This was more serious business as befitted, he supposed, the grey-green bulk filling the area, crude and forthright in the way it opposed the sky above it and the other buildings which framed it below. Yes, there were spires from other churches, but nothing to compare with the great mass of St Paul's. As for the rest, they were cramped sheds in comparison, hutches and outhouses. Dwellings for animals, he supposed, as should be right for the home, at least in London, of the Shepherd.

Challis doubted that He visited much.

He walked, munching his apple, over to where the crowd-sounds were coming from. Not much of a show was promised, perhaps, but it might provide distraction and opportunity for reflection before the afternoon's labours.

Better that than be harassed by the booksellers who swarmed round the stone as though their meagre offerings could attract some of His glory by dint of proximity alone.

Better that than go inside and find himself appalled by the pious, insulted by the clergy's scandalous touting for offerings and disgusted by idlers seeking cool shade and a place to snaffle their market luncheons, gnawing chicken bones and spilling cider in His house.

No. Outside would suffice.

#

There were steps up to the column of the cross. Not many, but enough for both stage and a pulpit. A preacher stood there, full in his oration. He was winding up; spittle on his chin and a black book in his hand. He jabbed out towards his congregation, promising damnation. A few at the front were rapt, revelling in the torments yet to come. Tom knew their like, half of them sent mad by their losses in the plague, a quarter driven to lunacy by the pox's effects on them, the others disappointed that the Lord had not yet gathered them on account of their past wickednesses.

Beyond the front rows of ragged faithful, the crowd had grown listless. Hectoring hadn't been to their taste; it was hot enough outside without the promise of flames to come, and those for all time.

The preacher finished. There was applause. Some threw coins, though not all of those were meant in charity. The preacher scrabbled in the dust for the money, kissed his Bible and was off.

The crowd was already melting, like ice sprinkled with salt. Some of the faithful moved out following the preacher. They must have been acolytes, driven to following his version of the Word. Daniel strode up the steps at speed, tossing the crate before him. It landed bottom side up, the way Daniel must have wanted it. He turned to face out, then stepped up and back onto the box. Tom thought for a moment that it would give under him, but it held. The extra height gave Daniel vital inches; he cast his arms wide and shouted to those gathered.

'Peace!'

His voice was loud, yet clear. Not shrill nor wheedling, it gave nothing of the desperation of the penitent, or the anger of those whose righteousness seemed fuelled mostly from within. It was a call to listen, and listen well.

'Peace, I say to you! There's time aplenty for the tearing of garments and the exposing of flesh! My first message to you is one of peace and of hope. Yes, there's the promise of never-ending agonies for those who fall by His wayside, but first I say to you, brothers and sisters, Londoners and travellers, righteous and corrupt, tenant and propertied man alike one word; peace.'

He did not shout the last word, but let his voice drop. The crowd around Tom, perhaps thirty all told, grew about him, coming nearer.

'You there,' Daniel crouched, almost nose-to-nose with the closest of the listeners, 'what is it that you seek?'

Tom did not hear the man's reply. He tried to shuffle in, but bodies around him allowed little space.

'Be not afraid,' Daniel said, louder, so the rest could hear, 'but speak with pride and conviction. Are we not all friends gathered here?'

'Peace,' the man said, repeated himself with greater confidence to the crowd. 'Peace.'

'Peace, he says. Peace! Is there anyone who does not desire that most of all? Peace from working long hours with little reward? Peace from the nagging wife at night-time or from the insistent husband in that most precious hour of sleep before the dawn? 'Peace from taxes, from the rent collector, from the hot sun, from your piles and your pox and your children?'

'Aye,' someone shouted, 'and from heat-struck would-be martyrs too!'

Daniel laughed. 'Right enough, brother. Be assured I've developed no taste for the whip. I'll not have myself or others around me indulge themselves overly in self-recrimination. Neither flagellation of the body nor the mind-' Tom felt himself pinking up at this '-shall we countenance today.

'So what is there to discuss? There is trouble ahead, brothers and sisters. But it is trouble we can escape from, trouble we can protect ourselves against. And neither by means of Popish incantation nor by means of old wives' chanting. Neither the rosary nor the cauldron shall we be forced to turn.

'My tale and my warning concerns London and therefore concerns us all. There are signs which point to the dangers ahead, signs we have avoided facing and understanding, in part because, I fear, we know them to speak true.

'And do you sir,' Daniel offered to one in the crowd behind Tom, 'and do you, pretty mistress,' indicating a girl with charcoal hair and tired rings round her eyes, 'or yet you, goodwife,' this time to a burly woman in headscarves and aprons, 'on occasion disregard plain truth because you fear its consequences?'

Some muttered assent. Others had latched onto the throng, there being, Tom guessed, fifty now listening with purpose and perhaps a dozen more who'd paused, being caught in the net of his brother's words.

'And I too. For does the truth not on occasion stand in our porch-way and is introduced as such to our faces? And too often we deny him, for we are afraid. We close our doors to the truth, as though the truth could harm us. But surely, even though we may not like the truth, it in itself cannot do us mischief. It is coming anyway, the truth. And it will not be denied.

'And that is my purpose this all too sunny day. To tell you not just of the smoke-clouds up ahead, and the heat which will rise, but of how we may remove ourselves from its path, how we may find ourselves redeemed. How we will, in short, gain that peace which we crave and which, God willing, He will bestow upon us.

'First, the cure, so that you may understand what needs to be done. Second, the illness, so that you may determine what ails the city and its dwellers. Third, the consequences for us all if we keep our gates barred to the truth.

'Some would advocate that what I propose is naught but foolishness fraught with danger. But hear what I have to say and why I say it, then think again.'

Daniel had not looked to Tom for some minutes now. He seemed lost in his oration, being swept along by his words and the passion behind them. There were more in the crowd; not yet a hundred, but surely not far off that.

Though the way that Daniel held the audience together under the roof of his words might have been impressive, Tom was lost as to his intent. Not knowing where his brother was leading made him further afraid. And there was something else. Like secret knowledge, meanings for one lone person in this dusty gathering.

Daniel was preaching to them, but speaking to him.

'The Province of New York,' Daniel said. 'Latterly removed by the grace of Charles Stuart and the Dutch West India Company from the control of our Netherlander foes. A new world, a fresh beginning, where men and women alike can begin again, free to practice their faith as their consciences dictate, yet also make what commerce or homesteading they desire, for the opportunities are as broad as the mighty rivers which cross the territory. The new world cries out for us to tame it, to make what profit we can from its bounty. To bring the benefits of English law and civility and also the freedoms that distance and opportunity invoke. Land for those that want it, trade for those who desire that, and more beyond. In a word, peace. Peace to start afresh, with the best that the old world has to offer in our hearts and memories, in our possessions and in our letters home and yet the best that the new might instil in us. Here is the place to do God's good work in raising families, communities, building churches and school-houses, bakeries and taverns. Building trust and,' he emphasised, 'peace.'

'That is my offer to you. The sea lanes are open again after our besting of the Dutch and after the terrible disease of the last years.

This is the moment to seek passage to the New World and to feel His warm embrace once more.'

Daniel paused, and it was then his eyes found Tom.

Could this be what Daniel wanted to say? An offer to leave, to travel across the ocean?

'Now that the plague has faded it is safe to board with others and we'll not now be troubled by the Dutchman.' Sounds of varying assent to that, at least, came from the crowd. Daniel held them still. No-one was leaving.

'But we have to act soon and with surety. Time passes, friends, and it passes right quick.' Daniel dropped his voice a touch. 'Listen to what I have to say.'

Tom stepped forwards with the crowd, bumping into the woman in front of him. He mumbled an apology as she tutted, recoiling when he saw the lice roiling in her hair. There was another collision, Tom stepping onto toes behind him. He did not glance back, though he raised a hand in apology.

'I'm sorry,' Tom said.

#

'Think nothing of it,' Challis murmured in response.

He didn't glance a second time at the clumsy lad in front. Challis made no indication that he was wanted. He wasn't going anywhere. Instead, Challis kept his focus on the speaker.

The way he was maintaining the crowd's attention interested Challis.

'Who among us has not lost someone dear over the last two years of plague? Perhaps a neighbour? Or worse, your mother, father, husband, wife. Your child? None of us has been free of the shadow cast over the city.

'It was then, when many fled to country cousins, or camped out beyond Highbury Fields lest they suffered the sickness, or else chanced their luck or their very faith and stayed in their homes and lived or died as He wrought, that a notion struck me.

'It is well known that the number four holds significance in our lives.' The preacher held up his fingers in emphasis. 'Four gospels, four winds, four cardinal points to the compass. Four elements, the ancients taught. Four humours. Four seasons. Does not St John the Divine prophesy of horsemen, four of them? Listen.'

Challis found himself chewing the skin on the inside of his mouth. He licked the blood that prickled there, warm salt on his tongue. The lad in front was breathing heavy, almost panting as though he'd sprinted to get here, afraid of missing the preacher's precious words. Around, others were likewise rapt.

'I dare not call it a revelation, but a realisation came to me. Consider this. Three times in the past years, within perhaps the lifespan of the very oldest among us, disaster and strife has visited.

'Once by air, in the foul contagion of the plague, which struck so many that the churchyards flowed over and doctors roamed, beaked and gloved against the noxious vapour.

'Once by the very earth itself. Was not this country torn in two by the wars between roundhead and royalist, parliament and crown, brother against brother? By the earth itself.

'Was not our nation threatened by water, latterly by the Dutchman but more satanically by Philip of Spain, who would have invaded Elizabeth's England as the Norman French and the Romans both did? Three times we have been threatened; by air, by water, by sea. And each time this city, the capital of the land and the seat of power of both monarch and parliament is challenged most. For if London falls, so does the country.

'That leaves a fourth element. Fire. The time of fire is coming. Astrologers now reckon the comet which prefigured the plague was a harbinger, a warning of the boiling flames to come. The flames draw nigh, brothers and sisters, the flames draw nigh.

'I spoke of the four horsemen. And I shall give them names. The names of archangels, for they do His work. The first of the four is Gabriel, borne on the west wind. Did not the Spaniard come from the west, around France and along our coast? White is Gabriel's colour, he who signifies the might of God. Were not the white sails of the Armada a sign of that might, and also their destruction a sign of the greater might of God that we should heed, heads bowed? But we heeded not, and another warning was sent.

'The second warning came from Michael, Christ's fighter against heresies. Red is Michael's colour and was not the soil of England stained ruby for a generation? And did we learn from those battles? We are here with a King right-wise on the throne and his parliament and ministers about their business as before? I know not what the state may demand of a monarch, but I know this as a humble man, a baker's son no less, that life goes on as before.'

A baker's son? Challis seized the information; they were brothers. His hand curled around the vial in thanks. The lad in front of him shuffled forwards. Eager to be closer, doubtless.

Eager to be closer because he was the brother. The realisation caused Challis to let the bottle go. Left hand to right sleeve. A grip on the shoulder in front and walk him at knifepoint somewhere discreet. Or he could do him here. Riddle a kidney with steel and slink out of the crowd backwards. He'd be away before Tom's knees hit the ground.

The preacher continued. 'So have we learned from the terrible battles Michael decreed we should fight? What outcome from the slaughter?'

Talk me through the bloodletting, preacher. Let me anoint your apocalypse poem. I will print it in the reddest ink.

Handle gripped, though still sheathed and sleeved, Challis held fast for auspicious wording.

'I say we learned little. Because a third trial was sent. A trial that has cost us more than the two previous. Black is the Archangel Raphael's sign, and was not the colour of the city, of the country, black for the year the plague ravaged us? As black as fear in the night, as we huddled fearing that any cough or sneeze, ache or boil would evidence the contagion. That we'd die helpless and alone, or worse, stand over our children while they swelled with the visitation, powerless to do aught except hasten their end by our own hand. That we'd be nailed inside our houses for fear of transferring the plague to others. We all crossed ourselves and hurried past such marked and sealed properties, wondering which was worse, a house with cries from within or a house that was silent.

Challis slipped his grip on the handle. No sign had been given. This was no longer a blood invocation.

'Today we see the plague's effects all around. We put on brave faces and we get on as best we can, ignoring the derelict dwellings and the lack of trade, ever wary of strangers and those with bulging goitres. For the plague year our lives have been weighed in the balance held by that third angel, the black rider named Raphael.

'And we gathered here have been allowed to live. For what reason? He above knows, but we should know in our hearts. He punishes us and at sends us signs that we might understand that the judgment hour foretold by the Divine is right soon.

'So to the New World, I say to you. To begin again, with an English Bible and the best of what man has made and spoken of foremost in our minds.

'And what if we do not, if we deny these truths, as proven as His love for us and as real as the stars and the moon? The Divine John's words are clear in the sixth chapter of Revelations. The first three horsemen are by way of warning; with crown, with sword, with scales of justice in hand. Totems which, as we have seen for ourselves, represent the trials we've suffered under Armada by water, under civil war by earth, under disease by air.

So Tom was another temptation. More than that, he was a living symbol. But of what? That whoring woman had been an exemplar. She was the city in dissolute miniature. The signification was clear.

What did Tom mean? What was he, Challis, being challenged with? This needed reflecting upon. A close study, perhaps.

Oh, that was it. And Challis might have laughed in rue had he been less circumspect. The provocation was the thing. The lad was a threat. He had to be kept close. He could not die. More than that: he could not be killed. Not yet. Not yet.

'And that fourth horseman? What does he offer? There can only be fire. Is that not the fourth element, and the one by which we've not been tested? Fire is the manner of our judgment. The walls of our city will be a stone crucible for damnation's flames.   And those flames will be lit by the last angel, the pale rider, the one coloured as the brightest burning coal, Uriel, the Fire of God himself. Uriel will come among us and he will burn us. Is it not so written? The Divine, in his mercy and compassion, shows us the sign by which we shall know the hour of our final judgment. Here is wisdom, says the Good Book. Let him that hath understanding count the number of the beast: for it is the number of a man; and his number is six hundred threescore and six.

'What plainer direction do we need? The very number of our annihilation, printed clear and in English in every Bible resting on every lectern in the land. Three sixes. The year, brothers and sisters, sixteen sixty-six.

'The warning is clear. God has sent, for his own good reasons, his angels amongst us. And three times we have been warned, and three times we have not heeded the instruction; that it is time to move on. That England as she exists, love her though I do with all my heart and soul, is in mortal danger. The answer is, brothers and sisters, simple. To begin again in the colonies. A new Eden in the New World.

'Who is with me?'

Three or four in the front row had fallen to the ground almost as soon as the preacher had finished. To his left and right, Challis saw others silent, thoughtful. An ugly white-whiskered man and his wife were forehead to forehead in quiet but anxious discussion. Others shifted forward to toss alms, offer a hand to shake or a prayer. Some went about their business now the free show was over.

The smaller and presumably younger of the brothers stood as still as an empty gallows.

Challis kept still too. The sermon had left him with ideas; slivers of thought to copy into his pocketbook. He had not considered the nature and level of feeling around him. Truly, what was to come would be awe-inspiring, if all went as he intended.

There was much to do, and that meant making his way back to the docks.

First though, a word with the preacher, and then to attend to the brother.

The ugly couple were at the preacher's side, patting him as though he were a prize-fighter they'd won money backing. There were hearty smiles all round, the preacher's face shining with exertion, and then the last of the converts, acolytes, hangers-on, left.

The preacher came over; stepping down from the height offered by the box he'd been perched on, descended the steps from the cross to the square. He nodded to Challis in deference to someone who'd listened with serious interest. He put his hands on the younger one's shoulders, and whispered to him. His words were fast and they did not carry.

Challis let them have their moment. Uriel, he thought. He liked that.

#

'The New World?'

'Yes, brother.'

'But what about Father?' Even in speaking, Tom did not feel that Farriner deserved the consideration.

'And what of him? He has all he desires in this world. He has the custom of the King. You know what else he has.'

Alice. 'Yes.'

'He has us, brother. Us.'

Tom kept his head down. 'He cares nothing for me. A pair of hands to fetch and to carry. That is all I am to that man.'

'Do you truly believe so?'

'And why should I not?' Tom's head rose at this, reddening at his brother's stupidity. For all his fine words he could be so blinkered. 'He works me hard from six till six. Never a word of thanks nor praise do I receive, yet you are free to wander wherever you will, pitching in or not as your calling dictates.' The words started to tumble from him. 'Are you not his firstborn? Isn't the business yours to take on when the time comes? Farriner and Son. Surely that's his intent. To leave you what he's built. And I labour while you're allowed to be free. Free for your distractions, for your preaching, for your fancy talk of leaving London and all you know and loves you for the New World? What need have you of freedom of faith and of conscience there when you have that here, in these streets, while your brother provides your bread and your father provides your roof?'

Daniel held his hands up as though Tom were apt to swing at him. 'If my actions have caused discomfort or uncertainty, brother, then I can only beg forgiveness. I am not certain I can explain this to you.'

'Try,' Tom barked.

Daniel's hands came up further, to his nose. He let them rest, adopting the stance of a praying statue. Why did he always do this, play the righteous man, the conscience-driven sinner seeking redemption? Why couldn't he just stand there and tell him?

'Tom,' Daniel started. He rarely used his name. 'Thomas.' And rarer still. He was forever "brother"; something that sounded religious in intent, but vague as though he did not care to know his name. 'Why do you think that father is hard on you but soft on me? Why does he work to make you work, where I am, as you say, free to roam? Baker Farriner is a practical man, is he not? Surely not one to let productive hands lie idle when there's orders to fulfil and money to be earned? He knows what he does. The question for you is, where's the profit in him for it?'

That was simple. So simple Daniel should have confessed to it and be done with the matter. Have the words spoken plain, here, in front of this church.

'You don't have to pay your son. You work him hard and you work him long hours for a roof and a meal and all in the name of family. You're allowed your freedoms because he loves you. He loves you and he doesn't need you; not while I am there.'

Daniel shook his head. 'That's not it, brother. Not it at all. You have the world turned in your mind. I-' he cut his words off there, before re-starting. 'Think of it in this fashion. He works you hard, yes?'

'Yes.'

'And you resent him for it.'

'While there are others around who could do that work, but are free to do otherwise. Who know the trade yet are not compelled to it.'

'And who would want to be a baker?'

The question made no sense to Tom. 'What do you mean?'

'I ask you again: who would want to be a baker? And, if not a baker, then a farrier, or a cooper, a fuller or a walker? Who chooses such trades?'

'All men have to make a living.'

'Yes.'

'And men often do as their fathers before them, be it working the same land, driving the same beasts to market or carrying on in the same manner of industry.'

'Yes,' Daniel said. 'And what of that?'

These riddles agitated Tom. His brother would persist in this stage mountebank talk though he had no more education than him. And yet he had no answer to his brother's question.

'Why persist? You can jaw with the best of them, and anger me too. But in the end I'll be the one with oven heat in my face, and you'll be the one charming money from strangers.'

'Don't think ill of me, brother. This isn't a circumstance that can be explained to you. You have to understand it for yourself. If I spelled matters plain, you would not take my word. But if you determine for yourself, then that knowledge will be yours and you will act on it right wise.'

'And until that beautiful day?' There was bitterness in Tom's tone.

Daniel's hands were now on Tom's shoulders. 'Until that day, I'll do what I can. Around the ovens, I mean. I've almost enough money saved. Enough for two passages. You and I brother, if that's how our lives are destined to go.'

Tom hated Daniel when he was like this. Loved him and hated him in equal and opposing measure. Nothing was ever straightforward with him. Part of Tom thought this offer of passage across the ocean was part of his fancy trickery, nothing but a ruse to divert his anger.

But then, what if the offer were real? Tom had no reason to believe that it was not genuine. And such an offer would make things so much easier.

Alice. He could leave her and the flour and the sweat to his father. He could take what skills he had and begin again, and be seen for the man he surely was, in the New World.

Daniel stood back. 'Where else does this money go?' he said, indicating the coins he'd collected. 'All in the pouch for my travels.'

'Just talk, then? The flames and the angels?' That would be like his brother; a storyteller, like father had once been.

'Talk? Not a word of it. The signs are there for all who've got the wit to stare beyond to see. Of that I'm sure. Do not our history and the Bible confirm this by their conjunction? I fear for this city, brother. His judgment is come, and that right soon. Each of these tests, these messages, comes quicker than the one before. A generation and more from Armada to the wars between parliament and King. Then only a handful of years from Charles' restoration to the plague. The intervals are falling faster, quicker, each time. Do you see? The fourth angel will walk among us. The signs are there. That's why I preach as I do; to spread the word, to try to clarify the message the scriptures and our past conspire to provoke. And if, in doing so, I can raise the funds to begin again, to perform what good works I may and purchase bunk and board on ship now the plague restrictions on travel are lifted then where's the harm caused?'

Daniel continued. 'Think on it, brother. But think fast. There's vessels sailing and I mean to secure my journey sooner rather than later. Before the winter closes the shipping lines, now we've done with sea-battles with the Dutch for the year. With luck we'll pick up some tattle from Father about the Navy's intentions, and we can use that to our advantage.'

Daniel's words seemed so certain that Tom found himself caught up in it. And what if it was running away? What if it left questions unanswered? Those questions, like the people who provoked them, would be countless thousands of miles away, here in London, where they would pass into and then perhaps from memory.

Tom found himself with his hand outstretched. Daniel took it, and they shook. Tom fancied that his grip was as strong as his brother's.

#

Challis had already decided he liked this pairing. The taller and, he presumed, the older one, had the gift of holding a gathering and being convincing both to a group and when talking man to man.

The smaller, younger one was a gawky creature; on the adult side of life, but still incomplete. He had three or four inches to grow and he had not yet filled out. There was a wiry strength in his movements, but he was still a galloway - a pony, not a full-grown horse - and with the spiky temperament to match.

Challis now understood why he'd been abroad late at night spying on a whoring corner, and also why he'd not raised a hue-and-cry or provoked other suspicion towards Challis.

He was curious.

'A fine sermon, pastor,' Challis said, coming forward, beaming over the same shoulder he might have grabbed and held tight as he stabbed and stabbed into the small of Tom's back. 'You know your signs right, I fear.'

And now Tom turned.

In Challis's open left hand, two shillings. Enough to capture attention. Not too great a donation to make him seem either a guizer or a fool. Challis let the coin jingle as Tom's head came around.

That's it. Eyes down to the noise, then up to my face.

You see me now. With your paling face and your now-uncertain stance. Challis wondered if Tom would withstand the fainting imperative.

'I'm no pastor,' the preacher replied. 'Just a humble man with an important message.'

'And does the message reach its intended?'

The preacher smiled; there were levels of amusement there. 'Daniel Farriner, at your service,' he said. 'And this, my brother Thomas.'

'Rufus Challis.' Challis nodded to the younger. 'Thomas.' Respectful, the lad returned the gesture with caution.

And very wise too. You might fall over otherwise.

Daniel offered his hand. Challis took his right from his pocket, fixing Daniel's gaze as he did so. The eye-lock and the combination move of bringing the left hand over the handshake did the trick. Challis patted their shake with the left, allowing the monies to find the pastor's palm as he withdrew his right. The upper hand and the money reinforced the attention and, evidenced by the way Daniel shuffled, feet apart and hands surreptitiously sheathing the coins, dominance.

The preacher still had gambits to learn.

'Do your flock pay heed?' Challis prompted. Keep the preacher talking. Let his brother stand and wonder.

'These are stray lambs, wandering common pastures. Some say that they hear truth in my words. Even so, it's easy to preach damnation and to gather those who yearn for it, who welcome the promise of infernal and unceasing torment. All I can say is that I know these truths to be just so, truths, and I would save those I could, for I believe them to be plainly writ.'

'So you desire a fresh life across the ocean?' The notion appealed to Challis; vessels of pious and God-shocked English fleeing their country and its arrogance. Risking seas, shipwreck, privateers. Starting again in stockaded huts, one eye on their Bibles and another on glints from sharp and hungry teeth in the strange uncleared forests beyond their encampment.

'The New World is an opportunity for salvation given to us from above. We would be remiss to ignore such a boon.'

'Remiss indeed.' Challis turned to face Thomas. 'And you're agreed? Is your destiny the Americas too?'

The lad did not speak at first. A scuttling at his Adam's apple. Then calmness was imposed over his face. Even then he gave himself a breath or two.

Good. He was not as ready to please as his brother, had not followed into the preacher's trap; the becoming of a jeremiad or a prancing entertainer, a frothing dog for blood or a quack offering panaceas of the life everlasting. And he had some reserve of self-control.

'So it would seem,' Tom said at last. 'If what brother says is true, then there is little alternative.'

'Then perhaps I can help. I've errands to run and but a short time to perform them. My knowledge of the city is uncertain. I need a guide for the afternoon. In return for such services, which will be concluded by nightfall, I'd be most generous.' Money was not, after all, an issue.

Challis slid a coin across his palm, letting the colour of the coin provoke. 'If you're agreeable, I'll even pay now.'

'Leave the money with my brother,' Thomas said, without pause. That was creditable. You are a curious one, are you not? 'He'll hold it for me.'

Challis mentioned a sum and it was agreed. The concord was well-judged; cautious enough to hide excitement at what the money could bring. A berth or, more likely, a hammock-space on a vessel. Security in his good faith for the day.

These were God-fearing types, after all, not God-loving. Their actions were driven in spite of the Redeemer, not because of him. And if they could help in Challis's bringing even part of Daniel's sermon towards realisation, then perhaps they would see the wider truth for themselves, and be brought closer to the light of His radiance.

'Then our bargain is made.'

Thomas turned to his brother and asked him something about covering at home. Doubtless he had neglected chores; God knew he'd ignored his own father's impotent demands for respect enough times. The elder assented, promising to make good whatever was needed. There was still the thick spin of heavy coin in Daniel's head. He would have promised anything, and meant it too.

'Where to?'

'Walk me to the dockside, Thomas. Or Tom?'

'Tom.'

'I've got someone to meet there. And perhaps you'll see the vessel that'll transport you to the Americas.'

#

The meeting was true enough. Saturday, on the afternoon tide. That had been the agreement. The ship's name was unknown to him, but how many would arrive from France in one day? He would not be tricky to find.

They walked around the cathedral and the hubbub around it, the stalls and the wheedlers, the once-fresh fruit and the ripening meat. Being Saturday there'd soon be that additional urgency in their entreaties, stock needing to be sold by the end of the day.

Some would make their price, sell and be gone. Others would be haggled down by the thrifty, by those who liked nothing better than making tradesmen sweat. Let them take their pleasures while they may.

Challis stopped. 'Which way?'

The lad pointed downhill.

#

It was difficult to breathe. Tom's throat felt clogged as though he'd been stuffed with forcemeat. The world shimmered when he blinked. The ground felt untrustworthy underfoot.

Challis had come for him. He had followed them through the streets and had listened to Daniel's sermon so that Tom could be found and – and what?

To offer some work?

He had made no sign of recognising him from the bakery, so perhaps this was happenstance, and an opportunity to make some money. But the docks were not hard to find and London was not so big that you couldn't navigate it.

What was in this man's mind? He who had killed Lizzie Corbet less than two days ago, and who Tom had tried to have beaten sore in comeback, was within stabbing distance.

The man was odd in appearance, in his heavy leather coat and his dark demeanour, but this was London. The fell was commonplace and the sensible man paid little attention to the foibles of others, else he brought similar unwanted attention to himself. There was an expectation of privacy in the bustle of the city.

Tom was not sure he believed in coincidences.

But he was going to have to start believing in opportunities. To take some initiative in life. A chance to earn and to find out more. Who was this man, and what was his business?

A chance here to test himself too. To prove that Tom Farriner was more than cheap labour. More than an easily-ignored youth.

The earth below him redefined itself in solidity. Tom swallowed, shifting the blockage in his gullet. He blinked and saw clear.

The risk was worth the opportunity. And perhaps - just — a chance to do something in Lizzie's memory.

The man strode, though he did not know where he was going. Tom sped up to overtake. He was now leading again, but had to move at a pace to keep the half-step ahead that would indicate, not least to himself, that he was the guide and not the follower.

Rufus was tall, too. Half a head at least taller than other men, taller even than Daniel. He was unadorned, needing neither fancy wig nor decorative sword. A necessity, a purpose to his dress. It was there in its plain dark, in the quality artisanship evident in his boots and coat. His gear had cost.

And he was flush with coin. The money nagged again at Tom. What he'd paid was plenty, but what if there was more to be got? The quicker he and Daniel got their passage fees the better.

He'd show willing and take what earning opportunities came.

Perhaps not believing in coincidences was a good thing. This man was another sign, in the way Daniel had preached, that the colonies were his destiny. He was being provoked into action.

Tom crossed the road, cutting into an alley. 'This is quicker,' he said over his shoulder. The side-street was not long, thirty paces in all. The opening at the far end was clear and bright. No-one was slumped in doorways. Neither urchins nor rats lurked in the shade.

A moment's pause. This was a good spot for a killing. A hand over Tom's face and a knife in the back and that would be that. Tom found himself breathing through his mouth. Thirty paces. Opportunity, not threat, he told himself.

Nothing to it.

Tom led them through, emerging into Bread Street Hill. He regretted his new route at once.

A commotion in the road. A horse had keeled over and had turned the cart it had been hauling. The cart was over on one side, the underside wheels broken. Crates lay strewn across the cobbles.

There were two men with the horse. One was on his knees, stroking the beast's neck. It whimpered, the sound piercing with sharpness and desperation. Sweat streaked its neck.

The other man, heavyset and with a switch tucked into his belt, laboured to rescue his load. Crates. Animal bones. Sharp white lengths streaked with blood and sinew where the butcher's cleaver had been imprecise.

A gaggle had formed, enjoying the distraction. Some peered into the boxes. The fat man did what he could to shoo them away, all the while collecting crates to the roadside and shouting across to his companion.

Rufus had stopped to take the sight in.

Tom held off from making to leave. Let him watch.

A lass around Tom's age came through the onlookers and spoke quick and fast with the fat man. He thought for a heartbeat, and then nodded. She made off just as quick, returning with another man in tow. More words, a handshake. A swift once-over of the still-keening animal, then money was exchanged.

The fat man went to his companion. He would not get up, wanting to stay with the horse. But the fat man was insistent, hand on hip. He pursed the money and might have gone for the switch had not the other eventually stood, head bowed, and run back off up the hill.

'Gone to borrow another horse and cart,' Tom said.

Rufus nodded, distracted, attention on the horse.

The fat man went to his boxes, counting the crates up. Then he unbuckled the harness still attaching the horse to the cart. Some of the leather strapping remained under the animal. That wouldn't be a problem for long.

This was the way of the city. Every journey a potential hazard. Cobbles were slippery with piss and shit. There were leavings and discarded waste, rain and thrown-out wash water, spilled beer. If you were near markets, there'd be slaughterhouse blood, fish guts, rendered fat. A thousand possibilities. Horses and driven livestock could bolt, carriages might throw a wheel or you might trip - or be shoved - and fall under hooves or axles.

The city brought its own solutions though. Theft or trade in most instances. Even a dead horse was worth something, and better to make a deal and get on than harbour grudges about ill-fortune as well as have to shift a carcass.

Already the blades were out. The first cut took the horse's breath, a leather jug pressed to its neck to catch its blood. The horse's huge soft brown eyes rolled back into its skull, up past long lashes and into whatever heaven waited for beasts of burden.

A second jug was swapped for the first, but the flow was already lessening. Besides, there was urgency to the business. The road could not remain blocked for long, and amusement and wonder would soon turn to name-calling and stone-throwing. Better to get on with what must be done.

The butcher's girl had brought others; one with a saw, one with a drag sled to pull the chunks of slaughtered animal away.

The three men set to their task fast. The girl stood back at first: Tom thought to watch, to play no part. But no, she rolled her dropped sleeve up so it matched its partner and pushed her hair back out of her eyes. And then she weighed in, wrist flexing and twisting with each stab and cut.

The way her skin stretched over her muscles was beautiful.

Once it became clear what was being done, tradesmen went back to their stores, pedestrians moved off. Those who'd been obstructed by the disruption would surely relax, because their inconvenience was coming to an end.

Blood stained the cobbles, finding paths both straight downhill and zigzagging out to the runnels. Tom trod carefully as he made his way past. Heavy meat smells were building. The drag sled was heaped with haphazard sections of flesh. They'd need to make a second trip.

The girl shouldered the sled harness. She slipped it on: she'd done this enough times to make it an unthinking movement. She caught Tom watching her, and stuck out her tongue.

Tom grinned back at her.

She tugged on her load. Nothing at first, then it shifted. There must have been something under the sled to make it slide easily. Not wheels. The girl came past, close enough for her elbow to scrape him. She kept eye contact until she passed.

Leather pads under the wood where it met the ground at the back: that was the trick. There was a wooden lip around the sled to prevent spillage, but one of the others followed behind, hand out to prevent the load toppling. He now met Tom's eyes, stopping him from seeing the way her shoulders took the burden. How her muscles strained below her neck.

He had his hatchet, still red, in his other hand.

'Don't fool with a man with a knife and a girl to protect.' Challis loomed over his shoulder. 'Not unless you're certain the risk is worth the reward.'

'Sometimes it might be.'

'Assuredly so. But measure your fight, and know your ground.' They had begun walking again, but slow. Tom reckoned that Challis did this so that they would not catch up with the girl.

Challis continued. 'Think of it this way. You see a pretty girl.'

Pretty? Tom wasn't sure. What he saw was her tongue, her cheekiness. And the way she was strong. How her skin rippled with each little movement.

'She's got some spark to her, yes?'

Tom didn't say anything. Her hair was dark brown, lustrous, like well-worn and much-loved oak.

'Yes. There's a light within. And you're curious. You want to see what makes the shine.'

They turned left, from Bread Street Hill onto Thames Street. Up to the left was St Michael's Queen-Hythe, and beyond that St James' Garlick-Hythe. The churches were the best route markers hereabouts, though Thames Street was easy enough, the road shadowing the river from Puddle Dock behind them to the west to the Tower ahead in the east.

The girl and her companion had by now crossed Thames Street. There were warehouse premises on a street corner, the first of many leading from here to the water and the berths at Queen-Hythe. Cleaver-man opened a set of double gates for her, holding one side back for her to pull the load through into shadow.

If she checked back behind her, she did so from darkness.

'He's got her home safe enough,' Challis said. 'And now you know where she lives.'

Thames Street was busier, being the main thoroughfare linking the docks and the water with the rest of the city. It was wider too, yards of clear sky between the rooftops. This meant that there was no escape from the sun.

'So consider his perspective, your friend with his hand-axe. He's wary of other men around his woman. Why? Perhaps she's not his woman at all, but his sister or other relative, and what you saw is protection from a family member. But let's suppose that this is not the case.'

'His woman?'

'Such possessive terms. His woman. Maybe that is how he feels. That she is his. His to use as a man uses a woman. But his to protect. To roof and clothe. Complicated, yes?'

Tom knew how "complicated" felt.

'Now say he's a kindly man. Respectful and God-fearing, charitable and generous. Such a man would not countenance disrespect nor would he express vile attitudes towards his woman, so protection is his mindset.'

Challis's pace had picked up. He was moving as purposeful as his words, striding in the dry runnel, kicking up plumes of dust. Tom stuck to the road-side, the walkways by the shop premises being too cluttered to maintain step with him.

'Now let us surmise he's no such paragon. A beater of women. A drunkard bully who can only service his woman when he's fat with meat and blurred with ale. Such a man will act to protect too. To protect his own selfish interest. He cannot afford for his woman to determine other possibilities for herself. So he will keep her busy, with housework and childrearing and his demands. You see how she took to dragging that horseflesh? Perhaps that was part of it.

'But a third possibility presents itself. The woman's a jade, a slattern, a doxy. The word is not important, but the consequence is. She does as she wills, swive who she fancies and cares not whom she insults nor disappoints, betrays nor makes an enemy of. Again, note the way she harnessed that load. Did that speak of her independence, or her mischievousness in doing a man's work in public to shame her husband, to further proclaim his cuckold-ness in the midst of his peers?'

Consternation at the bottom of Dowgate Hill. A brawl had spilled out of an alehouse. Shouts about being cheated of money by a whore. A woman leaning out of one of the tavern's windows. She was laughing so hard she kept a hand to her chest to stop her paps falling out of her clothes. She wasn't helping by waggling a little finger at him. He made for the door again, but was caught and held by two others. It was hard to tell if they were cronies of his or of hers. Either way, she ducked back out of sight and the commotion ceased, some returning inside, others staying out with the man. He'd taken blows to the head; his face was already swelling.

'A point made as if by Providence's design,' Challis remarked. 'It is everywhere, all around us.'

'Yes.'

'This is the city. Back to our butcher friend. Three possibilities linked by the one factor. Which is?'

'The man himself.'

'And what do we know about him?'

Tom thought before answering. It was fell how it was easier to exchange honest words with a stranger than with kin. 'He works as a butcher and with horseflesh. So he's comfortable with heavy hand tools. No fear of blood and guts.'

'And what else?'

'And he knows it too. This is-' Tom struggled for a word.

'This is how he presents himself.'

'Yes.'

'And so?'

The conversation was beginning to fluster Tom. That and the chance that he was being tricked somehow. That he was suspected. Of having seen Lizzie's murder, of having set those footpads on him.

'I'm not sure.' He had to speak louder; the noise from the water under the bridge as well as the tolling bells - that was St Magnus's - made it hard for his words to carry.

'So why should a man present himself in any manner?'

'Because that is what he is.'

'Or?'

Tom thought. 'Because that is what he is not; or that is what he lacks?'

'Precisely.'

'And?'

'Well,' Challis said, 'that would depend on your intentions, both towards him and the woman. His bluster indicates lack of confidence, not assuredness in his unity with the woman. That might be advantageous. But it also indicates a willingness to protect, if necessary with violence, or at least with the threat of it.'

'And?'

'And he has two things to lose. His respect, and the woman.'

'Then he would fight?'

'On his terms he would.'

'What terms would those be?'

'If challenged in public, for example. Or in front of her, or the company of family, friends. The challenge would be too great. If with his weapon to hand, whatever cutter he favours, he were to come at you, what manner of fighter would he be?'

'He would not be a fighter. A killer. That's his understanding, the cleaving of flesh. He'd swing high or wide, and always for the finishing blow. The head or the neck, that's where he'd aim.'

'Good. And what else?'

'He moves meat all day. Animals, carcasses, hams and joints. He's strong. He won't tire easily.'

'What would your strategy be?'

Tom laughed. 'Not to fight him at all. He'd cut me in two.'

'He might.'

Tom's thoughts picked up speed. Maybe it was the acrid oiliness of the air hereabouts greasing them. They were not far from Billingsgate. Oyster-houses, fish smokeries and salt-houses everywhere. 'It would have to be on my terms. I'd have to know it was worth the risk.'

'That's more like it. Let's assume that she's worth it. Aren't they all, in their own way?'

'I suppose.'

'You suppose right. How would you tackle him?'

'I couldn't beat him.'

'Are you sure?'

'He's too strong; he's used to cutting bodies open. He works with a heavy blade all day. He'd be angered and violent. I'd never land a blow.'

'And?'

'And he'd likely kill me as a consequence.'

There was an amused twitch to Challis's lips.

'What is it?' Tom asked.

'You're happy to engage in this conversation, about taking on this brute to secure passage to that girl's gusset and yet you seem dully insistent on one thing.'

'On what?'

'On some kind of fair fight. A duel.'

He was right. Tom had. Squaring off, man to man.

'Where's the sense in that?'

'Isn't that how these things are done?'

That smile was there again. 'In olden times perhaps, Tom. Your chivalry does you credit, but it won't wet your pizzle.'

Part of Tom riled. There was more to life, to women, to Lizzie or to Alice than simply tupping and wenching.

Part of him knew different. He wanted the experience, the knowledge, the sensation of bedding a woman he loved. Not a woman who took his money or allowed him access for companionship's sake.

And not the woman he once thought he loved. Something had died for him with the understanding that Alice was ordinary.

That was the word.

He had built her up into impossibility, something she could never be. Alice Corbould was a normal girl, an ordinary woman. The same needs, hopes and conflicts as all others.

It was Tom that was wrong. Wrong for indulging in childish hopes and dreams. He was little better than a baby and had behaved as such.

This was his punishment, to be told this by a stranger. To have the caul pulled from his face so that he could see the world the way it really was.

Tom should have had this very conversation with Daniel.

No dreams, no stories. None of the bedtime yarns his father had filled his head with. Just dry ground under his feet, dryness in his mouth and the low throb of hunger in his belly. This was all there was: body, not soul.

There was nothing here for Tom.

They walked west to east along Thames Street, the stones and flags of the Tower growing in the sky ahead. And to their right the shouts and crashes, the neighs and whinnies, laughter and threats and promises from the wharves along the river, backed all by the lapping of water against boats and over mudflats, and the dull thump of swaying ropes against mastings.

They were closing on the dockside.

#

Challis checked Jephcott's watch. Enough time for a stop-off. 'A drink,' he said. 'Beer?'

There was no shortage of inns and taverns to choose from. One with the sign of a Tudor rose, white and red, seemed hospitable enough. Challis beckoned Tom in.

Challis ordered ale and a platter of fried fish to share. The food arrived not long after the drink, a sizzling heaped bowl of bread-crumbed whitebait. Challis gestured to tuck in. This was grub best scarfed fast enough to burn the roof of the mouth, the better to enjoy the beer's cooling.

The fish did not last long; the pair of them soon left sucking salty fingers and taking long pulls on their drinks. Challis motioned to a serving boy for refills before resuming.

'Our imaginary fight. How would you go about it?'

Tom hadn't wasted his eating time by not thinking things over. 'If there's nothing to be gained in a fair fight and I had to have the girl, then it would be murder.'

'Murder?'

'Something deliberate.'

'And is your soul not jeopardised by murder, not to say your neck?'

'Death is all around. If not the plague, there's a score of other sicknesses which might carry a man off. There's a hundred ways to be killed otherwise by accident or design.'

'You're not afraid of death?'

Tom shook his head. 'I'm not afraid of futures I cannot foresee. If I were to murder a man, to have his blood coat my hands, then I should expect and deserve the noose. That's not to fear it, but to see it as a necessary part of the killing. I would not welcome it, but not be either frightened or aggrieved if that was the route He took me towards.'

'He? And what of Him?'

'If my heart and my soul are the one and the same, and if that man with the cleaver were the monster we've supposed, then his death would be kindness, both in preventing further harm to that woman and in punishing him for his sins and crimes.'

'So you would be Christ's instrument?'

'In such circumstance, then I suppose that would be His design. The test might be capture, I reckon. If it was foul murder done for selfish gain, then the tree at Tyburn would be assured, and He would ensure that.'

'And if you got away with it?'

There was care in the reply. 'Then the actions would accord with His will. The girl would have the reward of a good life. I would have her as reward for acting right-wise. The brute would receive the punishment that constables and judges had not provided. A good would have been done.'

Challis would have called for more beer, but it was rich, strong stuff, and he needed all wits in full function for the afternoon.

'And the deed? How would you do it?'

'I've no skill at brawling, or with swords. In a knife-fight he'd best me, through force if not finesse. I could,' an intake of breath taken to disguise a pause, 'hire ruffians to do him in, but that's expensive and

I don't know who to ask.' And out again. 'Plus it's cowardly not doing it yourself and it leaves others knowing what you've done.'

'Witnesses. Sneaks who'd rat you for a shilling.' Challis said this soft. He was not sure if he intended Tom to hear it or not.

'If I were to kill a man, I'd want to do it myself. I'd want to face him so he knew it was me. So that he'd know why.'

'Would you say something, make your statement?'

'You ask a lot of questions.'

'It's the best way to find things out.'

'I'd hope,' Tom said, 'that I would not have to. That he would know this was justified, and accede to it.'

'You've never seen a man at his last, I take it?'

'No. Not in the way you mean. Dying of disease and old age, yes. But not by being met by violence.'

'Men are not so accommodating or as stoic as you hope.'

'Perhaps not.'

'And your method of dispatch?'

'A firearm,' Tom said.

'Why?'

'It's quick and safe enough to use at a killing distance,' Tom said. 'And certain if aimed true. I've no wish to see a man suffer.'

'Not even to take back some the pain inflicted on that poor girl? To make good the balance?'

'No,' the lad said. 'The act is enough.'

'You sound like an executioner,' Challis said. 'The hand of justice, not its arbiter.'

'I suppose so,' Tom said. 'But this is all just a pipe-dream. Does life ever arrange itself in such ways?'

'One must be open to the possibility. And if it were to, for the sake of that lass, and others of her kind, one would hope that you'd act in accordance with your words at the crucial moment.'

'And what of you? What's your business in the city? Where do you need to go this afternoon?'

Challis didn't flicker at the lurch in conversation. 'Me? I'm just a humble trader. I import and I export. I meet with an acquaintance coming from the continent this tide. A fellow I've no wish having my competitors observe me dealing with.'

'So I'm to locate this man for you and bring him to you?'

'A sharp one, you, as well as being possessed of an acute sense of justice. Just so. And for that service I'm happy to consider our business concluded and you can be on your way.'

'Where are your premises?'

'On the bridge. I'm latterly set up in commerce there.' Challis gave Tom the details.

'And the gentleman I'm to find for you?'

Challis had met him just the once, earlier that week. He hadn't spoken except to introduce himself; his English had not been good. Perhaps that was reason enough for his reticence. Then again, they had been in Antwerp; there was no reason to expect a conversation in English. The Romans made it simple for themselves, he thought. One empire, one language from the Scottish borders to Egypt.

'A little thing, he is. The appearance of a simple man made good, this being precisely what he is. Not much taller than yourself, with dry sand-coloured hair. He's not likely to be wigged. He will almost certainly be wearing a hat, something with a brim wide enough to throw shadow across his face. He's cautious, somewhat bashful. I fancy he had some accident at birth or shortly afterwards, because his eyes bulge a little from his skull. That, combined with his unfortunately thin and distinct nose, one which could do with breaking, makes him individual in aspect, and simple to determine.'

'He sounds easy enough to find.'

'I don't doubt it. There's just one more thing that's of value to understand.'

'And what's that?'

'He'll probably hide his hands. Perhaps he'll wear gloves. If he doesn't, then he may well keep them deep in his garments. It might be a kindness to offer to carry his bag.'

'Is there something wrong with his hands?'

'That I couldn't say.'

'Why not?'

'I've never seen them.'

'And his name, if I have to ask?'

'Piedlow,' Challis said. 'His name is Stephen Piedlow.'

#

Tom followed Challis out of the inn.

Challis said he would point out Piedlow from a distance, and then leave Tom to bring him to his premises on the bridge. He'd go on ahead, and meet them there.

Challis, he said, was importing coffee from Turkey. Piedlow was in charge of the transit of goods across Europe to wherever the prices were best. Coffee being valuable, and there being much profit involved, Piedlow liked to check in at all stages of the deal. He was not a man to leave matters to correspondence. Challis had it on authority that London coffee prices were higher than Paris or Amsterdam's present offers, so he had contracted with Piedlow to bring his load to England.

'These new crops being traded in the explorers' wake are the coming truth,' Challis said. 'If you go ahead with your migration to the Americas, then maybe, like Raleigh and his contemporaries, you'll find fresh sources for cocoa, tea, tobacco or coffee. Or perhaps as yet unimagined crops, leaves and beans for man's use.'

Behind them now were the fish docks. Here, moving off the main thoroughfare of Thames Street and away from direct sight of the Tower, were the principal wharves and quays for the reception of incoming goods and the outgoing of manufactured and processed materials. They had cut across the road, and then down the narrow smoot called Bear Key, to the docks themselves.

It was hard to credit the amount and variety of labour being exercised. Yes, there was loading and unloading, onto carts for movement or straight into warehouses for storage. But there was also a great milling around of passengers, dock workers, chandlers' men, shipwrights and their woodworkers and apprentices, plus hawkers, barkers drumming up business for this inn or that tavern, sellers of patent medicines and whores of all stripe. Confident fancy women, all cheekiness and exposed flesh. Dark-eyed boys, slim and wary. Creased hags, offering economy and experience in lieu of beauty or youth.

And the ships! Some battered, ill-patched and sealed, scarcely creditable that they were judged seagoing at all. Single-masted vessels little bigger than a rowboat through to grand three and four-masted beasts perhaps a hundred feet in length. There were ships in the open water, and others moored. Rotting wood skeletons embedded in the clay, clustered with limpets and hovering clouds of midges.

A customs agent shouted and pointed with a billy-club in one hand and a sheaf of papers in the other. Goods were being weighed and measured. Barrels were tapped for inspection, an officer tasting samples to appraise that the goods in the cask related to their branding and documentation. Black faces were dotted among the sunburned browns and the flushed pinks, there being many an African who worked the ships; cabin lads, carpenters, translators and guides, workers of metal and stone, experts in crops and in foreign materials. Colours paraded everywhere; ships' insignia, merchant designs, a complement of musket-men that Tom presumed were either guarding some moving treasure or had been detailed to show force along the waterfront, some badge of officialdom over the frantic trade being conducted.

Tom saw his chance like a living dream.

Challis was pointing with his left hand, his coat swishing around behind him.

The pocket still bulged, the leather not yet relaxed back to true.

Tom dipped Challis the way he'd seen done a hundred times; his own left hand into the pocket, his right onto the mark's right hip. A shove at the right, enough to suggest clumsiness rather than malice. Enough to distract.

Challis grunted as though the nudge had pained him. He turned back, fast, shoulders tensing, his eyes alive.

'Sorry,' Tom said.

Challis didn't say anything.

On that turn, Tom had tucked - just - whatever it was that he'd grabbed into his waistband. It was solid against his gut.

It was easier with two people. You needed one to dip and then hand-off straightaway to your accomplice. Good crews worked in threes, with the third as both spotter and a second hand-off man if needed. Once you knew what to watch for, you saw teams working all across London.

Tom could scarcely breathe. A posset of fear of getting found out, exhilaration at his own daring, worry that he'd lose the trophy.

It wasn't coin, whatever it was. Less than three inches long, a cold cylinder. Maybe metal, perhaps glass. Either way, the man had money on him; there'd be value in the trinket.

And Challis couldn't have felt the dip. Tom even had time to tuck what he'd filched out of sight because the man was distracted.

'There,' Challis eventually said, momentarily out of breath as if still pained, over Tom's shoulder. 'Do you see?'

And there he was, perched on a wall, legs swinging against the brickwork, a satchel dangling between his legs. Another stood by his side, head bowed. He was toying with something in his hands, but from this distance, Tom could not make out what.

'How do I convince him that I am your man?' Tom was now cursing inside. Doubt had snuck in. Whatever he had snatched was not coin. Had he risked himself for nothing?

'Simply use my name. That will suffice.'

Tom nodded, and was glad to be gone.

#

Challis watched the lad dart through the throng.

Piedlow was maybe a hundred yards away. He waited till he was sure that Piedlow had not moved off, nor that Tom had got mistaken and gone elsewhere.

That might have caused problems.

He ran a hand across his brow. He was warm again, despite the drink. He'd take another soon. And he was sore. He could have done with a dose of the tincture.

No. Temptation was the test. That was the easy way out. It was not to be taken lightly, and then no more than once a day, upon retiring. He'd been given solemn instructions from the apothecary on his first visit. Treat with caution. The poppy is a seductive mistress. And use only when necessary. The solution might bring relief from pain, sleep unaffected by dreams until the waking hour, and sensations of bliss, but the bottle contained deception and need, and would suck up your time, your resolve, your being if allowed control.

Nevertheless, it would have been a comfort even to feel the cool glass in his palm.

But no. That would have to wait until night-time prayers. He would not yield to the enticement. Challis kept his right hand in his pocket, balled up, not letting his fingers drop to the pocket's bottom where the vial would be lying.

Ah. The lad was upon Piedlow. They were talking.

Good.

#

Tom stood in front of the man. Sitting on the wall, Piedlow was slightly raised from eye level to him.

The other fellow was still to Piedlow's side. The device in his hands, a padlock. He opened and closed it, not with a key, but with a slim bent pin. He did it over and over. He was practicing.

'Rufus Challis sends regards,' Tom said. 'I'm to guide you to him.'

Piedlow dropped from the wall. His feet didn't make a sound hitting the ground. He shouldered his bag.

'Lead on.' There was an accent to Piedlow's voice, Dutch rather than French, Tom believed. 'Robert?'

The man with the padlock turned to face them. 'Oui? Yes?'

'Time to leave. Come on.' Piedlow then spoke to Tom. 'He comes with us.'

Tom felt panic prickle him. Challis hadn't mentioned a second man.

'He is my-,' Piedlow paused. 'My apprentice. Robert Hubert.'

Hubert was simple; Tom was sure of it. He had that clarity about him, plainness and the welcoming open face that Tom had recognised before in the well-kept fool.

'Robert,' he said, indicating himself with the pin he held between thumb and forefinger.

'Tom.'

They moved. Piedlow had the only bag between them, Hubert possessing nothing except the padlock and the wire. Tom thought that it would have been the apprentice's place to carry his master's bag, but on observing him further, Tom took that back.

Hubert had some palsy to him; his walk was lopsided and his shoulders drooped unaccountably. He looked older than Tom. His apprenticeship at such an age must have been either on account of the feeblemindedness or else some family obligation being addressed. He was proficient in one thing, the mastering of his lock. Tom had seen children fascinated with a carved wooden toy, a doll, a swatch of cloth. Perhaps the same followed for this man. This was his solace for his damaged body and mind.

They were a strange coupling, indeed.

Challis was right about Piedlow's manner. He kept the hat brim low. It might have been a disguise; it might have been because of shyness. It might have been because he was ashamed of his looks. If Challis was correct about that, it was hard to tell; the shadow covered much and Tom was not about to begin staring.

If he was a merchant, then he was the oddest that Tom had come across. Tom had seen many strange people, but few as strange as Stephen Piedlow.

Piedlow's clothes were both rough and plain. There was no sense of the sophistication in dress, even if the cloth was cut simply, that adopted the trading classes. Were not one's garments both a badge of success and by extension both evidence of His blessing upon your transactions and an element of security and future profit promised to your trading party? He was travelling incognito perhaps, but this was being taken to an extent that Tom would not have credited.

Piedlow's skin was dry, yellowed. Waxy-looking and brittle, like fat on a long-stored ham.

Challis was right about his hands. They must have been sweaty, being gloved in leather and one pocketed deep, the other fast around the luggage strap.

Should he offer to carry the bag? Kindness or not, Tom decided not. The grip around the strap was sure. The leather was wrapped not once, but twice around and then through his fist. Where Hubert had his metal toy, Piedlow had his luggage for security. An experienced traveller might well have learned the costly lesson to keep close watch over one's personal possessions. Perhaps that was the situation here, caution in a busy port when feeling protective about one's presence.

Tom led them back the way that he had come. Bear Quay to Thames Street, Thames Street to the bridge. Neither of his companions seemed curious about their surroundings in any way. Piedlow kept focused dead ahead except for occasional glances to Hubert, who stayed two steps behind them, accompanying them with the click-snip of the unlatching and re-engaging padlock. They fell into a routine, a pace dictated as much by the percussive snap of the metal as their heels on the road.

The sole break came when they turned left onto the bridge. With the shift in direction back towards the river both Piedlow and Hubert became more animated, the latter scurrying forward to his master and gabbling into his ear. Tom caught enough to determine that Dutch was being spoken rather than French or English. Piedlow nodded and beckoned for Tom to stop.

Piedlow gestured around. They were stood at the north gate to the bridge, by St Magnus's. 'This noise? What is it?'

Tom took them to the side of the road, where there was a gap between two buildings. He pointed down over the side to the water. 'Wheels,' he said. He wasn't sure if his meaning was getting across. 'Three,' he said, holding that number of fingers up. 'Under the bridge. One under here,' he said, indicating below them. 'And two under there,' he continued, pointing under the next arch. 'See the water?'

The water rose between the wooden starlings that guarded the stone arches. The starlings served both to break the water and to force it through and under the bridge faster. He supposed this would propel the wheels round all the swifter. 'And above. See?' Tom pointed up. The buildings here were three storeys tall. Above that a tower, perhaps another three storeys higher, as though someone had built a church here in oak to compete with St Magnus' stone.

'The tower provides,' Piedlow halted before continuing, 'the pressure?'

Tom shrugged. He had no idea how the contraption worked.

'It pushes the water into the city? Through pipes, yes?'

Tom nodded. Yes, that was it. The wheels weren't turning. Maybe whatever mechanism was inside the building - something like the workings of a windmill, Tom supposed - was disengaged.

Piedlow took time to explain this to Hubert. Hubert became excited – no, more than that, he was agitated. He craned over the side. It was as though he was working the idea into his mind. He traced the path of the water with the pin, down river and through the bridge supports, then round and up and along. He was excited by the notion of water being piped into the city. He laughed, making exploding splashing sounds, like a child remembering being barefoot in puddles.

Piedlow took him, arm over shoulder like a much older brother, and whispered fast to him. Hubert stopped immediately; the scolded younger sibling.

Tom gave them their moment, and then they were ready to cross the bridge.

They were at the address Challis had given in a handful of minutes. Hubert had become excited again momentarily at the bridge's disrepair, but the earlier talking to Piedlow had given him must still have been echoing, because a sharp movement of Piedlow's head was all it took for Hubert to calm once more.

There were many fine properties on the bridge, particularly towards the centre, which had always been considered the most prestigious of locations if you did not count Nonesuch House just to the Southwark side of the crossing's centre. Like a Tower of London in miniature it was, both grandiose and imposing yet precariously positioned on the narrow causeway.

Challis's premises were nothing like that. It was plain to the point of seeming long-abandoned. The door bore signs of boarding up, in paint and in nail holes. This had been a plague house.

Nothing had been done since to revive the property. Lord knew there were many houses which still stood empty, though many others had been taken over by fresh arrivals or inheriting relatives from out of the city, if only to clear out what goods they dare recover and sell or arrange to let the property on. Perhaps Challis had come by this house for a bargain. He was self-assured enough to take on such a place, premises that others might shy from living in or trading from.

Tom knocked. No answer. He knocked again. Again, no reply. Tom wanted nothing more than to be away from here.

Then Tom heard a scraping, and Rufus Challis was at the door.

#

Fuck and how the hell could he have been so stupid? Was this some other test? Leaving that body sprawled out for any window-nosing lurker to happen upon, some yawning neighbour made curious by that morning's deliveries? It was a slim chance admittedly, because the rooms were dark enough and barrels blocked some of the windows, but even so. Plus, there was the question of Tom. What if he had blundered in? What if he had seen?

Challis had been busy in the few minutes he'd bought by racing ahead of Piedlow. Slinging off his coat he'd made for the barrels at once. Something on the docks had perturbed him, something that he needed to check.

The customs-house officers inspecting casks of brandy, doubtless to ensure that all was right with the goods in terms of revenue due to them for its unloading. It made sense for some to label goods as low-rated when they were shipping something which carried a higher charge. That was one of the attractions of coffee; it was expensive. Plus, the aroma was distinctive and it carried, particularly when the beans had been roasted prior to travel. Not that, he supposed, anyone would actually send the stuff on journeys of any length in such a condition.

He found what he was searching for on the first floor. Two separate barrels had been opened. Both had been forced at the pitch and rope-sealed end, having been first jemmied and then tacked shut.

It took a precious minute to open the casks again. But it was worth it. The customs agents could only have glanced inside, perhaps stuck a hand in a few inches down, then, finding precisely what they expected and what the papers told them - coffee - they had moved on. Besides, was there not always wine or harder liquor to sample? Perhaps one of them had done as Challis now did, and taken a bean and let its rich flavour infuse his mouth. The roasted taste roused him, and brought Jephcott's corpse back to his mind, and just in time.

Back down the stairs then, to drag the body out of sight; he laid it on the bottom few steps on the stairwell, kicking Jephcott's boots against the wall as he swung his coat back over his shoulders. He did this last movement between the first knock and the second, by which time he'd got to the door, had jammed it with his boot-cap while he sleeved himself; and then he opened the door which, damn his utter whoreson foolishness, was nothing more than latched shut.

'That was speedy, Tom,' he said, with the blankest face. He then saw Piedlow and he could not have failed to have registered something amiss. Not at the ugly Dutchman; but that he had brought an unanticipated friend.

'Tom,' Challis said again. 'Would you be so kind as to entertain-,' indicating Hubert, 'while I briefly discuss a private matter?'

He supposed the lad made some reply. He knew not for certain as his attention was with Piedlow, who passed his knapsack to his travelling companion as he stepped inside.

Once Challis had made sure that the blasted thing was discreetly but undeniably locked, Challis' hand went to his coat-lining. He did this on the spin, using the lock as an excuse to bare his back and shield his movements.

Piedlow already had a firearm in his hand. It was low-slung, probably holstered under his coat to his thigh. Obviously his pocket was open-ended; he'd made something of a virtue from the necessity of having to shield his hand from gaze. It must have rested on the stock of his piece all day. The barrel stuck out of his cheap coat like he was a rapist.

Challis clicked his hand-cannon from half- to full-cock.

'Stephen,' he said.

'Rufus,' Piedlow said. His thumb was over the pan, but he was still at half-cock.

Good. He was on the defensive.

As well he should be. Challis countenanced unpredictability, but better on his own terms. He was the random factor here. That was what he was paid for. That was what He wanted of him. Christ's right hand in these peculiar times.

'Who's your friend?'

'Robert?'

'I don't care for his name. I want to know who he is.'

'He travels with me.'

'And is this any time to go on pilgrimage with your catamite?'

Piedlow held his hand up, the one without the firearm. 'May we discuss this as men? Take your weapon to half-cock and I'll lower mine.'

'And take your hand from the stock.'

'If you follow directly.'

'You lead.'

'That doesn't work, Rufus. Stand your weapon down and then we can talk. I've made it a rule of mine never to trust a man with a corpse in his stairwell.'

Challis brought the weapon to half-cock. He laid it on an adjacent barrel. Better a live handgun within reach than a deactivated weapon in your hand.

Piedlow smiled. 'You were always a cagey one.' He let his gun click safe.

'And hand off the grip, if you would.'

'Take a step to the side. Away from your fowling piece.'

The man had a nerve on him. That firearm had cost plenty. Nevertheless, for the sake of expedition, Challis made the step away. Piedlow lowered his in return, the barrel flicking back under the opening in his coat.

'My understanding was that you would be alone.'

'Things change.' Piedlow looked aged before his time. Skin like smoked fish; a glassy yellow.

'For whom?'

'For all of us.' Piedlow took his hat off. That was a neat ruse, but Challis wasn't ready to fall for it. Expose the hidden eyes; make clear contact to show trust. Well, he'd see about that.

'He's a soldier of the cause. Like you or I, Rufus.'

'A soldier perhaps, but not like I nor, do I fancy, you. Stephen.'

'Be that as it may. Robert-'

'The dullard?'

Piedlow took exception at that. Not anger but more of a resigned acceptance. That was it. This was a man long-used to defending his colleague. 'He's going to be of great use,' Piedlow said.

'I've no space for ballast on this voyage.'

'I assure you. When the moment comes, he'll be more than willing and able to play his part.'

'And what part is that?'

Piedlow told him. The explanation took five minutes. Challis heard him out, and then asked for clarification. Piedlow said the same incredible thing using different words.

'I'm still not sure that I believe you.'

'Then put him to the test. He'll prove reliable and acute. He knows what he's doing, and more important, Rufus, he's clear about why.'

Challis let that jibe slide by. If accounts needed settling, then they could be attended on later. Piedlow's motivations had always been straightforward enough. He was in the munitions business for the gold of it. Judging by the way he looked though, he would not live long enough to enjoy it.

'A test it is then.'

'You have something in mind?'

Yes, thought Challis. I've got the very thing. He said nothing, but went instead to let the others in.

#

Hubert had gone back to playing with his padlock. He kept his eyes off it, blankly staring down the bridge towards Southwark, all the time working that sliver of metal in the keyhole.

What to say to this creature? But it was soon clear that Challis and Piedlow would be discussing their business for more than a few seconds. He couldn't stand here dumb forever.

'You're very good at that,' Tom said.

Hubert didn't move. Except for his hands. Snick, click and the lock was open. A firmer shutting snap then sounded, and he began the process again.

'Is that your trade? Locksmithing?'

'Watchmaker,' Hubert said. 'Clocks and watches, watches and clocks.' There was a sing-song lilt to his words. 'Our workshop is watches and clocks. Wheels and levers and hammers and springs.' His accent was thick but even so, his English was much better than Tom would have managed in any language other than his own.

'You make these?' He didn't seem capable in his mind, but his hands spoke otherwise. Hubert was two different people soldered together.

'I mend and I make, I open and I close.'

'Repair? You fix locks and timepieces?'

'If God wills it fixed,' Hubert shrugged. He seemed not to care one way or the other; he was separate from what his hands were doing.

'Does not your skill account for the mending of a broken lock?'

'It is not me who mends these items.'

Tom thought he understood Hubert's meaning. Did he really consider himself God's agent? That His hands would move through this awkward foreigner, seemingly content close and reopen the same fastening?

'Could you open this?' Tom asked, indicating the door.

Hubert snorted. 'You could open that.'

He did not have time to elaborate though, as that was the point when Challis reappeared.

#

'My apologies. You'll understand that certain confidences must be kept. Now, Tom,' Challis said, extending his right hand. 'You've done more than creditably. Go with God, and trust in the opportunities that He may elect to cast in your direction.' He held the lad fast in eye-contact, in part so that little attention would be diverted to his hand. His phantom thumb throbbed all the more. 'Be on your way, and I'll be sure to call upon you before I leave.'

Then Challis made his move, dropping his eyes for Tom to take his hand. Tom did so and Challis shook it.

It was important to Challis that Tom saw his scar. It was important that he felt it. He did not flinch or start, which spoke of benefit to his character. Then Challis disengaged, breaking off the grip.

The lad, uncertain for a count of three, then went off back towards the city.

'Monsieur Hubert. Come in quick.'

Once inside, Challis took the man's topcoat and swapped it for Piedlow's. Then he gave instructions, quick and precise. Piedlow repeated them, in simpler English, then again in French. He asked Hubert to repeat them. He did so. That was good. Better to be absolute.

At the last, Challis popped his own hat on Hubert's head. He looked stupid, but no less than he did without it. The ruse would suffice.

He let the ungainly hare loose. Back into the city.

Challis was hit by a bolt of nausea the moment he locked the door behind Hubert. Bile rose, bubbling up behind his teeth. He covered it with a cough.

His thumb screamed. The day had been hard on him; the threats, the blade-work and the gunplay for were difficult enough to bear. Let alone the blow his hand had received at the docks.

He could, just, have resisted, but he did not this time.

His right hand dived to where the vial was not. He checked again. Right pocket, then left, and then the right again. It was not there.

Where could it be? He'd not taken it out of the pocket since he'd put it there this morning. Why had he let himself be tempted to bring it? Surely this was His reminder upon him, not to yield to malign influences.

Its loss was nothing in itself. There was another in the tavern. But to have suffered the loss was something else.

He'd been bested once, near that puppet-show, by the boy who'd targeted him for robbery. Had he been taken for a mark a second time and had the item lifted in some crowded place? Surely not. He'd had his hands pocketed the whole day. There'd only been that moment when he'd been barged into by the quayside when he'd been pointing out Piedlow to Tom.

Oh, he was a fool.

And this was his correction for his idiot ways.

The lad had surely dipped him, taking him for some turnip-head.

Challis swallowed to clear his mouth of the last of the bile's taint.

#

Hubert was back within half an hour. Piedlow looked at him askance.

'I'm sorry I was so long. I did stop again on the walk back to,' he fought for the word, 'examine the water wheels once more. They are beautiful. So big. So clever.'

The French imbecile couldn't deliver in even the simplest of tasks, let alone this great one that Piedlow had promised.

'Where does he live, Robert?' Piedlow asked.

Hubert struggled with shedding the unfamiliar garments. He was wet and red with the heat. The afternoon was sweltering enough without the cumbersome disguise, Challis conceded. Or was it fear mixed with stupidity that made him blush and sweat?

Hubert spoke in monotone as though remembering something learned by rote. 'He lives but two streets away. It is across the bridge, under St Magnus' archway onto the long hilly street crossing the one which shadows the Thames. The next street over to the right is a narrow lane, which extends to the north. There is your bakery, by an inn with the sign of a White Hart.'

Challis knew then that Hubert might yet deliver on Piedlow's astonishing promise.

Even the great cities are small, he thought. And they are pulled in yet smaller by the draw-string of His design.

'You saw him enter?'

'I did.'

'And he did not notice you following him?'

'He did not.'

Piedlow broke in. 'Are you certain Robert?'

'He faced forward throughout except once, when he saw a pretty girl and he watched her cross the carriageway where the hilly road away from the bridge meets the street which copies the path of the river.'

Piedlow slapped Hubert's back. 'Good man!' Then to Challis: 'And so?'

'Very well. That'll be enough for the moment. But I've a second element to this test.' And in the process, thought Challis, remove an end which had become rather too loose. 'That's for later on perhaps,' he said. 'We have much to do, and little enough time to fulfil the tasks ahead of us.'

They started on the barrels.

#

Tom's father didn't ask where he'd been. He was in an odd mood, half bad-temperedly stabbing at his food, half trying to keep laboured conversation going around the table.

Daniel was of some use here, weaving tales of his preaching and of how well he'd been received. He spoke of Challis, but only in passing terms, and said nothing of either the money he'd paid or the work that Tom had done for him.

The four of them ate, passing innocuous comments and compliments on the table's load. Saturday was invariably a fish day. There was a memory of the popish practice of not eating meat on Fridays about the city, simply shifted a day later in the week to take the brimstone stink off it. For another, stallholders were desperate to be rid of stock on Saturdays. Meat might be cured, or sold green and cheap for pie-fillings, but fish? It was either cured on landing or set aside to be sold fresh and pink-gilled. Poor fish was poor fish; smoke or salt would not improve it. No, the judging of stock was precarious for the fishmonger and the eel seller, and their miscalculation was often the Farriners' suppertime reward.

Alice said little, but kept busy with small errands; unnecessarily filling the salt bowl, fetching another jug each of water and ale, working the butter a little more because it was straight up from the cellar and had not come to spreading temperature.

Eventually they finished. Tom and Daniel gathered the plates and the knives, this being their usual chore, taking them through to the kitchen for Alice to soak and leave to dry.

Tom wanted to say something, anything, but he was afraid that his words wouldn't penetrate the thick air in the house. It would be like shouting under water.

Eventually Daniel spoke. 'How was it this afternoon?'

'Fine.'

'Not you as well? It's bad enough with those two sulking without you deciding to join in too. They've been like it since I got back.'

Tom didn't say anything.

'Well thanks for that insight, brother. Your money's upstairs, by the by. It's safe. I'm going on Monday to enquire about passage. Think about that; leave them to themselves. They'll be happier. And so will you with an ocean and three weeks' voyaging between you and them. You'll find that I'm right. In New England.'

Daniel left. Tom heard some pleasantries exchanged, then the creaking of footsteps up.

Tom went to the back of the house. He'd no wish to go back through to see those two right now, nor yet to follow his brother up to their bedchamber. Instead he went out into the yard and hoisted himself up onto the water butt by the back door. The butt was empty save for a layer of filthy-smelling dark slime in its bottom. Maybe a sparrow had drowned and rotted in there. Perhaps that was what happened when you left anything for long enough; it turned thick and stank.

Tom held his breath as he clambered up, boosting himself up off the rim of the butt and onto the low pitched roof at the rear of the building. He took care; he hadn't done this for some time. Besides he wanted to make no noise. He might be stronger now, but he was heavier too, and the last thing he needed was to jam his foot through a roof slate, or cause one to slide and smash below.

Only the back of the house was slate-roofed. He supposed it must have been a later addition. The rest, which he scaled up to now, was thatch. And old, brittle thatch it was. Twenty years; was that not the lifespan of a thatched roof? He had little idea when it might last have been touched. Then again, it was in no worse a condition than any of the others up and down the hill.

Tom clambered, now on all fours, until he reached the apex of the roof. There he sat. He knew that with a little care he could shin down the other side and wriggle into a window somewhere. Failing that, he'd just go back down and in through the back door. And if that didn't work, if Farriner had locked up and gone to bed himself, then he'd stay up here. The evening was bright and clear, though still with some of the day's heaviness about. But this was the honest weight of a hot day in the city, not the stifling fug that lay under the roof-space.

Tom sat on the roof, scanning the river from the Tower and beyond, over the quays and Billingsgate, over St Magnus' Church and the bridge. There were boats on the water, but these were the small lightermen craft ferrying swells from one side to the other. A boat crossing was invariably quicker than the bridge, either because of the bustle on the bridge itself, or the additional journey to and from it.

It was not dark yet, and with the clarity of the sky it would remain light enough to see for some time to come.

Tom shivered. A breeze had picked up. That was good; there had scarcely been a mouthful of air for days. The wind played with trails of coal-smoke from those few burning a fire. The smoke blew in puffs from Tom's left to his right. Upriver. Inland.

It formed little low clouds.

Soon the clouds were blown more, until they were wisps and then not even that.

More lights came on, goodwives lighting lanterns and perhaps a small fire to heat water. There was street-noise and sounds of distant drunkenness; sharp bursts of shouting, laughter and music then, just as sudden, dips in volume. Taverns kicking out pissheads.

Tom lay back and let the sky circle overhead. He flipped over onto his belly, pointing now in the direction of St Paul's. The cathedral stones had caught the very last of the light in the west. Golden orbs, haloes, skittered around the topmost points and then were gone.

Something dug into his guts. Tom lifted his body enough to free the item; the spoils from his dipping of Challis's pocket.

He'd put it out of his head, discounting it after coming to the conclusion that there was no coin there. And there had been so much else to take in. Daniel's sermon and his offer, for one thing. Then that which had provoked it; Alice and her – "dealings" was the word coming to mind - with father. Challis and his provocations, his tempting words to murder so Tom might acquire the cheeky brown-haired girl. And then there was Piedlow and Hubert; Tom was sure they were no coffee traders. Last, the matter of Challis's hand. Challis had not shaken Tom's hand in confirmation of a job well done, but in some show of superiority in displaying his lack. He'd wanted to provoke. Disgust, unease. Fear.

Tom wished he'd had the wit to make up an address. Would Challis believe that he'd been stolen from? Was there value in the prize? Might Challis connect the theft to him? More than that, would he feel compelled to act upon this and seek some justice?

There was a head-full of reasons to leave the city behind.

Tom stood the stolen item in the thatch in front of him. At first he thought it a solid tube of metal that had been painted red, then he understood better.

A stoppered glass capsule, with a well-made and expensive-looking sense to it, sat before him. A thickish dark liquid filled it. This might have been blood.

Tom opened it and sniffed. The smell rushed out. It was rich and acrid, both sour and sweet in the same intake. He guessed at first that it was wine, some imported and well-thought of variety. But there was not enough here to use as a sample for salesmanship, let alone as a flask for refreshment.

He wondered if it might have been a medicine, some patent remedy brewed up by a mountebank with the promise of cure of all ills. But Challis did not seem to be the sort to be persuaded by patter or flummery. He'd not fall for stage-tricks.

Then a truth fell on Tom. This must be sacramental wine, some priest-blessed popish tincture, and that Challis carried it for idolatrous purposes.

Tom shivered once more.

It was just the breeze again, he told himself.

He put the open bottle to his lips and let the fluid wash against his tongue. It was not pleasant, but it did not taste of much other than ill-kept wine. Tom tried not to swallow, just in case, but a little trickled down his gullet nevertheless. He coughed as it hit the back of his throat, spitting the rest back into the container.

The wine was stronger than he'd thought possible. He felt its effect within breaths, though he'd surely taken only a sip's-worth. He stoppered the container, taking two goes to get it right.

Tom tucked the vial back away to where he'd secreted it earlier. A third shiver came, that was both inside him and outside him simultaneously.

Tom needed to rest.

The thatch was warm underneath him, and it yielded enough to make a nest. Tom tried to put the stolen item out of his mind and closed his eyes.

Women shifted behind his eyelids; his mother, long dead. Alice, so alive. Lizzie Corbet, her face up close, laughing and leering. The other girl, tongue-out, then turning away, as if leading him onwards somewhere.

Their faces overlapped, twisted, then formed one woman of parts of themselves, then they broke apart free of each other. Tom knew he was caught in that half-dream between waking and sleeping and surrendered himself to it, to them.

#

It was Piedlow's idea to tip out the coffee beans onto something – they decided on Jephcott's coat – and to top up the barrels with powder from others. That way they'd have fewer, better-filled casks. This was useful, Piedlow asserted. Explosions depended on the dryness of the gunpowder and on proximity. So be it; he was the expert. The coffee would go into empty barrels in due course.

That was the first stage. The second idea was Challis's. He located the latrine hole, and suggested disposing of the coffee beans there. The empty barrels could be smashed up and used as kindling: more to burn.

#

The removal of the coffee took less time than Challis was expecting. This was very good indeed.

His hands stank of the stuff. He was at the point where he could not smell coffee, but knew nevertheless that the stench was all around. The others were little better, hands coated in the oddly oily dust that the beans transferred.

They were left with repacked barrels full of gunpowder. A decision had been made to leave them on the three floors for the time being. There would be time to move them later if need be. Piedlow was still in two minds as to their configuration.

There was a pair of matters to resolve. The first was the fetching of victuals. And, thought Challis, his own possessions. He needed to get back to his room. Specifically, he needed his Bible. And he did not fancy leaving these two to their own devices for the night.

No, he'd sleep here.

'I'm going out for an hour. I'll return with food and drink. In the meantime, Stephen, I'd be grateful if you'd manufacture some grenades.'

'Grenadoes? Why?' The pronunciation that Piedlow affected irked Challis.

'I'll tell you over supper. Besides, wondering will keep you busy while I'm gone.'

#

Challis headed straight for the Welshman's tavern.

Taff's place was busier than on either of the previous two nights. He had help in over and above the vaguely whorish girls that had been there before. A hefty woman, her gaze askew because of strabismus. The ale-wife, he presumed.

'Plain food, and drink,' he told Taff. 'Enough for a lusty pair, if you take my meaning.'

'That I do, though not personally you understand, not since I fell for my Daisy.' He rolled his eyes, presumably to communicate a gentlemanly understanding that wives ought not to know all that engaged their husbands. Challis nodded back, intending to come across as complicit rather than contemptuous. He was not sure he'd been successful. At any rate, the man hurried off to attend on him.

The puppeteer and his barker were here as usual. The former sat placid with a pot of beer and an untouched platter of beef and bread. His companion's beer-pot was upended, the trencher all but licked clean.

The barker was not with his friend, but was cornered with one of the house whores, the thin one. Her right hand was under the table, pumping with vigour. Her left hand held a rock which she licked. Her eyes betrayed distance from her task.

The little fat man gasped, his mouth as wide as a cannon-muzzle. He waved to Challis, eyes bright, laughing, as Challis turned up the stairs. 'The Bottler's nearly there, he is, oh yes!'

Gasps and grunts followed Challis up the stairs.

Challis retrieved his Bible first, pausing only to reassure himself that nothing in the room had been tampered with.

Challis shouldered his bag and took it down with him.

Taff had a small well-filled sack waiting for him. The clink of glass from within when it was moved.

Challis golded the man and intimated that he expected to be back very late at best, and perhaps not till the following day.

'I'll expect you when I see you,' the barkeep said. Challis bristled; there was mocking scold in his tone, and the man must have recognised that too because he was away to other duties without further words, head bowed.

Challis watched him go. He wondered what he would look like if made to suckle on one of Challis's pistols.

#

'A grenade,' Piedlow said, mouth full of cheese, 'is beautiful. Simplicity itself to construct and to operate, but if made right, a devastating incendiary.'

Piedlow had taken his gloves off to eat. His left hand was ribbed and puckered, as though he'd had it in water too long and it had dried the instant it had been removed. His right was the same, except for the nubs which were all that remained of his smaller two fingers. Tendons flexed when he moved his hand, as though they believed they were still connected to full digits.

Piedlow caught Challis looking. He held up his hands for plainer inspection. 'Some lessons cannot be taught. They can only be learned,' Piedlow said. There was melancholy in his tone.

His gloves lay nearby. The left was unremarkable but the smallest two fingers on the right had been stuffed to give the impression of a whole hand when worn. It was the removal of these gloves on their first meeting that had compelled Challis to secure Piedlow's services.

Piedlow took more of the cheese, and ate before continuing. 'Now, if it's a fire you want, there are a dozen ways to provide. Lob a torch. Throw a lantern. A timed fuse. One way to make such is to fill a quill with powder, but the burn is quick and the timings are hard to estimate.'

Piedlow gestured as he spoke. Challis found the combination of movement, subject and the burned beauty of his hands enchanting.

'Better to proceed by soaking hemp or twine in pitch. You lead one end to your powder or kindling and wrap the other around the base of a candle. Take care to cut into the candle's base so the pitched twine contacts the wick. The candle burns down in its own time, then the flame reaches the twine. Flame travels the string to your fuel and there you have it. You can improve the burn by having the candle low down and the twine pulling up and away, so increasing the burn rate when it ignites. There are many advantages to this method. It's quiet. Simple. It's effective as long as there's no draught. A grenade is not so delicate a creature.

'Your fuse is short, for one. You're present for the detonation. There's the explosion itself. The best grenades are made with fine stoneware, Dutch porcelain if you can have it, the thinner the better. Airtight and delicate but sharp when broken, useful if laceration is your intent. Fill the vessel with powder, and then you stop it up tight. Cork is best, but first take an awl and drill a hole in the stopper for your fuse. Hemp, thick twine, wadded cotton or suchlike, all will work as well as each other for fuseworks. Then you light and depart. The bigger your grenade, the greater the detonation. But these are weapons better suited to siege-craft and to man-traps than to setting a fire. What's your intent?'

This was a time for specifics. 'And that's what you've come across from the continent for? To wrap a thread around a candle?'

'No,' Piedlow said. 'I have something more exact in mind, which Robert possesses the secret thereof. I will show you presently. First, though, to your grenade.'

'Think of it as a second test, another trial. I'm minded to create a diversionary incident and I also need intelligence. I want to see what happens when a strong fire begins. How do the people react? Will troops be called? Is there an official response? Will there be panic?' Challis wondered about the note he'd had couriered from outside Jephcott's. Was it yet in play, or was the letter still mouldering in some secretary's pigeonhole awaiting attendance after the Sabbath?

That note was part of his design. The other part, the one involving the incendiary, he might have regretted had its necessity not countermanded that emotion. There was a need for the intelligence he'd outlined, but there were other reasons too.

The baker's son knew something. Challis was sure of it. A curiosity leading to theft from him. This necessitated action on Challis's part. An event to distract Tom Farriner. Something potentially fatal. The precise outcome could be left to Providence.

'How will you set me my fire?' Challis asked.

Piedlow thought about it. 'You have more wine?'

Yes, there were two more bottles in the bag. Challis pulled them out.

'Let me open them,' Piedlow said.

'And the other matter?'

'The mechanism for the bridge?'

Challis nodded.

Piedlow beckoned to Hubert, who rummaged in Piedlow's belongings, extracting a plain wooden box. It might have been a baby's coffin.

Hubert took a knife and levered the lid off. He did this with fast skill, the way an oysterman opens shells.

He set the lid down, taking care to put aside the removed nails. There was precision in his movements. The he pulled something out, brushing off an outer layer of straw packing from around the item. The thing itself was wrapped in soft yellow cloth.

Hubert uncoiled the binding, using the material to cradle its secret. He seemed proud of the work; he didn't want to get greasy finger-marks on it.

It took Challis a moment to understand. He looked to Piedlow, who was face-full with the broadest grin. Then back to the device again.

'Is that what I think it is?'

Silence. They were enraptured by the contraption.

Challis again: 'And it works?'

'Would you like to see?'

'I would.'

Hubert's hands glided over it and he set it to go. And work it did.

Piedlow was a genius. The clock-face, the alarm mechanism. The way it was simple in design yet made with care and expertise.

The genius lay not just in the machine-work, but in the idea. In the marriage of timepiece and flintlock. The tick of the clock mechanism as the alarm was triggered, the whip-smart activation of the hammer, the sparking of the flint and the flash of powder in the firing pan, in turn setting off whatever fuse-works Piedlow attached.

'My design,' Piedlow said. 'But Robert's skill in the manufacture. He is my hands.'

'Yes,' Challis said. 'Open that wine.'

#

Tom reached out to pull his blanket over and was puzzled to grab at nothing but thatch and air.

Of course; he was still on the roof, hunkered down in a slight hollow caused by the age of the roof and the dryness of the straw. Plus, he supposed, his weight. He wasn't a child anymore.

Tom sat up. Wind ruffled his hair and caused him to shudder. Somewhere below there was creaking; porch lanterns swinging. The Lane channelled the wind like water through the bridge starlings.

Other noises. Laughter and cackling. A scold's shrieking. He fancied he heard lusty grunts and moans, but soon turned into the wind so that his ears were occupied instead with the rushing breeze.

There were some sounds that he didn't want to hear.

The wind blew down the mouth of the river into the city, east to west. Tom shivered again, but he enjoyed the novelty of the cold. He had been hot for too long.

His head was thick, but the drop in temperature had roused him. He did not fancy slinking back into the house

He wished that the Hart next door and the tavern on Fish Street, the Star, which backed onto the Farriner bakery, were more alive with sound.

Tom focused on the bridge instead. From up here he could see over the Thames Street warehousing and so had much of the bridge in view. The spire of St Magnus blocked his line of sight to some extent, but the church and the water tower over the wheels acted as twin pillars marking the entrance to the crossing clear enough.

There were many ships moored along the Legal Quays between the bridge and the Tower of London. More than had been there that afternoon. Tom wondered if any were bound for the New World.

Was it cramped on board? Did it stink? Was it full of sailors who'd fuck anything with a hole and eat anything without a heartbeat? Would he have to sleep with one hand on his knife and the other on his arsehole? Would he be a passenger, or be expected to work? Would he end up tending fires, baking bread in portable ovens on deck, enduring endless jibes about ships' biscuit? Would he spend his days high in the rigging, watching for whales?

The bridge bothered him. He'd made easy money in the errands for Challis and his odd companions. That was it. The odd companions. Tom knew London and he knew merchantman. He knew the selfish disinterest they had concerning others; they were not like Challis who seemed too ready to indulge in conversation. And what conversation; talk of grabbing opportunities was well and good, but the way he spoke of measuring probabilities then acting with violence if justified both by the logical benefits and feelings within?

This was not the banter of a man wishing to while away a few minutes. It spoke of experience and hard-won knowledge. In seizing chance and taking life. Something executed - that was the word - and not reflected upon.

Tom wished that he had not stolen from him.

And as for the Dutchman and the Frenchie, London was a lodestone which drew all manner of corrupted ore to it. Though there was war afoot and dead mariners on both sides this summer, the place heaved and surged with a hundred nationalities and as many languages. Foreigners in the capital were as everyday as locals charging over the odds for the cheapest. Cheat: they called the paupers' loaf that for a reason.

These three were no coffee traders though.

So what were they up to? There had been the whiff of coffee about Challis's premises. Why would a place smell otherwise?

One of them spoke of murder for gain, if the gain was evident, and one had apprenticed as a locksmith. A metalworker, someone useful with delicate tools, with picks and mechanical workings.

Something was amiss. The more Tom considered it, the more he became convinced.

The bridge was stillness itself compared to the water. In one of those houses there was something awry. But what to do about it? Tom had nothing but assumption and suspicion. Were his ideas nothing more than the usual speculation?

Tom had an idea. He'd present himself on the pretext of seeking further work. At worst he'd be sent away. At best, he might find something out. Something that could be reported.

Better still, something that could be acted upon, and a reward paid for diligence. There'd be ample monies for passage then.

Rest now, and in the morning, skip church and slip away.

He'd brazen out any challenge from Challis about the curious glass container. Surely no thief would willingly turn up on the doorstep of one he'd stolen from the day before?

Despite the wind getting up, Tom decided to stay on the roof.

Besides, he was sleepy. There was still some thickness from that odd wine. The cold would wake him all the earlier come the morning.

He closed his eyes and somewhere, midnight was called.

SUNDAY 2ND SEPTEMBER 1666

Rufus Challis believed much that he knew some found peculiar. Direct communication with God, for example, with no need for intercession.

The Almighty only spoke to a select few these days. Or, all-knowing, He understood that it was not worth the trouble. So if Hubert was the man that Piedlow had intimated then he was a rare beast indeed, and one to be treasured for the short time that they would have together.

'Come,' he said to the others, hatting himself. 'Let's away.'

The bridge was quieter than Challis had anticipated. Midnight had been called just before leaving, and the curfew was called at nine, was it not? That would mean the streets would calm for a time, and then the night-people would slink out.

They crossed the bridge in silence. Hubert paused once more by the north gate; his fascination with manufactured contraptions knew little boundary.

Piedlow put his hand up. He wanted to stop. Challis nodded. Piedlow went to the stone arch by the church and rummaged at his cods.

Challis walked to the Thames Street intersection. He'd no wish to listen in on a pissing man, and certainly not by holy ground. The act spoke of effrontery, though such things and worse; open gambling, seduction, argument and gluttonous indulgence of all manner were commonplace nowadays within church precincts. Was not St Paul's used to stable horses and billet troops during the wars between the Commonwealthers and the King's Men?

Piedlow came alongside. A questioning face; Challis pointed the way.

Pudding Lane was indeed a blood sausage, a tight-packed dark snake, eaves almost touching above them, the chequer-board of once-white walls and soiled wood to their sides.

Hubert pointed out the bakery, but it was an unnecessary act. The low scent of yeast now bloomed; the corn-sheaf sign confirmed the same. Even the front window construction, a shutter dropping down to make a shelf-cum-stall in the daylight, was testament.

Piedlow took his gifts from his pockets.

Challis regarded Hubert, then Piedlow. Remove all traces. This was the discipline. He nodded.

Piedlow motioned to Hubert, who moved close to the shutters.

Challis considered that he might have asked more about fuse timings, but substituted that for taking a step or two back.

Piedlow had, after all, explained this earlier when discussing grenades. There was a natural philosophy to it, and one similar to a firearm's operation.

A gun works, said Piedlow, the same as a grenade, or any explosive armament. Even water works on the shared principle; the path of least resistance. Water flows downhill because it's easiest. A cannonball or a pistol round flies down the barrel because of the same; it's simpler to go in that direction than through cast iron. A grenade differs in that its purpose is to explode itself out, pushing its constraints away fast and thereby causing damage. Fire ensues, and fire will transmit itself. In a gun, that force is put into propelling the ball. In a grenade there is both the force of the fire and of its constraints. So the holdings must be secure enough to hold the charge and allow the pressure to build yet be fragile enough to give. To give with venom is preferable.

Glass is both fragile and sharp.

Piedlow had turned their supper-time wine bottles into an arsenal.

Challis's instructions were simple. Burn the Farriner bakery; after all, dry powders of all manners had combustible properties, and flour was no exception. Tom would in all probability suffocate or burn in the blaze. If he survived, he'd be preoccupied with the aftermath - his preacher brother, whatever other family he might have - the ruin of their home and livelihood. Another link to Challis snuffed.

There was no opening the window from outside. It was barred or locked from within. The door was as secure as the window. Hubert would have no chance to prove his lock-skills here.

Then Hubert snapped his fingers. The authority of the motion intrigued Challis; then it exulted him. Let the man play.

Piedlow handed over a knife.

Oh, that was good.

Hubert took the knife and cut a hole in the wattle-and-daub about a foot above the top of the brickwork running up to the underside of the window. He thrust deep then sawed fast and round, a yawning half-moon slice in the wall.

Challis threw his new tinderbox to Hubert.

Hubert had a flame in his hand in moments. He cradled it over one of the bottles. White-yellow brightness flared over the off-green neck.

Hubert thrust the bottle into the cut maw. A brief nothingness then a rolling and a one, two, three, and –

#

At first Tom thought nothing of the sawing sound; it was strange, but in his half-wakefulness, not troubling.

The next sound could not be passed off so easily. The rasp of metal on fire-steel. Then ignition; working with ovens, you knew that soft gasp anywhere.

Where was it coming from? In the street below. Tom crawled along the apex of the roof to see.

Three men? It was hard to tell, because they were close to the

185

walls, where darkness was thickest. A huddle of hats and cloaks. Then all stepping back a pace, describing a wider semicircle.

One, the slightest, held his hand up. He wanted silence from the others. But for what?

There was little light. There were still-lit lanterns above front doors further up and down the lane, but none here. Tom could make out little specific. But what of that sawing noise? Fumbling with fire steel? Perhaps innocent, but where was their lantern, where were their tobacco pipes?

What was being lit?

No, that wasn't it at all. What had already been lit?

The three differently dark smudges took second steps back.

And then a light brightened the alley beneath. A thin strip of yellow-whiteness scarcely broader than the end of a horsewhip. The man nearest came forward as though inspecting the source. Then movement again; the three of them shifted out of sight further up the Lane.

The streak of light was gone. Perhaps it was nothing more than a fumbling with a lantern, and its eventual acceptance of flame. That would account for the light and their walking on. It was windy enough, gusting more than it had been when Tom had got up here. Sometimes the narrowness of thin streets like Pudding Lane was a blessing in providing shelter. Sometimes a hindrance; stupid pigeons would get caught as though in a church, and would flap themselves to exhaustion rather than find escape. Likewise, with the wind, being focused and channelled, gusts turned into gales, flicking at faces and tearing at drying washing.

Tom tried to settle again, but there was little use in it. Whichever way he laid he bared either arse- or his face-cheeks to the Thames wind. It had gone from cooling the day to turning his skin to fish-flesh.

It was past time to go inside.

Tom swung himself over and grabbed at the casement. He got it firm on the second swing; the wood was still damp with dribbles from the last piss-pot to be emptied from it.

Tom hoisted himself over, window now nudged open, legs first. He'd probably land on Daniel. If he could still fit through the window-hole.

Damn but he was longer than he used to be. His knees folded in the wrong place to make the manoeuvre easy. Holding tight to the eaves he had to lift his body, taking his weight by his hands as his legs fumbled for purchase.

It wasn't that far to the ground, but he knew sprawling over the cobbles hurt. It was easy enough to be killed by a trip; a drop from here would as likely as not do for him.

Sweet Christ but he was heavy. His fingers slipped, becoming slicker with sweat. Then pain, a nasty jab, and a different kind of oiliness, but at least he had grip.

Tom got his legs in and half-swung, half-sat on the window edge. The street was clear and quiet. The passers-by must have gone.

And then he was in, shoving forward with his feet, which had buttressed themselves against the inside of the wall. He prayed that he had the strength to lever himself to within grabbing distance of the window's sides.

There was, just, but not without cost. Tom's hand ripped as he let go. He stifled a grunt, one of surprise as much as of pain.

He crawled over Daniel, trying not to knee him in the ribs. Tom made it to his own bed, there to crouch and check on his injured hand.

There must have been a jutting nail and Tom had stuck his hand right on it. A fat round of hurt in his palm. A red eye weeping.

Lick it. Someone had once told him - his mother - to lick your wounds. Like a cat, Tom. Like a cat.

Have you ever bitten your tongue and tasted blood? Or burned your mouth on soup? Yes, of course.

And have you ever wondered why it heals so fast? No, never.

They say your spit has healing properties. One of God's smaller miracles, one that no-one gives thanks for. Do not men spit in their hands when shaking on a deal? Do they not spit when disgusted or when a little lubrication is needed? All these are other little signs; saliva can cure, gives meaning, helps ease the day along.

There'd better not be nail-iron stuck in the wound. Splinters were bad at the best of times, and those from iron were the worst. Like dog-bites, they were. Lockjaw could result, and death as sure as sunrise following midnight.

So clean your graze as best you can, Tom.

'What?'

Tom's hand was in his mouth.

'First you mount me, then you leave the blasted shutter open, then you huddle there like a goblin with a chicken bone.'

'I've cut myself.'

'Good.'

Tom held his hand up, as though Daniel could make anything out in this light.

A pause. Then: 'Is it bad?'

Yes. 'I'm not sure.'

Daniel muttered something, the words not carrying, and he closed the window. Then a scuffling and a fresh immediate light; Daniel held a nub of candle. He set it on the floor.

Tom held the hand out for inspection. Daniel grimaced at it.

'And that was you on the roof?'

'I went to get cool.'

'Thought you'd outgrown that.' Daniel checked the hand again. 'Close and open it.' Tom did so. 'Everything works. You'll survive. I'd give it a wash all the same and try to keep it wrapped up clean. You don't want to drip pus in the dough, do you?'

'Might give it some flavour.'

'Aye, it might at that.'

Tom wondered about saying something about the men in the street, but what would Daniel say? Shall we summon a constable? Rouse the army? No, leave it.

There was a soft rumbling from downstairs. 'He been drinking again?' Tom asked.

Daniel blew the candle out. For some seconds, the wick glowed with the last of the flame's heart, illuminating the tallow-smoke from underneath. 'Only a proper skinful. Pleased as you like about something, that man is. Could hardly get up the stairs, and she was little-'

'What?'

'Nothing.'

Then there were snores from below; they hammered holes in Tom bigger than any roof-tack could gouge.

Tom lay down on his mattress, fingers exploring the wound in his hand. The heat that felt red at the outside, the dull insistence closer in, then the jab of ice at the centre of the pulsing. Tom brought his fingers together; they were already tacky. Good, he thought, as he licked the last of the drying blood from the finger pads.

He was so caught up in this it was some time before he realised that he could see in the darkness, and not because he had adjusted to the grey, but because there was light coming under the door. And with it, a sound that wasn't snoring, and a smell like dry wood-sap.

Tom shouted 'Fire!', but his mouth was dry and the word came out like ashes.

#

Challis had half expected Hubert to cast the bottle, lit rag-wick and all, through the slit he'd forced in the wattle. There'd be the shatter of glass, and then the rush of flame; they'd be undone by the sound alone. Glass made a din universally attractive to the curious.

Hubert didn't so much surprise Challis as exceed his expectations.

First, there was the matter of ignition. Fire-steels were awkward and unreliable at best; the curled metal was better carried as a knuckleduster for fistfights than as a reliable method for creating fire. But Hubert'd done the job using the knife's spine to spark off the iron; a showy piece of skill.

He had not lobbed the bottle. Instead, Hubert had not only taken time but made use of the bottle's shape, and rolled it.

He was rising in the ranks.

It would be a shame, Challis reflected, to lose him.

Hubert waited by the split he'd created, watchful over his new-born. Then he stepped back. 'The fire. She will take.'

They'd moved off, Piedlow jumpy at some sound or other and fearing that the house had already risen; but there was no cry forthcoming.

In walking off - not down the hill, but up - Hubert asked one thing. 'I would like to stay awhile. Here.'

'For what purpose?'

'To see the work done.'

That made some sense, Challis supposed. He'd proved capable despite Challis's earlier misgivings. If he wanted to invest precious sleeping time watching shopkeepers panicking that a house-blaze might spread to their premises then, considering his particular circumstances, that was understandable.

'An hour, no more. Bring no attention to yourself. Watch and remember, so you can report how they react.'

Hubert nodded. They shook on it and then Piedlow went off to the top of the lane and turned left into a wider thoroughfare, Eastcheap. Right would take you straight to the Tower. Left then left again onto Fish Street Hill and straight on to the bridge.

They left Hubert there.

'No rest on the Sabbath for us, Rufus.'

'Hmm?'

'No rest.'

'How long will you need?'

'To move the barrels, perhaps half a day. How long did it take them to be installed?'

'The same, though these were London carters labouring. It will take us longer than that, I fear. And then your mechanism?'

'The device is ready. One more complete test to be sure; perhaps two. The work of an hour I would have thought.'

'So we'll be set by nightfall?'

'I see no reason why not. Your communication is sent?'

'Yes.' That so, Challis wanted to ensure that the maximum effect was achieved. The note he'd had despatched, even if it had not been read already, would surely be in Arlington's hands by Monday morning. It was important that it was known this was no accident. 'Stephen?'

'Yes?'

'What's the busiest time of the week for most people? When are they facing the trials and tribulations of their lives the most?'

'On a Monday morning, one would suppose.'

'Just so. And what is the date on Monday?'

Piedlow gave a low laugh. 'In England, September the third. Is that significant?'

'Numbers are strange. Men can find meaning in all manner of ways in them.'

'Always riddles with you, Challis. Speak straight, or not at all.'

Challis shrugged. 'There are those who mark the third in their own way, and there are those who would watch for evidence. The third is the anniversary of the Roundhead victory against the Scots at Dunbar. There's many a republican who remembers such battles.'

'That is ancient history. What of the common man?'

'And the third is the anniversary of the battle of Worcester. The battle that gave Cromwell his Protectorship. That secured the elder Charles's appointment with the headsman, and had his son, the present king, scurrying to the continent.

'And also,' Challis said, 'the anniversary of the death of Oliver Cromwell.'

'That,' Piedlow said, 'would seem worthy of commemoration, if only for mischief. Such fireworks I shall give you.'

The date was naught but coincidence, but it had its potential. Bennet would be twitchy enough, half-expecting some kind of protest. London would run with the possible significance. Mistrust would rule.

They crossed the bridge in silence. Challis saw a lighterman

191

rowing off to the right, crossing with them, London to Southwark.

His boat was otherwise empty.

#

Was he right, though? There'd be the Devil to pay if Tom woke the house without good reason. But the yellow flashing between door and floorboard; what else could it be?

He rose fast, pulling his clothes back on, shoeing himself. Careful, quiet, he tipped the latch and went out.

It was quiet as only a house at night can be when creeping abroad. And there was light coming from downstairs, a strong flicker. Perhaps a lantern, conceivably an unattended hearth. But who would light a lamp then leave? Who would leave a fire burning in the grate this summer?

Checking the fires was Farriner's nightly ritual, as natural as locking the front door and shuttering up. Still, if he had been drinking more than usual, an amount enough to leave most spewing into their chamber-pots, there might be something missed.

He had made it to bed. The snoring from his room made that obvious. So he wouldn't be slumped over the kitchen table, buttered cake in one hand and spilled wine on the floor beside him.

Down again, and then Tom knew it. In his griping guts. Shit turning to water. He knew it in his ears, the rushing and cracking. In his nose; a smell like baking, but more so. Wood and flour and candlewax and something else, not tar but of that ilk.

But he had to see.

The floor was alight. Rush matting covering over the floor at the front of the shop was burning. There was more; wood faggots stacked up by the oven were already burning freely, as was the work table they kneaded their dough upon. Fire cut the room in two, barring Tom from getting through into the back rooms. There was water there, enough in the pannier for the kettles and the first of the new day's cooking and washing. The fire had spread to one of the walls too, licking up at the front of the house. There was a split already showing there; the heat must have forced a crack.

There was little smoke, or so Tom thought. But there it was, pale with burning flour and so could scarce be seen at first, rising and curling under the ceiling, where pots hung from hooks in the joists.

Two places where the fire was not. The hearth. The oven. He checked again. The grates were clear.

It made no sense, but this was not a time for how or why.

Flames shifted, seizing on the pile of empty sacks stored in the gap under the stairwell for return to the miller, empty for full. Tom grabbed one from the middle of the stack as yet untouched by the flames.

Tom held the sack like he'd been shown. Fire needs air, his father had said. Air and something to burn. To raise a fire or to kill it you had to know to control it. The right fuel, kindling and something drier and lighter is needed to start a fire. You built a fire in layers, the small and light material underneath and inside, the larger and heavier on top and around. That, plus flint and tinder for the spark, and an adequate supply of air.

To kill it, the opposite. Fire is hungry; you have to starve it. Either air or fuel: ideally, both. Then your fire withers and perishes.

Tom struck out at the advancing flames, yellow-red snicks beginning to consume the sacking. There was a room full of air for the fire to play with. Tom lashed with the hessian, beating on the flames. At first it worked, the impact snuffing the fire. But there was soon more, then more again. The whole of the room was on fire; an upright beam smouldered darkly. The stack of oven logs toppled, causing sparks to leap out. A bottle, cracked and already charred, lay on the floor, glinting green against the reds and yellows. Maybe that was the source: that Farriner's carelessness while in his cups had caused this.

Tom tried again, but that was all. Trying. He was flailing at it, getting desperate. He struck again, only serving to cast bright fragments of burning hemp into the room.

Smoke now rolled around the foot of the stairs, and Tom knew his choices were but one.

He backed to the stairs. The way behind him was clear, but in front, much of the shop and kitchen areas had flames filling them. Only then did it strike Tom just how much of the house was filled with materials that would burn. Sacks, barrels, wooden furniture and crossbeams. Cloths of all description; washing and cleaning rags and towels, wall-hangings, bed covers, clothes. The few books; the family Bible, the one volume of poetry his father owned, the sheaves of invoices, orders, and other documents. Sea-coal in the bunkers, oil for lamps and frying, candles and rush-lights. A lidded bucket of pitch for little waterproofing jobs.

Everything that was not metal or stone would burn.

Tom ran up the stairs. Smoke was rising like an incoming tide around his ankles as he went up. This was thicker, darker stuff. White smoke had already gathered like clouds at the ceiling. It rolled round where the ceiling met the stairwell gap. It would find its way into the rooms above. Where smoke went, fire would follow.

'Fire!' Tom shouted at the top of the stairs, rounding on the landing to cross the three or so steps to his father's chamber. 'Fire!' He pounded on the door, hard enough for the latch to bounce open. His last blow caught the door already ajar; it thudded back against the upright. The frame cracked at the hinges.

Tom winced, but not at that.

His father was laid naked because of the summer heat and because of her. One arm was looped over Alice, who was half-hidden under a once-green blanket that had been Tom's mother's favourite.

Alice's legs stuck out from under the blanket, crossed right over left. Her hair was mussed around, and even in this light Tom could see she had a sweat on.

Farriner grunted, not awake, not asleep. His hand came over his side and then under the covering. It must have fallen between her hips and waist. He shuffled, flitching as though a bed mite had nipped.

There was smoke in the room already. It streamed from below, cutting between board-gaps, feeling its way out.

The house was on fire.

She was there like it was any other night.

The house was on fire.

'Tom?'

Daniel, from above. His sleepy voice.

'Tom?'

The second call got Tom shouting. 'Fire!'

Tom wanted to be running, to be getting out, but he had to be sure that they knew. He went to the bed and even though his father was already rousing, propping himself up and shifting his arm from around her, Tom put his hands on him.

His father's eyes opened.

Farriner was all action, fast and immediate. 'Get your brother,' he said. 'Now!'

Tom bolted. He ran back along the landing. The downstairs smoke was thicker. Tom couldn't see the bottom of the stairs. The smoke rolled and boiled, aglow with red and orange.

'Daniel?' Tom stumbled through the door. He put his hand out to protect himself as he fell. He landed between the beds, wrist out and palm down. Tom grunted, scrabbled back to his feet. He caught himself on the corner of his own bed.

At least the crash served some purpose. Daniel rolled over. 'What is it?'

'Get up, quick. The house is alight.'

Daniel's mouth opened as though to automatically gainsay this, but something forced him silent. Tom craned behind him to see what had shushed his brother.

The doorway, fully open, rippling with rising smoke.

'Father?'

'He's awake. Alice too. Quick!'

Daniel dived into the clothing he'd been wearing the previous day. Tom stood, awkward. What to do?

The answer came from below. 'Tom? Daniel?' His father's shouting stopped, paused by a coughing fit.

Tom went to the landing then down to the first floor. His father wasn't there; the bedroom was empty. Where was he? Where was Alice?

Sounds from below, from where the smoke was now rich and black. For the first time, Tom could smell the depth of the burning. Heavy with dark wood, stinking with oil and tar. Tom gagged on it, taking in a mouthful as he tried not to catch it in his nostrils.

He got to the top of the stairs. Movement in the smoke; shadows between the grey wall of the burning and the flames beyond.

Tom didn't think.

He went down the stairs too.

He didn't get further than the step before the bottom. Farriner had one hand clamped over his mouth. There was a rag in it. In his other hand he had some papers, one of the smaller ledgers too. The newest one. The papers were curled, but otherwise untouched.

Alice held nothing. Her eyes were bright red with the same heat that was scouring Tom's face. Something else as well; panic. She rushed past Tom, heading back upstairs.

Farriner grabbed Tom with the rag-clenched hand. 'Get your brother into the street. Quick while we can get out safe. Any longer and we'll end up being trapped upstairs.' He was urgent but controlled. There was nothing in his tone to suggest panic, not anger, nor yet surprise or even guilt at the fire's presence. This was the Farriner of the stories, the man who'd once stood on a battlefield and who served a king. 'Come on!' Then puzzlement. 'Alice?'

He charged up the stairs calling her. The bottom step was alight. Tom stamped the flames but it caused a draught, pushing them back and encouraging them forwards again. Tom stepped up a stair. The bottom step was now well caught, the wood blackening, offering succour to the burning.

Tom took the rest of the stairs in twos. Daniel was babbling something about them getting out now, and Father was shouting back about salvage. 'Grab what you can. Money, anything precious and small. Leave the rest.'

Leave the rest? This was it. The house was lost. Bakery, business, his home in the city. It was going to burn. No. It was already burning. This was happening now.

So what should he take? What did he have? None save the money he'd got together, and the larger sum that Daniel held from Challis.

'Daniel?' He got no reply. He shouted again louder, to make himself clear above the noise of the fire. It had been silent minutes ago, but now the ground floor was roaring as it was consumed.

A gust of flame shot up the stairwell. Tom staggered back, hitting the wall behind him. The wall, thin laths of wood smoothed over with lime mixture, buckled. Tom fell, rupturing the wall further.

Another shot of agony to his hand. Tom hit the floorboards side on, keeling over. He laid there just long enough for the stabbing in his hand to lift. The floorboards reeked of smoke. The wood was hot.

Then he was up, dragged to his feet. By Daniel. 'Are you hurt?' he said.

Tom shook his head. Daniel's hands were full. His purse, Bible, some papers. The papers were wedged into the book as though they'd been used to mark a page.

The boards creaked under them, moaning under the heat combined. But the house must have stood for hundreds of years. Pray God that it held some minutes more.

Farriner was at the door to his chamber. He was red with exertion; whatever he'd been doing had been interrupted by the house-noise.

'There's no time,' Tom said. Farriner had stooped to pick something up. A crowbar, a jemmy. 'We have to get out.'

Alice was there too, but at the other end of the corridor. She must have gone to her room – her old room at the back of the house - salvaging whatever she might. She had a sack at her side. It bulged. She wasn't looking at Tom, but past him. To Daniel? Her mouth was wide open but she gave no shriek.

The stairwell gave way, dropping to the floor below. A series of crashes, then a mad flume of sparks and smoke and fresh lively flame.

There was no way down. No way down and the house was burning. Alice was not trapped, but the landing was now alight where the stairs had fallen. The gap between them was not much, but a leap rather than a step.

The smoke was so rich it was hard to tell where solid boards ended and oily insubstance began. 'Up and out boys, up and out!' Farriner shouted.

Alice was as still as a tree. She was day from the flames and night from the smoke. Her gaze was still caught, but not on the gap where the stairs had been torn away. She was haloed in red. It was as though she was melting.

'Get out!'

'Alice!'

'I'll get her. You go!'

Daniel, who must still have had firm grip on Tom, pulled him back to the stairwell. 'Come on!'

Alice was maybe four feet away. She had dropped her bag and was rapt in the fire. 'Alice!'

'Come on Tom!'

If she reached out as well, then their combined grasp would be enough. Tom could pull her over if she jumped at the same time.

'Leave her!' Farriner, from behind. The jemmy was still in his hand. 'I'll bring her.'

'Tom.' Daniel's voice dropped. It scarcely carried in the tumult around them.

She was framed by light. Her feet were shrouded in smoke. A joist was on fire by her side, but she did not notice. She was crying, dribbling. A red glaze.

'Out!' Farriner shoved Daniel and Tom as one to the stairs. Daniel took the momentum of the blow and used it to pull them upwards.

He bundled Tom into their room. She was down there all alone.

\#

Tom retched from the smoke, coughing up nothing but spittle and bile. His throat stung with acid.

'He'll bring her up,' Daniel said. 'Now, we have to get you out of here.' He was calm now, so calm. It was as though he was privy to Tom's mind.

Daniel left Tom to recover. He opened the little window Tom had shimmied through earlier – had that only been an hour ago? Less? 'Come on. Help me pull this apart.'

They wrenched at the frame. It gave easy, the window pulling off its hinges, the nails popping out rather than snapping in the wood. Tom chucked it aside.

He looked out. There were people in the street. Not many, five or six. They were watching, calling. Tom shouted down. 'Ladders? Do you have ladders?'

If they had, no-one said.

The front of the building was alight. Someone was coming, huffing along with two buckets. They threw water at the walls, but they did little except splash smoke and send onlookers scurrying back.

'It's well aflame. So we go up, over the next roof then drop down to the street. It's the only way. We jump and we might land in the fire.'

'Aim for a neighbour,' Daniel said. 'A fat one to break our fall.'

'You go first,' Tom said. 'I'll guide you out.'

'No. You first.'

'No brother, it's easier for me and we have little time. I can get out faster than you if need be.'

Daniel said nothing, but kissed his Bible and tucked that and his money into his breeches. Paper stuck out over his belt.

He hoisted himself out onto the ledge. Then he was out and up onto the roof.

'Now you!'

Tom ran back to the doorway and shouted down. 'Through the attic room!'

'Yes!' His father was panting.

'Tom?' That was Daniel from outside.

'Have you got Alice?'

Nothing.

'Father?'

'Yes! Now go!' There was scuffling from below, like someone being dragged. And then a sudden rush of heat from downstairs - a hot wall of air - pummelled Tom.

Daniel's arm hung down. Maybe he was thinking of climbing back in to find out what the delay was.

Tom had to go.

Tom went back to the window, batting his brother's hand away. There were more people in the street underneath, some of them half-dressed, all of them engrossed. One or two gasped when they saw Tom, shouting him to jump quick.

Tom slid out. He thought about going the other way, about hanging off the window-hole and dropping into the street, but he'd have landed too close to the house. The shutters were burning as were the walls above the brick line.

Tom upped himself onto the roof. Daniel was there, breathing hard. Smoke leaked up through the thatch. 'We can't go off the back,' Daniel said. 'See?'

The rear of the building was fully ablaze. Already fire had forced gaps where there were cracked roof tiles. Flames grew like weeds round cobbles. Tom fancied he might have been able to scrabble across it even so, crossing over the back alley and ending up on the tavern on Fish Street Hill.

But no, the clearest path was across, then down.

They were shouting in the street for him and Daniel to save themselves. 'Over one, then down, yes?' Tom yelled over to Daniel. 'You go first.'

Daniel chucked his Bible over, then half-stepped, half-jumped over the slim gap between buildings. Where the roof met the walls, there was smoke.

'Now you!'

Tom shook his head. 'I'll help them out. You get down and try to put the fire out before it takes everything.' Perhaps something could be salvaged if they acted quick.

Daniel nodded, and then disappeared from view. He must have slid down the far side of the roof.

Tom hitched himself back over to the window. They were shouting for him now down in the lane, bawling for him to risk the jump.

Where were they?

Tom swung himself and it must have looked like he was going to make the leap, because the crowd quieted. But Tom instead rolled himself over, trying to peer in upside-down while hanging onto the roof-works.

He brought his head down to the window-space. There were flames two feet away. The fire had taken control of the first floor. His father's room must be well alight. Where were they?

Then a face came into view, startling Tom. Shocked, he almost let go. His father, almost nose-to-nose with him, upside down.

'Out of the way,' he grunted. Tom shifted back over, his hand screaming at him. It felt wet and shredded.

Then a harsh rasping, a crunching immediately below. Farriner was smashing at the wall around the window, making the space bigger. An iron bar stabbed the wall. The force of the blows made the front of the roof quake; Tom crawled back onto the roof to get out of the way.

A mighty crack resounded, and the roof moaned. Tom was rocked, lurching over. He stumbled again, and his right foot went through the thatch. Tom gasped in surprise. His foot was in thatch to the knee. He struggled to gain support. His father was not to be seen; he still hadn't got out. Daniel was gone, and if Christ willed it, he would be safe on the street and organising aid.

Tom reached to push himself out of the hole, but his hands were greasy, one with sweat and the other with blood. He fumbled, desperate for purchase, grabbing at loose handfuls of flaking straw.

He tried again but the roof was weaker than Tom had understood.

It gave, and Tom went with it.

He dropped rather than fell, landing on something soft – mattresses? – in what had been his own room. He saw his father swing one last time at a hole in the wall where the window had been. The gap was crude, but big enough for a hefty man.

Then Farriner stooped to pick something up. He had to drop the crowbar to do so, to pick up his chest, the one from the end of his bed, and force it through the hole.

He shouted out to those below. Smoke occluded the room. The rush of the fire, like water over mill-wheels, made it hard to hear. Curses to the outside world, threats not to touch or interfere.

Then Farriner's shoulders relaxed; he'd dropped the chest.

Alice was not to be seen.

The fire was up to the second floor now. The hole Tom fell through acted like a chimney, clearing enough air to let Tom see his father clamber awkwardly half-out of the gutted window, then turn to hang on to let himself down rather than to jump outright.

Farriner was staring right at Tom. And then he dropped.

Sparks surrounded Tom. One of the mattresses was alight; the stink of horsehair made Tom gag. The corridor was full of burning. His feet were hot from underneath and the floor groaned with each step. Underfoot, the boards flexed. They were going to give.

Tom went for the door. Alice was trapped somewhere and he had to find her, drag her out if need be, carry her out.

The boards were crackling. Not cracking, though that word-sound was in there too; they were crackling, as brittle and yielding as roasted pig-skin. Yellow spurts of flame sprung between his feet. Smoke was everywhere.

A board buckled under him. He stepped back from the charring edges. Fresh flame shot up through the new hole. It caught the surrounding wood fast, the door-jambs and lintel taking to fire. And then the wall around took the burning willingly, craving to be consumed.

Tom's arm came up to protect his face. He listened for something, anything that might have been human through the din of the fire. There was nothing but shouting from outside, a crowd pleading for him to come out.

He hated himself for making for the window. He hated himself for not doing more. Getting out, Tom stood on something solid; his father's improvised crowbar.

It glowed.

No, it didn't. It glistered, bright with firelight from the burning room, white with the wall debris that stuck to it, and red with the wet blood that stuck it there.

The claw end was slick with blood, some of the gore covered by powdery lime. The wall around the window-space was flecked with it too, where Farriner's hacking had been frenzied.

Father must have hurt himself, like Tom. Caught himself on something, maybe the Claw itself, in panic or just in plain fumbling in the smoky black.

Tom got out of the window; what was left of it. His father's gouging had made the hole much larger than it had been. Tom doubted he'd be able to reach to the roof.

He was right. He was now too low. He couldn't sit on the bottom of the hole and reach the roof-beam. The frame gone, the laths and plaster just didn't have the strength to support him. Twice he tried, each time his foot serving to push out fresh chunks of material.

His face was blackening with smoke; it scratched his face, dried his eyes. His pores were silting up.

Then Tom reached for the crowbar. It was only then he realised quite what the tool was; the kitchen implement, the Devil's Claw.

It was rich with blood, baked in solid redness but yet bright with it. Tom grabbed the tool, brought it through the window-space, and swung it up.

The claw made contact, fixing itself firm into the thatch, and then biting down around something more solid. That was enough.

More shouts, pleadings from the street.

Tom held on for a count of three to the window, then let go. In one, he gripped hard with his left hand and swung and reached with his right.

Tom made contact and just kept going. Right hand over the roof-beam and then he pulled, pulled, pulled, switching his weight from one hand to the other. His damaged right hand screamed at him. Tom kept on, swinging back and bringing his left up. He flailed at the beam, overshooting, hand burying itself into the now-smoking straw like the Claw before it.

Tom pushed up, and then got one leg over onto the roof. He rolled and gave himself another count of three to recover.

The roof wasn't safe. He'd already learned that. One thing before he moved though.

Tom reached out and retrieved the Claw.

Then he crawled away from the front of the house. He skirted around the hole he'd made earlier.

The room was red with burning below.

Tom continued crawling, over the apex and down the other side. The newer rear of the bakery was well alight. Tiles had popped with heat from beneath them, splitting along their lengths from the nail-holes downwards. Fresh-sundered halves dropped into the blaze.

Tom got to the edge of the roof. There were sparks around him, rising from where he'd been. They floated in the rising heat and smoke. Some settled on the roof of the building next door, on the tavern.

Tom's right hand was throbbing, aching, stinging all at once. Shards of ice-direct pain and the lower rumblings of nausea, some kind of fever brought on by the fire.

He kept moving on, he had to. If he didn't, he'd die. And there were questions, so many, pushing out against the inside of his skull. But if he dwelled on them now he'd be lost to the inferno.

He was too tired to think if what he was going to do was a good idea.

Tom sat on the edge of the thatch where it butted up to a chimney stack. He dropped the Claw to the ground, picturing its clatter as it hit the earth, holding that in his memory so he'd know where to reach. The wall hadn't burned through, not yet. He hoped the mortar had not been corrupted by the flames.

Tom angled himself and jumped across, landing opposite the chimney stack. Yes. Then he left himself fall back, hoping he'd judged the distance right.

His back smacked against the wall-work. Again, yes! Then Tom walked, back solid against the wattle, sliding as he moved his feet left over right over left onto the opposing wall and then down.

It worked. His clothes rode up and his back was scratched, then grazed, then torn, but it worked. He stopped where he could, shuffling to adjust his clothing, and then moved again. In this way he walked down the wall until he could see clear where he would land.

Then he let himself go.

Tom hit the ground hard. He landed on the balls of his feet then pitched forward, scuffing his elbows on walls. The Claw lay in front of him. Tom snatched it and ran out of the alley.

He went to find the bastard.

#

Challis could not sleep. Part of it was the tightening knot of anticipation in his gut, that day-before-battle feeling that he knew wouldn't loosen until the first swing of the blade, the first cannon. Part of it was uncertainty.

And that was the pleasure of it too. Plans were all fine and well, but it was in His chaotic moment that He revealed Himself and made the space for His will to be made manifest.

Part of it was the pain. His absent thumb throbbed as though it was filling with blood to the point of bursting. Challis used his breathing, steady and even as he could, to bring the fullness under control.

Silent, he got up from where he lay and found his belongings. He picked out his Bible. It rattled as he crept up the stairs. Challis paused and steadied himself, careful not to rouse the dozing Piedlow.

The man had worked for maybe an hour, then had slumped, complaining of fatigue, and had nodded off, all the while declaiming that he was a light enough sleeper to be disturbed the instant Hubert returned.

Even so, Challis went only as far as the first-floor landing. There was a little light here from sky reflecting on the river. He opened the Bible and took the vial out.

He would have to be careful, and part of him thought that this was a temptation, because Piedlow was not an altogether known quantity, and Hubert was not back, but on the other side of the coin, it was late. Past Challis's usual retiring hour. Past his time of prayer and contemplation.

He took the bottle and let its coolness soothe him. Having it in his hand was an ease in itself. But the vial soon warmed, as it always did.

The stopper came out with the slightest scrape of cork on glass. It squeaked rather than popped on release; the heavy scent swam out. Like the richest wine, something Spanish and expensive reduced over a low flame, augmented with heavy spices, mulled with an apothecary's hand, then the opium essence droplets added. A shake and it was done. Sydenham's Elixir, it was called.

A half-dose would have to suffice. A full serving would bring on blessed sleep, and dreams of immortality. A taste for now then, just enough to grease the gears of the night-time hours.

Challis prayed for the morning. He prayed for the flame. He prayed for the success of the mission and of his part in it. He prayed forgiveness of the trespasses as he forgave the trespasses of those who auctioned against Him and Challis, thought and deed, will and action, jury and executioner.

He prayed that the apostate Charles would have word of the message he'd had passed to him brought near, and with that intelligence still in his ears be yet informed of what else had passed in His name.

In revenge for the English attacks on the Dutch navy and of their boastful gloating thereafter. In return for the cowardice in the burning of Schelling, in Holmes's sea attack on an undefended seaport; all the while the English claiming that they were trying to sue for peace.

Peace.

Challis tipped the vial on his lips. Saffron and cinnamon, cloves and sherry. The scent belied the taste of it, bitter harshness through the heady sweetness of the liquid.

Redeemer, save us all. Sweet Christ, save us all who profess your one true faith and who act in your name and in pursuit of your everlasting mercy.

Challis swallowed. He felt the red juice trickle down his gullet, warming and expanding, coating and soothing. Its effects were as ever almost instantaneous, another indicator surely of Providence in its formulation.

A tightening in the lungs sufficient to allow the imbiber to be assured that he was in the tincture's embrace. And then a secondary warmth, a relaxation. Spreading outwards from his stomach, around the heart and ribs, to the head and brain, then lastly to the limbs. Thigh then lower leg then foot. Gut to slackening bollocks and relaxing prick. Shoulders to arms and, blessedly, to hands.

Challis stoppered the bottle. It was not easy; his hands being numbed somewhat by the elixir. Nevertheless, he allowed himself success in replacing the shut capsule back in the Bible which in turn was laid, like a babe to its cot, to rest.

He drifted. He flexed his right hand, watching the way the muscles worked under the skin. If only, he thought, if he could take his blade and prise out the canker that afflicted him, scrape away the human rust inside. But would that not be an affront to His design? The awkwardnesses his hand presented were as nothing to the stigma He had been given with the crown of thorns and with the sign they had hung around His neck. And the pain Challis experienced held no comparison with His passion upon the cross.

Challis was blessed. Blessed with purpose and with insight. Blessed with an earthly mission and with the wit to determine His hand in matters. Blessed that He gave sanction for both Challis's acts and his omissions. Surely capture, a temporal trial, imprisonment and in all likelihood the rope would be forthcoming otherwise, and then the judgment everlasting soon after. No. Challis was certain, because the facts of his continued existence and success served to justify that certainty. He would receive but one assessment, and then he would receive his permanent reward and a place at His table.

Laid back now, eyes shut. He was tired and could sleep. Surely, he thought, a few minutes' slumber would be no disgrace. Piedlow was downstairs and Hubert would be back soon. What harm could come in the night?

And he might well have convinced himself that the lazy course of action was in the circumstances justifiable, and even well-earned, had he not had the wit, or have been guided by some grace, to stretch out. And in that stretching, he had swept his sleeve over some obstruction, some minor barrier to what comfort he could manage on the bare wood.

One touch of the leather was all that it took. One glancing contact with his father's disembowelled Book.

He might have expressed ruefulness in his countenance, had there been someone there to observe.

Challis got himself to sitting upright, grabbing and pulling on a baluster to so do. He shuffled forwards, hand still on the upright, perching himself on the very lip of the upmost stair. He balanced himself not just between comfort and falling but between befuddlement and wonder.

Some part of him was cognizant that he'd let slip too much of the liquid into his throat. Some other part of him revelled in it. Usually, sleep was claimed through prayer, not this waking dream.

Challis felt outside of himself, the way he'd heard wounded battlefield veterans talk of it. A feeling, a sensation of floating outside their own bodies before being snatched back to life by some field surgeon's skill, or eased back into wholeness through some greater design.

The building was uncertain around him. The plain facts of timber and glass, the prosaic realities of the solid were being re-inscribed around him. Edges shimmered, corners danced. His body was numb as though needles-and-pins swaddled him entire.

Had he not sat on his own legs more than once as a child to try to force the sensation upon himself? He fancied he could see through walls, between gaps, under bolted doors and despite and through banks of fog.

He could hear the night; lovers' midnight desperate secrets, magic curses, fell sounds of giants stirring under the soil. His mouth was still painted with the linctus; its ingredients disassembled on his tongue, the taste of it separating out as each flavour in turn were presented to him and then stirred, his maw a cauldron, the brew coming together with a final circular flourish.

He could smell the subtlest odours of the city. Parchments and silks. Milk not yet turned to sour. He knew the smell of diamonds and the perfume of gold, the scent of bodies in motion.

And then he smelled something else; fresh air, and with it, the residue of bonfire.

There was then clatter downstairs. The front door closing, and being bolted with relish. The draught and the new airborne flavours had come from without.

He pinched himself hard on the pad of his thumb. Not enough. A second time, the more so.

Still outside himself, though the more aware of the fact, Challis made himself rise and prepare to descend.

Hubert had by this time roused Piedlow and was jabbering to him in some flux of Dutch and French, eyes wide, hands supplementing his flustered and breathless speech.

The man stunk of what he spoke. Of fire and burning. Of flame.

Challis, affecting the mildest confusion of weariness, asked the man to repeat himself. He felt like a fraud, like he was a drunk pretending to be sober. But no-one noticed. Not with what Hubert had to say.

#

Tom rounded the corner to find a swelling crowd with its back to him. He forced himself between two bodies, seeing his brother and father on the other side of the half-circle that had formed, dumbstruck by the fire consuming the bakery.

Alice was at the shattered window at the top of the house. There were flames from the window below her, from Tom's father's room. The ground floor shutters were alight. Smoke was rushing out from wherever it could. There was red fire behind her, more smoke at her sides. The smoke was not rising far, because it was being buffeted by the still-strong winds. Sparks, flakes of smouldering lath and thatch rose and flew with each gust.

The crowd was crying for her to jump, to climb out, anything. Alice put her hands to her head, not to sob, but to wipe blood from her forehead. She'd taken at least one blow. A gouge as livid as the fire around her stood out across her temple, bleeding unimpeded. She served only to streak more red over her face, mixing it with soot and grime.

A rumble, something deep from within the house's innards. The crowd shouted again for her to jump. Tom found himself shouting, screaming too. Daniel stood silent beside him, hands clasped tight.

It was the house that answered. The thatch caught fully, a flume of fire bursting up, in all probability through the hole Tom had made in his fall. The fire ran like water and the whole of the roof was alight.

That was the moment when the crowd shifted, the signal to them that this might spread. From one roof to another, from one place of business to the next, from someone else's home to theirs. There was not panic yet, but there was now distraction from the immediate tragedy in waiting. They were starting to think about themselves.

They did not have long to wait.

There was no way up to the window. No-one had anything like a ladder or a cart high enough to allow anyone to reach near the window. There was no way to climb up. The roof was burning well now; no escape that way seemed possible. The girl would have to jump and take her chances.

But she would not. She did not even scream now, or she did, then Tom was shouting too loud to hear anyone else's utterances. Perhaps she said something to herself, because, hand still to her temple, blood still leaking through her fingers, her mouth moved. And then she dropped out of sight.

She must have fainted from heat or injury. There was a gap in time between her disappearing from the window and the collapse inside. Afterwards, they said that the floor gave way under her and she fell to her death. But that was not what Tom saw.

She fell out of sight. The onlookers were shut up by her vanishing, and then the crash.

'Alice?' But Tom's shout was for nothing. There were two great noises, two floors dropping in turn under the fire's assault. Second floor to first, first to ground. With the latter, the whole structure quivered; fresh flames roared where once had been shutters and windows. They had been blown out or otherwise buckled under the onslaught.

Farriner had murdered her. The proof was in his hand. Tom wheeled about to face his father.

'You killed her.'

There were people all around but no-one was giving them attention. Tom said it again. 'You killed her.'

Someone grinned at him from the crowd, teeth reflecting red in the fire. A fat little face, blushed with heat and drink. Behind him stood another, taller, impassive. The round-faced one clapped his hands, gleeful.

Tom jabbed the claw into his father's gut. Not hard enough to break the skin through his shirt, but hard enough to make him grunt. The impact left a dark smear behind. 'What did you do to her? Beat her away because she was holding your escape back? Did you lash out in fury at losing your precious king's bakery? Why?'

Farriner grabbed him by the shoulders. He spoke both quiet and harsh at the same time. 'I did no such thing.'

Tom relaxed his grip on the claw. 'Look at it. Look at it! Blood on this and a wound on her head.'

'I saw no such wound.'

'Liar! The blood ran down her face!'

'No Tom. You're mistaken.'

'Then explain the blood.' Tom held the claw up now. 'Look at it.'

His father glanced down. 'And what of it? We've all got cuts and scrapes. Look at your own hand. What's to say it's not your own blood running?'

'I saw you.'

'You did no such thing.'

'I saw you. Not strike her, but in our room, making your hole to rescue your lockbox.' The chest was at Farriner's feet. The lid had broken open; it must have smashed in the drop. 'At least your treasure's safe.' Tom lashed out with a foot. The box barely shook.

Tom continued: 'You were striking at the plaster, forcing a hole big enough.'

'And what of it? I had to get our money out, Tom. It's all we've got. And not much either. Not enough to start again without assistance or charity, that's certain.'

'Is that all you think of?'

'And is that what you think of me?'

'I saw you. I saw the blood on the walls. It didn't get there from my hands. It came from this,' Tom said, claw still in hand.

Part of Tom wanted to bring the iron tines down on his father's head, to smash open his skull and gouge out his brain. To pound his lying trap until he dribbled broken teeth, until his jaw cracked under the hammering, his mouth a red and white commemoration of the day he'd fled in greed and selfishness.

He might have done it had not Daniel intervened. He came between them, pulling on Tom's wrist as his did, twisting and prising the claw from his grip. The shaft was slick with blood, the hole in his hand refusing to stop its weeping.

'Enough,' Daniel said, all calm. He threw the claw back into the bakery. It disappeared through a burned-out window. 'It's over.'

Daniel's eyes were red-rimmed and wet. There were smoke and tears there. He pushed the two apart, Farriner knocking into the chest in the process. 'There's time for this later. Your differences can be settled then.' His tone was distant. 'Look.'

The house - their home - was done for. But there was more. Flames had spread through spark and fire and by part of a wall collapsing to the next building. The White Hart to the other side was not yet touched, but it would not be long before it was afflicted. Some of the onlookers had scattered, no doubt to secure their own possessions. There were a few buckets around, not many. Some attempts had been made to douse the fire, but there'd been no success, and Farriner's was now beyond saving.

Taff had rolled barrels out into the street, partly to protect his stock, but partly for resources with which to fight the fire. He opened two, cracking the upended barrels with a device that could have been the brother of the claw. 'Come on, lads. Do what you can to soak the walls. I'll not lose my property to your carelessness.'

John Wardley and Widow Grimes, who were all but living together these days, joined in using jugs and buckets to scoop ale and drench the adjoining tavern wall where they could. Upstairs, Taff's wife was leaning out of a window, reaching up to the roof, a haphazard mix of thatch and tiling like the Farriner building. Though some of the water she was chucking up there found its mark, as much did not, falling uselessly to the ground or vanishing hissing into oblivion.

Farriner was bridling at the suggestion that he'd caused the fire. His muscles at the neck were tensed and he glared at Taff.

'And what of it?' The landlord was bright with rage. 'I say you've not doused your fires nor checked your oven. God knows you were pissed enough not to care last night.'

'I'm a fucking baker,' Farriner snarled. 'Fire's what I know.'

'And don't we bloody know it.'

'All my fires were out in all the hearths. I'll swear to it. We've not even had a hearth lit upstairs all summer, just kept the oven for trade and the kitchen alight for our hot water. It's been the same for all of us. Has it not been too hot a summer to need our homes warming?'

'You've a warm enough one now, Farriner,' someone yelled out, and there was a resigned laughter from some.

That was when the roof gave in. Tom heard it rather than saw it, a vast creaking, the way he'd thought a ship at sea might sound under pressure from the ocean. The roof, by now a field of fire, dropped into the heart of the building and with the floors having already collapsed; there was nothing to break its fall.

Alice's body was in there.

Fire leapt into the street, chasing whatever fuel it could. Smoke and sparks were flying all around, chased out by the mighty blow from inside. A roof beam jutted out of the front window, its wood blackened here, charring there, livid crimson elsewhere.

'That's no ordinary fire,' Daniel said.

Someone else took up his cry. 'The preacher speaks right. This is arson.'

'No,' Daniel said. 'That's not my meaning.' But his words didn't carry to those still trying to save the tavern. Not to the innkeeper, not to their father, not to the few still lolly-gagging.

Farriner was still locked with Taff, the pair at once doing what they could to both fight the fire and argue the reasons for its cause. Distracted doubly, they didn't see the third man come in and dip a scoop into the upended, opened ale. Instead of flinging it at the fire, he took a draught.

Tom knew his face. He saw it clearly for less than a second, because he was shrouded by shadow and other bodies, but at the instant he brought drink to lips there was no doubt.

And then he was gone, hidden by the shadows the fire was causing to be cast.

'What did you say, Daniel?'

'That this is no ordinary fire.' Again, that distant tone.

'Perhaps you're right.'

'We are judged, brother.'

Tom was staring into the black. There were rushing noises all around him, flickers and murmurings. The wind was up again, gusting east to west over the houses. The smoke, rising only to rooftop level before being ushered westwards, confirmed this.

Then a dark sense of movement. Someone approaching slowly. With caution. Tom shielded one side of his face, partly so that his vision would not be affected by the brightness of the burning. Partly to disguise his face.

Someone coming to have a closer look. Someone who couldn't bear to not see the conflagration.

But why?

It seemed to Tom that Robert Hubert could only be here for one reason.

#

'Were you seen?' was Challis's first question.

'No. I am sure of it.'

'How so?'

'All were watching the house burn. The whole street. And not to put the flames out. Watching. First the flames and then the death.'

'Death?' Piedlow interrupted.

'A woman. In the bakery. She fell into the fires. She's roasting there now.'

Challis came back in. 'And the bakery lad?'

'He was trapped in the house. I saw him climb onto the roof but he fell through. I did not see him after.'

'And what of others from the house?'

'Two escaped. A younger man and an older. Son and father, I would say.'

So some people had got free. And Hubert couldn't confirm Tom's death.

'Tell me more about the fire.'

Hubert became more animated, gabbling and switching to French or Dutch where his vocabulary failed him. Once or twice Piedlow corrected him, but there was enough English to make sense of sense what he was saying.

The gist was plain. First the bakery had burned. It had taken some time for the fire to take firm hold, but when it did, it burned fierce and fast. The building had collapsed in on itself.

Neighbours had been roused by the fire but had through confusion, malice or lack of thought, largely been satisfied to let the building burn. What efforts that had been made to quell the flames had been haphazard, poorly organised, and ineffective. Some pitchers of water thrown, nothing more.

'And then,' Hubert said, by now having picked up fresh words from Piedlow's interruptions, 'when the roof-beams fell, there was such a rising of blow-devils-'

'Sparks?'

Hubert nodded. 'Sparks with motive, as though commanded by witchcraft, made to operate through-' he waved his hands as though trying to summon the word "articulation" '- the four winds.'

'How so?'

'The winds blew sparks onto the house next door, and next-but-one, and the one after that. A second house fell, and a third. And with the wind, the flames and the sparks, by the time I left, they were fearful for those properties linked to them at the rear.'

'The street along?'

'Yes.'

'In which way?'

'To the west, the direction the wind is focused.'

Challis was already getting his coat on. He checked that his pockets were appropriately full. He shut his eyes for a heartbeat. The elixir was strong inside him. Purples and greens throbbed behind his eyelids. His thumb did not hurt and walking felt as though he were elevated, like standing in stirrups at full charge.

'This is not the devil's work,' he said. 'This is a signal for us to read right. Our work is blessed, like with like.'

Challis opened the door. 'I would see this burning for myself.'

\#

The fire had spread to half a dozen properties on the west side of Pudding Lane. That half of the Lane was well alight, and Tom and the others had retreated as far as the top of the street and the junction with Eastcheap.

It was moving methodically, with purpose. Wind and burning thatch was the main culprit at first, sending bright flickers of flame into the sky embedded in hot gusts of smoke. But the wind was too strong to allow the smoke and fire to rise harmlessly; instead it made the smoke skim rooftops until the sparks found purchase. From the top of the street you could see this clearly; the still-burning gap where the bakery had stood until minutes ago, then fresh conflagrations where the fire had taken hold.

People had come round from Fish Street to watch and wonder. One, who Tom recognised as the landlord of the Star Inn on Fish Street, was panicking, pacing and muttering about his outbuildings backing onto the Lane, and who'd pay if there was damage to his sheds or his coopering workshop.

Tom took in only the gist of the oaths around him. He wanted the claw back in his hand. He wanted it melded to his hand, adhered there in solid gore. He wanted it there until he got his answers, his revenge.

His father, still arguing with anyone who'd come near, repelling them with curses when someone tried to suggest he'd been responsible. Tom knew the attitude. He'd seen it a thousand times, the use of force of mouth and bared teeth to scare off would-be aggressors. Putting on a show like a cornered dog.

That was his father, nothing more than a threatened cur. Snarling and growling because he knew he was caught and didn't have the brute strength, the guile or skill to fight his way out.

Dogs didn't seem so threatening now.

He was nothing. Maybe he'd killed Alice in his panic or cowardice in the fire. Maybe he hadn't. There was no way of proving either way.

But he was defensive about something, and Tom knew that it wasn't the fire.

Even if drunk he wouldn't have started a fresh fire or left a lantern unattended. It was ritual with the man.

The anger that would have followed an unwarranted accusation was a purer thing, something distinct from the pink-faced, neck-tensed, shoulders-braced presentation here. If confronted with a baseless charge, he was a mix of calm and smug. He was at ease with the allegation and would take calm delight in watching his accuser squirm when presented with counter-evidence, or asking to present some substance to back up the intimation. But he was tense nevertheless. He was beset with trouble that threatened him. And he had not looked Tom in the eye for some time.

It could only be Alice.

Daniel sat on Farriner's lock-box as though acting as its new security, his head bowed, both hands joined under his chin. Perhaps he was realising, as Tom was, that they had no home. He seemed to be at prayer.

Sitting around was pointless, but there was nothing else to do. No-one seemed interested in fighting the fire unless it directly threatened their own livelihoods, and then their thoughts had soon enough turned to salvage. No-one wanted to be like the baker and his sons, cast into the night with nothing but the clothes they wore and what they'd carried out.

Taff stood, arm around his wife, a crate with random possessions bundled in beside her.

Tom had nothing. Maybe Daniel had his purse and his Bible. Their father had his precious chest.

'Stand up,' Tom said. Daniel didn't respond. Tom kicked him on the shin. 'Get up.'

'Huh?' Daniel made no move.

'I want to check.'

'What for.' His brother's voice was without inflection.

'Just move.'

Daniel got up. There was a clattering behind them, good shoes and metal on cobbles. Something being set down. A sedan chair.

The chairs had been in use in London for years, but only the richest, laziest, or those most affected by gout used them. True, they were quicker than coaches, being relatively slim and nimble despite the corpulence of the best-dined passenger, but they were expensive to hire and an easy target for shit-lobbing urchins. One here at this time of night was not good news.

Tom used the arrival as pretext to drag the chest across to one side. There was a kerfuffle around him as the chair opened up and some fat toff got out, all walking stick and harrumphing. He was attended by a couple of flunkies; Tom wasn't sure if they were the ones who'd chaired him across town or if they'd trotted along in his wake.

They bundled past and made their way downhill. This arrival caused consternation; Farriner quietened up and followed them.

A moment's relative peace.

The fire was both close and livid enough to make a lantern or candle unnecessary. Tom wanted to see what was so precious in his father's chest.

Some clothes, the good ones, some rolled up documents bound with a long ribbon, wrapped around the scrolled-up papers several times, the business's current ledger. A purse, thick with new gold coins. A second purse, more modest in contents. A pistol, a knife, and at the bottom, folded, the standard.

That was it. And what else would he have expected to find in there? Perhaps there was something in the papers, but these would be deeds to their property, agreements to service the navy requisitions. If the coin was precious above all things, why not just snatch that from the top of the casket? The pistol looked ordinary enough, but Tom knew little of such devices, not enough even to tell if it were loaded or not. He assumed not.

It had to be the standard. It was at the bottom of the chest after all, and might have been mistaken for lining or padding, some old bit of cloth used to cushion valuables.

But it was not. This was what Farriner valued above all; a rag. Enough to risk his life by not fleeing without it. Enough, when pressed for time by oncoming flames to the extent that he dared not simply unlock and extract the standard, but he'd taken the whole chest and damn the repercussions. Even if those consequences meant he couldn't help the woman he bedded.

Tom took the standard out from the chest. He untied the ribbon from the documents and made a roll of the standard, tying it off with the ribbon. There was plenty left, so he made a sash with it, so he could carry the rolled-up cloth like a satchel. This he looped over his head.

Daniel had been beside him throughout. He was without expression. His lips were moving, but no sound issued. Tom assumed it to be prayer.

Prayer?

That could wait.

#

Challis led the others back across the bridge. Hubert had by now ceased his gabbling, but was alive with pride at the mischief he'd claimed to have caused.

That was one thing, and it was an unexpected benefit, but Challis had to be sure of something else. He needed to know that the bakery lad was dead. Providence sometimes needed assistance.

That, after all, was his function. He was neither an incendiarist nor a deviser of contraptions. Being not unknown in intelligence circles, he could not, except through an intermediary, risk alarm by the purchase of armaments nor the leasing of property. He was no base close quarter murderer, though he'd done more than his share of blade-work, and poison was beneath him.

If Challis had a specialism, it was in organisation. And if he had an allied specialism within that, it was in execution. In as many senses of the word that Challis could summon, medicated though he was.

Hence the renewed interest in the lad. Challis was too old, too scarred, too experienced and too justified to distrust anything than utter surety that no paths led back to him. Aught else was folly.

The fire was a good enough ruse. But fire is an unpredictable beast, and unwieldy for plain murder. Yet sometimes the direct method was not politic, or would cause undue angst. So fire in the first instance was useful, both as a check on Hubert and Piedlow's professional abilities, and as a diversionary tactic. And besides, accidents happened in and after fires. A man might easily get killed; in rescue, in running away through fright or guilt or in seizing the opportunity for larceny. Quarrels were not unknown, blame and counter-blame leading to blows and butchery. Panicked city streets were loci for summary justice.

And if the loss of home, work and loved ones were not enough to fill a man's mind, that gap would be expanded with questions. Questions might lead to answers, or at least good guesses.

So, in the first instance, had the lad perished? And in the second, if not, then what?

A lead ball in Tom's head might be the better for all concerned. Quick and painless for the lad, efficient and irrevocable for Challis.

They were passing the water wheels when Challis saw the fire. In truth, he wondered that he did not see it sooner, though he knew that the elixir, in modest doses, led one to introspection and contemplation of matters of the soul rather than concrete observance of surrounding physicality.

The elixir's wonderment was turned on its head, taking its odd effects into the world. But for his companions' reactions, Challis might have doubted his vision, assuming that he was seeing images that had no correlation to the actual city. Was it not Plato who talked of worlds beyond worlds, of the world of forms beyond that which mortal man could determine? Such was that sight.

The street rose, so that rows of houses, shops, guild halls, churches were staggered up the incline. Rows cut across left to right, following the road patterns, bisecting those streets which pointed away from the Thames. One of those streets was lit from within, low-hanging clouds of what could only be fire-lit smoke marking the area that they'd been to earlier that evening.

This was no single structure on fire. The whole street must have gone up.

And there was more. The fire was spreading, and it was easy at this distance to see how. The wind had picked up in the night. Already there were shadows of people standing further up Fish Street, and those shadows were not being cast by nothing.

Hubert and Piedlow were struck likewise, stood in the middle of the road, arms crossed, dumb.

Challis beckoned them over. 'Do not speak when we come close,' he said.

'Why not?'

Piedlow struck Hubert, a hand flicking out from his chest. 'Your accent will betray you, as might mine.'

Challis led the way.

At the sign of the Star Inn on Fish Street, he stopped. The inn was alight at the back of the premises, and there was much confusion and panic from within. There was little attempt being made to stop the burning, though. Instead, the frenzied activity was concerned with salvage. A horse and cart had been procured, and was now being loaded, partly with household goods, partly with barrels, presumably of the better stock. A haphazard selection was being taken through from the front of the tavern; chairs, rolled hangings, bundles of clothes, papers, a viol. There were children and women huddled in awe of the flames. Menfolk were running and hollering, or grim-faced and silent. Some were praying, out loud and with curses interrupting the flow. From somewhere, an old woman had been carried out and been dumped like a sack of peas. She had pissed herself, either from her natural incontinence or in fear.

If nothing was done, the island of buildings from Pudding Lane to Fish Street would be lost. One man had a fire hook in his hand, but was being held back by another. They were arguing about pulling down a house, but neither could decide if the certain risk of damage by hook-work was worth the risk of possible damage by the oncoming fire.

This indecision would cost property and lives, and Challis was both glad of it. They would boggle their heads while around them their world was consumed. This was their red right punishment.

'What caused this?' he asked of a woman, naked and barefoot under a man's overcoat.

'They say it's the Dutch, come to destroy the city in revenge.'

'Who says?'

The woman looked at him in puzzlement, as though Challis was new to town. 'They do. Everyone.' She cast one arm around by way of wide-sweeping indication, the other keeping her garments closed in a grip to her neck. 'Started in the King's baker's in Pudding Lane. And who would tend a fire better than a baker? Who would know to watch his embers? This is popish work, sir. The brimstone stink of foreigners is all over it. Why, sir, even the mayor's been roused from his chamber to oversee the fire and to make his arrangements. Too late for this side of the street, it's feared.' There was little emotion in the way she communicated her words. Challis concluded that she was here for the show, and was already tiring of it, there being little in the way of carnage for her other than the slow procession of the burning. Maybe she'd been expecting it, and was receiving her confirmation with resignation.

He pushed past her and the cart, now fully almost laden. A boy was blinkering the horse, which had become jittery. He was trying to calm it as he worked the beast, whispering and stroking. Behind the cart, another argument, this time between a huge bald carter and someone else; Challis assumed it was whoever'd rented the contraption. Danger meant extra was the gist of the conversation. The usual rates didn't apply, and there was no point in calling on past business dealings because it seemed like he wouldn't have any more business to call upon in future.

Challis passed a set-aside sedan chair at the Eastcheap cut-through. Here were clusters of men, partly debating the fire, partly hanging on to the word of some stuffed shirt in the centre of a ring of people. More shouting, threats, pleadings. Some wanted buildings to be torn down to make a firebreak; others said this was unnecessary, that the fire would burn itself soon enough when the wind dropped, and there was no sense in destroying property for the sake of it. In the centre, the bewigged fellow, all fancy garments despite his unshaven face and need for a stick to stand aright, as much for being the worse for drink as for a gouty foot, was growing agitated; suffering the prattling of tradesmen for the sake of good order, but not for much longer, if the quivering hand on the pommel of his stick spoke true.

There was no sign of the lad. His brother, the preacher, was there, sat hunched on a box. Perhaps he was considering his earlier words.

Folk darted here and there, bundles and casks, boxes and clothes in hands. The west side of the lane was burning; each house was either full alight or showed some evidence of the flames. One or two on the east side had been caught too. Before long, whole houses would collapse under the burning, and the fire would fully cross the road-gap.

There was red and there was pink. Crimsons, scarlets, rubies. Burgundies, clarets and sherries. Cherry and apple-reds. Cerises and carmines, cinnamons and blood. Then there were the oranges; auburn and chestnut, sand and ginger. Yellows and golds, blondes and butters, bright and shine, glitter and polish all of it.

The fire had all of these and more. A hundred rainbows could be constructed of the shades on display here and he would have the words for none of them. There was work being done here, and not the work of some moonstruck arsonist, however talented he might be.

This was something else. This was other. And Challis was humbled to have been privy to the insight.

He needed to talk with Hubert and Piedlow. And he thought that they might not like what he was going to suggest.

There was the question also of the lad. But his world entire was being consumed about him. If he yet lived, as his brother did, then he would be surely distracted; Challis would not rate consideration.

No. That was a fool talking. The kind of devilry that would see you in the Tower and then dancing at Tyburn for the crowds.

But why go searching? If Tom Farriner had survived, and had the wit that Challis felt he possessed, then he'd go searching for answers that would only be certain if they were experienced first-hand.

Challis walked to the still-crouched preacher, coming from behind. A cautious hand went between his coat buttons, but this was more the habit of years than at any present anticipated threat.

Onto his haunches, then, and words whispered into the brother's ear. 'What caused this?'

'Man's folly.'

Challis kept his silence.

'My pride, my folly,' Daniel continued. Did I not preach of this? Have I not called down the angel? Uriel's mighty wings beat, giving sustenance to the fire. His wrath is around us and all for my vain words, shouting out my sermon of devastation, promising the end of times and for what? I have brought the pale fire to the city. My sermon was my invitation and I have been answered with the call of woeful guests.'

'You have lost family in this?'

Daniel stuttered a little before answering. 'A serving girl, beloved of the-' his voice broke, then re-asserted itself: '-family.' And then he was lost to silent tears, his shoulders rocking as he coughed up his grief.

His self-pity.

His vanity.

Challis spoke. 'Then perhaps you are in some dark manner blessed not to have suffered further loss. If family remains, then surely hope survives.'

'And what hope is there for Tom and I, or our father?' There was more in that vein, but Challis was already backing away, and let the words dwindle into the hoarse rush of fire-sounds.

Passing the cluster of still-arguing worthies, Challis saw the centre of this group's attention raise his arm. He was summoning his chair-porters. He'd had enough.

'And who will pay for pulled houses to be built anew? You? You?' This man stabbed around, poking one fellow in the jowl. 'No, this will run its course and be over and done with by morning.' He backed back out of the circle and made to turn.

Challis caught him at the elbow and muttered quick words to him before stepping out of the way.

'Indeed, sir,' the man was bellowing, 'some sense at last.' The others were still remonstrating with him as he got to his chair. He got in and stuck his head out of the window. 'Enough!' he exclaimed. 'A woman could piss this out!' With that he rapped hard, metal-pommelled stick on wood, and the chair was righted around, presumably to go back the way it had come.

Back to Fish Street, where the Star Inn was well alight. A chain of men had formed, passing buckets back and forth to as near to the fire as they dared; water sizzled and steamed on contact with each throw, causing the closest men to back off before advancing again with caution. Sometimes the thrown water had the opposite effect to that intended; forcing more sparks into the sky.

Something crashed, a further house collapsing on Pudding Lane. There was a series of deep rumbles, and then a great spurt of flame struck into the air over the top of the Fish Street rooftops. A shop three doors from the Star rocked. The falling walls must have hit it hard. A second arc of flame crested the roof, as though fanned by a mighty bellows. It rose like fountain water before falling into the street and onto the roofs on both sides of the road. Where it landed, a bright fire-trail lay.

People ducked for shelter and stamped out the fragments of fire that had fallen on the cobblestones. But that was not the danger. Challis looked up and could see where the fire had landed on the rooftops. This side, then the other. Some had found thatch; some had fallen on clinker tiles weatherproofed with tar. And they were burning.

Challis gestured to Piedlow, who grabbed Hubert. He motioned for them to follow, taking care to keep under overhanging eaves where possible lest more flame jump out and strike. The heat was great; passing the Star it was as though walls of hot air were being pushed out to crush him. There was fire fighting going on, but he could see there was little point in it. Others had done as their compatriots in the street over had already done, and were salvaging what they thought prudent to do. The cart had long gone, and there was at least one householder crying out for transport.

Challis held up his hand to pause where Fish Street crossed Thames Street.

'Look,' he said. 'Look.'

There were dozens of properties aflame. A red cloud hung over these streets, growing as it was blown to the west and fed by the blaze underneath. 'Now,' Challis said, 'do you smell it?'

The others nodded. The air was thick and hot to the nose-hairs, even at this distance. And such scents were flowing; wood-smoke and straw, thatch and hay, roofing and fodder for animals. But also oil and tar, pitch and grease.

'The docks are full of it,' Piedlow said. 'Wood and spice, caulk and brandy. And all of it will house the flames.'

'It will do more than house them. It will feed them and give strength. It will spread them further, through the grace of God and through their own selfishnesses. This fire will punch a hole in the city.'

'And then we will blow the bridge and cut its throat,' Piedlow said.

Challis didn't add anything. That could wait. Instead, he gave his back to the fire, and returned along the roadway to the bridge.

He wondered if he was right about Tom. His hands glided over the pistol handles inside his coat. It was time to find out.

#

Tom got to Challis's house on the bridge to find it empty. It was hard to see inside. Tom hadn't brought any light with him. The lanterns left after closing above shop premises had long since exhausted their fuel.

Tom's heart pounded, his arms and legs tingling with a mix of anger and grief, exhilaration and curiosity. Hubert had been there by the fire. Tom had seen him, as plain as he was standing on this bridge now. There could be no other reason for him being in Pudding Lane; he'd been the one that had started the fire.

The consequences of that made Tom sick. His mouth filled. Tom coughed and gasped, but succeeded only in expelling a thin trail of acid drool.

His father might yet have been responsible for Alice's death, but that seemed less likely if he hadn't been the cause of the fire in the first instance. Farriner would have had nothing to hide, thus no reason for killing Alice, if he had not set or, more likely, failed to douse a fire which had got out of control.

And would Alice have had any cause to die, no matter what might have occurred between her and Farriner if there'd been no initial fire?

There was still the chance that Farriner had been seized with a fatal choice: rescue his precious standard or his woman, and that he had selected the former.

But that didn't explain Alice's wounds. She'd taken blows to the head. From the Claw. Farriner would have used his fists.

That just left Daniel.

This would have to wait. Would have to.

Tom refocused. One matter at a time. First the fire, then Alice. If he lived through this he'd deal with his brother.

If Hubert had caused the fire, then why? Did this make the stories true, that foreigners stalked London streets with popish mischief in their hearts? The like of Guido Fawkes? Was this one lunatic's work or an element in some greater design? Was Hubert a spy sent from the continent?

And Piedlow and Challis? What was their part in this?

The rush of questions dazzled Tom. He had no evidence he could present, no confession, no plans. And such evidence might not exist.

But Tom had to know. For Alice's sake, for Lizzie's - and how long it seemed since she'd been killed, yet it was less than three days ago - and for his own sake. He had to determine the truth. That meant finding a way into Challis's house and uncovering something.

A vacant house has a different feeling to a house where the occupants are sleeping or simply out of earshot to the knock. This place had that empty feeling. There was no-one in.

He could determine through the dusty window-glass that the house was full of goods. Barrels, those he'd seen delivered – and was that really only less than a day before? – were stacked up to the walls, covering the better part of the window-panes. There was a doorway through to a room behind, and some items on the floor there; discarded clothing, knives and bread, a box. Even with straining, and with the palest light coming through from the rear of the house, that was all he could see.

So people had been here, and had eaten here, but were not here now. If they'd taken lodgings, then they'd have taken their supper there.

Challis's accommodation had burned down. The White Hart was lost alongside their bake-house.

They were abroad in the city.

So perhaps they were involved in some way.

Tom knew he would have to get in. But then what? He had no idea.

The first question was how. How to get into a locked house? The door and windows to the front were locked, and there were no windows open above. Forcing an entry would mean noise, perhaps a hue-and-cry and would certainly leave evidence.

But if the house was empty now, then this might be the only opportunity he'd have to gain access. If they were about mischievous errands, then they could be back at any time. And they would think less than kindly to someone prying.

It had to be now.

There was a gap a couple of houses along which gave access to the river. It was barely wide enough to squeeze down and it was rank. Tom trod careful, because there was likely as not rotting filth in the blackness among the shit, loose timbers under his feet and nothing at the edge, no guard rail or walling, just a rectangle of blue-grey murk standing upright between the grey-black tightness to each side of him.

At the edge, he paused. He stood thirty feet? more? – above one of the stone feet supporting the bridge and around it, the wide wooden starling protecting it from the constant river.

There was no point thinking about it.

Tom jumped. He hit the starling dead on, right in the middle of the wooden platform. Timbers cracked as he landed and rolled over. He laid there, the Thames water a bedlam in his ears.

He lay there long enough to understand that half of what he heard was his blood pumping around his head.

He was fine. Tom got up and made his way over to where wood met stone. Climbing was easy enough, the rough-shaped stonework giving plenty of choice for hand- and foot-holds, but he was tired. Each fresh grasp made his fingers ache. He scuffed his right hand and the wound, which had scabbed over, began to trickle again.

In a strange way, that helped. Tom focused on the pain from his hand. Left hand, right foot, then hold. Right hand, quick, then left foot up again and hold. And breathe.

He was up to the buttressing woodwork under the houses. The buildings jettied out twelve, fourteen feet as owners had extended their properties one of the two ways they could. If not up, then out. And each was supported by complicated-feeling trusses and bracketing, oddly like the underside of a church roof. Tom got inside and was able to perch himself between two such roof-beams.

He sat there, gathering strength, letting his legs swing. He reckoned he was under the house next to Challis's. He could walk along the timbers, keeping his head low to avoid the flooring above, and he'd be there in no time.

The wood was crumbly with dry rot, caked bird crap and, as he'd hoped, human excrement too. Tom put another hand out, and almost lost his grip and pitched forwards before righting himself. He'd put his hand in an old birds' nest, a crumbling mass of twig and downy chick feathers. There was nothing resting there. And then he was under what he guessed to be the house that Challis was using.

Now he had to feel anew. It was too dark under here to see anything subtle with any confidence. Tom's free hand, the right, ran along the woodwork above. It took some time before he was certain. But there it was. His fingers traced the shape, two feet by two feet square.

If you had a house on the bridge, you didn't chuck your waste into the street, and you had no cess-pit. You used the river. Tom had counted on there being some trapdoor or hatch which would be used to empty kitchen leavings, brimming chamber-pots and the like out from. And here it was.

Tom braced himself against the wooden beams underneath and, with care, brought both hands up to opposite corners of the hatch. He pushed. Nothing happened.

There wasn't the slight give-and-then-metal resistance that would have indicated that the trapdoor was bolted or otherwise locked from above. No, there was no movement at all. Tom tried again, putting what muscle force he could into the shove, but nothing. Something hefty had to be sat on it.

He would have to find another way in. And that would mean climbing some more.

He didn't know how far he'd be able to climb. Once already he'd felt the dryness in the mouth that told him that his body was craving sleep. His arms and legs were still tingling from the exertions of the last hour or so, and his fingers were strained from supporting his weight. He was losing the stringiness of youth, he knew. He'd had to get new clothes recently; he was filling out, broadening across the chest. He was getting heavier.

Tom blew on the wound in the middle of his hand. The cool breath was the smallest comfort.

The supporting beams under the flooring extended about a foot beyond the point where the floor met the outside wall. That would have to be enough. Tom moved fast; there was no other option now.

Below him, the water. He was beyond the wide reach of the starling here. If he fell and was lucky, he might twist and catch some area of the stone arch or its wider supports and have a quick death through impact. Otherwise, he would surely hit the water and drown. The river would carry him under the bridge and he'd wash up somewhere on the far side of the Tower, else on the Southwark foreshore, just another body for stripping by the scavengers.

That wasn't going to happen. Not tonight. He'd been through too much to be stopped by something as ordinary as falling.

Tom edged out along one of the rising beams as far as he could. It narrowed to where it was jointed to horizontal supports and that in turn to vertical joists forming part of the building structure above.

He felt around the corner. There was a lip, not much, just a couple of inches, but enough.

He flexed his right hand slow. It felt full, as though his hand was nothing but a gelid blister from wrist to nails.

He cupped his hand anyway, half-forming the shape he needed before he shifted his body. And then he moved.

Hands up onto the thin ledge. A pressing for fresh purchase there in the grime. Then up; legs pushing off the struts below him, right leg swinging up to meet the jutting joist – yes! – and then pushing again off this, keeping hands tight to the lip until there was somewhere better to reposition them.

A window. A simple casement, centre-opening, leaded glass in diamond patterns. Tom caught the sill with one hand, then the other.

He waited, not daring to breathe too deeply lest his expanding chest push him back off the wall into the water. Cold glass on his face, moistening with his now-hot breath.

Careful as he could, he made for his knife. There was nothing to the window mechanism; a simple lever operating a catch. Tom couldn't tell from the hinges if the window would open in or out. He begged for inward opening.

He snicked the blade down the middle of the window. Would anyone think to fit an elaborate lock to a water-facing casement?

Tom flicked the blade and the lever on the other side of the glass looped around. The two halves swung blessedly in. He braced himself against the upright sides, hoisted himself inside and sat, gasping, on the floor.

Eventually he got up and closed the window. He kept his eyes closed as he did this, not wanting glitter off the water to disturb the way his adjustment to the dark. The house was silent save for distant lapping, the creaking of wood and nails against wind, dust settling.

He dared not risk a lantern, though there were two on the floor among the meal leavings. Christ, but he was hungry. There was a bag with some untouched cheese still wrapped in muslin. Tom decided to risk it.

As he unwrapped and started to chew, Tom took in the rest of the room. Barrels stacked floor to as close to the ceiling as could be on the front side of the room. Those barrels left over were stacked up against them, forming a secondary wall. There was passage through to the front door, and window-spaces had been left somewhat unblocked, but the rest was filled with casks. The heavy smell of coffee clouded all around. Tom paced out, figuring where the trap door ought to lie.

And there it was, weighed down by another of the barrels.

Some other articles lay about; bags with clothes or some such, he assumed. Tom left them and crept up the stairs.

The first floor was as the ground, rooms to the front of the building filled with coffee casks. Tom continued up to the second floor. Confident now, he made up the stairs two at a time. They could return at any moment; he had to be quick.

At first, the second floor seemed as the two below. The rooms to the rear, smaller and cramped with low pitched roofing, were empty. The first one he tried to the front was stacked with more barrels. One room to check, and Tom expected to find more of the similar arrangement.

He unlatched the door and went in.

It was as though Tom had been punched hard in the gut.

A man. Staring right back at him.

Tom did not move, and neither did the man. It was impossible that he could not have heard Tom or could not make him out.

Tom held his breath, and so, it seemed, did the man. And then the truth of it came upon Tom and he did not know if he ought to be relieved or further disturbed.

He was dead. Propped up, as though sitting on a cask. And then Tom could smell death on him, cutting through the sweeter tones of the coffee. Blood and puke, harsh notes which confirmed his end. There was staining to his front; he'd been stabbed or perhaps slashed across the face and under the chins. There was piss and shit-stink too. The man had voided at the last, crapping himself as he bled out.

He'd been well-to-do, judging by his shoes and the wig on the floor nearby. A merchant, perhaps the man who owned this building. Tom touched him on the hand. He was cold and waxy, like a long-snuffed candle. There was stiffness in his muscles still. He'd been dead some hours but less than two days.

Tom had learned that from the house-cleaners after the plague. Different teams had different habits. Some liked to move them after the stiffness had gone and the rotting set in; soft was easier to shift. Some liked to move while the rigor, as they called it, was yet upon them. A common idea was that the contagion could be communicated by the breath trapped inside a dead man's body. You moved them while hard, there was less chance they'd fold and gasp their foul last lungs-full on you.

So there was murder here. But what did this have, if anything, to do with the fire? And what connection was there, if any, to Alice's death? To Lizzie's?

Tom patted at the man's garments, thinking there might be some clue. But there was nothing save a little money, which Tom took, and a wadded silk handkerchief, which he left.

Of course there was nothing important there. If there had been, then the murderer would have taken them.

Tom turned to the casks. Nobody killed anyone over coffee, surely? He knew it was valuable as a commodity and a stylish substance to be trading in, but even so. He tried one of the casks; it was shut up tight, ends sealed. He'd need either to break in or lever the caulked lid somehow.

Tom pressed around, hoping to find a cracked panel, but there was nothing. The barrels were done up tight. He would have to break one open.

Again he checked himself, listening to make sure he was alone apart from the corpse.

The simplest way seemed to be best. Tom got on his knees and slid the knife-blade in between two slats about halfway up the barrel, and began working the metal back and forth. It didn't take long. Four or five movements and there was a splintering of wood, clear and loud in the room. A couple more twists and the end of a panel broke out, releasing a stream of black grains. So that was it, coffee? But there was no additional coffee smell.

Tom put his hand to the powder, which continued to flow from the punctured barrel. It left a black stain on his fingertips; there was charcoal in it. And the sulphurous smell which came off the stuff. This was gunpowder.

The house was full of the stuff. Three dozen barrels, perhaps more. Enough to do what?

And then Tom had it.

That must be their design, Tom thought. To blow the bridge and with it London's only road connection to Southwark. This was like Catesby, Fawkes and the others, the Catholic traitors from before Cromwell's time. This was treason and spycraft, the work of foreigners. Of Dutchmen retaliating after their summer defeats.

Tom went back to the body and lifted the handkerchief from the man's pocket. It was stuck together with snuff-crusted snot. Tom peeled it open and poured a handful of the black powder into it, then tied the parcel off. He stuffed this deep into the wrapped-up standard he still had strung around him.

Challis had used him, in some small way, to secure elements of this plan, if only by guiding him to the docks. His payment for this was the fire which Hubert had started, which must have been set to kill him and Daniel off; removing evidence of anyone who'd come across odd-acting strangers with barrels being offloaded. Doubtless the stabbed fellow behind him had been part of this too and had paid the price for his knowledge or assistance.

Challis and Hubert were responsible for Alice's death. They had murdered her, as sure as if they had walked up and gutted her in the street like a pair of common footpads.

Tom's path was now clear. He had to stop them. He had to find them and stop them and ensure that they hanged.

The only question was how.

Tom tilted the barrel onto one edge and rolled it round so that the burst side would butt up to the wall. He shovelled as much of the powder as he could out of sight behind other barrels. He coughed as he did this; it was acrid stuff, almost as bad as breathing in fire-smoke.

Christ, but it stung as well, the grains finding their way into Tom's battered hand. He bit the side of his mouth, fighting the urge to moan out load.

Done, and he swept away what he couldn't scoop up with his good hand, hoping it would scatter or settle into the board-cracks. That would have to suffice. As best he could, he had made the room look undisturbed.

The powder was the evidence. The standard was the key. That, used with the Farriner name, would give him credibility. With the Navy Office first, and if he was not heard there, then with someone at the Tower. Farriner's precious cloth would finally have some use.

Tom was closing the door behind him so that the room would be as he had found it when there were sounds from below.

Unlocking, chatter.

Eyes shut, Tom could picture their movements in the cramped ground floor rooms. Two men talking and a third who was silent.

Shit. Challis and the others must have returned.

Tom's thumb was still on the latch mechanism, the bar half-lifted. It would make a sound no matter what he did. He dared not breathe.

Voices again, still indistinct.

Tom could not remember if he had shut the window behind him when he had broken in. He must have done. He must have done.

Neither hue nor cry. No suspicion that their enterprise had been intercepted. Scuffling and shuffling from below, the sound of boots being prised off, and at one point a little crack of laughter that was just as quick stopped again. Then there was quiet.

And then another sound he could not mistake. That of footsteps on stairs coming upwards.

That was the noise that made Tom need to pass water. The sensation under his belly: bloated pressure from inside.

Ten, eleven, twelve steps up. Then the footsteps stopped.

Tom figured that must have been to the first-floor landing. Someone had left the others, to give them space or to find himself privacy. Sounds again; heavy items being laid down with a careful hand, more boots being wriggled off and then something softer, perhaps a coat being wadded to act as a headrest, being plumped up for comfort's sake.

There was someone bedding himself down on the floor below. Tom, as careful as he'd been about anything in his life, let the latch bar down, with him on the wrong side of the door.

#

Piedlow and Hubert had done nothing but jabber in Hubert's mixed-up language, flitting across tongues to find the handiest word to summon up their inanities. Challis had been content to let them carry on, buzzing annoyance though the sound of them was.

It gave him time to think. No, more than that. It gave him time to imagine. He knew that there was still some of the drug in him, and so that he would have to discount some of his ruminations come the sunrise, but the fire had provoked such possibilities. One of them was so beautiful he did not want it spoiled by exposure to undue scrutiny just yet.

There would be time enough for that come dawn on the Lord's Day.

They were back at the house on the bridge and he'd soon left them to bed themselves down among the barrels on the ground floor, twittering with excitement like children before a carnival.

There was none of the mix of riotous bluster and grim introspection that accompanied soldiers' camps on the eve of battle. Some men took their strength and solace in the words of Christ, some in the bottle and a whore, some in the promise of victory and plunder, booty and gain. Often as much there was a blend of all of these and others as well. The very young would have naïve hopes and the very real and understandable fear of the unknown. Old soldiers would exhibit resignation; that their fighting days could not last forever one way or another.

Those who carried wounds or nursed fears about their condition, their kit, their opponents' might or their own side's inadequacies tended to keep their counsel to themselves. They would busy themselves with checking their weapons, attending to their horse, or they might use prayer as a mask for solitude. Oftentimes there'd be a focus on the ordinary; little rituals like shaving, juggling or tossing a coin, and so seek to determine some insight into the future from the silver's fall.

Challis laid on the first-floor landing and made himself as comfortable as he could given the bare boards. He brought the vial back to his lips, taking in a little less than he had earlier. There could be little darkness left in the night but he wanted to sleep some. Doubtless the two below would rouse him with their blundering, but he did not want to have to rely upon that. He promised himself as he swallowed, the rich blessed liquid coating his throat, that tomorrow night he would lie in a bed again.

He held his breath, enjoying the sensation of the warmth from the tincture. He stoppered the bottle and shifted one of his pistols so that it lay well within reach. Then Rufus Challis surrendered himself to Christ once more.

#

Tom stayed still until he was as sure as he could be that everyone was asleep. Time's true passage eluded him.

Whoever it was on the first floor had not moved; Tom would have heard him.

That meant that if Tom shifted, he'd have the same chance of being detected.

What Tom did hear, though, was snoring. It was gentle; the way Daniel snored if he slept on his back and had taken too much ale.

Tom re-opened the door. His hand was still on the handle and was glad of the movement. At least the bleeding had ceased. The door swung open as far as Tom's arm would permit. It did not squeak. Then Tom took careful steps back into the room with the old man's body in. With each footfall he checked, but there was nothing below apart from snuffling and slumber.

He dared not risk going downstairs. He was stuck here until morning. And that surely was not many hours away. Tom did not know if that notion was pleasing or not.

Piss thumped inside him every time he took a step. It bulged against his skin demanding release. Tom closed himself in the room, the slumped corpse again his for company.

He would find a way out in the morning. He would rest till then, and maybe even sleep. Perhaps he could climb out somehow, or jump. There was a chance they'd go to church and he could sneak away. The dawn would bring inspiration.

And what of the fire, of Daniel and his father? He would find them too. He would get word to the authorities.

He'd get some justice for the women killed.

But he needed to piss. Tom could hold himself no longer. He considered voiding himself, letting his piss soak into his clothes and so pass water in silence. No. An alternative presented itself.

Tom got down onto his knees, grabbing the wig that had fallen off the body. The dead man had blood all over him, but there was no great spilling of blood on the floor hereabouts. He'd been killed elsewhere and the corpse brought up here. That gave Tom cheer; maybe it meant that this room was not to be disturbed. You didn't hide a body somewhere where you'd be working and living, even if it were only for a short time.

Keeping down and shifting careful, Tom got himself into the near corner. If someone came in, he wouldn't be in their line of sight, at least not at first.

Then he took himself in hand and, using the wig as wadding, let his piss out into the hair. It was near silent but oh the relief of it.

He was gasping when he was done, open–mouthed and empty. He left the wig where it lay, trusting that it would soak up his spoil. Then, using the rolled-up standard as head support, he lay down, curled himself up on one side, and did not have to pray for sleep to come.

#

Challis was troubled by his dreams. Ordinarily, he was rapt in the comfort they offered and in the visions they showed him. Such were the dreams he had at nightfall, with the spirit within him and the elixir guiding his thoughts to Christ. And if there were further dreams in the night, or in that uncomfortable half-hour before rising, when it was difficult to ascertain if one truly was with the living or with the dead, he did not remember them.

But this morning he was vexed by visions. Visions which did not clear until he had sat himself up and had reached for the reassurance of his closest flintlock. Only with the feel of the wooden stock, warm with the contrasting cold of the metal ornamental plates upon it, the scent of oil and powder, the reality of the weight of the weapon, did the trouble subside.

He knew it was the tincture's effect. But knowledge of the contents of a room in the dark does not make the room, unlit, less daunting to a child. So it was with Challis that morning. His mind was a patchwork of terrors; of fire's bite and brimstone breath, of screaming women and silent infants in their arms.

Challis bid the images fade. He mouthed the Lord's Prayer and the Nicene Creed. The truth in the words gave him clarity. He stood, free hand out for support at first, and murmured a commination against sinners.

Cursed is the man who putteth his trust in man, and taketh man for his defence, and in his heart goeth from the Lord. Cursed are the unmerciful, fornicators, and adulterers, covetous persons, idolaters, slanderers, drunkards, and extortioners. Cursed is he that taketh reward to slay the innocent.

O Lord, save thy servant, that put his trust in thee. Send unto him help from above, and evermore mightily defend him. Help me, O God our Saviour, and for the glory of thy Name deliver me; be merciful to this sinner, for thy Name's sake.

O Lord, hear my prayer.

And let my cry come unto thee.

Challis's hand was now steady. He did not shake. He was without pain in his thumb; neither did he feel hunger in his belly nor yet the malicious stirring in his bowels which often accompanied over-application of the elixir.

It was the morning of the Lord's Day, and Challis prayed that he'd be forgiven lack of strict observance for the greater praise of His name.

He laid down the firearm and shoed himself, and then clumped down the stairs, the better to wake his fellow travellers.

#

Tom knew he was awake because he was half-dreaming of piss. The room stank of it, sour-sweet and cloying, like an uncovered honey-jar, the contents exposed and congealing.

He lay there listening, ear to the oak boards. After giving time to discount both his breathing and his heartbeat, he could hear descending footsteps – the stirring of the sleeper on the landing below must have woken him.

The quality of the incoming light from the windows, so clear and orange, told him it was yet early. He had slept perhaps a couple of hours, and maybe less than that.

And then there was commotion, not a fight or an argument, but nevertheless a sense of great consternation and rapid movement underneath him. The front door below was being unlocked and then there was bustle out into the street.

Tom risked it and shifted across the room. And then, checking below and seeing not just the three that he'd been pursuing but many others also in the street, stood staring, he understood, following their gaze north by jamming his head tight against the window, why the dawn seemed so orange that day.

#

It was a miracle. There were no other words to describe it. The terrors he'd experienced before waking were simple premonitions, demons fleeing from other people's dreams. He had intercepted them because he was attuned. As one of His servants he was privy to such happenings. That was what Rufus Challis now understood. He was a focusing point, the way a lens might be used to ignite tinder. What he'd dreamed was the smoke from that burning.

The fears of the city. The realisation of the godless and venal, the earthbound and the corrupt, those that put their trust in a mortal leviathan or in committees of men rather in the temple everlasting. They that worshipped gold or trade or books or titties; and all of them craven upon their knees, if not now then right soon.

His dreams were their spoil, their shit-breeched panic, their hopeless tears and their selfish tardy protestations to the Almighty.

That was what he'd dreamed, what he'd been privy to. And Challis now knew not fear but exhilaration. And the idea that had been fermenting, like good wine he had not yet served, was about to be brought to table.

He wanted to get closer first, though. And then he would be sure.

People, slack-jawed in their fear, some wet-eyed and fearful, some angered and shouting, others yet dulled by incomprehension, had gathered around and behind him. Challis shoved his way past them and went back to the house, beckoning Piedlow and Hubert to follow.

At the door he could not resist another glance. At the city burning. At de Witt's divine revenge.

This was no ordinary fire.

This was so much better.

#

Tom didn't hear them re-enter the house; he was too struck by the little he could see from the small window. He wanted to see more. He needed to get down there.

Tom made it as far as the first-floor landing before he was betrayed. And not by something as prosaic as a loose board or a squeaking hinge. The row was incredible; a solid thumping, heavier the first time, then less so the second. The third one, though, was the biggest, a great crash that could only have been a stacked barrel toppling somehow off the cousin it had been piled upon, and breaking open on impact.

He didn't have time to think. Tom made for the nearest alcove, three, four steps to the right and stood praying that he was buried in the darkness.

#

Challis, who was behind the others, merely raised his head. That was instruction enough to the others. Piedlow took up the stairs at pace while Hubert cast into his bag and took out a nasty-looking awl that would double as a slim little stabbing weapon.

Challis drew one of his pistols and brought it straight to full-cock. What was the cause? He didn't have the patience to wait for Piedlow's report.

Piedlow had carried on to the top of the house. Challis went after him, his coat catching once on a nail as he swept up. A snag, a little rip somewhere behind him. Damn.

He found Piedlow, hands on knees, half-gasping for air, half-laughing. 'Nothing but your friend,' he said, indicating the mess that had sprawled over the bare boards. 'I think he's still sleeping.'

Indeed, Jephcott's corpse was curled, hands together, on one side. Doubtless the body had fallen – slipped? – from where it had been quickly and - in hindsight, with lack of care - stacked alongside a second, upper tier of casks. In dropping from its perch, the body had evidently slumped against the barrel it had been leaning on to the extent that it had tumbled down with the corpse. The coopering had split open, tiny dark gunpowder beads had disgorged over the clothing, the skin, on the floorboards. Too early for the rank wetness of decomposition, the place smelled of firewood and sulphur. The powder even clumped around Jephcott's wig, making it look even tickier than it had been during its wearer's sybaritic life.

'Drag it into the corner if you can, then leave it.' Challis checked around. 'Are these barrels staying here?'

'No.' Piedlow was already manhandling the meat, half-dragging, half-carrying the bulk across the room. 'As much is to be arranged in the ground floor rooms as can be done. The first floor materials can be left. There will not be the space for them, but these barrels should be with the others on the bridge level.'

'Then that's your task.'

Piedlow nodded, wiping his sleeve over his brow. He did not look well.

'Will that take long?'

Piedlow shook his head, strands of hair sticking to his scalp. 'I think not. To carry up, that needs strength. And skill, practice. Down is easy.' He mimed rolling.

'How long to accomplish this?'

'And to engineer the fuse?'

'This first, then the fuse.'

Piedlow sucked his teeth. Air whistled in the gaps. The kind of trick Challis might have expected of a barber-surgeon haggling for extra payment. 'With care, four hours. Less care, three. Another hour for testing the mechanism, and an hour for the fuse.'

'And you can manage this?'

A smile, somewhat rueful. 'This will be my life's work.'

Challis turned. 'Be quick, then, and wait on my word.' He went down the stairs fast, one hand on the wall as he went, the other rubbing his eyes. Keep him busy: that was key. Let him move his barrels, prime his fuses, worry about his part on the inside of the building.

But Challis needed to be out there. He needed to be closer to the flames.

Hubert was downstairs, crouched over an open hatch, attending to his morning motions. He must have shifted a barrel to get to it; the bottom of the stairwell was blocked off by one, necessitating Challis to squeeze between the cask and the squatting Frenchman. He wondered at the reason for siting a hatch in that position; then he saw that it made a kind of sense if occupants were emptying their chamber pots from above and their kitchen waste also.

He gave Hubert some privacy, wincing at the man's grunting and splattering.

He walked out into the street. Again, residents were standing around, discussing, pointing. Mischief seemed to be the belief of many, at least those who felt confident enough in their opinions to express them out loud.

'Catholics, and on the Sabbath too. Shouldn't they be crying to their virgin?'

'This is the Dutchman's work, mark you. Can't fight us at sea so they send their agents on land to burn us in our beds.'

'Bollocks, it's just a fire.'

'Just a fire? Do you see it, man? Do you see it?'

Indeed, it was scarcely credible that human agency could have wrought this. It had been burning for, what, six hours? Challis checked Jephcott's timepiece. It was not yet seven o'clock. He examined the device, finding its winding-point. A key-hole in the back plate. He did not have the key. Jephcott had not kept it hanging on the same chain as the watch. Perhaps it was still in one of his pockets. It would be a shame to lose its use. Inaccurate as they were,

245

Challis knowing such mechanisms lost or gained a quarter of an hour a day unless checked against something more authoritative, they had their uses. And it was a pretty enough bauble. He made a note to check the man for the key, or at least get Hubert to rig a dupe.

Hubert appeared at his side, struck immediately by the activity at the far end of the bridge. His face split open into an excited smirk.

'Stop that,' murmured Challis. 'And mind your tongue unless you've a fancy to being hanged in the street for this so soon.'

Hubert nodded. His hand was busy in his pocket.

'And leave that rosary alone.'

Challis weaved through those who lived on the bridge, who stood in the roadway and conjectured. Hubert tagged along behind like a submissive dog.

There was traffic, but it was one-way, north to south. Already some Londoners had abandoned their homes, carrying sacks, dragging children, pushing barrows laden with possessions, goods, valuables. Some were having a hard time getting through, being stopped and questioned at intervals by the curious or the desperate, eager for knowledge of loved ones, of the fire's spread, of rumours of its cause, of news about what was being done to arrest its progress.

The river was becoming spotted with loaded boats too; little skiffs, scarcely bigger than coracles, weighed dangerously low in the water with bags, boxes and families. One held a keyboard instrument, virginals or harpsichord – he had never been sure of the difference between the two – lashed with ropes and half-covered with sacking, its owner clinging to the precious box as the boat he stood in rocked under its ungainly cargo.

Having now cleared the central inhabited part of the bridge, and not yet reached the new houses and the water mill, Challis could take in the glorious vision in full.

Whole streets must have been alight. Sheets of red and orange described lines up, down and across. Not lines indicating the roads and alleys themselves, but the housing that bracketed them. Had once defined them. The fire had spread far in the few hours he'd rested; he guessed that four or five streets to the west of Pudding Lane were now affected, and perhaps one to the east. North-south was a trickier thing to estimate, partly because of the great wall of fire rising at least to the height of the dockside warehouses, and behind them, the north side of Thames Street was aflame, and the fire was reaching downhill - south - as well as to the west.

It was hard for Challis to understand the fire as anything other than a beast, a creature, a living thing with motivations, goals, desires. Intent. And what did it want, this creature which roared before Challis?

It wanted to burn. It wanted to purge. It wanted to blister the city, to scour it of its wickednesses and its sins, its idolatries and its licentiousness. It wanted to demonstrate to London, to England, to Charles and his papist brother and their statue-worshipping lackeys, lickspittles and grovellers that the true faith will not be denied. That London, which stood for all that was wrong in the world, had been judged and found wanting. That its denizens had not heeded the signs, had not opened their hearts to Christ's truth in the ways that the preacher-baker had oh so rightly been working towards; that fourfold was their punishment and that this was the final judgment. What water and air and earth had not revealed, let fire sweep clean. Let the blessed flames raze the city, bring it not to its knees, but prostrate on the ground in front of His altar.

Challis knew that this was his mission. That these events had conspired to wreak a majestic weirdness, a torment for the city much greater and more terrible than that which men could have devised.

He motioned for Hubert to stop.

'What is it?'

'Didn't I tell you not to speak?' Challis did not take his gaze from the fire. From the hot red smoke rising then shifting westward and to the river in one.

Silence. Good. 'Back to the house, and quick.'

#

Tom stood flat against the wall in the dark corner. He'd had to shift at least once, scared that he'd be found by someone coming down the stairs. He didn't need to think about what might happen if he were caught; the body in the top room was all the indication he needed.

Challis had gone, and he thought Hubert had gone with him. The third man was busy shifting casks around. He'd toppled one over and had rolled it down the stairwell, bringing it down step by step, using his weight to brace against the mass of the barrel. He'd rested on the first-floor landing, breathing heavy, leaning over the cask. Tom had been sure that he would have been found out then; but he was not.

The man, clearly unused to heavy lifting, was too focused on his work to pay attention to aught else. He cursed; a jibber-jabber of harsh foreign words, and then got back to it.

His labour resounded through the building, solid clumping down the stairs, a regular thumping like the beating of a massive drum.

There was no point in finding Daniel or anyone else now. Tom knew he had to act first, and then seek assistance after. That would mean racing back up to the top floor once more.

He waited until he was sure, by counting the thumps, that Piedlow was out of sight on the stairs, and then he spurred himself. Tom didn't care about making noise. Speed was the trick here, and his only danger was that Challis and Hubert were still within earshot and would respond to any cry for assistance.

Tom hastened down the stairwell to the first dog-leg. He did this quiet as he could. Then he turned, running up the stairs, stamping, and was almost to the top by the time he was sure that Piedlow had both heard and was after him. But the man wasn't running himself. 'Robert?' His accent was thick; the name spoken in the foreign manner. 'Etes-vous là? You there?'

Tom slammed the door shut. The latch rattled into place. He didn't have time to roll a cask behind it as a barricade. Besides, it would have been counter-productive for what he had in mind.

He readied himself, trusting to sound as he could not see well.

The door opened.

'Rob-'

The rest of the call was cut off. Tom, standing with the corpse propped in front of him, shoved the body at the open door-space.

Piedlow shrieked, the body knocking him back into the hallway. He was yabbering something, arms up in defence, when Tom hit him full-on. Tom caught him, both hands still out after pushing the cadaver forwards, square in the chest.

Piedlow's arms came up higher as he over-balanced. Tom doubted that he really saw who or what had hit him.

Piedlow staggered back, one step, then two, and went backwards down the stairs. His head hit the wall halfway down the stairwell, punching a hole in the plaster and exposing thin wood underneath. He bounced, landing at the bottom of the stairs in an unnatural pile of limbs.

One leg had broken, shinbone stabbing through his clothing. He was face down, a thick gash already bleeding through his hair where he'd hit the wall. The man groaned; still alive.

Tom went down to him, almost falling himself in his rush. He tugged the man over, exposing a ruined face. The nose was flattened. Blood masked his mouth. He coughed once, a mix of air and more blood bubbling out of him. Tom knew that sign; he'd broken at least one rib and a lung had been punctured by the bone. That would mean death for the man for certain.

Tom had worked out their plan for himself. He didn't need to ask about that. He got the man by the neck, throttling him with his good hand. 'Rufus Challis. Where is he?'

Piedlow gurgled. There was no focus in his eyes.

'Where is he? Did he start the fire?'

His lips moved, but nothing but more red froth came out.

Again. 'Answer me!' Tom squeezed harder, desperate to get something, anything, from this murderer before he was sent to Hell. 'Where is he?'

Tom squeezed again, forcing Piedlow's head against the wall. He banged it hard, and Piedlow's eyes rolled to white. Something gave:

there was a relaxing of tension under pressure. The bubbled spittle ceased flow.

Tom crouched over the dead man long enough to spit in his face. Now both of his hands hurt.

No longer working through his thoughts, but acting like an animal, on instinct rather than reason, Tom returned to the top room. There, he took the bundled standard and laid it out.

This precious rag.

He nicked the centre of the top of the standard and used the weak point to tear through the cloth. It was difficult, and now and again Tom had to saw through some of the more intricate embroidery. Then it was done.

Tom opened the window just enough to get his hand through the gap. He pushed one half of the standard through then re-closed the window, trapping some of the cloth between the frame and the underside of the windowpane. He made sure it was caught tight. It would not fall and would be hard to detect from inside unless one were searching for it specifically. Tom cut the excess off. He had a use for that.

He prayed that no-one would look up from outside. Unless they'd been instructed to.

Now to get out.

There was little point in trying to remove the casks. There was far too much gunpowder to try anything single-handed, such as pour it through the trapdoor into the river. He'd considered it when cowering in the shadows earlier, but that was a fool's task.

No, the best plan was to raise the alarm. But with the fire burning, surely all resources would be distracted. But then again, with the fire burning, the fire was where all the resources he needed would be.

Sure that he still had the handkerchief pouch he'd filled with gunpowder, Tom secured it inside the rest of the standard and strapped that on as before. Tom stepped over the wigless body splayed out at the top of the stairs, and went down.

Further down, and Tom strode over Piedlow's corpse without

pause. He had no private prayer for him.

At ground level, he paused, taking in the scene. There were bags, the ones they'd carried with them from the docks, and others.

The first one contained food; a pulled-apart loaf, cheese.

This he cast to one side. He busied himself with the other bags. Tools, various kinds of fire-making equipment; steels, flint, a small metal box that he presumed would contain tinder or some other easily-combustible substance.

The third bag stunned him. Tom lifted the contents out with care and set them in front of him. He had not seen the like before.

The object was like a clock, except not. There were things missing from it, a mechanism for striking the hour, for example; and where this element was gone something else stood in its place.

A flintlock mechanism, except one not connected to any other parts of a handgun. Its purpose seemed clear enough to Tom. This was conjoined to the timepiece, and thus the clock could be set. Instead of striking the hour, it would activate the flintlock, flash the powder in the frizzen-pan and ignite whatever fuse had been devised.

Tom held an image; this thing ticking to its ultimate. A fuse, perhaps nothing more sophisticated than a thick line of gunpowder. The hour would strike, but instead of a pleasant bell-sound, there would be the first of a series of ignitions. From spark to fuse, from fuse to barrels. And then the maelstrom.

The bridge would surely fall.

Tom opened the hatch. He bundled the - "flintclock" was the only word he had for it - back in the bag, then dropped that through the hole in the floor. The sack opened as it fell, exposing its contents. Then the sack hit the water. It sank straight away. Tom blinked and it was already gone. Little choppy waves clustered by the starling underneath.

The fuse mechanism machinery signalled to Tom that these rogues did not intend to be present when the conflagration erupted; he hoped the loss of their invention would be sufficient to thwart the plan.

But was it enough? And in any case, if the fire was as terrible as it seemed, what if it made its infernal progress along the bridge? The fire would do the job that these villains were now unable to do.

So the path was clear. The fire might well do the bridge great damage on its own account. If it was not challenged with success, this house would become consumed and the powder would detonate and with it the bridge.

Help would be in the city; there would be by now some element of organisation surely. The army would be mobilised, there would be soldiers at work pulling houses and creating firebreaks.

And in the middle of this would be Challis, taking in his pleasure in the destruction of the city.

Tom made to leave. And then the front door opened.

#

The round knocker-cum-handle turned without resistance. Challis could not remember if he had locked the front door or not.

There was increased activity on the bridge already. More were waking and being greeted by the shocking news that their city was alight.

He gave the street one last disparaging look and opened the door.

A rush of something at the trapdoor. Challis pulled his pistol, stepping in and closing the front door behind him in one move. He cocked and fired. No response. The room filled with smoky discharge from the weapon, rising as Challis ran through to the hatch. He'd blown a hole in the wood by the little recessed metal pull-ring.

He stuck his head into the space below. Nothing. Then he checked left, then right. And there he was, clambering in the support beams under the overhanging bridge structures.

So that was where Tom was.

He considered a second shot, and was already reaching over for the other piece holstered under his armpit, but decided against it. It was too difficult; the beams and cross-braces would make the shot a hopeful guess at best. There was no value in it. Besides, one gunshot might be explained away. Two was always more of a challenge.

Hubert was in and charging up the stairs, his little pig-sticker in hand. There would be nothing up there.

From above: 'Challis?'

Hubert was back soon enough, shaking his head.

Really? Piedlow was dead? Challis decided to take a look at this for himself.

Piedlow was crumpled in a pile at the bottom of a flight of stairs. His head was a mess and his neck had been crushed. Challis knew the signs; the bruises around the windpipe, the speckled pinpricks of blood circling the eyes. Whatever else had happened here, he'd been finished off by hand.

That was impressive. It was one thing to kill at a distance, quite another to do your work close-quarters. And to take a man in your fingers and choke life from him; that took determination.

'And this is a problem?' Hubert, now pragmatic.

'No.' And it wasn't. Challis recalculated. Tom had saved him a task, if not a reload.

'He will raise alarm, no?'

And what if he did? Who would believe the ravings of an urchin who'd lost everything in this fire? And who would take time to attend even if he did? Challis shook his head. 'Perhaps, but I think not.'

'Then it is time.'

'Quite so.'

Hubert stood there, as though he expected something more. A salute, a handshake, a brotherly embrace. Challis relented; it could do no harm. He shook the man's hand.

'You're a braver man than I, Robert.' And that was true.

'To die for what you believe in? That is not courage. Merely honesty.'

Well, every man was entitled to his opinion, and Challis was not going to gainsay this fellow's certainties.

'God go with you, then.'

'And you.' And with that, Hubert went.

Challis took the precaution of locking the door behind Hubert once he'd left. He lowered one of the barrels onto its side and sat down, enjoying the rocking motion as he pondered. He let his legs push-pull him back and forward gently as he reloaded.

He should leave. He'd been vague enough in his promises to the Dutch for them to have no doubt he was responsible for this act of destruction.

He would allow them to believe that the London fire was his design.

And Hubert should, assuming he carried through his second element of the greater design, both reinforce those points and underline to London, to Charles, to his retinue of whores and pimps, to all those who'd treated this country as little more than one great stew to fornicate in, that Europe was watching, and that both the earthly powers and those whose realm was everlasting and without bounds in glory, had passed their sentence on the upstart monarch and his papist gallants.

Yes, Challis reckoned that he should leave, and be glad at the job of work done.

But even so. Some little bastard of an apprentice, some half-man, had robbed him of making that decision for himself.

It would have been pleasing to have returned from ascertaining the spread of the fire and determining that the bridge's destruction would have been the greater disaster. That leaving the work undone was not merely unnecessary, but could even be counter-productive.

If the bridge went in the flames, so be it. That would be God's decision, and thus right and proper.

But to have Challis's decision wrested from him, to have his kill taken from him? That was less forgivable.

If he'd been the man to end Piedlow's life, letting him set his powder as he'd been commissioned to do and then done with him as being surplus to the new requirements, then his death would have been sanctioned by Christ. Piedlow's soul would be guaranteed entrance to heaven and there would have been no sin on his own back, as Challis would have acted as His fatal messenger.

But now? Piedlow would be weighed and judged along with the rest. The lad carried the sin of murder on him.

And someone had fucked with his plan.

Challis could not see how that could be forgiven by the most generous of men.

He checked the vial. There was some of the precious juice there, red and cloying in the bottom of the bottle, but he would need more soon. Perhaps there was a day's dose. Enough to sleep tonight, or enough to power himself through the next day as he'd done the last. He'd need more tomorrow, whichever route he decided to take.

After taking the time to roll the barrel he'd sat on over to the hatch that had served Hubert as a close-stool and Tom as an escape – and presumably an entry – route, he upended it, weighing the hole closed. No-one else would be clambering in.

He checked that he'd not left anything of use. No. He had his weapons, his paper cartridges, and his vial. That was sufficient.

He locked up behind him one last time, then, when he came across a gap between buildings, he tossed the key to the property into the smoke-and-blue sky between, and was satisfied that it had gone over into the water.

Then Challis strode against a growing human tide, panicked and screeching women, bawling infants and snuffling children, sullen men and their pathetic bundles of preciousness, marching himself all the while into the fire.

He was owed a kill.

#

When Tom clambered out onto the bridge, the first person he saw was Robert Hubert. But Hubert was already ahead of him, not searching him out, but walking steadily and with purpose towards St Magnus's church and the north side of the river. He did not pause to stare at the water wheels. He was not gawping, like so many others around him, some at once escaping the fire yet, head-over-shoulders, unable to draw their eyes from it. His head was straight. Any fool in him was gone.

Tom fought his way through one of the partitions erected where there were no houses. Such antics, which on any other day and particularly on any Sunday might rightly have caused questions, barracking, even worse besides, this day provoked nothing.

He could not see Challis behind. No sign of his distinctive black coat. That had to be a good sign. Tom thought Challis wouldn't attempt something so rash as to shoot at him in public, but he could not discount it entirely.

Another thought came. What if Challis was at work even now, priming the explosive powder for detonation? He did not seem to be a man who would willingly sacrifice himself for a greater cause. But then, he was no coffee-trader.

Tom trained himself on Hubert some thirty yards ahead. No point in worrying about something that you could not affect. Focus yourself on the matters which you can have an influence on.

Find Daniel. Even, yes, find his father. And find someone with men to command and men to spare. Someone who would listen.

Hubert was at Thames Street. He disappeared into a rush of men and fire. Tom couldn't figure out which way he'd gone, but gone he was.

Good. Pay attention to your own advice. Keep your mind and what abilities you have on the task before you. Nothing else matters.

'Tom!' He wheeled about at the shout, distant but distinct in a fragment of quiet, but could not determine where it came from. 'Tom!' again, and a little closer. Who was calling him?

Tom cast all around; at the crossroads at Fish Street Hill and Thames Street. He felt rather than heard that his name was being shouted again, but there was no way to be sure. Such noise! The fire had advanced as far as where Fish Street Hill met Thames Street on the north side. The high warehouses and dock suppliers, traders and wholesalers that made up much of the business hereabouts were alight on that side of the street.

Some attempts were being made to quell the flames, but they seemed to Tom sporadic, uncoordinated. On one side of him there was another chain of buckets being passed, full one to a warehouse, thrown, and then passed back empty along the same row of hands. Frantic action at street pumps; the whole point of the water mill was that it forced water along pipes into the city, but with the wheels being still, it could supply nothing. There was a hand-pump. Two men were at it, sweating more than the device could provide. The pump wheezed, spluttering water out rather than jetting great amounts with a single thrust on the handle.

A team had tried to attach a portable pumping engine, complete with huge water tank on the back of a cart and pump-handles of its own, to a thick hose of stitched leather. But the arrangement had already been abandoned as useless, the bowser being used simply as another water-source for buckets.

These attempts were the exception rather than the rule and seemed driven largely by those who had a vested interest in particular properties being snatched from the inferno. You could see it in the tension in their grimaces, in the tight knots in their necks and shoulders.

Salvage was the order, and some had decided already to abandon their livelihoods, taking with them what they could. There was no question of grabbing keepsakes and loved ones, but raw materials, sellable stock, the fixtures and fittings of trade.

Some were loading carts, but transport was in short supply, and fights had broken out over the rights to use and the price to be paid for the transport of property. One man lay battered and dazed, bloody face and shirt, as panic surrounded him.

Then Tom saw the liquid. Thick and black, some kind of caulking agent, pitch or tar perhaps, flowing from some unknown source. The flowing in itself was unusual; it could only have been heated up and become runny, the way treacle might over a pan of hot water. Somewhere there must have been a cauldron of the stuff, some premises devoted to its usage, and that crucible had tumbled over in the fire.

Then a burning spar dropped, a winch collapsing from a

warehouse building. Fire coated both the wood and a rope still attached and tied off to it, one end weighted with a hooked iron pulley. The rope slithered as the pulley fell, the heavy end smashing into the ground sending splintered cobbles flying. The rope uncoiled after it, snaking into the black pitch.

Fire sped over the top of the tar, blooming out. In a heartbeat a fire-river ran at the bottom of Fish Street, spitting out gobbets of flaming tar. Where it hit wood or plaster, fresh smoke rose on contact. A woman running down the hill was distracted by the fire-stream ahead of her. She panicked, and Tom saw her drop the crate she'd been carrying. It landed in the running flames. The impact splashed fiery tar onto her legs, her face, into her hair.

She screamed twice, the first one in shock; the second was with the pain. Her hair was burning, her skin mottling, rippling.

Tom ran into her, leaping over the fire-stream now pooling in a pot-hole. He used the standard, beating the fire in her hair. The stink of it; pitch and hair and flame as one, made him gag. It was out in seconds, leaving a scorched, blistered patch above her forehead. Tom did what he could to swab the tar off her legs too, but she was thrashing about, hands all over herself trying to swat the heat off her.

She staggered off, one hand in what was left of her hair, the other still flapping at her thighs.

The still-rolled standard had been smeared with tar. Tom slapped it hard on the ground, extinguishing the last of the burn. It was holed but still intact. Good enough. Matted hair, pitch and what might have been skin was streaked across it.

The woman was gone. Leave her; at least she was alive.

Tom promised himself something; not to get distracted like that again. He couldn't save everyone, not in a fire like this. What he was doing was too important be diverted from his efforts.

He hoped he was as strong as that.

'Tom!'

And he did not have to look around because the voice was in his ears and one arm was about him, all lopsided. He knew that voice, its rough tones; that smell, the mix of sweat and flour, yeast and salt.

Farriner.

Father.

'Son, I thought I had lost you.'

'When you seized your chattels rather than save a woman's life?'

'I thought you were burned.' He wasn't listening to what Tom was saying; this was some rote script learned, practiced, to be repeated as meaningless litany when the time came.

'You killed Alice!'

'No, son, not I.'

'By your inaction, by not saving her!'

'I saved what I could for you, for your brother, damn him. We can start again, you and me. People will always need bread.' There was fire all around them and with it a curious rushing sound. The blaze, greedy, was sucking air towards it.

Tom snarled. 'Stay here with your ashes and your gold and see what mirth you can make with them.'

Farriner seized Tom with both hands, great meaty hocks on his shoulders. In doing so he'd had to slip his burden. His precious chest, tied up with baling twine. Farriner held him fast, but kept the chest between his legs. 'Listen to me. Even if it has to be for the last time son, listen to me. I did nothing to that girl.' He couldn't even say her name. 'I never could have.'

Flames were closer around them now and not red as much as orange, and not orange as much as white. Heat prickled Tom's face: like a sun-burn in an instant.

'Believe what you want, son. But ask the same of your brother. He'll tell you. He'll tell you before he dies.'

'What do you mean?'

'He's gone. His mind is broken. Not by the fire, I reckon, but before. He's made his confession to me, and now he's gone. Gone to make his confession to God.'

'Where?'

'St Magnus.'

Why there? Their family church was St Margaret's on Fish Street Hill, but even in thinking these words, Tom could see the steeple of Margaret's. It was coated in smoke from the outside, all red-black and gold. Flames leapt from the slats which let the bell-sounds out. Its bell was tolling, but not the steady ringing of the other churches beyond the limits of the fire. Neither a warning to parishioners nor a crazed summons of the faithful to their devotions, it spasmed as though whoever was on the rope-pull was caught in some fit. And then a wrenching crack, a crash, and the bell was silenced.

Farriner shook him. 'Tom, he's gone to make his peace. I'll not stop him in that. I can't. You're my only son now. But you might want to, and I'll not forgo you the chance to do right.' He then stooped to rummage with the chest.

'Spare him if you can,' he continued. 'But it's a martyr's death he seeks. And he might yet deserve it for what he's done, that's not for me to say. Spare him the flames or an arrest if you can.' And with those words, Farriner thrust the flintlock from the chest into Tom's ravaged hand.

'If we get lost in the fire, meet me. I'll be at the Tower at noon each day. Now go!'

He wrenched Tom about, facing him back the way he'd come, back towards the bridge.

Tom spun back. 'And what about you?'

'I'll stay and do what good I can here. It's fire-breaks we need, not water. Hooks and charges to bring roofs and walls down, to create gaps that the broadest flame cannot span.'

'You'll need an army.'

Farriner smiled at that. 'Right enough, and an army's what we'll have once Charles hears of this. Already the Navy Office have sent word, and if that's not enough, all His Majesty'll need to do is poke his head out of whoever's chamber he's woken up in. Now go.'

Tom was caught and he knew it. The choice between the two; the city and Challis's design on the one side of the scales. Daniel on the other.

He wished he hadn't vowed to not allow himself to be distracted. Because then he wouldn't have to break his word.

Tom ran to the church of St Magnus.

#

He'd crossed the bridge how many times? A hundred? Three? And during each crossing Challis had wondered about the stupidity of it.

It would have been a beautiful target.

Because during daylight or when there was some festival or high service, or when the poltroon Charles had ordered another of his interminable celebrations, the first consequence was that the bridge became impassable. If it wasn't fruit-sellers and meat-roasters cluttering the walkways, it was promenaders peering in glovers' shop windows, or holding court in milliners' doorways. And if it wasn't those it was traffic; carriages and sedan chairs, carts and hand-barrows, horses and donkeys and livestock being driven across. It might take an hour to struggle through the perspiring, preening, swearing, spitting, drink-stinking, slow-footed throb of humankind who wasted their days at a stream-trickle of a pace, rather than mimic the full-blooded river below and sweep along with purpose.

That was what Challis was faced with now. Even at this hour, the city was up and about, curious and expectant, thronging to see the fire or yet had come from the north side of the river and getting between him and a clear run at the city.

Little wonder that those who could afford the fare took a lighterman across the river. Ten minutes in a rocking boat with some opinionated half-drunk – it seemed those that offered personal ferry crossings did so only when their brandy-coin had run out and worked only to gather enough silver to consign them to their cups for another couple of days – was a sacrifice worth making to avoid these masses.

It was like squeezing through the crowd at a bear-baiting to secure the best view. They stood there, at what they yet considered a safe distance, begrudgingly letting through those that had decided not to stay.

Challis was the only traffic intent on not merely seeing the conflagration for himself, but wanting to get involved with it.

He thrust himself through three, four rows of those who'd congregated in the last few minutes in the gap between the new houses and the old. He put a hand out to force a passage, to make a hole, and found his wrist soon gripped.

'Watch it!'

Challis rotated his wrist, shifting enough to have the cur loose his grasp. Then, hand now over the one that had tried to restrain him, he snatched out himself, twisting back around the other way.

The arm led to a burly oaf who smelled as smoky as a coal-merchant's labourer. He might have been strong and used to getting his own way, but he had no guile. He yelped as though nipped by a small, fashionable dog, and swung about. But he was slow and hemmed in and did not think to check for either a restraining hand on the shoulder or a knee to the cods.

The man went down fast, folding over. Hand quick now to seize the man's scalp, then a second blow, knee again, this time into the face. A crunch, and something sharp to Challis's skin. He must have had his mouth open.

He stepped over the groaning felled oaf. Challis didn't check back for any uproar. He marched on towards the hot burning stink.

Oh, the smells; a hundred different kinds of immolation. Meat and sinew, bone and fibres, strong drink and spices, hot turds, pitch, wood and boiling piss. The sound of it too; hissing and spluttering, roaring and grumbling, scrapings of metal against its own kind. Church bells and panicked horses, shouting men and squalling dogs, and behind all of it the irresistible hungry crumple of the fire.

The words he summoned were those of ravenous sin: there was licking and stroking flame, caressing and coaxing, teasing and corrupting, defiling and raping. There was greedy fire, eager for more to armour itself, to gorge, to enrich, to push beyond satiety to – yes! - the inevitable release of destructive joyous explosion. There was gluttonous burning; consuming, biting, eating, smearing flame. Fire drunk in the air and snacked on timber. It made its own roast for its feasting as it travelled, snatching for morsels, tidbits, crumbs, before reaching anew. There was wrath embodied in its remorselessness, in its lack of pity, in its whole destructive capability. In its intent and purpose.

Not twenty yards off, shuttered warehouse doors collapsing outward, scalded bales of unworked hides leaping out after, falling and being violated by the flames, crushing one man, breaking his bones then smothering him in dead leather and live firelight. Another bale toppled out fully enrobed in this new light, striking the ground and bouncing, tumbling, from the north to the south side of Thames Street.

This is how the fire would transmit itself from wall to wall, not just from house to house, but from Roman gate to Roman gate; by spark and by smoke, by debris and by collapse, by accident and incident, by man's foolish ineptitudes and by his vainglorious pride.

There was envy and pride here too. In the few steps Challis took, he could not but recognise it, acknowledge it, be enthralled by it. Pride and envy in that a man would not help his fellow, lest he lose what he had. Envy in that if one man's property were lost, what would it benefit him to offer Christian assistance to another? Charity, faith and hope be damned for these men, for they cared nothing but for themselves. See them scurry now, like rats from a broom.

And the heat! Already the air between him and the flames rippled. There were waves and pulses, throbs and gusts: both movement and solidity in the sky. No, not waves of water, but those of glass, ill-formed and not yet cooled, solid but transparent, hot and dry yet holding the illusion of liquidity.

There was design here; thought, purpose, beauty and intent. And there was also motion.

Another sharp report, then a series of dull thumps. Beams were collapsing, structures rupturing in the streets ahead. A boom, and a great upsurge of fresh rolling smoke, black atop and underlit in yellows and orange, was propelled into the air, spearing itself on some jutting spire before being coughed to one side by the wind. Shards of fire erupted below, sharp daggers of light.

Challis could have stood here forever.

Then a figure cut across, moving fast, keeping low. The runner had a shadow cast from the second low sun burning behind him. The target. Tom.

Challis tracked him left to right and closer, away from the fire and crossing Thames Street. Was he fool enough to attempt to re-cross the bridge? Surely not. He had a destination in mind; there was a purpose in him. He was making for the church.

The lad disappeared behind stonework. His direction gave Challis certainty. He was after sanctuary.

Not from me.

Challis made for the north side of the building. Where he knew the porch would be.

#

Tom had expected the church to be cool. He was anticipating a few precious seconds of relief from the rising, oppressive heat outside. But the fat round door-pull which gave him access was warm to the touch and clammy, as though hot panicked hands had grasped it.

The door was heavy; as heavy as a church door should be, and its bulk and its slow movement was a fleeting provocation of protection. Then the scent. Wax and dust, chased-off dampness. That too was a reassurance, but there was a baked flavour to the air Tom took in with the first gulp behind the closed arched wood.

It tasted wrong.

There was something else wrong too.

Daniel was standing before the altar, cross in hand. He was facing the east window and the sacred table underneath. A black-robed man lay sprawled on the steps leading up to the altar. Candle-sticks were strewn around him. Perhaps he'd been setting them out for that morning's service, or maybe he'd been trying to rescue them from the burning world outside. The man was at Daniel's feet. He might have been prostrate before Christ, but there was evidence otherwise.

Blood was spreading across the stone floor, collecting where the blocks butted to each other, taking the course directed to them to the first step down, then trickling over and beginning anew.

Daniel shifted the cross in his grip, placing his other hand under it to give more support. It was gold for the most part and had a wide base. One arm of the cross dripped red.

Blood collected by Daniel's toes.

Tom, fascinated and appalled at once, did nothing. He stood in the half-empty nave, in the vacant portion where the poor would assemble behind the pews reserved for those who could afford to pay for such luxuries.

A cracking noise. The east window occluded. It bulged. The stained glass loomed inward, something both dark and light pressing hard against it. There were flames on the other side of the glass, probing. Little patches of coloured brightness danced on the stones between Daniel and the altar, the crisis outside turning the mosaic image in the window from a rising Jesus triumphant, his angels and archangels to his sides to something fell, something other, something changed.

Daniel backed away, the cross still clasped in his hands. He was off the steps now, almost retreated to where the pews began. To his right, a lectern with Bible opened. To his left, the pulpit.

A second crack and the lead holding the glass in the East window behind the altar gave in, a burning wooden spar projecting obscenely through from outside.

And then Daniel bowed to the altar. Or to the fire which now dripped onto it.

'Daniel!'

Tom shouted his brother's name again, but was sure that he was not heard. A third time, louder, and now the walls echoed with his calling, the word resounding off the stone uprights.

Someone might have entered the church at that moment; Tom was not sure of this until later.

Tom came forward, the gun awkward in his grip. He tucked it into the rolled standard hanging at his side and flexed his hand in relief. Daniel had started praying, head still bowed. His words were audible but indistinct.

There must have been some covering on the altar. Some fine bit of embroidered linen. It was not Good Friday, after all. Fire took the material and chased itself along it, then down its sides. The cloth ripped under the weight of the burning and the altar, wooden, not more stone as Tom had assumed, was smoking. It had been polished so many times with beeswax; there was no doubting its odour.

Daniel had finished his prayer. Tom came forward, but Daniel was moving fast, and was at the pulpit steps before Tom had gone three paces.

Daniel had to turn when making the ascent, and in doing so, curving around and up the dark wood to the pulpit stand, there was no mistaking that he knew that Tom was there.

His eyes darted from Tom to the back of the church and then back to Tom. And then he closed them. 'A congregation,' he said. His eyes were bright.

Some sound from above gave him pause. A rustling, like sifting your hands through clumped flour to make it useable. The rustling moved, the sound now more like rat-claws on sacking, vermin wrestling, trapped in hessian, a dozen of them, then a score, then a hundred, then a hundred-weight of the beasts, ripping and tearing and scratching and biting free.

The roof was catching. Soon it would burn.

'Brother?'

Daniel clutched the cross tight to his chest. Blood scraped across his cheek in the doing so; it might have been a fresh cut from the cross, it might equally have been excess spatter from the caved-in skull of the church-clerk.

'My prayers have been answered, brother,' Daniel said. There was a distance in him. He was already on the journey to wherever he was going. Only his body lagged behind.

'We have to get out.'

'You may.' Daniel let his head tilt to one side. 'I am at home.'

'No.' Tom grappled for what to say, the words that might coax his brother back. 'The New World. Settlement in the Americas. You and I, once we've got the money saved from your preaching and what other work I pick up. Setting ourselves up again, baking bread and delivering the gospels. It was your idea!'

'The time for ideas has passed, brother. Events have taken over from fancies.'

'It's not a dream. But we have no time to stay and talk this over. Outside, yes, till our tongues are blistered and our ears numb with the conversation, but not here.'

Daniel ran his fingers along the underside of the cross's outstretched arms. He then examined his wet finger with curiosity, sniffing then tasting the red richness he found there.

Tom winced at the wet-lipped smile that followed. There was sadness in Daniel's eyes. The kind of sadness you saw in the old. The sadness of experience.

'You don't understand, brother. And I don't even need to forgive you for it, for there's nothing to forgive. You weren't to know. You weren't supposed ever to know.'

'I don't understand.'

'Why America? Why the New World, with its diseases and savages, the risk of the crossing and the uncertainty of the existence? Why there?'

'Tell me, then. Come down and tell me.'

Daniel was crying. Another old man's trick. The soft shake of the head. He was aging by the minute, as though the rising heat in the church was curling the pages of the book of his life. 'Because it was far enough away.'

The altar was blazing, great plumes of coloured smoke, dappled by the melting stained glass behind it, rising and collecting in the eaves. Window-lead dripped like ash-coloured candlewax, splattering on the stonework around the consecrated table, impacting with splash-cracks like stones pelted through thin ice.

A door to one side, an opening that must have led to a side-chapel or an entrance to the crypt, was already buckling. Iron rivets were baking in their holes, the wood around them twisting against their touch.

This place would burn, and burn soon. Tom had to get his brother out.

'Then let us get away again. Right now. Somewhere else, somewhere new. It doesn't matter where.' Just out of here, please.

And then Tom stopped. Another thought came to him. 'Far enough away? From what?'

'Not what, Tom. From who. She was mine from the first Tom. And now she's gone. The first of many that'll die tonight, I'll warrant. I'll see that she's not the last.

'Don't you see, Tom,' Daniel continued, head still to one side, still nuzzling the gory crucifix, 'that this is my doing? He knows, because He saw. He heard my words and they have come to pass. Did I not preach brimstone and destruction, an avenging and purifying fire to sweep through the city?'

'But they were just words, a show, hellfire and apocalypse for the masses. An entertainment for the money. You must come down!'

'You might have thought so. And I might have considered that in part. Poor in spirit is the man who prefers his meat unseasoned and his drink over-watered, after all. So why not give them a show, eh? But it is I who has been shown, shown by the Almighty the power of words and the hubris of careless prophecy.'

'Daniel. You did not cause this fire.'

'It earned us the money, brother. That sermon, with the coin your travelling man gave me in trust for you; there was enough there and more besides with what I'd already sequestered.'

Tom tried to repeat himself, that the fire was not Daniel's fault. He did not summon fiery angels or whatever guilt-ridden unmentionable was coursing through his mind. He had not caused this.

'And so I thought myself free, brother. After the preaching, after the coin. Yea, and after you'd toddled off with him about his business.'

He paused long enough for Tom to wonder about the way his brother was phrasing his words.

Above them, the scratching had ceased, at least for the while. But fire was all through the east end of the church. The altar and the whole of the sanctuary were ablaze; wood, cloth, books, all of it. Roof beams were burning above them and fire was travelling rapturously along their spans, dodging carvings and coating then rupturing painted surfaces. Some walls had been plastered; this too was alight, being built up on thin slats of wood or sheets of woven, nailed reed then skimmed over. Yellow-orange leaves now grew here, shedding dust, smoke and sparks wherever.

'And so I went to her, brother. I did that thing that you could not.'

Please no.

'And I confessed that I could not be without her and yet live in England. I put my hands on her, as she'd let me do before, thinking that she'd see the benefit of a younger man over an old.

'But she did not. She laughed at me. Said what use was a workless man, a man without a trade. That my preaching was well-dressed tinkering, not honest work. That father left me alone, did not chastise me as he has chastised you so many times because he knew that it was not worth his while. That I could never be his son in the ways that you could be.'

Flame coiled round the lectern, reaching up for the Bible. Faded gilt-edged pages shone anew, briefly.

'What did you do?'

'I didn't mean to.'

The sound of drums in his ears. The noise from the rafters and the lead roof above. Again, but louder, more insistent, faster. 'Daniel. What did you do?'

'Father was away, desperate for his strongbox and so I went to her. You were not there. And we spoke, or I spoke and she laughed me off, telling me how she'd gladly take his prick when he got back, pissed and lusty, a hundred times over, while I cried myself to sleep, praying all the while. I only meant to scare her.'

And Daniel's head was upright, as though he could now bear the weight.

'To brandish it, just the once. I meant nothing by it. I was angry you see, and she was but a serving girl when all was all.'

'You hit her.'

'I offered to save her from the fire.'

'You struck her down.'

'Once. Once only, I swear it. I reached out, not knowing even it were within my grasp, that claw-shaped thing you pull the trays with. And I hit her.'

Tom was shaking. But he wanted to hear it all. And Daniel wanted Tom to hear this. This was a confession, some grasp for absolution. 'What did you do?'

'She did not even fall. She stood, agape. Struck dumb.'

'But then the fire.' The shaking was worse. How could he? Daniel, of all people. How could he?

'Sent as retribution. Not at my request, but because of my request. Because of my lust for her. She's dead, because of me. The bakery is lost, because of me. The city is burning because of what I've wrought.' Spittle flew with each "because", such were the force of his words. 'It's only fair that I should atone.'

Daniel looked up then, and Tom followed. The roof was buckling. It was on fire above and below, and the weakening roof-timbers would not take the weight of its burden for much longer. Already the eaves were alight, some charred and coal-like, glowing themselves and feeding fresh flames that were boiling the roof-space.

Tom pulled the flintlock from the standard rolled at his waist and brought it to half-cock. The device had already been loaded. Father must have primed the piece.

He was shaking too much, though. He could not keep the firearm steady with one hand, so he brought the other up for support.

He was not sure what would happen when he pulled the trigger.

'Don't do it brother,' Daniel said, his voice unnatural in its calm. 'I'll not have another murder on our hands. Just walk away. Wait outside if you like.' He checked up and almost smiled. 'I won't be long. I just have to find my own way out.'

'No,' Tom said. And his shaking stopped. The Bible on the lectern was now fully alight, pages scrunching and frying, then floating off, little grey-white slivers of the gospels. They flew up and about, buffeted by heat, thousands and thousands of them. Hot snowflakes, angel-feathers. Rising to the rafters and spreading out to the aisles beyond the pews.

Tom raised the firearm from chest height to above his head, aiming straight up at Daniel some ten feet away and raised perhaps half as much by the pulpit. He tensed, not wanting to kill his brother but both needing to do his father's bidding and to avenge Alice's death. His right index and middle fingers curled round the fat trigger, pulled and -

#

And Challis brought his arm up from below, knocking the weapon up as it discharged. The lad would in all probability have missed anyway - the gun he was using was ancient-looking, probably stolen off a battlefield corpse in Cromwell's time and not cleaned since - but it was better not to take those kinds of chances. And besides, if he'd have struck down rather than up, there was the likelihood of someone losing a foot.

As it was, the damn device actually fired, a shot-ball whizzing off into the roof. That wasn't the best outcome, but Challis was in a different frame of mind to the one he'd been in ten minutes earlier.

Tom reeled from the combined force of the upward blow and the recoil, staggering back a pace or so.

His target, the preacher-brother, was lost to it all. His eyes were now shut and he had some altar-iron in his arms, hugging it as though the gold in it would buy him entrance to heaven.

Challis grabbed Tom, stepping back with him and steadying him in one move. He brought out a gun of his own and slid to Tom's chin, the better for him to hear the click to half-cock.

Tom struggled, but Challis's grip was sure.

Tom's spent gun dropped from his hands.

'Bear witness,' Challis said.

The shot-ball had been the last test for the roof over the pulpit area. A hole had been punched through the roof-works, bringing down a flurry of plaster already crazed by heat from above, exposing a small but perfect new circle.

Challis switched grips, taking Tom by the hair. Now he held him by the head with his chin elevated by the gun barrel. He raised Tom's head so there would be no question that he would see what Challis wanted.

'You don't get to choose this, Tom. His decision. His life, right or wrong.'

Tom struggled, but it was no use. Challis had him firm.

'Then let me kill him.'

'Oh, I think not. He needs to suffer. He needs to taste the everlasting torments in advance. He needs to know how the woman he murdered felt in her last minutes.'

'No, he doesn't.'

Challis twisted his grip in Tom's hair. 'Stop your flailing, man. Look at him. Just look.' The preacher brother gazed skyward. The hold he had on the cross seemed relaxed; there was little of the previous tension in his shoulders from bearing the weight. It might have been heavy, but he didn't feel it anymore. 'Do you not see? This is what he wants, what he feels he deserves. Who are we to deny a dying man his last wish?'

The lad still writhed, but the fight was running out of him. Maybe the sense of it was getting through to him. Perhaps he was just tired; resigned to his brother's burning and to his helplessness in witnessing his immolation.

It would be instructive.

The hole in the roof poked through by the shot began to drip molten lead. As it dripped, the hole widened. Not by much, but it would in time, Challis was sure.

The first droplets hit a stone sarcophagus to the left of the pulpit from where they stood. Someone must have paid dear for so prized a spot in eternity. The first couple of drops merely hissed and smoked. The next few cracked the flat lid, splitting it on impact. The drips travelled left to right as more fell. The lid cracked again as it split, chunks of stone dropping into the coffin-space. These impacts raised plumes of dust immediately. Whoever was in there was nothing more than brittle and friable matter, dry bone and scraps of burial finery. Fire erupted in this grave. Musty stink rose at once. The drops gathered pace, now more of an intermittent stream. Challis guided Tom's head again.

Daniel, lost in his rapture.

The roof, now a slash where there had been a hole.

The molten lead, burning on contact.

The coffin, now rupturing in flame and steam-smoke, breaking down the side facing them, disgorging its contents.

The burning skeleton, teeth and hair and last clinging garments alight, spilling out of the puking, overflowing coffin onto the ground, bony half-hand reaching for the nearest pew.

The hand, unsupported, falling and shattering.

The lead, streaming now, moving further across to the right. Hissing on the hardwood steps up to the pulpit, on the curving handrail burnished by years of contact, splitting the wood and setting it to torch on the spot.

Tom started to struggle again. Challis made sure he was going nowhere.

'Do you know your Bible, Tom?'

And then to Daniel, still dumbstruck in the pulpit, a hot grey rain now falling by him. 'Preacher? Knowest you your Bible? Book of Isaiah, chapter forty-seven? Verses thirteen and fourteen?'

Daniel cut him off. 'Let now the astrologers, the stargazers, the monthly prognosticators, stand up, and save thee from these things that shall come upon thee. Behold, they shall be as stubble; the fire shall burn them; they shall not deliver themselves from the power of the flame.'

Molten lead splashed on him from the pulpit; he rocked but did not waver. Tom would have shouted, but the muzzle was tight under his jaw. Instead he snuffled, a snotty whinging sound.

The preacher's clothes were alight.

'And your Psalms, preacher Daniel? Twenty-one, verse nine.'

Challis leaned in even closer to Tom. A check to the man in the pulpit, who hadn't yet replied. Maybe he was past conversation.

The preacher buckled. 'Thou shalt make them as a fiery oven in the time of thine anger: the Lord shall swallow them up in his wrath, and the fire shall devour them.' Lead was now raining down behind and around the man. His clothes were burning and his skin must have been puckering underneath. His face was pale, so pale, with sweat-beads standing out on his brow as though they were unpricked buboes.

'Oh, that's right preacher. Not long, just one more now and you'll be released. Quick now, and clear. John's Gospel. Chapter fifteen, the sixth verse.'

The response was immediate; the voice wavering. That wasn't surprising. 'If a man abide not in me, he is cast forth as a branch, and is withered; and men gather them, and cast them into the fire, and they are burned.' He was crying. Challis did not think that the tears were caused by any physical pain that he might be suffering.

And now, mouth to Tom's ear, close enough to reach out with his tongue and lick the lobe should he have been minded, Challis whispered.

'Now you have a choice.'

Challis de-cocked the flintlock. He pulled Tom back so he was behind him, and then spun around so they were facing each other.

'Look at me. Not him. Look at me.'

Challis flipped the flintlock like a juggler with one club. He grabbed it by the barrel, and then offered it, stock end out.

Challis said the words again. 'Now you have a choice.'

#

Tom pulled the gun out of Challis's hand. It was released without resistance.

The roof crackled, a second hole having burned through. The roof-space was filling with smoke, the hole apparent only because of the fresh melted metal eating its way outwards then pouring down a stone pillar. The stone cracked on contact, spitting out mouthfuls of rock chips and baubles of scalding lead.

Daniel's mouth was wide open, but with the noise of the burning all around it was hard to be sure if he was screaming or not. Maybe he was just breathing hard, trying to suck some goodness out of the searing air.

Challis stood not two yards distant, hands still outstretched as if they were going to clasp Tom in fellowship. His hands were empty.

Kill the man who'd brought devastation to London or end the misery of his tormented brother? Daniel was dying anyway; he was roasting in front of him. He deserved to burn in this life and the next for what he'd done.

He couldn't kill his brother.

But he could kill a stranger. He was sure of that. He'd proved that today already.

Yet his father had understood Daniel's design and had as much reason as Tom to want him to suffer, more perhaps, yet he'd pressed on him that old-looking weapon anyway to ease his brother's passing.

Or Tom could put a hole the size of his fist in Challis's head. He could drag his body out and they'd quarter it and spike the chunks for jeering public display.

The roaring of a dozen different fires. Above him, the roof slumped, the ceiling bulging and distending, held together only by custom and the last of the strength in the buckling timbers.

Tom's mouth was dry; he sucked in air but it was clogged with Bible-soot and the stink of flame on flesh. His nose hairs were singeing, his skin both slick with sweat and crisping up with hot scrutiny.

He cocked; took the flintlock in both hands.

Challis winced and Daniel screamed. This time he could be heard.

Tom fired.

#

Challis reeled, dropping to his knees. His hand came up to his chest.

The lad stood over him, still-smouldering firearm in both hands.

Behind him there was the sound of a body tumbling down stairs.

Challis blinked; there was something in his eye. Powder residue, some fleck of wadding perhaps. He was sure he'd cleaned the barrel thoroughly.

One ear was buzzing, sound pulsing in and out. That wasn't natural. Not unexpected, but unnatural nevertheless.

It occurred to him that this is what it would be like to die. He kept his hand moving, tracing across his clothing for a fresh wound.

He knew then that he wasn't hit, but it was wise to have the secondary confirmation.

All dry. Good. The hand kept going.

Challis rose and drew as one, standing and pulling his other flintlock.

The lad was still. Then the spent, still-smoking weapon was dropped. It clattered between them.

Challis risked a glance. The preacher was collapsed at the bottom of the pulpit steps, his body doubled over. It was impossible to tell if there was a gunshot wound or not. The body was on fire.

Quick now. The church wouldn't remain in this state for long. The signs were all around, all senses urging him to shift.

It might already have been too late. There were flames on three sides of them, and a hot grey curtain that was both falling and expanding. The roof was going to give, and soon.

Stone boomed; a support pillar cracked laterally, the top half shearing sideways by a foot. This sent ructions through the edifice. The roof would come with it and perhaps the spire as well.

So be it.

Challis knew that his mission was not done. The works he'd been set on this earth to do had to be completed. Thus, he would survive.

He had his doubts about Tom though.

'You owe me a killing,' Challis said.

Challis indicated the pointed gun. From the firmness of the returned gaze the weapon might have simply been some plaything whittled from driftwood. 'I owe nothing. You've had your killing for today.'

'You could have shot me. You'd have been a hero.'

'I couldn't leave my brother to die like that.'

'His death served nothing.' Challis was shouting now, not from the stupidity of the choice, but because of the thunderous sounds all about them. 'That ball could have taken my life and with it you'd have brought the King's revenge and justice against our enterprise.'

'No.'

'How so?'

And then Tom smiled. 'Because this isn't your enterprise. What would you call this if you were being honest? An unintended consequence? This is better than your petty scheme. The whole city burns, not just a mere bridge, and burns in such a way they'll not be sure if it were by design or accident. You've got both proof of your intent in your planning and yet you can deny your dealings with a plain face because you did not intend this destruction.'

Oh, that was good. 'And what of it?'

'It means that I'm no obstacle to you, because I never was. You can walk away and say what you like to your paymasters and they'll believe you and pay your blood money twice over for the majesty of your havoc. And though you might have shot at me on the bridge, you'll not do it now.'

Challis wanted him to say it. Say it loud. Say it before Christ on the Sabbath while his temple burns.

Tom continued. 'Your conscience allows you to kill in the name of your enterprise, because you believe you work for a higher power. The sins you have not yet committed are already absolved. But that doesn't grant you letters of credit for wanton murder.'

'And that is why you didn't shoot me?'

'Murder is murder, be it in the Lord's house or not. If you deserve aught, it's a trial then the noose; your life is not for me to take.'

'And your brother?'

'Daniel was already dead. That was merciful release only.'

Challis took a step closer. 'We can all find ways to accommodate the things we've done.' He snatched with his free hand at something fluttering in the air. A scrap of paper being buffeted by waves of heat.

God's words, freed from their leather-binding prison. Challis smiled at the serendipity.

A half-pace forward. Tom was surrendering to him, his arms stretching out to either side. Blood dripped from the wound in his hand. His head was crooked to one side, lips parted.

'How many commandments have you broken, Tom? How many? With your unchristian talisman around your neck. Does that praise God? Your father on his knees in the road outside. Is that honour? Have you not cursed and sworn? How many lies have you told? To me? About me to others? To yourself? And what have you coveted? Money? Secret knowledge? Who have you coveted? That pretty piece who stuck her tongue out at you? The bakery girl? And murder, in the Lord's house. Of your brother, no less. And all on the Sabbath day. Not forgetting theft, because I know what you took from me. All of the commandments broken but adultery, Tom. All except adultery. But still, you're only a child, aren't you?'

Challis slid the paper into Tom's mouth. The words lay on his tongue. A new sacrament.

Then Challis murmured something, clear but low. A murmur, he knew, carried differently to a whisper.

The words on the paper.

Tom nodded at what was said; and then Rufus Challis shot him.

#

Challis did not stay to see the body fall.

The pistol's report set off an echo. An echo that filled the church entire. It had to, because the sound was not that of the shot at all, but of the roof giving in.

Challis made for the same north door that he'd entered by, firearm still smoking in his hand. He'd expected that when it came down, then the roof would go from the sanctuary end, from the altar, because that was where the great stained window had been shattered by falling debris. That end was where the lead had started falling first. He had not reckoned on the steeple.

Whatever load-bearing capabilities the building possessed were exhausted. The world was folding inwards, the roof support beams splintering out and racing towards him under force from the failing masonry from above.

A momentary image, a fragment from his past; a chicken carcass being torn for sharing at a campsite cook-tent.

Challis ran.

The north door was a boon. Diverting right to go towards it in all probability saved him; the wit to do that was further proof of the Almighty's trust in his competence to carry out His works. He made it to the porch way, the roof half-melted, half-distorted out of true by fire damage and by pummelling from the steeple-blocks, falling, crashing behind him. At the last he dived, not caring how or where he fell, just so long as he was those precious few inches further from the sundered rock.

He waited after the falling, curled up and cloaked twice over, once in leather and once in dust and plaster, wood and stone.

He did not feel injured. He checked anyway, a quick pat all over as soon as it was still enough to gamble the move. Too cloudy to see: fire-smoke and noxious metal-working stink rising with the lime dust of plaster and shattered glass all about.

He was entire. Challis stood, careful as you please. The building, half-standing and gaping open to the heavens, could complete its destruction at any instant. Fire patrolled the rubble, taking residence on any matter which would support its tenancy.

The north door, burnt itself with splashed metal-juice, was off one hinge. Challis elbowed it open enough to get out.

Someone came running over; he stashed the firearm in time. They fussed, exclaiming how fortunate he'd been and God be praised and all that. Challis brushed off the inanities, though took time to swig from an offered flask and to pour more of the brackish water over his face. It felt good to have the grit sluiced from him, and he thanked the man for it.

No, he was as well as might be expected and no, he needed no more assistance, kind Samaritan.

He turned about, shaking the last of the water from his brow. If he'd troubled himself to put a hat on that morning, he'd lost it. No matter.

He wanted to see the extent of the burning. Thames Street was alight on both sides, up and downriver from where he stood. Fish Street Hill was lost, and two, maybe three streets over as well. There had been a church there, St Margaret's. Challis remembered it from previous occasions as a peaceful place. Not now.

St Magnus's? Naught but a crucible, a pot full of fire. There was a gap in the sky where the church had stood. That was power indeed, and evidence of His intent to bring destruction, yea even unto His own house.

Sometimes events unpeel themselves in a way that cannot be wished, dreamed of, foretold, strategized for.

What was it that Proverbs said? Trust in the Lord with all thine heart; and lean not unto thine own understanding.

Chapter three, verse five.

Challis curled his coat around him, hands deep in pockets despite the heat and the smoke. It would not do to be seen hereabouts; a fire like this would already have raised questions at the highest levels. And there'd be more besides once the blaze was put together with that little note he'd sent.

He loped rather than ran, quickstepping flames, rubble, exhausted fire-fighters, fleeing locals, the lot of it all, as he made way to the bridge again.

The houses this side of the break would be doubtless lost, for no-one had the wit to pull any down. That meant the water-wheels would go too, and with them any chance of using their power, if they could be repaired in time, to force piped water into the heart of the city to quell at least some of the burning.

The old fire-damaged section of the bridge might, and there was an irony, serve as a firebreak; it might not.

That didn't seem to matter anymore.

Job done, Challis strode across the bridge. It took time, what with the tearful and the fearful, the vengeful and the dumbstruck serving to clutter his route with their salvage and their fretting. He looked back the once, to see the hulk of St Paul's half-shrouded in smoke lit from underneath, great clouds of it scudding low over the burning city in the cathedral's direction.

Now to see that burn! But that would be too much to pray for, and so he did not.

He passed the house Jephcott had procured for him and gave it no attention. Instead, he kept his head down and his hands in his pockets, rolling the vial over his thumb scar and enjoying the little peace the manoeuvre gave.

He should have continued with Proverbs, he recalled, as he went under Nonesuch House, and thus firmly on the Southwark side of the water. The sixth and seventh verses of the third chapters went, if he remembered right, and he flattered himself that he did: In all thy ways acknowledge him, and he shall direct thy paths. Be not wise in thy own eyes: fear the Lord, and depart from evil.

And amen to that, Challis concluded. Then his thoughts turned to more practical matters; putting up with tavern-dwellers on the Southwark side, and indulging their hunger for tales of the fire.

He'd trade the information for breakfast. Fried eggs and bacon collops perhaps, and then sleep. Besides, he now had a day in hand to get to Folkestone and his boat to Holland. There was little point in rushing.

#

It was only later that Tom realised he wasn't dead.

281

Challis had shot him, yes. But he'd spoken before he'd fired, more of his Bible words. 'Genesis four, verses ten and eleven.' Then he pulled the trigger.

It hardly bled, his shoulder. That was where Challis had shot him, and there'd been no mistake or faulty aim about it. He'd pressed the mouth of the gun square on the bone before shooting.

It didn't hurt either. And Tom knew why. He was in a stupor, he had to be, some half-dead trance. He was standing at some lych-gate to the heavens.

And he was being refused entry.

The turning back came with pain. That was life, such torment. And so it was. With pain and noise and confusion and thunder and heavy, heavy rain. It was only when Tom had laid there, under the pew where he'd fallen back after the shot's impact, the pew having itself been tumbled over him by something, falling roof-work he supposed, for he knew not how long, that his senses came back in some kind of order.

His shoulder was fucked; there'd be no argument there. It wasn't bleeding because it was fused, a great clod of muzzle-scorch and clothing and punished flesh had combined to seal the pellet's damage, at least for the present. He could feel no wound nor dampness from the ball's passing. It must yet be lodged in his shoulder-bone. That'd need digging out and the shoulder cleaning and soon, or he'd die from infection.

That idea made him croak with laughter out loud, and the comic sound, so close under the upturned pew, made him fear that the wood would splinter and he'd be crushed under whatever had impacted on it.

The laughter brought in turn coughing. He almost choked, foreign matter catching in his gullet. Another cough expelled the blockage; the paper Challis had pushed into his mouth.

The air was foul with poison fumes and the dogs' breath of metal-smoke and a dust ten times worse than any flour-mill.

The heat was no bother to him. He'd been up close to fires all his life; that at least was no new sensation. But heat meant the chance of more fire and he'd not yet peeked out to see what the chances of that were.

He was on his back and had to shift himself around to try crawling from under what had protected him. Tom levered himself up enough to flip his body onto his good side, fearing for his left shoulder if he put any strain on it.

With one good arm, it nearly worked, but he went over clumsily, smacking the shoulder-blade on what had been the pew seat as he went round.

He cursed through his puking, little more than scrappy dribble, as though he'd reached down his throat into his guts and wrung them out.

The ripe acid stench he'd gobbed up gave him further cause to hustle. Anything rather than breathe that in.

He snatched at the paper he'd coughed out. He did not let it go.

Tom crawled out, hoping he was headed in the right direction. And he was.

The church was ruined, the tower or steeple or whatever it was having collapsed into the nave. Doing so had torn a great gash through the roof, which was caved in utterly. Parts of it seemed like a rotting boat, the kind he'd seen still stuck in Thames silt years after being abandoned. Except for mud there was lead, sheets and tiles and strips of it, giving off steam-smoke and drizzling searing liquid where it could, in turn boiling grave-slabs and stone coffin-caskets, splitting stone and scalding what wood remained on contact.

No sign of Daniel, neither of the other man, the churchman laid on the steps to the altar. Just rubble and smoke and steam and fire.

And no evidence of Challis. He might be crushed under a hundred tons of gargoyle and lead pipe too, but Tom doubted it. He was not going to risk picking through the debris to check the truth of it though.

He stooped the once, to retrieve his father's gun. He slid it back into the remnants of the standard still slung around him. It came in useful, Tom resting his broken arm on it as a makeshift sling.

He clambered over and through the remains. Fire still burned, but it seemed lazy, as though its work here was three parts done. Perhaps the collapse had snuffed some of it out.

The north door hung half-open, one hinge remaining. Tom got himself to the door and, not wanting to hurt himself any more than he had to, kicked it open and ducked through the swinging gap hurriedly.

He made it five, six paces outside before tumbling over, of all things, a discarded bucket. People were all around him at once. They must have seen him emerge. One had water, thank God, and fed him fat mouthfuls. Another had his arms in the air, waving others closer to see the lad who'd escaped the falling church.

Tom pulled on the standard, and they started, fearful, when the firearm clattered out of it, and he tried to make them see the sense of what he was saying about the bridge, he really did, but it was difficult enough with the pain in his shoulder and the faces pressed in and him holding the standard in his good hand enough to shake it free so that it fell open.

He was sure he made himself plain at the time, and he was sure he was heard, not just with the amazement of the story of a lucky survival against whatever foul odds Mother Nature might have thrown up, but with seriousness because of the standard that he held and the importance that at least some of them saw in the cloth if not in the fire-wracked, red-eyed, shot-punched youth that gabbled about the house on the bridge, and he was sure at the last, before he went to the lych-gate a second time, and this time for longer, that he was heard in a different fashion.

At the back of the huddle, but barging through fast, he was heard by another, older man. Tom was not sure if he was heard with love, but he could see as he was fading that he was heard, one man to another, father to son, with respect.

Light capered in front of Tom's eyes. He went to rub his brow, finding the slip of paper still in his hand. It was curled, scorched.

'What hast thou done?' Tom read. 'The voice of thy brother's blood crieth unto me from the ground. And now art thou cursed from the earth, which has opened her mouth to receive thy brother's blood from thy hand.'

There was more from the fourth book of Genesis, but Tom could not read for the tears.

A cry: 'My son!' His father's voice.

Tom did not know who that cry was for.

EPILOGUE: MONDAY 29TH OCTOBER 1666

Mondays were hanging days. Executions were an extension to the Sabbath, another day's break from labour and the only place to be if you were able. And if you were a trader, the opportunities were like no other.

Men had thirsts to be slaked as the hangman was cheered, demanding brewers to be on hand with cartloads of barrels to be tapped.

For the harassed mother in need of some gewgaw to amuse impatient children in the bustle before the drawing, there were tinker-girls with trays of little peg-men; dandling by their peg-necks on strings from twig gallows.

And for everyone, child, woman or man who'd not thought to bring food with them or had said to the devil with it, it's a festival, we'll treat ourselves, there was meat of all stripes, roasting and frying and dried for chewing on. Fruits, codling tarts and sweetmeats, cheeses and poultry, eel pies and cake.

There were whores who'd tumble you, or boys if that was your fancy. Conjurors and fire-swallowers, bearded woman and donkey-cocked midgets who'd flash you their pizzle for a penny. There'd be palms read and teeth pulled, dirty jokes and laughter of all kinds.

There were all kinds of raucous noise and amusement in the air, not least from the puppet-show opposite.

But first and last there was drink, Taff chuckled to himself. It had been worth the early start. There'd not been an execution since before the Fire. Almost two months ago. You couldn't fail to make money if you had beer to sell. Taff grinned over at his Daisy and she grinned back. She loved a hanging, the wife.

He was going to take a fortune. And then he would treat his Daisy some, and Taff was sure that she'd do likewise come night-time.

They'd do well out of the day. They'd treat this like it was St Bartholomew's Fair reborn, and with the money they made they'd look to build a new tavern, bigger and maybe with more stabling than the one they'd lost.

#

Tom had no wish to be here, but they needed the money. Starting again takes coin. Yes, there were new orders from the Navy Office, in part because stored ship's biscuit in the navy stocks had been doled out by the King's order to feed those made homeless by the Fire. But the Navy was never a quick payer.

Camps had opened up on the fringes of the city just as when the plague had been fled. Demand for bread was higher than ever, but working premises were needed, and the Farriners needed money to start again with, contract with the Navy Office or no.

The first stage of that had been acquiring ovens.

Getting ovens had ended up being a simple thing. In the week after the fire, when baker Farriner and his bandaged son had been to the Tower of London for questioning dressed up as bland statement-taking, they'd been able to arrange the loan of two portable cast-iron bread-ovens, military stock covered in cobwebs and brick dust, relics from Civil War days. They were the kinds of contraptions with which Farriner claimed to have learned his trade. The Navy Office might not pay well or on time, but having the connections had proved useful.

The ovens were simple devices, being little more than metal boxes with a hinged front opening. You'd load them with fire, wood being better than sea-coal as the smoke-scent was easier on the loaves, bring it up to baking heat, and then check by spitting on the outside. If the spit sizzled, you were ready for baking. Scoop the fire out with your flat shovel and in goes the bread. Close the door, seal it with leftover dough and give it an hour. Having two ovens was the trick; you could switch back and forth, moving your fire and always having hot bread ready, and hot bread's what'll draw in and sell to a crowd.

With the gathering that was here, and ovens being in short supply, bread was fetching three times its usual price.

Farriner had shook on the loan with the quarter-master; they'd drunk hot wine to seal the contract, and if there ever any arrangement made to give the ovens back, Tom never heard of it.

Queues had already formed. Tom whistled to the new serving-girl, who was over quick-smart, smiling and handing over what should have been penny and halfpenny loaves, taking their money, wishing customers a good day. Aye, she was more than capable at her new job.

Tom did little but stand. In truth, with one good arm, there was not much more that he could do. Farriner senior took up the donkey-work; Tom kept an eye on the queue and did what he could with the oven. That was the unspoken arrangement. Every day he tried again, working to strengthen his shoulder by turning and twisting it, by seeing how long he could hold a full pint-pot at arm's length before having to swap hands or risk dropping his beer.

He'd been seen at the Tower by a military sawbones, some half-retired brandy-blossom who they'd kept on out of comradeship's sake. He was gruff and was forever tippling, bringing a delicate glass-and-silver flask to his lips throughout the consultation. His lips were wet with unwiped phlegm and raw liquor, but he was good at doctoring. No infection had set in, and Tom would be left in time, he was promised, with a scar that'd look like a second belly button, no more than that. Just keep up the exercise or it'll go stiff on you in no time, the physick said with a lecherous wink.

It was the standard that had bought these kindnesses, that and the minor reputation of being a naval supplier. If they ever checked out

Tom's story about the house, he never heard. The bridge survived the Fire right enough, the flames being halted by the break caused by the previous burning. But that seemed small consolation to many, two-thirds of London having been consumed, from the gates of the Tower to Temple Stairs on the river, and from the Thames to as far north as Cripplegate. From the Sunday night through to the Wednesday it had raged, until the wind finally stalled. Those that could had fled, many back to the same places they'd camped when waiting for the plague to exhaust itself.

But before the Fire was fully out, indeed there were great patches still smouldering even now, people returned. Partly to salvage and steal, partly to reclaim their land and ensure no-one filched their birthright, partly because that was their life and where else could they go? Everywhere, the talk was of Charles and his brother James, how they'd laboured like common men when the need arose, like great generals when direction and the command that comes with title was needed.

The talk was also of the baker who'd come home pissed and let his midnight snack burn the city down when he'd slumbered in his cups, his griddle untended. Talk that Farriner had fought with his reputation, with bluster, with his fists at least once, and by packing himself and sundry cousins onto the jury that had got them all here this day. That jury had bought baker Farriner a verdict, official proof that he was without stain in the matter.

That didn't stop tongues wagging in the tavern-tents in the camps though, and both Tom and his father knew it. Farriner struggled with the gossip. In the days he buried himself in work, happy to have Tom's injury as excuse to run himself to breaking point. In the evenings he put down his tankard and picked up his spirits cup, having opted for the Bristol Milk cure, sitting alone until his bottle of sweet sherry was done, all the while talking with no-one but himself.

And though there was talk of conspiracy, of Catholic revengers seeking to complete their incendiary mission begun under James, Charles' grandfather, and also of Protestant militants from the Low

Countries, there was, in truth, always such talk. It seemed every man picked his convenient enemy and adapted their animosity to the news of the day.

In those days at the Tower when the Farriners had been questioned – it was civil enough, but questioning nonetheless - and stiff-necked secretaries had scribed their statements about the fire's beginnings, Tom had been by his father's side.

For the most part. He was sent first to the physician and on a second occasion he was directed to a private garden.

The man who met him there was well-dressed and seemed important, given the way he was treated by the others, who deferred to him with speed and courtesy. He was quiet-spoken and contemplative and wore a curious black plaster at the bridge of his nose. It covered, the man mentioned, a wound from his soldiering days.

He bid Tom sit down and share an apple or two, and tell him his story and leave naught out.

And so Tom did, from the sermon to the gathered crowd outside the wrecked shell of St Magnus's.

The man, who had asked to be called simply "Bennet", listened and said nothing throughout. He sat there on a low wall, paring slivers of apple with a dainty but sharp-looking knife from time to time.

Each time Challis's name came into the conversation, one-sided from Tom bar Bennet's nodding though it was, he cut himself another slice.

At the end of Tom's story, Bennet slipped his hand into a pocket, consulted a handwritten note he found there, then slid it back.

'I'd be most gratified,' he said, 'if you'd send word if you hear anything of your Challis again. Anything at all. Or of anyone resembling him. Most gratified. In fact, Tom, I'd be pleased if you'd take me into your confidence regarding any such persons you might chance upon. England has her enemies, and we can always do with another clear and true pair of eyes.'

Bennet stood, leaving Tom on the wall. Where he'd been sitting, there was a purse. Tom opened it. It was full of gold coins, the new twenty-shilling pieces with the milled edges. They said the gold came from Guinea, and was the purest.

'Will you do that for me Tom?'

'Aye.'

With the money was something else. A single shilling, a coin just as new as the gold. The coin had four holes punched through so that it resembled a button.

'Wear this.'

'Why?'

'As a token of your service.'

The purse was on him now, and he'd not spent a penny of it, nor had he a mind to. He'd hold it on account, he had decided, to be used when needed. He'd mentioned nothing to his father about this, and if Farriner knew aught of it, he'd not brought the subject to bear.

The money was heavy on his hip, stitched into an inside pouch. Its weight gave reassurance, the way a flintlock in your hand might.

Around his neck, a pouch. Not the yeast he'd worn there before, his personal mark as a baker's apprentice. He'd emptied that out and replaced it with the gunpowder he'd taken as evidence. Bennet hadn't asked to see it – why would he, it was just black powder after all – and even if he had, Tom thought now that he would have preferred not to hand it over.

That was worn for Daniel. He'd not die like his brother had. He would never allow himself to suffer in such a way, nor be beholden to another to end such suffering. There was sufficient charge in the pouch to take his head right off if it came to it. He'd not be trapped by fire again and be left to burn.

Tom had taken the shilling and threaded it onto the same twine as the gunpowder pouch. He had seen similar coins a few times since that day; worn as a brooch, as an unnecessary top button; once, one set as if it were a gemstone on a ring.

The King's men were abroad in the city. They, like Tom, were here even now.

The crowds - and there *were* crowds, great swathes of people - were rippling with something. They sensed it; the centrepiece of the day must be coming through.

Somewhere out there, a cart was being drawn with the prisoner chained in the back. He'd be stripped to the waist, and probably bruised by thrown fruit, turds and rocks, being scratched at by harridans, had dogs set on him, all the usual kinds of last-trip torments.

But this one was special. The man who'd confessed to causing the Fire.

He'd have been given a last drink at a tavern on the journey from wherever he'd been held, the Tower itself for all Tom knew. His next stop would be the triple tree, and his Tyburn appointment with hangman Ketch.

Farriner had gone up there somewhere at the front of the throng; as part of the jury he'd been allocated a good view, standing on a wagon tethered up close to the gallows. There must have been dozens of similar wagons and carts, each of their owners charging a shilling or more for the privilege of an unimpeded view of the Frenchman's dandling.

Let him enjoy the show, drink his worst and come home maudlin.

Tom had no desire to see a man die today. Besides, he was busy minding the stall, and he'd have enough of a job on with the oven-work.

And in any case he got to spend time with her. The girl he'd sought out to take over from Alice. The girl who'd stuck her tongue out once and caught his eye.

She had a name. Rebecca. Hair like burnished wood, tendons that danced under her skin when she turned her head.

He'd gone hunting her out as soon as he was able. He'd not taken no for an answer, no matter who he asked the question of concerning her whereabouts.

Despite what he'd said to Challis in the conversation they'd shared through the streets of London, in the end he didn't need a firearm.

Tom had found her man off Thames Street. He was boastful, in his cups late at night, leering to Tom – who he did not recognise - as he bragged of his woman and her artful tongue, in the way that strangers sometimes will.

Tom had pushed him against a part-collapsed wall and struck him for his disrespect. When he got up, Tom hit him again, and did so until the man, learning the lesson, stayed down.

Tom gave it half a day before he went to find the girl and take her for his own. She stuck her tongue out at him as she'd done before, and came along willingly.

Rufus Challis had been right about one thing, though in perhaps not the manner he'd intended.

Tom's actions now held little consequence. He could act, respond, even provoke, but it was all a sham. A puppet-show for others.

This was freedom of a sort, as actions held little fear of repercussion for Tom these days. He would do as he pleased, take what he wanted and fill the rest of his hours with work and noise to try to drown out the screaming from the earth.

Dogs no longer stalked his dreams. Instead, it was Daniel's shed blood that would not be silenced.

#

Challis knew there was minimal risk. Of course Henry Bennet, the Earl of Arlington, would have his spotters out; his spies and his turncoats and his squealers. But there was little chance of Challis being seen in a crowd of this size, and Arlington would have known it too. He'd have sent his men abroad anyway – he could scarcely do otherwise given the nature of the event – but he'd not be expecting a return on his outlay.

And Challis was not intending to let him have that satisfaction.

He was back in England, but only as a detour. He was expected in Scotland, where another dour band of Protestants were making preparations for some kind of rebellion. He could easily have sailed up to Newcastle or Edinburgh, and might well have done so, had not the news come through from London about the execution.

The pamphlets had been full of little else but of matters concerning the Great Fire, as they were now calling his work. Theories about its cause. The extent of the damage. The resolve demonstrated by Charles and James in combating the flames.

He had heard nothing through his usual contacts from de Witt, but the Dutchman could not have failed to have been pleased. The continental handbills were obsessed with the notion that this had been divine justice at work.

Challis strode through the crowd, ploughing a way through with resolute gait and a face that would not brook argument. He wanted to find a position to see all, and not be seen from.

He found one at last, a little way apart from the thrust of the crowds. To one side, the three-sided framework of the hanging place. All around it, the milling throng, the pitched tents and wagons.

Challis blinked, each time fixing on something new. A blind man being led by a small boy. A circle, with a fistfight inside. A cart, brightly ribboned, upon which capered a little fat man making lewd gestures to the audience crammed in around him. A mock-up of a stage behind him on the flat bed of his vehicle. The curtained-off stage rippled, and a little wooden puppet head squeezed out. It scoured around as though seeking someone out.

The puppet stopped; all big nose and falling-forwards bonnet, facing Challis direct. A gloved puppet hand joined the head. It waved.

Challis shivered, and then blinked once more. By the time he'd refocused, the stage-wagon was bare.

Challis turned back to the triple tree. This would be the spot from which to wait for Hubert.

Robert Hubert had more than played his part. It would have been a thing indeed to have seen his and Piedlow's watchmaker skills put to destructive use; that invention was indeed ingenious. But it was not of genius. That quality lay within Robert Hubert, and the miracle of him was in his convictions.

Challis did not share them, of course. He had his own reasons for doing what he did, his own set of guidelines which happened to accord from time to time with those he allowed himself to be sponsored by. It was alms-giving in a way, charitable donation, because it was indeed the Lord's work.

But to do what Hubert had done, was doing even now? That commanded respect. To let himself be caught, to allow his own capture in the full knowledge of what was to come. That was little shy of brilliance.

That was what Piedlow had confided. Hubert was more than Piedlow's hands. He was a living bomb, an incendiary made flesh. He had come to Piedlow half-formed, a talent for mechanical constructions and a direct and unwavering view of the world. So Piedlow had worked on him, polishing his faith. Making it shine. He was Piedlow's last, and greatest, device of war.

They'd thought him a lunatic, a raving suicide who wanted attention, of course. Until he led them to the point of the fire. With that and with his adamant confession, what else could they do? They gave him what he wanted. If a Frenchman demands to die, you let him.

The city, thinking itself absolved from sin because the burning had been laid at the hands of someone who was either a madman or an insurgent, and in either case a foreigner? They'd run to the hanging.

And here they were. London, dispossessed. In the background lay the city, still smouldering.

They'd beg for their hot snacks and their spiced ale. They'd wet their cocks in doxies or dry them in catamites' arses. They'd gorge and carouse, flirt and swear, cheer and grope and laugh. Pickpockets would dip and drunks would be rolled. Pie men would overcharge and hawkers would short-change and drop lead slugs instead of hard coin. They'd fight and they'd puke, cheat each other, debase themselves and their kin and kid each other it was all in the name of sport.

And in the middle of it, the execution. It would be not too long now. They'd take Hubert from the cart that was bringing him across the flattened city and they'd have whatever final prayers might be scrounged for his damned papist soul.

After, they'd hang him and he would dance, slowly strangling till he was all but still and then he'd be drawn, guts out and heart plucked, and there'd be such a cheer raised at the death of the culprit that you'd hear it in Southwark. And that would be the end of Robert Hubert.

Except it would not. Because of that moment between the last amen for his soul and the hangman's noose-tightening. That moment when the mob would shush itself, a quiet not out of respect but of anticipation, that it might hear the snap of his neck if he went quick or his final voiding if he went slow.

And in that hushed moment Robert Hubert would be the highest man in London and would have an unparalleled view across these fields.

And he would see them and they would see him.

And he would have their attention in ways either fire or detonation would never have attracted.

And in enough of them there would be doubt. There would be fear. Some would not bear to look at all, but would hide their faces in shame.

Because some of them would see the world not through Hubert's eyes, and not yet through Challis's, but with their own, anew.

Their own eyes, but attuned to a different sensibility; not opaque with cataracts of hate for the man before them, but clear with the possibility that they had in some way been responsible themselves, that their actions had begun some chain of events, that if there were monsters here in the city, they were not all bound and due to hang that day.

That they had brought this upon themselves.

How Challis envied Hubert that moment.

ABOUT THE AUTHOR

Eamonn Martin Griffin lives in Lincolnshire, England, where he was born and raised. He's worked as a stonemason, in a plastics factory, in a laboratory, in a computer games shop, and latterly in further and higher education. Historical crime thriller *The Prospect of This City* is Eamonn's first novel.

Eamonn's online at www.eamonngriffinwriting.com and is on Twitter here: @eamonngriffin

Printed in Great Britain
by Amazon